SILENT NIGHT

SILENT NIGHT

CHARLES ELLINGWORTH

QUARTET BOOKS

First published in 2010 by
Quartet Books Limited
A member of the Namara Group
27 Goodge Street, London W1T 2LD

A catalogue record for this book
is available from the British Library

ISBN 978 0 7043 7212 2

Typeset by Antony Gray
Printed and bound in Great Britain by
T J International Ltd, Padstow, Cornwall

2

For Amanda; without whom, ashes

1

GERMANY

Silesia, Eastern Germany. Christmas Eve 1944

Silent Night. *Heilige Nacht.*

Treble voices and taut wind in the dark caves of a church roof; coughs and shuffled feet against bitter draughts eddying among Lutheran benches; candles guttering. There are catches in the women's voices as sadness tightens vocal chords and the keening wind speaks of winter wastes, bitter steppe and the homesickness of men choking on the memory of warmth and children in a frozen dugout or Gulag hut.

Holy Night.

As the carol ends, it is only the children's voices that are left. The women have heads in hands or shawls pulled tight around faces to hide their tears from curious children, a sisterhood of sadness with a collective drift of imagination empathetic with men of flesh living with steel and terror or hopeless captivity. Smaller children look questioningly; older, more knowing heads fix their eyes forward and sing.

There are only four men in the crowded church – three of them silent and bare-headed, encased in outsized greatcoats. They watch, one stifling tubercular coughs into his sleeve, another staring at, but not singing from, a leather hymnal, the third, mouth hidden by a turned-up collar, drips desolate tears on to clasped hands.

The pastor, old enough to avoid the clutches of even the *Volkssturm*, the Home Guard of a desperate cause, looks downward as he greets the Christ-child, almost apologising for the good news that he is proclaiming – a hollow promise in the bitter sadness of separation and fearful expectation. Sensing the dislocation, his blessing is short and, without waiting for the traditional acclamation that he knows will not be forthcoming, he stoops his way to the door amid shuffled, sobbed amens.

In normal times the porch, freezing but surrounded by coloured lanterns, would be the stage for hugs between friends, kisses on the heads of excited children and masculine shoulder slapping. This night, gun-cold and lit by a single paraffin flame, only anaemic shadows grasp briefly at each other and whisper the traditional Christmas greeting, pulling smaller wraiths into the protection of cloak or coat before heading into the darkness pricked by pins of light.

A woman, alone, fur-trimmed collar holding a brush of dark curls below a felt hat, stops by the pastor, her posture contrasting with the widow's back of the aged priest. His greeting is one of respect, with a sideways bow and kissed hand. She uses her other hand to raise him, accepting a benediction as he painfully straightens. As the light catches her face, tears gleam.

She leaves the church alone. With folded arms clasping her coat and leaning into the wind, she follows a frozen road for a quarter of a mile, through opened gates and into a house of towering shadows that suggest turrets and gables. The hall is cavernous, with painted stalactites of plaster piercing a gloom broken only by two lamps illuminating heavy furniture and portraits of bewhiskered overlords, with consort chatelaines in crinolines and lace. The woman walks quickly up the staircase, on to a shadow-furrowed landing and into a bedroom glistening with the dancing warmth of an open fire, leaning the door shut with evident relief. The stuffy warmth is womb-like and she turns herself in front of the fire, enjoying the heat as it seeps into her chilled body.

A four-poster bed dominates, its posts and roof losing definition in the shadows of the ceiling. Against one wall there is a desk, piled with books and papers. A sofa and chaise longue, heavy with velvet, lace and imperial solidity, mix with boulle chests and sandalwood chairs, elegant and delicate. The woman, now without a coat, in a grey skirt and high-collared hussar jacket, shakes her hair and, face in hands and fingertips on eyelids, rocks backwards and forwards in the light of the fire, lost in reverie.

There is a scratch, a knock perhaps, on a door. She rubs her eyes,

8

quickly stretching and composing her features and hands into an expectant state. It is one of the men from the church, swathed in a greatcoat and clutching a forage cap – but not in servility. He has a high forehead and deep-set eyes that take in her distraction and sadness. He clasps one of her hands in his and with the other caresses her cheek as her tears run down the ravines of his fingers. Slowly and carefully, with the intimacy of a long-standing lover, he undresses her and leads her to the bed, helping her under an eiderdown where she lies facing away from him while he removes his own clothes. The white of his body is waxy in the fire-glow as he joins her spoon-like, naked.

They lie together lost in their own thoughts; Christmas thoughts of family and friends; ghosts from another life haunting them from across a frozen continent. In time they make love, but with the sex of comfort rather than abandon, tenderly stroking each other back from where they had been into a cocoon of present warmth.

They sleep as the fire settles.

2

Breslau, Silesia, Eastern Germany.
Three months earlier. September 1944

Mimi von Hedow frowned in irritation as a soldier's kitbag knocked against the table, spilling hock on to a tablecloth that had seen better days and much soap. He waved at her in apology and she forced herself into a gracious smile that she did not feel. Her eyes scanned the milling square as she lit a cigarette, tapping the lighter against an ashtray that already contained three butts crowned with lipstick. The sun still radiated heat, enough to make the jacket she was wearing uncomfortable, but not enough when it disappeared behind puffball cumuli to make her regret her decision to continue wearing it. She picked up one of three books on the table and toyed with its pages without conviction.

'Not here yet?'

She frowned. 'He's never been known for punctuality.'

'He'll be here, don't worry. Have some more wine.'

She turned and smiled at the huge man poising a bottle over her glass. 'Thank you, Herr Reinhart. You spoil me.'

He bowed. 'Always a pleasure.'

She shaded her eyes to allow her to see him in his entirety, the vastness of his belly straining against the buttons of his waistcoat, his chins cascading over the stiff collar and overwhelming the knot of his tie.

'May I join you . . . until he comes that is?'

'Of course.' She leant over and pulled out a chair, the seat of which disappeared into the folds of his behind. He poured himself a glass and they both contemplated the scene before them. Market stalls – barrows overlaid with crude canvas – lined both sides of the gabled square. A corral containing sheep surrounded the water trough. Tethered to its rails were mules, working horses and a pony so small that an Alsatian could have looked it in the eye. Boys and old men in *Wehrmacht* field-grey sprawled on haversacks, smoking and sharing water bottles, dipping rags into an upturned helmet and squeezing the water they contained over their heads.

'Of course he'll come. He's in love with you.'

She arched an eyebrow at him. 'We're friends. Very old friends, that's all.'

'And I'm very old, my dear. Old enough to know about these things.'

She threw back her head and laughed, the tension of her previous suspense evaporating. She composed herself into *faux* severity. 'I hope you haven't been saying that to everyone who comes to your café. I'm a respectable married woman.'

He held out his hand and rocked it from side to side, accompanying the gesture with a dubious expression and a shaking of his head. In sympathy with the passing cloud that cooled the air and eclipsed the sun, her previous pensiveness returned.

'I haven't seen him since . . . '41 . . . just before . . . yes, it was just before we invaded Russia. He's been through a lot, hasn't he?'

The old man nodded.

'And?' she asked.

He shrugged. 'I can't tell. I didn't know him before.'

'I wish you had. There's no one sweeter. Really. And talented. The fun we had when we were in Berlin together! I've really missed him.'

'Us provincials not good enough for you?'

'Webbed feet and potatoes.'

'Nothing wrong with potatoes.'

'But webbed feet?'

'It's why we have such big shoes.'

He raised a huge two-tone shoe and the odd couple laughed again. Just as the sun reappeared, flooding the gables and bell towers with crystalline light, another shadow fell over the table, that of a figure wearing an officer's cap.

'Grafin von Hedow, I presume?'

'Max! Max von Sheilditz!'

Mimi sprang to her feet in delight to take in the face of her old friend who had his arms out in greeting. They hugged each other with childlike enthusiasm.

'Let me look at you.' She held him at arm's length. 'Without the cap: it doesn't suit you.'

He removed it with a flourish and posed his profile. She studied it with the precision of a practised joke.

'You still look fifteen.'

There was indeed something boyish about him that the uniform failed to age – but also a weariness that disquieted her. He clicked his heels and inclined his head.

'May I join you, Grafin? And Herr Reinhart?'

The café owner was already standing. 'I'll leave you to it. But you'd like your usual schnapps, I presume, captain?'

'Thank you.'

The two friends smiled at each other and for a few moments neither spoke as they allowed themselves to readjust to each other. She accepted a cigarette and they smoked and eyed each other shyly. The breeze flicked a lick of his chestnut hair and she noticed that the buttons on his cuffs, as well as two on his tunic, were undone. He had never been able to look smart even in the most tailored of suits.

'It's good to see you, Max. I've missed you.'

He reached over, took her hand, and kissed it. 'And me you. It's been a long time.'

'Being a soldier doesn't suit you.'

'Different skills from music and writing. I haven't touched a piano for . . . a year. And poetry? Not much inspiration or opportunity where I've been.'

'Why didn't you tell me you were here?'

He pulled at a running thread in the tablecloth. 'I was going to. Of course I was.'

'You've been here a month.'

'Don't exaggerate. Three weeks.'

'A lifetime as far as I'm concerned.'

There was reproach in her voice. The customary levity of their exchanges was gone and the *joie de vive* had departed his face. She noticed a tic in his left eye as he looked away and drew on his cigarette.

'I'm sorry. I wanted to see you . . . but . . . things have changed. I've changed.' As if to forestall any further revelations he reached for the books, holding them one by one as if they were items of evidence in a court of law. 'What have you got here? Dostoyevsky . . . Balzac . . . Turgenev. Didn't we used to have some good German writers? I always admired Mann. So did you. But he's Jewish, not German, of course. One forgets these things.' He placed the books on the table and looked at her to emphasise the irony before continuing. 'Any news? About Eric?'

'How did you know he was missing?'

'Reinhart.'

'Nothing.'

'Don't expect anything. And missing does mean missing; you do know that, don't you? There are hundreds of thousands who were encircled and captured this summer. He's almost certainly among them.'

They paused as barter became inflamed into an argument over a nearby barrow. Two soldiers were egging on the protagonists and within seconds a small crowd had gathered. They watched with amusement as the shouting subsided and the peasant farmer made hand-signs towards the back of a gesticulating woman.

'Are you happy here, Mimi?'

It was her turn to look away. 'What does that mean? Here in Breslau? Out east? In the sticks? Living on a farm?'

He shrugged. 'It's not Berlin.'

'But it's fine. Was fine, I should say. It's rather different now, as you can see.' She indicated the soldiers who were falling into lines at the approach of an NCO.

'It wasn't exactly exciting in peacetime, was it?'

'Better. A lot better. And I kept in touch, Max: with all the old gang. Eric didn't try to stop me. And everyone came to stay. They were fun those house-parties, weren't they? You enjoyed them. I know you did.'

'It wasn't the same.'

'Because of Eric?'

Max shook his head. In the chiaroscuro she could see the change: deep tiredness and a sadness at the core.

'Look, he's been a good husband to me, Max. He hasn't tried to control me or stop me writing. I knew that things would be different out in the country. They were bound to be. He's a kind man.'

'And dull.'

She looked at her cigarette, without demurring.

'It suits you though. You look wonderful.'

She averted her eyes as he studied her. She had been barely out of her teens when she married, and the dark looks she had inherited from her Italian grandmother had been sallow in an urban environment. Sun, maturity and an outside life had not made her beautiful but, allied to a natural animation, she was now an arresting woman.

'What about you, Max? What's happened?'

He considered her before replying. 'A somewhat over-developed sense of my own mortality: it's what happens in war.'

She reached over the table and took his hand. 'It's safe here. You're away from the front.'

He shook his head and sighed in exasperation. 'You haven't heard then? About the *festung*?'

'A fortress?'

'Doesn't exactly look like it, does it?'

Two sheep had slipped their pen and were trotting hither and thither, not wanting to be separated from their companions. A violinist launched into a Strauss melody further along the square.

'It's the new strategic master-plan dreamt up by . . . from the top, I'm told. And I'm part of it. The idea is that you take a city – in Russia ideally – and fortify it so that, when the next offensive starts, Ivan's then forced to make the decision as to whether he spends weeks or months taking it street by street, or leave it behind where it becomes a threat to his supply lines. The problem is that we've run out of Russian cities and have nearly got through all the possibilities in Poland. Breslau's the first city in Germany to be "honoured" with the title of *festung*.'

'So . . . you don't think the front will hold?'

'What with? Children and old men . . . like that lot?' He nodded towards the two lines that were now drawn up facing the café. 'I heard they've sent reinforcements to Warsaw. A specialist battalion. Apparently they're all deaf.' He offered her another cigarette. 'You've got to go, Mimi. Away from here.'

'Where to?'

'Anywhere in the West. Your parents. Just away from here. The Americans are nearly over the Rhine. Make sure you're in the bit of Germany that they invade.'

'But I have . . . responsibilities here. It's my home.'

Something changed in him. His fists clenched and his jaw tightened. She watched him with alarm as he spoke, straining to retain control.

'It's not going to be anyone's home soon, you idiot! Do you have any idea what's in store for us when Ivan gets here? Any idea?' There was alarm in her eyes as they darted from side to side to see if their neighbours were listening. 'Has Eric told you anything about Russia? Anything?' She began to reply but he brushed her aside. 'There isn't a city or town or village standing. Prisoners starved to death. Civilians murdered – or left to freeze in the open in winter, which amounts to the same thing. And it's not just the SS. I wish it was. We're going to get a taste of our own medicine when they get here – which they will. When? Who knows? Next month? Next year? But they'll be here for sure in the near future – and there's nothing that I, or that lot there, are going to be able to do to stop them. And, if they do to us one tenth of what we've done to them, Mimi, it'll be hell on earth here. Believe me.'

As he spoke he scratched his eyebrow. A smear of blood darkened the skin above his eye. His other hand trembled so much that, as he reached for the ashtray, the cigarette flicked across the table and on to the pavement. Aware of eyes on them, Mimi leant over and took hold of both his forearms, hard in spasm. She held them firmly and, after a few seconds, she felt them relax – the palsy still there, but subsiding.

'I'm sorry'

'No sorries.'

She felt a hand on her shoulder. Herr Reinhart was standing over her in concern. She signalled with her head that she was mistress of the situation and he retreated to the shadow of the awning.

'Better?'

He nodded. 'I can't control it any more.'

His mouth was puckered and his forehead knotted on the brink of tears. She lit a cigarette and passed it to him. He checked his hand carefully before accepting.

'Until this . . . this posting . . . I thought that there might be some chance of surviving. Not much – but some. The best I can hope for here is to become a prisoner. It's what they call Hobson's choice, isn't it? You're right. I'm a rotten soldier. Too scared.'

She stood and took his hand. 'Come. Walk with me. Reinhart will understand.'

He stood unsteadily and put on his cap, the low peak shadowing and hiding his distress. At the sight of the officer, the *Volkssturm* platoon snapped to attention with arms extended in salute. The acknowledgement was more akin to a wave. Though she took his arm, hers was the support as they strolled with the outer casualness of nascent lovers. They left the main square for the gothic shadow of the *Rathaus* where the privacy of a bench beckoned. She continued to hold his arm as they sat together, each conscious of the physical warmth of the other. She laid her head on his shoulder as she used to do in the cool dawns that followed pre-war parties. She remembered the smell of tobacco, cologne and other women's scent mixed into a cocktail of laughter. She felt his hand on her arm.

'You will go, wont you?'

She sat up and, still holding his arm, looked above the rooftops where brass-edged clouds rolled over the bell towers, amplifying the sun's glare – still summer, not quite autumn. She turned towards him and touched his cheek, almost absent-mindedly.

'I'll go.'

*   *   *

But she didn't. Autumn set in and a new centripetal force rooted her in Silesia, holding her in a huge and unheated house, alone apart from a single crippled servant and his silent wife – and the watching tribal portraits.

It started in a threshing barn, dusty, chaff-laden and dry-smelling of woodwormed timbers and stale horse sweat. Outside there was an October chill, thinned poplars, clear sun and the skittering of maple leaves. Inside there was men's work, lacking men – exhausted women hauling dried corn staves into the maw of a clattering thresher. Through the dust billows came four men, one in a military uniform with a shouldered rifle and the silhouette of rounded age, the others in olive trench coats and a medley of headwear from beret to *Wehrmacht* forage cap. All were worn and hollow-cheeked – one with a cough that pre-dated dust: a work detail of prisoners – hungry but not starved.

The grateful women pushed final staves into the insatiable machine and sat on a bench sharing apple juice, rough bread and rhinded cheese. Mimi, her dark hair tied away under a headscarf, cut four bolts of bread, keenly watched by hungry eyes, and offered them off a wooden platter. There was an attempt at dignity, but it was lost in the scramble for the food. Grateful nods and two '*mercis*'.

'*Vous êtes Français?*'

'*Oui. Et vous, madame?*' The tallest of the three checked his mastication to await her reply.

'*Je suis Allemande.*'

He considered this for a moment, improbable blue eyes above a stubble beard, trying to work out the antecedents of a Silesian peasant woman speaking faultless French. Despite his pallor and the scars of hunger on his face, there was a knowing energy that set him apart from his companions.

'*Bien. Merci, freundliche dame.*' His slight head-bow was free of irony but his eye-contact full of interest as he joined the others.

They drank apple juice, sharing an enamel mug, excluding the one whose hacking cough told of tuberculosis. No instructions were given, but work began with the men hefting stalks into the thresher and the women collecting and sweeping unthreshed ears and loose seed into hessian sacks. The men dipped surreptitiously into the raw corn, secreting handfuls into pockets and hats, observed but unremarked.

Conscious of eyes watching her, Mimi went about her peasant work, secretly enjoying, for the first time in months, the effect of her femininity. She turned suddenly, expecting the man's eye contact to disengage – but he continued to stare at her with disconcerting confidence and the barest smile. A bolt of sexual excitement contracted her stomach; a novel sensation that left her breathless and trembling. Confused and unnerved, she covered her blush with thespian coughing and reached for the dust-free air outside.

This was a new country for her. She sat in the chilled sunlight, flushed and breathing hard, shocked at the landslip of physicality that was outside her marital experience.

*   *   *

Two days later they met again in the *schloss*, now dark and eyeless, its sepulchral hall shuttered, with only a round window-light above an elaborate porch throwing a cylinder of light across its vaulted vastness. Her bedroom was now the only inhabited room in a house without servants, other than Herr Remmer and his wife who occupied the basement rooms. He had been wounded in North Africa, losing an arm and an eye. The military Kronos had been devouring his children fast, leaving only widows, cripples and echoing voids in its wake.

The day was one for light and cleaning; windows were opened to autumnal drafts that streamed cobwebs like Tibetan prayer flags, stirring heavy velvet curtains to leave a dew of dust on horizontal surfaces. Human activity raised the house out of its hibernation, and it rumbled into life again as furniture was pushed aside and forgotten corners shone to the brief sheen of a damp cloth. The library, collected and catalogued by Eric's grandfather during the time of the first Wilhelm, but forgotten other than as a smoking room by his descendants, had its shutters wide for the first time since the current Graf had gone to his war, the stale air still holding the smell of old leather in the face of the breeze that was visible in the dust-laiden sun-shafts.

She did not see him at first through the glare as she gathered cushions for an outside beating. Her first sight elicited a sharp intake of breath and the clatter of a dropped broom. As her eyes adjusted, she made out his silhouette and then the details of his face. He held a book – open.

'Baudelaire. I'm sorry to frighten you.'

He raised the book as an explanation and she nodded in acknowledgement, trying to cover her surprise.

'I love this bit. Would you like me to read it to you?'

Now in control of herself, she placed the cushions on the table between them and twisted an errant strand of hair under her scarf, thankful that the sun-shaft obscured him.

He read:

> *'Leave then*
> *And stand you here. Behold the past lean down*
> *Over heaven's balcony in antique gown*
> *While from the river's depths nostalgia smiles.'*

He glanced up at her; she continued:

> *'Beneath the arch the dead sun sinks from sight*
> *And in the east trailing her shroud long miles*
> *Hark, my love, hark, the gentle tread of night.'*

If he was surprised, he gave no indication. 'He knew he was dying of syphilis when he wrote that. I find it very beautiful, don't you?'

'Yes, I do. But Baudelaire's too melancholic for me: absinthe and syphilis aren't the best of companions unless you're feeling strong – and I'm not sure I am at the moment.

'Strong enough to do your own cleaning.'

She looked embarrassed.

'Please excuse me, Grafin; my curiosity is killing me. Your French is perfect. How?'

'My family live on the other side of the Rhine from Strasbourg – in Baden-Baden. I had a French nanny and went to school in France for two years. Not very clever, I'm afraid, just lucky. What about your German?'

'School in Germany: last four years. Not very lucky – or clever.'

She felt another flush warming her face. 'I'm sorry.'

'Don't be. I'm alive – so far – and intend to remain that way if I can scrape together enough food to get through the winter. I'm not sure that poor Pierre will make it though; his cough's got much worse and the cold's getting to him already.' He looked around the room. 'May I ask a favour?' She nodded. 'Can I borrow some books? The evenings are very long and I need something to stop Pierre's cough driving me mad. I'll return them, I promise.'

'Of course. What do you like?'

'Contemporary.' There was a real enthusiasm in his voice. 'Gide, Fitzgerald – in translation as my English is pedestrian. But if that's not possible, and I'm not sure it's that sort of library, then I'll happily run with the classics: Corneille, Racine; or with the nineteenth-century novelists . . . '

'Maupassant? Balzac? Flaubert? My favourites. But they aren't on this side. You'll find Racine in that corner. I saw *Madame Bovary* over there.'

Now absorbed in the search for literary treasure, she abandoned her cushions and, standing on mahogany library steps, she ran her fingers along leather spines, as if along piano keys, before triumphantly alighting on her prize. Still absorbed in the book, she turned towards where he had been standing to find him no longer the other side of the table but at the foot of the steps – so close that she could smell his unwashed clothes and the warmth of the air around him.

'I was worried about the steps, let me help you down.'

His hand was extended but she could not see his face in the glare. She held it, almost fainting in the consciousness of the pulse she imagined through the calloused skin. She tried not to focus on him as she handed him the book, squinting at an imaginary point beyond his shoulder. He stepped back out of the spiral of light and considered her carefully, his eyes travelling over her with a confidence that unnerved and excited her in equal measure.

'Thank you. I'll enjoy that.'

'You're . . . you're welcome. But why are you here? I mean here in the house . . . '

'I'm not supposed to be. I apologise. We were cutting firewood from the fallen branch in the garden and Hans-Pieter – you remember, our poor old guard – went to sleep in the sunshine: he does it all the time – weak heart. I saw the open doors and the books: couldn't resist. I'm sorry.'

'No. Please don't be sorry. The library's hardly used. But, tell me, how is the barn?'

'No doubt it'll stink once the cows are in but at least it will be warm. Better here than the camp. Anything's better than another winter of that.'

'Were you treated badly?'

'Us? No. Damp, bored, hungry, yes. But no beatings or starvation. Not like the Russians in some of the camps in Poland. Or the Jews. Most of the guards were a bit like poor Hans-Pieter – doing a job and counting the days until they could get home to their farms. Old, sick, reluctant – like us really: even wearing the same clothes.'

He held up his *Wehrmacht* forage cap as evidence but suddenly bought it to his chest and snapped an ironic bow, with a *Junker* click of the heels that she noticed was for the benefit of the gaunt Hans-Pieter, now framed by the French doors.

'*Danke, Gräfin.* You are too kind. I will return the book soon.'

The guard raised an eyebrow towards Mimi.

'Thank you. Corporal, your prisoner has been helping me move furniture around – for which I am very grateful.'

There was a shrug from the soldier and a bow and half-smile from the prisoner as he followed the guard through the open door. The Gräfin was left in a whirl of sunlight – and a welter of heartbeats and a trembling of the legs that even a thrashing of cushions failed to allay.

*   *   *

The last of the harvest drew them together in the threshing barn once again. Conversation was impossible either inside, with the rattle-clatter of the thresher, or outside against the detonations of the belt-driving diesel. Mimi worked hard, directing their efforts with hand signals and using her farm apron to wipe perspiration from her face. She felt, rather than saw, his eyes on her as she struggled with disintegrating stalks and contrived to look anywhere but in his direction. By mid-morning the need to grease the moving parts silenced the thresher and allowed the work-party to strew themselves around the barn. Some dozed, others smoked. Pierre, the tubercular Frenchman, pointed to the clipboard that Mimi used to record the tally of sacks.

'*Madame*, would you be able to spare some paper? Jerome will show you a trick.'

'Who's Jerome?'

She guessed the answer before he raised his arm. She tried to look again over his shoulder as she handed him the paper. From a pocket he produced a stub of charcoal and moved himself in front of Hans-Pieter who was snoring with his mouth open and a trembling dribble of saliva hanging from his lower lip. He studied the recumbent guard carefully and threw a flurry of wrist strokes over the makeshift drawing-pad. He briefly checked it before he pulled loose the sheet and balanced it in the crook of the sleeping man's arm. The other Frenchman sat up in smiling anticipation as Pierre nudged the guard with his foot. He jerked upright and looked around in alarm – before catching sight of the sheet of paper that had fallen on to his lap. He studied it without comprehension, then annoyance, before smiling ruefully as he held up a cartoon that showed a grotesque lower lip and a slavering tongue hanging from one side. The joke was clearly not a new one as the Frenchmen coughed and spluttered with laughter and the guard hammed it up good-naturedly. Jerome caught Mimi's eye.

'What about you, Grafin? Will you sit for me? I promise to show you mercy.'

'More than you showed him, I hope.'

It was his turn to laugh and it transformed him. The intensity of his usual expression evaporated as the frown of concentration metamorphosed into a good-natured boyish grin. The change was so startling that Mimi felt that she was interacting with someone entirely different.

'Shall we sit outside? The light's better and it's warmer today.' He held up his stick of charcoal as a question mark.

She nodded in agreement and they moved outside into the golden hues of an autumn day. There was sawn, but not yet split, firewood piled against the barn, two logs of which he rolled into position as stools, indicating that she should sit. He placed himself at a diagonal to her and studied her with what, she knew now, was his customary intensity.

'I'll make this a drawing . . . if that's what you'd like, of course. I could do a cartoon . . . '

'Thank you. Like most women, I'm vainer than I'd like to be.'

He signalled that she should give him a profile. She looked away with relief.

'You'll have to talk to me as I draw. It'll stop you posing too much.'

'Will you talk to me?'

'That depends on whether you say anything interesting.'

'A monologue then?'

'I'd rather not.'

She could see out of the corner of her eye that he was holding the charcoal at arm's length as an angle and measuring tool.

'You have a fine nose, Grafin.'

'You mean big?'

'No. Fine's what I said. And interesting eyes too. Your lids are splayed. Not oriental but something a bit like that. Sorry – do you mind me making these personal remarks?'

She looked round at him to be met by a flick of the fingers to indicate that she should maintain the profile pose. She tried to fix her gaze on a stand of poplars in the distance, sensing his eyes travelling over her even though it was legitimate in the circumstances.

'No. It's nice actually. I don't have too many people who make fun of me. It's a bit feudal here – as you may have noticed.'

'So who is here?'

'In the house? Two servants. Just Remmer – and Frau Remmer.'

'The cheerful one in black?'

Mimi laughed. Frau Remmer had never been known to smile. 'You see what I mean. Not the best of companions.'

'But you must have friends, surely?'

'In Breslau, yes. A wonderful man. Older. He owns a café on the main square. Very funny. No, that's not quite right. Very witty. Different.'

'What is the difference?'

She considered. 'My other friend, a very old friend, is also in Breslau. Not by choice. In the army. He is . . . he was . . . he's changed . . . very funny. A clown. God, how we used to laugh – so much that it hurt. With Herr Reinhart it's his sharpness – cynical, clever. He's a wonderful gossip too. I love that; but with Max it was like a bath in champagne.'

'A bit sticky.'

'You know what I mean.'

'Is that all? All the friends you have?'

'Here? Yes. When my husband was here we used to go to dinner, or parties, with families he was brought up with. But they're his friends really – and more of his caste. Most of them are older too – not that that should make a difference. All my friends are . . . they were . . . in Berlin. Now they're scattered across Europe – the ones that are still alive, that is. Only the men were killed at first – but two of the girls in my class at university died in the bombing this year. It may be a bit dull here – or so my friend Max says – but at least it's safe.'

She found herself turning towards him as she spoke. He made an irritated gesture with the charcoal again and she snapped back into pose.

'You're very dark. Unusual.'

She found it difficult to respond and found herself blushing again. He noticed and stopped scratching at his improvised canvas.

'I'm sorry. I get absorbed in what I'm doing and say whatever comes into my head. I'll be quiet.'

She forced herself to look at him. 'No. No, please keep talking. I've been rather lonely for the last few months. Especially since my husband went missing.'

'I heard.'

'Who from?

'Remmer. I asked him about you when he came to the barn to see what was happening. He does talk, doesn't he? Makes up for his wife, I suppose. I had the whole family history since Frederick the Great. Got a bit lost during the Napoleonic Wars.' He hesitated, obviously concerned to ask the question delicately. 'No news at all? About your husband?'

She shook her head. 'Max – that's my soldier friend in Breslau – tried to convince me that he's a prisoner. Who knows?'

He made as if to respond – but realised that any words of consolation would be clichéd and thought the better of it. She noticed this and was grateful. He scratched silently for a few minutes before she spoke.

'What about you? What did you do before the war? Are you an artist?'

He laughed again and she stole a glace at his once more transformed face, intrigued by the metamorphosis. 'If I was, I'd have starved in a garret years ago. No, I'm a journalist. On a local paper in Montreuil, my hometown in Northern France. I'd like to be a writer – but I have to earn a living, unfortunately.'

'Is it interesting?'

'It has its moments. But cattle prices and catfights in the local council only go so far. Frustrating. But better than being a prisoner.' It was her turn to avoid clichéd comfort. He carried on. 'And you? Apart from being a Grafin? You're not what I expected.'

'What did you expect?'

He shrugged. 'Something like the pictures in the library. Fierce. You've got the face for it.'

'Fierce?'

'No. That's the wrong word. Strong. Intelligent'

'That sounds better. I don't feel very strong at the moment though. Rather useless, in fact, with what's going on in the world. I read, run the farm and worry. It's all I've done for the last five years. Not much.'

'We seem to have a lot in common then.'

She looked at him. Instead of another flick of the wrist to indicate a return to profile, he looked at her with a neutral expression, the charcoal idle on the page. The now familiar surge of adrenalin stirred within her. He stared at her, blue eyes against a day's stubble and dark hair combed back from a high forehead. There was a restlessness in the pupils that flicked over her and a sensuality in the slightly too full lips that fought in the same face. He turned the drawing towards her. She looked at it in relief.

'What do you think?'

'Is my nose really that big?'

'No. Just relatively. And nor are your eyes that oriental. I'm a cartoonist – I can't help it.'

Pierre appeared at the door, saw that he was finished and beckoned the others over to admire. 'Nicer than poor old Hans-Pieter – but if I were you, Grafin, I wouldn't lend him any more books.'

They all laughed as Pierre gave the artist a good-natured shove that rolled him on to the sawdust-carpeted ground. He stood up in the sunlight, brushing down his shirt and flicking wood chips from his hair.

'I'm sorry if I've insulted you, Grafin. Hans-Pieter should have been a warning, I suppose.'

Mimi was laughing too, caught up in the good-natured banter. 'I'm flattered. I thought my nose was much bigger than you've drawn it – which must be good news. May I keep it?'

He handed it to her without comment.

'Thank you. I need to pay you for this valuable portrait. Perhaps you could all come for supper in the schloss tonight? The one thing we do have on a farm is food – so let's make sure that you have enough. Seven o'clock?'

*   *   *

It was an egalitarian meal of pork and turnips in the bowels of the house; the company was made up of the three prisoners with their guard and the Grafin and her two servants. Slowly they all softened to the schnapps and the mellow lubrication of the new century's wine. The cooking had a heavy Gallic input of garlic and herbs – watched with care by the prisoners and eaten with a fierce concentration that presaged discomfort for stomachs unused to a surfeit of food. The intermittent conversation petered into dozing by the warmth of an open fire.

Mimi and Jerome, either side of the rough table, smiled at the snoring forms around them. Proper distance had been maintained during the meal: respect shown by prisoner to captor, by guest to host and by one social class to another. Language had weaved for privacy between French and German. Jokes had been acknowledged with polite laughter, eye contact avoided and the subject matter kept to food and books – but safe in the past; contemporary topics they kept to the transatlantic, away from the political and racial fault-lines of the Old World. The personal or political had been avoided by unspoken agreement – partly to avoid the bustling disapproval of Remmer's wife, whose silence was known to harbour a fervent devotion to the Führer.

Eventually, satisfied by the Grafin's assurance of the chaperoning presence of the snoring guard, the Remmers bowed their retirement – but pointedly left open the door connecting their pair of basement rooms with the vaults of the kitchen. Pierre, dozing in an upright chair, leant sideways, half woke and jerked himself upright. His sleep-sodden eyes meandered around the bench and table before settling on the book open beside his friend. He pointed at *Madame Bovary*.

'That's a French book, isn't it, Jerome?'

'It's probably one of the best books ever written in French.'

'Never heard of it. What's it about?'

'It's about a woman called Emma Bovary, who marries a dolt of a doctor who bores her to death. She's read too many books and wants to fall in love and live among people who are educated and think about other things than pigs and the price of wool. She has affairs and ruins her husband before committing suicide.'

'Romantic then?'

'Not exactly.'

'A tragedy?'

'Yes. I suppose it is. Would you like me to read it to you? It's a good story.'

Pierre rubbed his eyes and looked around the room for a comfortable place to lie down, his gaze settling on the bench in front of the fire, towards which he shuffled.

'Thanks. I prefer my stories to have a happy ending: in love; married; happy ever after – that's my sort of thing.'

'So you're a romantic? I'd never have guessed.'

Pierre smiled an embarrassed smile as he wrapped his greatcoat around him by the fire. 'If you say so.' And his eyes closed as his head touched the pillow of his forearm.

Mimi's hand cradled her chin as they luxuriated in the somnolence around them. She glanced at Jerome across the table, at the orange silhouette of his face in the firelight. Now clean-shaven, his profile had a nobility that was at odds with the patchwork of clothes that he wore with the indifference of a vagrant. She found that the rounded length of his chin coming back into large lips that rarely closed held an intense beauty for her. These same lips occasionally puckered in concentration. At those moments they possessed a sensuality that sparked a charge of longing. She looked back at the fire, trying to keep her breathing steady, coping with an out-of-body sensation, swallowing surreptitiously to reduce the pounding in her temples. She forced herself back to Emma Bovary, aware of, and strangely excited by, the potential metaphor – the key of which they alone held.

She tested the waters. 'So how would you define romantic? Is it about getting married; a meeting of minds; a happy ending?'

'Exactly so: it's a conclusion. So I suppose you'd call Jane Austen a romantic as it all ends in marriage. That's the conclusion. Flaubert was writing about what happens afterwards; when you've got married; when the boredom sets in; when that "soul mate" is a degree duller than you thought. That's why it shocked so much: it was too close to the bone.'

She considered. 'Don't you think that most people, at the time, were scandalised by the adultery? It was about a bourgeois woman doing something that a bourgeois morality couldn't stomach.'

'Do you have a different morality?'

She found herself flushing with confusion, uncertain as to how this was meant. She glanced at him. His look was kind, but ambiguous.

'I'm sorry, that was rude.'

'No. But you have me wrong. I wasn't born a Grafin. Nowhere near. My father's a lawyer. My mother's family are academics. I "married well", that's all.'

'But you behave like a Grafin.'

A boundary had been breached, a direct and personal statement made.

'Thank you. Whatever that means, I'll take it as a compliment.'

He slid along the bench and faced her. 'Is Emma such a silly woman? If she was just silly, then she wouldn't be such a powerful character. Don't you think that for all her terrible irresponsibility there's something admirable in her longing to transcend the dreary reality of her stupid husband and her soul-sapping surroundings? I know what it's like to live in a place like the one she was stuck in. Awful. Do you know Montreuil? It's about eighty kilometres from Calais; pretty enough, with a château that was used by General Haig as his headquarters during the last war, and it was where Victor Hugo wrote *Les Misérables*. Nothing else exciting has ever happened there except the chopping off of some heads during the Revolution – and all that did was to replace those that had some education and intelligence with men like the dreadful Homais . . . remember him? – the fraudulent apothecary who sucks up to Emma's husband and spends his time spouting cod philosophy and posing as a rationalist and despiser of religion. At least Emma aspires to something. At least she wants to transcend where she is and who she is; to do something with her life rather than stew in a provincial pond of mediocrity. I'm not going to do that. Not any more.'

Without noticing it himself, his voice had risen, from an audible whisper used among sleepers to an angry half-shout that drew their companions on to the foreshore of wakefulness. There was stirring – and the sucking and clicking of dry mouths. He stared back at the fire, jaw working.

Mimi found his anger both disturbing and attractive in its demonstration of a passion that was absent from her nature. In the self-awareness of maturity, she was increasingly conscious of the strengths and weaknesses of her chameleon qualities, qualities that enabled her to move between the conventionality of her married life and a bohemian hinterland – but left the nagging fear that this made her a mere dilettante, liable to be exposed and illuminated in the presence of emotional or creative heat. The irony of human relations was that this duality of personality, that could swing effortlessly along the register of sensibility – even if that register was slightly shortened – gave her an intriguing aura that was deeply attractive to those whose personalities had formed at either extreme. He turned back towards her, his voice once more a near whisper, but the anger still there.

'What are you doing here? You don't belong on a farm playing the lady of the manor. Do you really want this for the rest of your life? Well, this sort of thing – because we both know this isn't going on for much longer. Do you want to live surrounded by peasants – and men like Homais? Stupid priests and greedy little shopkeepers squirrelling away dowries for their lumpen daughters? Montreuil;

here; no difference – just a different language and priests that wave a Bible rather than fiddle with a rosary.'

They looked at each other, both startled at the directness.

She bought time by retreating into a faint archness. 'Do I look that unhappy? Does my husband deserve to be lumped in with Emma's? Is this that bad? I don't think it is, I really don't. I'm not Emma. I don't believe in fairy tales, knights in armour or happy endings for everyone. Nor do I believe what the priest tells me, or that men like Homais have the answers, or that everything that's worth knowing is in an encyclopaedia. At least I hope it's not. I think I'm an optimist.'

'Someone who believes that the future's uncertain then?'

They both smiled and gazed at the fire, the joke rubbing the edges smooth.

'I suppose I empathise with boredom,' he continued, 'after all, I've had enough of it over the last four years. I can understand what makes Emma do what she does, the *ennui*, the feeling that anything's better than the present. You can allow me that, can't you? Given my circumstances.' He held up his hands in imitation of a man in handcuffs.

'Just don't transfer it on to me, that's all. I'm not Emma.'

'Sorry. I take it back. But if you take out Emma's silliness, can't you see what she does, her affairs anyway, as an assertion of her individuality – a statement that she's not just a possession, a cook or a bed warmer – which is what the bourgeois institution of marriage requires, doesn't it?'

'It could be about companionship, trust, loyalty.'

'Passion, intimacy, excitement. What about those?' He was now looking intently at her, the metaphor at full stretch, a charged arc of meaning flickering across the table. Holding her gaze, he stood up. 'I'm going to find the Racine we discussed yesterday. He's always been a favourite of mine. I think I know where it is, so don't bother to come – if you'd rather stay in the warm.'

His look at her was pregnant with invitation. She nodded – but hesitated to join him as, candle in hand, he was followed only by his shadow up the stairs.

Decisive moment.

Silence in the room, except for the receding sound of his footfalls and the rumbling grunts of dozing men.

Hesitation. Decision.

The sound of snoring but no one-armed enquiry from beyond the open door accompanied her as she climbed the stone stairs into the ecclesiastical cavern of the hall – so tall that the shadows lost all form as they counter-marched in magnified file through the Gothic vaults and on into the library, returned now to the stuffy stillness of inanimate leather bindings, with only a single candle on the table, scent but no sight in the gloom. She placed her candle alongside his and turned to search for him. He was standing, stock-still, watching her, half-hidden behind the door. His movement towards her had no sense of rush. His breath, damp with wine, was inside her focal length, the smell of his clothes and musk-sweat an overpowering presence.

The kiss was dominating, penetrating, drowning even, as she gasped for air, feeling his stubble's rasp over her lips and his staccato breathing loud in her ear. He lifted her long peasant skirt to her hips and pressed her back over the table with the weight of his kiss. She felt his fumbling, exploratory fingers among her underwear and pushed him upright to take control, shedding the silk but leaving the woollen stockings. As soon as her hands were free, his weight was back against her and the rough serge of his clothes was harsh against the soft skin of her upper leg.

Suddenly, he disengaged, pushing her back on to the table, and, before she had time to protest, she felt his hot, fast breath on her thighs, his rough beard – and an exquisite sliver of pleasure turning to warm waves against the insistent rhythm of his tongue. The escalation caught her by surprise. It was beyond her limited experience, clutching her in a crescendo that was threatening, frightening, out of control. So enveloping was the sensation, so sudden, that all power seemed to drain from her upper body and any effort to push away the catalyst of this physical maelstrom was a feeble failure as she felt herself tensing to a point from which there may have been no return and over which there was no check. Her own moan, loud enough to echo in her consciousness, broke the surface tension, and the waves receded in lapping

31

warmth, allowing back the sound of her gasping breath, and the alarm from across the hall and down the stairs.

As Remmer hobbled through the door, concern on his face and candle in hand, he found his mistress sitting on the table, a bare foot subject to the careful ministrations of the French prisoner, who was turning it slowly against a wincing resistance.

'Grafin . . . .'

'It's fine, Remmer. Thank you. Fine. Nothing broken . . . I think. Just a sprain. Missed a step.' She pointed towards the library steps.

The prisoner nodded in sage agreement with the diagnosis and indicated, without expression, to the servant that his judgement was required. A gasping flinch and nodded agreement.

'Shall I help you upstairs, Grafin?'

'Please, Remmer. That would be kind. Thank you. I'm really fine – but feeling a bit faint.'

As indeed she was, with an uncontrollable palsy of leg and hand, breathing that refused to come under control, swimming, lapping hotness deep in her womb and the remnants of erotic tension still undulating in her groin. Some vestige of normality returned once the concerned Remmer, not noticing the alternation of sprained ankle, had left her on her bedroom's chaise longue.

The formal copulations of her marriage had been domestic from the start, more a dynastic duty than an erotic exploration – not unpleasant, but leaving a sense of puzzlement as to why so much human creativity had been expended in celebrating something so prosaic. That sexuality could be other than missionary, that it could happen other than between the folds of bed linen or that the mere presence in a room of another human being could overwhelm all other considerations had never been in her adult experience.

Not until now.

3

Silesia, Eastern Germany. Winter 1944

Autumn moved to winter and a building sense of climacteric hung in the air. Distant from the bombers operating out of England, and away from the industrial heartlands of the Ruhr, the countryside surrounding Breslau observed its annual cycle of reap, plough and sow as it had always done – only now with foreign workers and prisoners taking the place of husbands and sons. Fronts, both east and west, were static through the autumn. The huge advances of the previous summer had shrunk the Reich from the Atlantic to the Rhine and the Ukraine to the Polish border, leaving Germany surrounded, with its enemies building their strength for the endgame.

A welter of propaganda seeped into the collective consciousness. Tales of the fate of villages in East Prussia that had been taken and then abandoned during the last gasp of the Red Army's summer offensive were salivated over by the malformed Goebbels – every detail of rape and torture, of bayoneted children and burned babies itemised and photographed. Roads rumbled under the weight of lorries and horse-drawn carts filled with adolescent soldiers with pink cheeks, barely broken voices and uniforms to fit the torsos of grown men rather than malnourished boys. They were filled also with bent *Volkssturm*, veterans of the trenches of the previous war, blinking with disbelief to be riding towards a holocaust twice in one lifetime. Occasional fighter-bombers, advance guards of an eastern nemesis, dipped their wings over church spires in search of convoys and trains that were unprotected by a Luftwaffe that was by now decimated and engaged elsewhere in a war of attrition with the bomber fleets to the west. All this was against a backdrop of peasant labour, bent in potato-picking under grey skies that merged in the autumn light, and horizons knitted together by bare poplars and isolated haystacks, stroked by parliaments of rooks and murmurations

33

of starlings; distant vistas of ploughed fields and slow ditches, mud-smeared roads, straining horses and the single-cylinder heartbeat of pump or thresher, puffing greasy smoke-rings to be snatched by steppe-chilled breezes.

Despite her assurance to her friend Max, Mimi remained in Silesia ignoring the appeals of friends and relatives to go west, to her parents' home in Baden-Baden, where, in the shadow of the Black Forest and close to the Rhine, she could have awaited the arrival of the Western Allies in a town untouched by bombing. She claimed duty and responsibility – which was partially true. But the real reason for her procrastination lay in the key to a turret staircase that led directly to her bedroom from the garden and planks easily removed from the back-wall of the barn. These had turned her bedroom into a nest of sensual adventure. Each evening, at an earlier hour every week as the agricultural day shortened, she would anticipate the sound of the Frenchman's tiptoed steps on the spiral staircase with an excitement that she had never known before. From untutored beginnings, her latent carnality had grown like a sunflower, opening and twisting into the light and warmth imparted by a natural sensualist, whose own winter years of drab, solitary boredom had given the process a particular pent-up potency.

*   *   *

The voluptuousness of it astonished her. She lay on her front with the dead weight of his exhaustion pressing down on her back, his breathing harsh and fast in her ear. She willed herself tighter round him and felt a trembling spasm deep within her and caught his sharp intake of breath that slid out in a long sigh of contentment. They lay enjoined with only the crackle of the fire competing with their synchronised breathing, its flickering light rippling over the bed and the room. Neither moved. She could feel him retreating out of her, his hardness diminishing, but his thighs still pressed against her. If she had to choose her moment, this would be it – a sensual intimacy that drained and stroked them into speechlessness; pure pleasure, culminating in a soft expulsion that drew from them both a light gasp of pleasure.

He rolled slowly on to his side, taking her with him so that they lay, still together, with the damp of his ejaculation trickling down her thigh, his lower hand cradling her breast and the other entwined with hers, fingers dancing to imaginary music.

'We never did this.'

He didn't answer for some seconds; his breathing was now steady.

'Who?'

'Eric. And I.'

'Sex?'

'No. This. This bit. He'd just pull out. And go to sleep.'

She could sense his incredulity.

'It's the best bit.'

'I know. I know now anyway.'

She shifted over to face him and put her hand on his chest, fingering his nipples and the fine hairs surrounding them. His hands lay slack and his eyes were half closed as her fingers traced a serpentine pattern down to his belly button. This unconcerned intimacy was also a source of wonder to her; the frank delight in every crease and crevice of the other's body, explored without embarrassment or hesitation, luxuriating in pleasure given and taken. He observed her and her hand as it fingered his hip.

'Were you happy?'

Her finger slowed as she considered his question.

'Yes. Yes, I think we were.' She was partially aware that she was talking about her husband in the past tense. 'But it was different. From this.' She placed her hand on his belly, touching the line of his pubic hair with her fingers splayed. There was steady pulse from a vein in the wedge of his groin. 'He was – he is – a lot older than me.'

'Did that matter?'

'No.'

'So why do you mention it?'

She considered this. 'Not so much in the years between us but . . . well, he's old in the way he thinks. Very concerned about his family. Duty. I don't know what he would have been like without it. It shaped him; a sort of mould that makes you come out rigid, channelled into a certain way of thinking about things.'

She hesitated. He stroked her cheek and lent forward to kiss her. She could smell the wood smoke in his hair. He lay back with his head resting on his hand, his eyes meeting her gaze.

'If you find it awkward, you don't have to talk about him. Maybe we should leave it?'

'No. I don't mind. Really. It's just that I've never talked about him to anyone before. Not even to my best friend, Eva. Embarrassed. Too embarrassed.'

'Why? Did he treat you badly?'

'No. God no. Never. He was always kind. I'm embarrassed . . . about myself.' She could not look at him now and stared at the Fragonard miniature on the bedside table behind his head. 'About why I married him.'

'People marry for all sorts of reasons.'

'But mine were the wrong ones.'

'You wanted to be a Grafin?'

'Yes.'

'And live in a big house?'

'Yes. Yes, I did. And be financially secure.'

She saw his shrug in a slightly raised shoulder. 'Women have married for worse reasons than that.'

'But they're not good reasons are they? Not reasons to feel proud of? Not exactly something that I would want to boast to my friends about? Or to you.'

'Everyone makes mistakes.'

There was something dismissive in his tone that rankled. She lent away from him and faced the fire. There was anger in her voice. 'They do. They certainly do.'

She felt his hand on her hip; steady. 'I'm sorry.'

She could sense the ingenuousness in his apology but waited until some of the hurt subsided. 'It's not just guilt, you know. About this.' The finger pressure on her hip told of his acknowledgement. 'It's about how I allowed myself to get here. Was I that insecure and superficial? If I was looking at me from the outside I'd say that I was.'

She forced herself to look back at him, biting her lip as she did so. His hair, normally combed back from the high forehead that framed and accentuated his blue eyes, was ruffled: she recalled her fingers raking his scalp only minutes beforehand and his tongue working between her legs. He reached out and stroked her ear. This gentleness still took her by surprise as it was not the attraction, the brutal sexual desire, that sucked her to him. It was his taut mind and whip-sharp body that had her enthralled: the dissonant tenderness awoke other feelings.

'I am looking at you from the outside. And I don't see superficial.'

'You're being nice.'

'I'm not good at nice.' They both smiled. They had laughed many times over his coruscating criticisms. 'You're too tough on yourself – and I don't really know why.'

She adjusted herself again so that she didn't have to look at him, wriggling into a foetal curl and resting her head on his stomach as a pillow, her view over the mound of his slack penis and her hand on one of his legs that she stroked absent-mindedly; intermittent gurgles echoed comfortingly in the ear pressed to his stomach. She allowed her thoughts to settle before she replied.

'It's confused. I was insecure before I got married – didn't know who I was, who I was supposed to be, in fact. My friends were writers mainly. Bohemian would be too raffish as they were nearly all educated and middle class – some aristocratic. I loved them, loved their company, but always felt that I was bringing up the rear. I could share their excitements – but couldn't add to them. Does that make sense?' She felt the faint squeeze of his hand on her upper arm. 'I was intelligent enough for them – but not creative enough for myself. And I feel a bit like that with you.' Her hand halted the stroking of his knee. 'Double insecurity.'

Her confession made, Mimi could feel the vein to the side of her head pulsing against the softness of his belly and his hand on her head. There was real affection in his reply.

'What do you think I – and they – think of you? Why do you think we want to be with you? Because you're interesting, interested. You know a lot. You're well read. You're funny. That's a good count. Not many like that. And for me there's the fucking. The best.'

'You're describing yourself. But thank you. It doesn't go away that easily, though. And it doesn't account for why I married Eric, does it? If what I wanted – needed – was money and position with someone . . . someone whom I liked enough but . . . ' she hesitated . . . it doesn't say much more than that I'm pretty shallow.'

She could sense the shrug again.

'We all have our insecurities.'

'What are yours?'

His hand checked the stroking of her hair.

'Money. I don't have any. Unlike you. And education. I never went to university. My parents couldn't afford it.'

The revelation of a chip on his shoulder surprised her. 'You don't need a university.'

'Easy for you to say.' There was a flare of anger in his voice. 'All I had was the bloody Jesuits – a childhood filled with terror. Damnation with everything. That's a pretty good insecurity, isn't it? Beatings and hellfire?'

'But now?'

'Of course I don't believe it.' The anger was still there. 'Or I don't most of the time. When I'm awake anyway. Asleep . . . well sometimes I still get the dreams. And the guilt. You'd think you could shed that, wouldn't you? When you know God's not there? What's the good in being an atheist if you still get the bad bits? Nothing at the end with guilt and nightmares to be getting along with in the meantime.'

He laughed a bitter laugh that she felt against her ear. She sat up and twisted round to face him, surprised at the depth of emotion that her question had unleashed. The cool and cynical rationalist had gone, to reveal something different, another facet to a complex polyhedron that reflected the different lights thrown upon it. She placed her hand back on his chest and lay on the pillow to look at his profile. His mouth was working with emotion, as it had in the basement on the evening of the communal dinner, and as then, shadowed and illuminated in ripples by the fire, it held a great beauty for her.

'You never told me about these dreams.'

'I get them. Not all the time. They come with . . . when I have my black times.'

This too was a revelation. She stroked the side of his head as she probed.

'Black?'

'It's what I call them. Normally I'm fine but every now and then, I don't know why or when, I get periods when I can hardly function. It's like carrying around a physical weight – lead-lined clothes. The dreams are usually the start.'

'Now?'

'No. I had a period in the factory: during the winter. They normally happen then. I dread Christmas. I'm fine now, don't worry. Maybe you'll make the difference.'

The confessed vulnerability deeply moved her. His intelligence and energy, wrapped in a carapace of self-reliance, had intrigued her from the start; this vulnerability, a deep self-doubt, was a new and moving thing that touched something akin to the maternal in her, a tenderness that added another layer to feelings that were already complex and multi-hued.

Mimi lent over and kissed him, slackening her lips so that they folded against his. She felt his hand cradle one of her breasts and a thumb circling the nipple that hardened in response, and the now familiar arousal surged upward from her abdomen and constricted her throat.

*   *   *

Mimi was a new experience for Jerome also. A natural, if not born, aristocrat, she had a poise and manner that he observed with admiration as she directed the workings of the farm during the day. Appearances were kept up: the Grafin and the prisoner exchanged daily greetings in the frosty mist of agricultural dawns. Polite discussions continued over rough lunches of cheese and bread. She gave orders in the form of requests, always polite, always grateful. Her possessions – food, clothes, blankets and books – she shared with the prisoners, always giving them the best and always with a smile that was never patronising. She was not beautiful in a conventional sense, but the sum of the parts, allied with an inherent grace, drew eyes to her. That was during the day. At night her frank and uninhibited carnality surprised, shocked and excited him in equal measure. The contrast between the public cool and the private abandon was matched by the range of her reading and the scope of her knowledge of the arts where, ironically, he discovered her insecurity. She was an observer, not an artist, and this knowledge made her defensive, as she acknowledged in him a creativity that she herself lacked. He was touched by this vulnerability, though he only partly understood it, as well as being irritated by it when she allowed her uncertainties and conviction of inferiority to surface in conversation. For both of them, this contained and intense liaison was a voyage of discovery.

Only Christmas allowed the past to intrude into their cocoon, a season redolent with domestic memories and dislocation. It was a time when separation roused guilt and regret from their slumber in the subconscious to wide wakefulness: complicated guilt, that had to be borne not shared, for a time overwhelmed their secret garden and bought silence to the public face of their relationship – a silence unremarked upon in the fog of self-absorbed apprehension. Christmas also bought a prick of conscience over her old friend, Max von Sheilditz, of whom Mimi had thought much, but whom she had failed to contact, since her promise to leave for the West those months ago. His presence in Breslau, a mere twenty kilometres away, had changed her usual behaviour, keeping her in the country, absorbed in the farm and her nocturnal escapades, and away from the bookshops and the cafés that had given her a provincial link to the cosmopolitan world that she so missed. She blamed the lack of petrol, the militarisation of the city and the needs of the farm – but the real reason was that she knew that if she went to Breslau she would have to try to find him and, if she did, then she would have to explain why she was still in Silesia. At Christmas, her conscience finally got the better of her.

So, with Remmer as coachman, on a freezing but clear New Year's Day, they heaved the old family landau from the back of a barn where it had hibernated since her wedding day, its leather seats cracked and speckled with bird droppings and threatening to split in the brittle cold. Instead of the shiny-coated black Hanoverian garlanded with flowers, a shaggy cart pony was drafted between shafts that sat over, rather than alongside its flanks. Swaddled in furs and blankets, she drove under Remmer's frustrated tuition – thwarted in his traditional role by one-armed impotence – along country tracks dusted with snow, parallel to the main umbilical road connecting the city with the West, calculating that their trotting progress would be better by the solitary serpentine lanes.

As they reached the edges of the city, the side-road options ran out and they found themselves behind a lorry of frozen soldiery, mummified in balaclavas and scarves, smoke from cigarettes mixing with the steam of collective breath and grey diesel fumes to form a cloud of resigned misery. At a walking pace they crawled through the open suburbs of the city, waved on by squads of *Feldgendamerie* – military police – brutal-looking men, with silver-chain gorgets and machine pistols around their necks. Their focus, they realised, was on traffic in the other direction, outgoing lorries and carts to be combed for deserters. Out of touch with the changes in the city, their first sight of a victim, knocking in frozen woodenness against a telegraph pole, caught them by surprise. It dangled by them for minutes as the traffic slowed to a halt, blackened toes at their eye level, turning in the occasional breeze with a limp hand missing a ring finger and an unnaturally elongated neck mercifully twisting the face upwards and out of view, its dark beard peppered with snow.

Shaken and wordless, the pony stopping and starting on cue without their intervention, they passed open spaces that had been parks or villas with wide gardens, last seen in tree-dappled summer. Now, with houses demolished to create free fields of fire, anti-tank ditches scarred themselves into the white bleakness topped with a fleece of barbed wire. Like termites atop their mound, occasional gangs of striped-clothed slaves hacked uselessly at the frozen earth, supervised by vulpine dogs on straining leashes – exhaustion apparent in each swing and skittering ricochet of pickaxe on unyielding ground.

In the winter sunshine, the dilapidated state of the city unveiled itself. Though there was no bomb damage, the concentric self-inflicted wounds of self-defence had left isolated rings of villas, abandoned by their owners only weeks beforehand, with the appearance of long dereliction. In the approaches to the old centre of the city, years of war-rationing of non-essential paint had left coloured gables a sour, peeling grey, and shops, that had spilt on to the street in peacetime plenty, retreated to boarded emptiness or the half-life of depopulated shelves. Everywhere there were carts, field-grey huddles, ragged, unshaven and dirty, and the hard outlines of ordinance.

The Ring, the old heart of the city, reiterated the grey of the suburbs; the former lavender and pink façades of the gables were scoured and cracked, their gold paint weathered back to wood, although the clocks still chimed with a peacetime timbre. Anti-aircraft batteries, spiked sandbagged tumuli, occupied the open spaces, creating a chicane of tents, carts and piles of ammunition for the pony to negotiate before coming to rest outside Mimi's favourite café, a favourite not only for its location next to a book-shop, but also for the paternal presence of Herr Reinhart. His multilingual irreverences, delivered *baritone fortissimo,* had always gathered an appreciative crowd, an impromptu cabaret that had customers laughing but also glancing nervously at their neighbours for the po-faced signature of the Gestapo informer.

Open, with its windows half-shuttered for insulation and its tall enamel stove making but a slight impression on the chill, the café shared the threadbare shabbiness of the rest of Breslau, its owner correspondingly shrunken, with great folds of skin empty of the customary fat of the peacetime trencherman.

If his flesh was reduced, his spirit appeared unaffected. 'Mimi, my dear, it's been too long.' This was accompanied by the sweeping bow of a Renaissance courtier, a kiss of her hand and an ushering to a small table by the stove.

'I can offer you *fischbratklops*, if you can stomach it – sounds like fish but looks a bit grey to me; coffee, *ersatz* of course; or the speciality of the house, *tunke* – made from, I'm assured, horse; though I would suspect that this particular horse had big teeth, a long pink tail and didn't eat much grass.'

'Coffee, Herr Reinhart, please; even if it's only hot water: I'm frozen through.'

He beckoned in the general direction of the counter where a thin girl, swaddled in coats, huddled close to the tall kettle.

'*Raconte, chérie, raconte.* Tell me all.'

She smiled a smile of great affection at this grey-jowled shrunken bear of a man with whom she had a friendship both paternal and *gallante*: he had always treated her as one of his many daughters but with an exaggerated courtly flirtatiousness that amused them both across a generational divide.

'Not much to tell as a farmer's wife. It's you who'll have to fill me in with what's going on. I only know about turnips and cows these days. I hear about the bombing from my parents but only propaganda from any newspapers that ever get to . . . '

'Newspapers! Paper maybe – but no news – just Goebbels's ink staining your fingers. Careful, though: if you read them too much they'll stain your soul the same colour as his. Did you know I met him once? He came hobbling in here before the war, surrounded by the fattest and ugliest collection of Aryan supermen you've ever seen. What is it about the Nazis that attracts such gargoyles? He had one of those particularly nasty brown uniforms they used to wear then – the only good thing about the SS is their uniforms, by the way. Not stupid, unfortunately, but a vicious little man. Not one for your *salon*, Grafin. Which prompts me to ask if there is any news of the Graf? Forgive me for not asking earlier, my dear; very insensitive.'

'No news; thank you – not that I expect any.'

He considered this but moved off on another tack. 'I have seen something – quite a lot actually – of your friend Captain von Sheilditz, who, I think, is a little bit in love with you, no? He's spent some time here – I'm pleased to say that all the good ones do – and he is a good one, I think; too good.'

The thin girl appeared behind him with a coffee pot and cups, chipped but elegant. They paused while a bracken-hued steaming liquid was poured, neither wanting to explore the insinuation.

'I came into Breslau to see him.'

'Filthy acorn muck! Coffee, indeed!' He glared at the girl as if she was to blame, stomped to the shelf behind the bar and produced a small jar out of which he twisted a spoonful of amber honey and dropped it in her cup. 'Better.'

They watched the honey dissolve.

'He's a dead man walking. It hurts me to say it, but I think you know it.'

She stirred slowly. 'He isn't expecting to survive a siege.'

'My dear, I don't think you realise how dangerous it's become here. It's martial law. Actually, that wouldn't be too bad as at least that would be law of sorts. You've met our charming Gauleiter Hanke, haven't you – here? I know you did. I remember him making me introduce you to him. Like most of those National Socialist men of the people, he's a snob – and was beside himself, in a masculine lather of excitement, to be kissing the hand of a real Grafin. He's now more powerful than any field marshal and swinging a scythe around him with abandon. Even I have to be careful. And your friend isn't careful, Mimi; not at all.'

'Have you seen him . . . recently?'

'Last night. Here. Drunk. Very drunk. Shouting drunk.'

They sipped the brown liquid, the sweetness of the honey a warming balm that worked outwards.

'Where is he?'

'His regiment's out near the new airfield that Hanke's building. But you won't get anywhere near it as a civilian. And I don't think you should see him, Mimi; it won't do any good. It would only make him more . . . worried . . . than he already is.'

'When I saw him in September, he wanted me to go West. I promised him I would, but . . . '

'Always "buts". It will be too late for "buts" soon, my dear. Let me tell you about some friends of mine. Lovely people, but . . . Jewish . . . and living in Vienna. No Ghetto Jews these: his father had been one of the Emperor's confidants and he a lifetime government servant with an Iron Cross earned at Ypres. Oh, how they prevaricated; how they procrastinated! "We're assimilated," they said. "Surely nothing will happen in Austria; not to us." I was with them at the *Anschluss*, sitting in their beautiful drawing room, when the scales fell from their eyes; when they suddenly realised that it was too late; that the fear of losing everything had now . . . lost them everything. Everything. Don't do what they did, Mimi.'

'But what about you? Why are you still here?'

'Old, I suppose: too frightened of poverty. All I have is here. This café is the remains of my rather reduced life and any prospect without it, homeless, destitute, isn't a life I want to live. Stupid, maybe. But there it is. I've made my bed and bullied my daughters to take their families to my sister's farm near Bonn. But you? You've no need to shackle yourself to a house that isn't even yours. Your friend's right. You should have gone long ago – and before the panic starts. What does that loathsome idiot Hanke think he's doing creating a *festung* with tens of thousands of civilians inside it? Surely he can't really believe that those poor children – and cripples – can hold the line on the Polish border. He can't believe it that strongly or they wouldn't be trying to make this place a fortress; in which case the last thing they're going to need is a large civilian population to feed and shelter. How are they going to get all those people away? Ice skates? Or an evacuation organised by that clown Göring with no planes and no fuel?'

In his anger and frustration he had been tapping the air with the honey-spoon and, at the last, he struck hard at the table, as if at the corpulent Reichsmarschall himself – but connected with a saucer that shattered into an inchoate mosaic, lurching the cup and its contents on to the table and floor.

It was as they were sweeping and mopping that the door opened and half a dozen uniformed men entered the café, the cold visibly clinging to them as a portable cloud, the spectacles of the rearmost steaming over in response to the relative warmth. They clustered around the stove as men accustomed to grabbing what they wanted without ceremony. Hard faces.

'What are you doing, Reinhart?'

The leader, obvious from the careless authority he exuded, leant over the table to address the café owner who was struggling to his feet with a cloth in one hand and shards of the saucer in the other.

'A dropped saucer, I'm afraid, Herr Gauleiter. Very annoying, as it was rather beautiful; from Meissen where an old friend of mine ran the factory and would let me have things that were slightly flawed rather than throw them away – as he was supposed to do.'

'I wondered where you got them from: too good for a café – even yours. I assumed that you'd liberated them from some Pole – or a Jew. *Guten morgen, fraülein.*'

He bowed towards Mimi, without recognition.

'Coffee, Reinhart, for all these gentlemen. And use this, will you.'

He tossed him a creased brown-paper bag. As the package retreated in the hands of the thin girl, the party spread itself in assumed ownership across two tables: brutal cropped heads, noses red and dripping, hands flexing in anticipation of the aching return of circulation. Mimi huddled by the stove, a slight brush of femininity against an assertive rumble of masculinity.

'Not much trade, Reinhart.'

As this seemed more of a statement than a question, the patron merely shrugged as he swept the last fragments of the saucer into his hand.

'New Year's Day is always quiet, Herr Gauleiter.'

'Not like last night, eh?'

There was a barb in the gauleiter's voice, acknowledged in Reinhart's blink and the attention of the shuffling men around the table, the instinctive antennae of bullies sensing a victim.

'New Year's Eve is always noisy, Herr Gauleiter – and some of my customers would have missed the curfew if they'd gone home. A few of them stayed on the floor overnight – which I judged to be safer for them than risking a bullet from the *Feldgendamerie*.'

'Very wise, Reinhart, very wise. But the noise is what I was talking about. Very loud. Keeping all those children who are manning the flak batteries awake. Shocked by some of the things they heard – weren't they, gentlemen?'

Nodded smirks.

'I only serve drinks, Herr Gauleiter, but soldiers do like to sing and shout if they have had a few too many: let off steam. God knows, most of them deserve a little relaxation after what they've been through – and it was New Year after all. And, I suspect that more than one of those boys out there had heard some bad language before, don't you?'

Hanke's expression stayed the same as the thin girl clumsily banged a tall pot on the table. Over the stale background sourness of the *ersatz* acorn version came the unmistakable and exotic aroma of real coffee – a distant memory of peace and luxury. In an instant, the smell transfigured the shabby room into a sophisticated oasis of furs, cigarettes in long holders, tête-à-têtes and cream cakes. The vision disintegrated with the hawking cough of one of the henchmen. Mimi noticed the condensation forming droplets on the damp hair tight against the gauleiter's skull where the rim of his peaked cap had pressed and a puffed, livid scar below his left ear; a brawling wound.

'Don't get smart with me, Reinhart. You know what I'm talking about. Soldiers get pissed – so what? They shout a bit and say things their mummies might not like – so what? There's a war going on. It's what the Führer wouldn't like, that I don't like: shouting that he's a bloody madman; that everyone should go home before Ivan arrives. Treason, Reinhart; fucking treason!'

The last was bellowed, accompanied by the smash of a clenched fist, a jangle of spoons and crockery and wide-eyed shock, as intended. The old man, still clutching the fragments of his saucer, slack-jowled and blinking, half held the gauleiter's stare, intimidated.

'So, Reinhart, who was it? Which of the little band of toffs and traitors that hang around here was it? You seem to be a magnet for them, don't you? Let's have his name so that we can cut out the gangrene before the rot sets in? Come on, Reinhart; out with it.'

No longer able to hold the hard stare, Reinhart dropped his gaze and his cloth to the table that he carried on wiping distractedly. For a moment he caught Mimi's eye, pregnant with concern and fear, his own betraying desperation – mental reflexes at full stretch, twisting like a coursed hare. His shrug was convincing, but his distracted inability to hold the gauleiter's eye negated the intended insouciance.

'It was very busy here last night: lots of singing and plenty of shouting. It sounds as if the traitor was outside if the boys in the batteries heard him. I was busy all night behind the bar or in the kitchen – not that there's much to cook, Herr Gauleiter.'

The attempt at levity was weak and relentlessly pushed aside.

'All right, Reinhart, let's jog your memory. Shall we say that this little shit has been a regular here for months. Let's say that he has a 'von' in his name. Let's say that he has a cousin who was pals with that traitor von Stauffenberg. Need more clues? Or are you too senile to remember half an hour of shouting inside your café last night, even if you failed to hear what he was broadcasting to all those impressionable boys out there. His name, Reinhart. I want his name. Now. From your fat lips.'

Slowly, he reached to his right side, unbuttoned the flap of his holster and placed a blue-black Luger pistol on the table. Maintaining his stare, he took a sip of coffee.

'Sit down.'

Still holding the china fragments, his Adam's apple pumping with the swallowing of fear, the old man obeyed, blinking eyes hovering on the coffee pot, flicking glances at his persecutor who carefully replaced the coffee cup on the saucer, palmed the pistol and leant forward on his elbows pressing the end of the barrel against the bare bald flesh of Reinhart's temple, the indentation it made going white with the pressure.

'Well? His name, Reinhart. I want his name.'

Blinking. Swallowing. Cold perspiration beading among the quivering folds of chins.

'Now.'

The click of a cocked hammer. Silence, other than the bubbling of the kettle and the short staccato breaths of mortal fear.

'Von . . . Sheild – ' the last syllable was gulped into the back of the throat with an intake of breath.

Very slowly, theatrically it appeared to Mimi, the gauleiter's finger tightened round the trigger, the gun jumping as the hammer was released.

Silence. Dud round.

The pressure was removed, revealing a livid red-filling indentation on the temple, the old man staring into the middle distance beyond the bar – a sob of snapping nerves from the thin girl and a mirthless smile from the wielder of the pistol.

'Silly me. How forgetful.' Metallic ratchet and the spring release of a spent round which spat on to the table, pirouetting drunkenly before settling with the finality of a roulette ball in between two cups. 'But good to know it wasn't wasted. That was the bullet that shot your friend half an hour ago.'

4

FRANCE

A mill-house outside Montreuil, Northern France. May 1945

The water was pearly grey as the first dribbles funnelled into the bucket below the mangle. The shirt, in damp pleats, sagged as it wound its way on to the draining-board, curling into itself in response to the exertions of the woman heaving at the handle, grunting with each revolution. Her breath was short and the fair skin of her cheeks was reddening with the physicality of her work. Her hands, with each brush of errant hair, showed that this work was not new to her – roughened, with a parchment texture to the skin between the knuckles that contrasted with the luminosity of a face that was framed by fair auburn-tinged hair. The room was as light as it would ever get – the brightness of the spring day outside visible but the north-facing window grimed, barred and cobwebbed, only admitting second-hand light that soaked into the bare stone of the walls. A cast-iron hand pump, the mangle and a wooden bucket were its only furniture; the woman's scarlet scarf its only colour; the squeak of the mangle, the dribble into the bucket and her sharp breathing, the only sounds.

Footfalls in the house beyond – not purposeful but shuffling, searching – were moving towards the washroom. The door opened and an older man, unshaven, with a collarless shirt open at the neck, looked at her for some seconds, allowing the soft flop of the squeezed garment on to the draining-board before speaking.

'Have you seen my hat?'

She carefully unrolled the nightshirt, and placed it over the mangle before answering – in a voice that managed to suggest that this was not the first time she had answered this question but was happy to do so again without rancour.

'On the dresser. Next to the flowers. I'm pretty sure I saw it there.'

He considered this, chewing his lip, his thoughts going back over his footsteps. She noticed how thin his hair had become, the silver in his beard and the rounded shoulders.

'Where are you going, papa?'

He looked up at her, or rather through her, past the mangle into the smears of sunlight outside. He nodded slowly in recognition of her question and its implications.

'Just for a walk. Nowhere near the *mairie*. Nor the café. I promise.'

'Good.'

'It's a lovely day.'

'Yes. Lovely. I'm going to take Philippe down to the river later. Will you come? As long as we go to the shallow bit near the weir, he should be able to paddle without getting into any harm.'

The man nodded as he stared at the mangle, avoiding eye contact with his daughter. 'Yes. That would be nice. Very nice.'

There was a long silence, with pursed lips and contemplation. She did not hurry him. Neither party seemed concerned about the silence, broken only by drips into the bucket.

'They're good these days, aren't they? Summer I mean. Outside days. Out of here.' He waved a loose finger that encompassed the room, but was vague enough to include the whole house. It was the grand gesture of the fallen aristocrat, acknowledging but not accepting reduced circumstances. Tired. Crushed.

The woman looked at him with gentleness.

'The sun will do us all good, papa. We'll take some wine and cheese and you can sleep under the tree. You always liked that – even when you were busy.'

Had her father been looking at her, he would have seen her bite her lip in regret at her words. She glanced to see if they had registered with him but he continued to stare at the bucket.

'Always liked sleeping in the sun. And drinking. Not too much though. Did I? Did I then? Always difficult to know. Others notice; you don't. That was Labord's problem . . . when he was mayor. It was why he lost the election, you know – not because the man was a Communist.'

'Papa, he was a Socialist.'

'He was a Communist!'

The transformation was shocking and sudden: choleric colour

surged into his face, eyes bulged and fists clenched. The woman glanced at him and then downwards, instantly softening to absorb his anger. Submissive.

'I'm sure you're right, papa. Sure.'

'Paid by Moscow. Everybody knew it. Everybody.'

'Everybody.'

'A traitor. Working for the Germans because Stalin told him to when he and Hitler were best friends in the early days; in that lovely summer, like today, lovely. Do you remember it? It was beautiful, wasn't it? Then.'

As quickly as it arose, his anger subsided, his shoulders sagged and the spleen trickled away into the creases of the rumpled jacket that seemed to overwhelm him. She took a step closer to him and put her hand on his arm.

'Yes, papa. It was beautiful then. It was.'

5

Montreuil. Five years earlier. Summer 1940

It had been an impossibly beautiful summer, that summer of defeat: days of puffball clouds rising during the afternoon into towering cumuli and red-skied sunsets; dusks of bat-skimmed stillness and nights of honeysuckle scent and stone-held warmth. The war had been heard but not seen; from wireless news-bulletins glossed by propaganda that tried to disguise the unravelling of the army and its vaunted Maginot Line; from the exhausted tales of stray refugees who had bucked the conventional wisdom of flight to the south and west; from the growl of aero engines low and offensive or spewing vapour-trails high against an azure sky.

As the catastrophe unfolded, the sound of renting along the traditional line of French politics could be heard – in absinthe-fuelled cafés; in the town hall and across family hearths and tables around the town – the Right searching for excuses among the godless traitors of the Left, and the Left pointing to the incompetence of an anti-Semitic army, hidebound by a Catholic conservatism. Generation and gender provided another front in this civil war, with women confronting older men – the younger men conscripted, killed or captured in the encircling battles to the east. Veterans unrolled maps overlaid with lines representing the trenches of 1918 and placed pins that moved daily westward in response to fragments of news, with an ominous gap appearing in the centre as the late spring turned to summer and the intensity of British aircraft activity indicated ground support for an army that could only be heading for the coast, leaving the heart of France wide open. Fragments of units cut off from the main British army appeared, unshaven, hungry and defeated; looked on with a mixture of contempt and pity as they ate silently in the café of the Grand Place, before striking north to the coast with the barest nod of acknowledgement or thanks.

Shame was a cloak worn by all. The news worsened and pins on maps remained unmoved as the front crumbled in an enveloping rout. Paris was abandoned and a provisional government formed in Bordeaux. *Les perfides Anglais* scuttled back across the Channel from Dunkirk. There was an uneasy hiatus in the sudden quietening of the skies that coincided with a humid closeness that amplified the sound of blame; blame for the shame that expressed itself in the near-lynching of a drunken Geordie deserter who pawed a respectable girl on her way to school; blame for the fear of occupation that seized a town that had been close enough to the occupied areas of the Great War to know its brutalities. The town emptied. Carts, bicycles, and cars that ran out of petrol within a hundred miles, headed south and west. Families of four generations, single women and men who had avoided conscription, all joined the chaos of that June during an exodus ahead of the *Wehrmacht* that contained death, looting and dislocation, leaving behind those too fearful to join the rout or too attached to their farms to abandon them.

Marie-Louise Annecy was pushing her bicycle up the cobbled hill when she first heard them. She had just closed the school and her focus had been on the heat and the visible patches of perspiration that shadowed her dress underneath her arms. She was self-consciously trying to smell herself as three bicyclists in German uniform, standing on their pedals, bells tinkling and laughing, swept by. One braked his steed into a skidding halt, put his steel helmet to his chest and bowed. The two others rolled to a standstill ahead of her, turned, and grinned. Boys.

'*Bonjour, mademoiselle. Je m'appelle Carl. Et vous?*'

Her first impression was of the green in the grey of their uniforms. She had been expecting the grey of monochrome newspaper photographs and also the shadowed grimness of visages under coal-scuttle helmets that had dominated the collective imagination. She had anticipated cruelty and brutality, but here were three boys: sunburnt, exultant, smiling, flirting – in the colours of youth. She smiled an involuntary smile that she forced into a frown, but not before they had seen it, forming a close escort as she purposefully carried on pushing her bicycle towards the town-centre, mounting it unsteadily as the road flattened, trying to pedal ahead of them as they easily outflanked her with sweeping turns, blowing kisses at her and laughing with each pass. She could sense eyes on her from windows and doorways and put on her angriest face until she turned suddenly into the gate at the side of her father's house, ignoring the shouts and catcalls behind her, running through the open door and into the sheltering gloom of the hall. She hovered, invisible from the outside, watching the boys as they laughed and drank from their corrugated water bottles, leaning against the pollarded lime trees of the Place Vert with unconcerned ease; victors.

She tiptoed up the stairs, having slipped off her shoes, and stood back from the window, still invisible from the outside but with a view over the small square. Surely they weren't the only ones? Across the street Madame Acarier was watching from a similar position. Their eyes met before their gazes both returned to the invaders who were now perched on the curb and sharing a sausage as they chatted, hand movements and laughter indicating the perennial male adolescent obsession. How old were they? Eighteen? Nineteen? No more. She felt old. Only twenty-six, but these soldiers felt like another generation: children. The nearest one, the French speaker, had his back to her. She noticed the sunburn on his neck, on the unprotected skin that had been covered by hair. He must have had a haircut in the last couple of days, she thought. The darkest of the three had his tunic unbuttoned and his shirt open to his chest. He was smoking and the sun caught the threads of smoke against the shadow of the building behind him. It was only a coincidence, but the spot they had chosen to eat, drink and laugh was where, in peacetime, the young men of the town did the same. She tiptoed back along the corridor and knocked on the door at the head of the stairs.

'Papa, the Boche are here.'

Almost instantaneously the door opened. He was fully dressed, with a shirt, stiff collar and tie but no jacket in deference to the closeness of the day.

'Where are they?'

She pointed down the landing towards the window. As she had before, he stood back, invisible from the outside, and watched, expressionless. He came back to where she was waiting.

'Where are the others?'

She shrugged. 'Behind. I don't know.'

Just then, the noise of a lorry engine could be heard, revs high, grinding its way up the hill. He looked at her, nodded, and went back into his room and reappeared in his suit jacket. He signalled that she should join him as he headed for the front door. The mid-afternoon heat beat down on them as they stood side by side in the gateway that formed the old coaching entrance to the house. The three young men were too busy doing up their tunics and straightening their helmets to notice them and were standing at attention as a staff car drove slowly past, with an officer and driver in the front seat and two soldiers in the back with machine pistols sweeping windows and doors. Behind them were two lorries, their engines blowing clouds of noise and exhaust smoke. Her father indicated that she should follow him as he tailed the second lorry into the square. Guns pointed at them from the shadows of the canvas-covered rear. Behind them, others were filing into the square, silent, formal, children holding parents' hands. Others looked down from windows or stood in doorways as the lorries fell silent and troops jumped down, falling into two lines, shadows cast by their black helmets giving a sinister mask to their eyes. She noticed how dirty their uniforms were, their boots dust-covered and the canvas of the lorries streaked with mud stains. In the second row she spotted her blond, sunburnt, smiling boy – now expressionless, a carrier of weapons, jaw set and eyes forward. A conqueror.

The officer stood in his car, one hand on the windscreen the other on his hip: young too. She noticed the hipped hand clenching and stretching – a nervous tic – and a hole in his tunic that bore the hallmarks of a bullet. His reddish hair was damp with sweat and, without looking anywhere but over the square, he performed a sign of the cross over his face with a grey handkerchief to mop the pearls of perspiration that trickled over his eyebrows. He waited patiently until the last boot scrape and dust-laden cough gave way to a final silence. She was expecting him to shout but he spoke in short sentences, halting for his interpreter, the language rather than the content harsh to the Francophone ear.

'This town is now under German military law. There will be a curfew, until further notice, between the hours of 8 p.m. and 6 a.m. All weapons are to be handed in immediately: failure to comply will be punished by death.'

He halted and wiped his face again.

'Military law applies to all troops. We are soldiers, not savages, and the strictest discipline will be enforced. You have nothing to fear if you cooperate. Will the mayor or senior government official please step forward?'

Without looking at his daughter, Michel Annecy walked slowly across the square. He halted in front of the car and saluted, something she had never seen him do before – his military days being over in her infancy. It gave him dignity, she thought proudly, as the interpreter said something to him that was difficult to catch. The officer in the car stepped down, and returned the salute, but with the out-thrown arm of the Nazis, and the two of them walked into the *mairie* with its tricolour rippling to the occasional stirring of the humid air. Sentries were posted as the troops were fallen out, some soaking their heads under the hand-pump, others lying against the wheels of the lorries and pouring the contents of their canteens over their faces, unconcerned by an audience that was observing them with unalloyed fascination. Two young boys, one holding a stick, edged closer to a soldier who was slicing a sausage. He held out a morsel to them, smiling a broken-toothed smile. The boy with the stick edged forward, one arm outstretched with the other being held by his friend as if to stop him falling over an imaginary cliff. The soldier kept drawing the prize back towards him, before suddenly thrusting it into the boy's hand with a laugh that was shared by his companions but which scared the boys into a terrified dash to the shelter of a tree from where they could inspect and eat their prize. Women stood in clusters and watched, Marie-Louise among them. One of the soldiers caught her eye and waved. Confused, she dropped her eyes. Her companions looked at her in surprise. She felt an accusation, and embarrassment.

'He was one of three who passed me on the road as I was coming back from school – on their bicycles. They're boys. Just boys.'

'Did you speak to them?' Adèle Carpentier always managed to

make a question like this have implications beyond the form of words.

'No. No, I didn't. He spoke to me. In French.'

'What did he say?'

'He said his name was Carl, I think.'

'Which were the others?'

Marie-Louise tried to look without appearing to do so, using the pretext of the sun to shade her eyes. The darker one was combing back his wet hair, a cigarette between his lips and water staining the front and shoulders of his tunic.

'By the hand-pump, combing his hair. I can't see the other.'

'Not bad-looking.' It was the turn of Ghislaine Proux to feel the questioning eyes of the other women. 'I said he was good-looking, that's all. He can be a Boche and good-looking, can't he?' She stared Adèle out, with crossed arms and a slightly raised voice – loud enough for the circle to hear but no one else. 'Stop giving me that crap, Adèle. It isn't going to be possible to ignore the Boche – they're going to be around for some time – and I, for one, am going to say *bonjour* if one says *bonjour* to me. And if you think that's the same as fucking them, then go ahead and think it. What do you think, Marie-Louise?'

'I . . . I think that courtesy isn't collaboration.' She looked nervously at her friend, who carried on – fiercely.

'Look, those are the same lot that may have killed Marie-Louise's Jerome and my Robert for all I know – so I'm going to ignore them. But if one opens a door for me, I'm going to say thank you. If we're going to be occupied by them, we might as well give them reason to treat us well. And, Adèle, if any woman who speaks to a Boche is going to be labelled a whore by other women, what are the men going to do? We're in this together – so for God's sake let's stick together and not give the Boche a catfight to watch. OK?'

Adèle gave them a look that didn't bode well, but the group overall nodded acquiescence. Marie-Louise caught Ghislaine's eye, indicating with a nod of the head that she should follow her as she made a move towards her father's house. They would have the luxury of privacy there: their maid, Bernadette, was visiting her grandmother, as she did every Wednesday.

They sat in the parlour, its heavy oak furniture exuding an airless stuffiness that even an opened window and door failed to stir, its taste seemingly absorbed into the wine and water that they drank. There was a comfort in their silence that was the privilege of a childhood friendship. They had always known each other – but it was in many ways a friendship of opposites. Marie-Louise had shone at school with a powerful intellect that had her teachers shaking their heads at the accident of gender that prevented her from climbing to the heights of the École Nationale. Even if the school had been open to her, it would almost certainly not have happened, because on the other side of her balance sheet was a laziness, or rather a lack of ambition, that kept her planted in rural northern France, a teacher in a *lycée* of moderate attainment rather than at a university tested by richer minds. Her character held a curious combination of cleverness and diffidence, intellectual assurance and lack of confidence, as well as an endearing, to Ghislaine at least, cack-handedness in personal relationships. As dark as Marie-Louise was fair, Ghislaine had been a tomboy as a child, an object of wide-eyed admiration to her timid friend as she threw stones with the boys and joined the roughest of them in any adventure. They, in turn, admired her and, as they grew older, flocked round her as she learned to drink, smoke and match their jokes. She possessed the gift of friendship that transcended gender, and managed to walk the tightrope of flirtation, without alienating her women friends who were, though they would never admit it, afraid of the direct stare that suffered no fools and the lash of her tongue that left a stinging mark on those who crossed her. There was something of an antelope about her, an alertness, a litheness and quickness of movement, that captured the attention. She had married the town doctor, a huge man ten years her senior, who everyone had assumed to have homosexual tendencies since he had shown no interest in any woman before he had proposed to her – and none since. He was devoted to his patients to the point of obsession, but it did not stop him and his wife being happy – much to everyone's surprise – though after six years they were still childless.

The two women listened to the sound of Teutonic voices, carried on the humid air from the square, fanning themselves with dog-eared magazines and sipping watered wine as they felt trickles of sweat running down their arms and the insides of their legs under their summer dresses. A clock, masterful in the corner, chimed the hour with a rattling of cogs and whir of springs, and a blackbird alighted on the open window's sill, bobbing in defiance of the closeness of the day.

Marie-Louise broke the silence. 'There must be some way that we can get some news, surely?'

'From Bordeaux? Or Vichy – which is apparently where Pétain is now setting up some form of government? I doubt they even have a telephone. What do you want to do? Ring up General Weygand and say, "Have you heard any news of two reservists who were in a unit north of Sedan?" And there's the small matter of the Boche. Maybe they'll take kindly to us trying to make contact with the French military headquarters – but I doubt it. It'd be a bit silly to get shot as spies, don't you think?'

Marie-Louise looked at her friend with annoyance, fanning herself faster. 'So we just have to wait?'

Ghislaine dropped her magazine on the table, stood and walked to the window, where a small stirring of air moved her cotton dress. 'We should have gone, shouldn't we? Joined the *exode* to the south? Chantal was right. It would be better to have options. We could have seen how things worked out. Now we're stuck. *Merde.*' She took a packet of cigarettes and started to rasp at the flint of a lighter, banging it on the table as a drift of smoke surrounded her, hanging in the still air.

Marie-Louise shook her head in exasperation. 'We've been through this many times. I stayed because of the school . . . and papa. And you because you're a trained nurse and the nearest thing to a doctor round here until Robert gets back. So we can moan about it – or we can make the best of it. Anyway, to where would we have escaped? Another part of France? What would have happened on the road? Bombed and starved most likely. Raped by some drunken Tommy or Boche. And what does Chantal do now? I'll tell you what: she comes right back here when the surrender happens – as it must do any time soon. Where else does she go? Across the Pyrenees to Spain? To

England in a fishing boat? I doubt it. The Boche are going to be all over France – so this is as good as anywhere. And they haven't exactly arrived shooting and looting – so far.'

'Oh, you're right. Always so bloody logical!' Ghislaine stamped her foot in frustration and marched around the table dragging at her cigarette. 'I just feel so . . . angry. You don't seem to understand how much I hate those bastards. How dare they invade France, drive into my town and start pointing guns at me! All you can say is that they seem to be a decent bunch. If they are so bloody decent, why don't they go back to Germany and point their guns at someone else? I know I had to stay here, but it doesn't make me feel any better about it – and no amount of soft fluff from you is going to make me feel any different about it – so stop trying.'

Just as she was stubbing out her cigarette, they heard the sound of the front door opening and masculine footsteps in the hall. Ghislaine glanced at her friend and made a face. She knew Marie-Louise's father hated women smoking – even though he chain-smoked himself. He appeared to notice neither the women nor the miasma of smoke that filled the room as he strode to the cupboard to pour a slop of Calvados into a tumbler. He walked to the open window and stood by it, looking into the street.

'Arrogant little shit.' He turned to look at them. 'But he's decent, I think. Not a Nazi.'

'Papa, did he tell you what's going to happen?'

'Yes . . . and no. More stuff about military law and curfews for the foreseeable future. "We're now the front line," he kept on saying. What I think he meant is that, as far as they're concerned, France is finished and they're turning their attention towards England – which makes us, only ten kilometres from the coast, the front line. Whatever happens we're going to be in a heavily militarised zone – which isn't going to be much fun: limited travel, billeted soldiers and our cafés filled with off-duty Boche. They'll loot, I'm sure. And you girls have got to be careful.' He nodded sagely. 'Really careful. Don't tempt fate by wearing tarty clothes. The Boche have this idea that all Frenchwomen are whores.'

'Why?'

There was something pointed in the way that he ignored Ghislaine's interjection and reached for the packet of cigarettes on the table without seeking her permission. For her part, she visibly bridled, jaw clenching and eyes narrowing. She reached over to take the packet from him, avoiding eye contact and lighting up as she looked out of the window but neglecting to offer him the courtesy of the same. He raised an eyebrow before he shrugged and reached into the depths of his pockets for his own matches.

'As I said at the council meeting last night, we must do nothing until we hear from Bordeaux . . . '

' . . . Vichy.'

He continued with only hint of a pause.' . . . what the Maréchal orders. There must be some sort of armistice soon. What a disgrace! They're cowards, the lot of them.' He shook his head sadly.

'You mean our husbands?' The anger in Ghislaine's voice was now on the surface.

'Of course not, my dear . . . ' He waved his cigarette dismissively, but not decisively enough to wipe away the imputation.' . . . the generals. How could they lose everything in six weeks when we, led by men like the Maréchal, held the Boche for four years and then managed to thrash them? Politicians. Communists. *Merde.* Maybe we were tougher?'

'Or more stupid.'

He looked up at Ghislaine, anger now flushing across his face. 'Stupid? What do you know about war? What do any of your soft generation know about it? Eh?'

'Enough to know that any war that resulted in the same thing happening again twenty-five years later was a stupid war – that's what I know. It's your generation the generals in this war belong to, *monsieur*, but it's our generation that's going to have to fight to get those filthy Boche out of France while you wait for orders from some vain old man who thinks he'll be the saviour of France all over again.'

The two of them were now staring at each other in anger and mutual dislike. Marie-Louise held up two hands, making the motion of pushing them apart.

'Papa! Ghislaine! Stop this now. Now, do you hear me? Stop. Both of you.'

They faced away from each other, furiously smoking, Ghislaine wiping her forehead on the shoulder of her dress, Marie-Louise's father using a monogrammed handkerchief to do the same.

'What is wrong with you two? Why do you always end up arguing? Anyone would think that neither of you were patriotic from the way you go at each other. Are either of you responsible for losing this war? I don't think so. So leave each other alone and fight the Boche instead. Come on!'

Ghislaine fanned herself furiously with a magazine, Marie-Louise's father attempted insouciance – but a tic in his eye gave him away.

Marie-Louise continued. 'Can we go back to talking about the Boche, please? Papa, we need to know more. Are they going to put a garrison here? What happens to the school? And food? Will they take everything? Will you remain mayor? Are they going to take hostages?'

He pursed his lips. 'No. I don't think so. Unless, that is, some idiot tries to be a hero and shoots one of them. Whatever deal the Maréchal can come up with for France as a whole, I don't think it will cut much ice here as their military law will apply. Me? I'll just be a transmitter of orders. They'll want to control everything – until the invasion of England is over, that is. Then . . . who knows? They may occupy the whole country. More likely they'll just neuter the army, steal the fleet and occupy Algeria. And use us as a Boche holiday camp.'

He got up again and looked out of the window as one of the lorries passed by, its engine making too much noise for speech. As the noise receded, he turned back to the women. 'Thank you for staying; both of you. I know you wanted to go; but I hope you understand why I asked you to stay. We must be careful though.'

He gave a half-formal nod or neck-bow and left the room. They listened to him climbing the stairs without speaking. How typical, thought Marie-Louise: admirable, maddening, arrogant, insensitive, disarming. How could all these things exist in one man? She realised that her friend saw only the negatives, his bullying arrogance and his dismissal of opinions other than his own. But that was why he was mayor and a rich man; rich by provincial standards, with a textile business that he had built from nothing through the depression of the previous ten years. His courage was legendary, physically in the Great War with a *Croix de Guerre* to prove it, and mentally in the way he had dealt with business disasters and the death of her mother who had been his counterbalance, a gentle and softening influence that allowed Marie-Louise to love as well as fear him. She realised that he hated the role that was now upon him – a mere receptor of orders from the Germans, rather than the giver of commands. She tried to explain this to her friend.

'Papa is in a difficult position; you must understand that.'

The ire was still in Ghislaine's voice. 'What's so bloody difficult? If he's so patriotic why doesn't he just resign and let the Boche give the orders? Then at least everyone knows that it's them doing it rather than us collaborating.'

'You know it's not that simple. Someone has to talk for us. We're in a military zone. The Boche could be completely arbitrary and ship us all off to Germany. Life's got to go on, and in the real world we have to talk to them and come to some sort of *modus vivendi*. You know he doesn't like it. He hates it. Admit it; the fact that you don't like him means that you refuse to see that. Please, Ghislaine, for me, understand it and try to see the best in him rather than the worst. I know the worst is bad, but there is another side; I promise you.' She reached across the table and held Ghislaine's hand. 'Please.'

'I'll try. But it's difficult.'

6

Montreuil. Four months later.
October 1940

Marie-Louise smelled him the moment she walked through the door. Over the faint cologne of her father was a new masculine aroma: pleasant; a combination of cigars and shaving soap. She carefully pushed open the door into the parlour. No one. She tried the kitchen where the smell grew faint against the familiar body odour of Bernadette. Up the stairs and on to the landing. Warmer. In the guest bedroom she could hear the sound of footsteps hard on the wooden floor, the unfastening of a metal trunk and the scrape of an opening drawer. Where to wait? She walked quietly to her room and shut the door behind her, intending to mark some essays and await a meeting on her own terms. She tried to concentrate but the movement along the landing vibrated her writing table, reminding her of the foreign presence in their house.

They had received the news the day before. Military personnel would be billeted with them, they had been told – numbers not specified. Here was the first. What would he be like? An officer: Luftwaffe; no other details. By now the Germans had become a fact of life, a life that had adjusted to their presence with the usual human adaptability that absorbs and makes humdrum the most extraordinary of circumstances. The initial terror of occupation had receded. Their grey and black uniforms, the guttural orders, the tramp of boots and their triumphal songs seemed to have always been there, life without them a receding memory. They barely raised a glance from the queue outside the boulangerie as they paraded in the Grand Place or smoked in groups and eyed any passing girl. The reverberation of aircraft engines still elicited a searching of the sky to the north, towards the airfield of Le Touquet, home to a wing of bombers engaged in mortal combat over London and the ports of the south coast of England. Occasionally, disabled Heinkels with shattered perspex and twisted metal coughed their way home like drooping-winged vultures, shedding oil and smoke. One dropped a wing and erupted in a column of smoke below the walls of the town, its broken-backed skeleton smouldering for days, its carcase guarded from curious children by a bored sentry. Food was becoming scarce and a mounting obsession. Winter was anticipated with foreboding as it became apparent that the season for invasion was over and that the war would drag on. The boredom of curfews, the attrition of shortages and the restrictions on movement were taking their toll.

While the presence of billeted soldiery was an added imposition, Marie-Louise was secretly intrigued. What would she say to them? How would they live together in the silence of antagonism? She had addressed it with her father.

'Polite. *Bonjour, bonsoir*. Please and thank you. That's it. We agreed at the council that they could make life intolerable if we boycotted them completely. But no conversation. Make sure that Bernadette makes coffee for them in the morning but lock the drinks cupboard. They can guzzle their filthy schnapps but I'm damned if they're going to drink anything civilised.'

The vibrations ceased. She tiptoed to the door and put her ear to the hinges the better to hear his movements. She heard a door open and the faint sound of song, phrase mouthed in half-voice, a love song perhaps, just audible above the knock of boots on stairs. She heard the door of the parlour open and close, and carpet-muffled steps.

She looked around for an excuse to visit the kitchen, alighting on the washbowl and jug on the chest. She glanced at herself in the mirror. Her hair was sensibly held back by two grips; grey skirt and sensible cardigan: a schoolmistress. She stretched her facial muscles and set her expression to neutral. Maybe a small frown? She discarded it as too contrived before setting forth with bowl and jug in hand. As she reached the parlour door, she transferred the bowl to one arm and reached with the other to turn the doorknob. Just as her hand fell upon it, the door opened, almost making her lose her balance. She took an involuntary step forward, to find herself at neck level with a grey uniform and a hand on her shoulder restoring her balance. She took a backward step of recovery, only then able to focus on the man in front of her, who, she was disconcerted to see, was laughing at her.

'*Pardon, monsieur.*'

She almost dropped the jug and bowl as she grasped them once again in both hands, flustered.

'*Pardon?* It is I who should be apologising to you, *madame*. Please, let me take that for you.'

He reached out for the bowl, which she relinquished. 'The kitchen?'

'Thank you.'

Feeling suddenly naked, she folded her arms to mask her confusion and watched him through the kitchen door place the bowl on the table and face her once again. He was taller than her by a head and pleasant-looking rather than handsome, with a smile that had the appearance of being his natural state of repose. That he would be a difficult man to dislike was obvious. He stopped two paces from her and bowed with a faintly ironic click of his heels, still smiling.

'Leutnant Kohl, Luftwaffe, at your service, *madame*. I am uncomfortably aware that I am not welcome in your house, but hope that you and your family will understand that it is not my wish to be here under such circumstances. If I can do anything to make my presence less of an imposition, I will do my best to do so. Perhaps I can contribute to the cost of your maid or help with some additional food? I am also aware of the sensitive nature of . . . conversation with the enemy . . . so I will not embarrass you, or your husband, with anything other than commonplace civilities – which I sincerely hope will not be misconstrued.'

It immediately occurred to her that his French was nearly perfect: in another uniform she would have had him down as an Alsatian. There was a formality in his conversation that she felt instinctively was foreign to his usual style.

'I should also let you know that my duties are mainly nocturnal and so I'm afraid I will be in the house a good deal during the day, albeit asleep. I understand that there may be another of my countrymen billeted on you. He might be living a more normal life so I am sorry to say that you may have one or other of us around the clock.'

He smiled and shrugged while raising his spread hands in a gesture that said that this was regrettably out of his control.

'Thank you.' She found it difficult to look him in the eye and focused instead on the kitsch watercolour that hung on the wall behind his left shoulder. 'My husband isn't here . . . a prisoner . . . but you'll meet my father. He's the mayor of Montreuil. The maid's name is Bernadette and she'll make sure you're looked after. Thank you for your offer, but my father would never accept it. I'm a teacher and will be out during the day, so we probably won't see each other very much.'

She stopped and there was an awkward silence. He nodded, continuing to smile with gentle gravity, while she looked out of the window into the gloaming of an autumn dusk with just the heavy ticking of the corner clock measuring the gap between words.

'I . . . won't hold you up any longer, *madame*.' Neither moved. 'May I ask a favour? You have a piano . . . and I do like to play. Nothing serious, I'm afraid – a misspent youth spent in jazz clubs. I would, of course, only play when you and your father were out.'

She looked back at him to answer. His chin had a pronounced cleft and his crinkly black hair was almost mastered by hair oil. Five-o'clock shadow accentuated his dark colouring. His age? Difficult to pin down – but there was an openness about him that was still youthful and an ease with her that suggested a life lived contentedly in the company of women.

'I'm afraid that the D sharp key is mute and it needs tuning. The piano tuner was killed last summer – but it's there if you want it. The parlour isn't much used as my father and I tend to eat together but spend our time independently in our bedrooms.'

'Thank you. I'm much obliged. And I do assure you, *madame*, that I will do my best neither to inconvenience nor embarrass you, as I am keenly aware of the . . . difficulties . . . in our situation. *Au revoir, madame.*'

She acknowledged him with a faint bowed inclination of the neck as he retreated to his room, leaving only the metronome of the clock counting out the evening and a single lamp subsuming the last dregs of autumnal light.

Breakfast two days later was, as usual, silent; the rustle of the turned pages of a two-day-old *Figaro* the only noise other than the occasional phlegm-filled coughs of Michel Annecy, whose tobacco-soaked lungs reacted badly to the autumnal fog and the sooty fumes of the town's coal fires. They still drank coffee, its source a mystery to Marie-Louise; her father simply dumped a brown bag on the parlour table without explanation – a lifetime of traded favours being the most probable.

They heard the sound of the front door opening, footsteps in the hall and on the stairs, another door shutting – and then the sound of movement in the room above them.

'What do you think of him?' Her father raised an interrogative eyebrow across the table.

'He,' she raised her eyes to the ceiling, 'seems decent enough. Better than that, I suspect. He asked if he could play the piano. I hope you don't mind, but I said yes – he promised not to when we're in the house.'

'I agree. We could have done a lot worse. A lot worse. He asked me as well. I was probably rather graceless in replying that he was in a position to do what he liked; true – but not particularly good manners as he really didn't have to ask. He seems well educated and speaks excellent French. He's going to be around for some time it seems – as long as England holds out. That can't be too long though; the Boche will simply starve them into surrender now that they've got their U-boats based on our Atlantic coast. Bastards.'

'Who?'

'Both of them. The Boche and the Tommies. They deserve each other. With friends like them, who needs enemies? How could any so-called ally open fire on our fleet? I don't like the Boche any more than I ever did – but we have to face the fact that they've won the war and that we need the Maréchal to negotiate the best deal he can with them – and get Jerome and the rest of them out of their camps and back home. The sooner the better, in my view – and the council's as well.'

Marie-Louise did not reply but stood to take the plates into the kitchen. Her father looked at her over his coffee cup. 'What do you think, my dear? Tell me, please. I'm interested.' There was no disingenuousness in his tone or expression, as she looked at him to check. 'I want to know, as I only hear the opinions of my generation. What do you and your friends think?'

She sat down again, surprised once again by her father.

'I don't know. I really don't. Of course I want Jerome and all of them back again. And yes, it does look as if the Boche have won – or it seems impossible for the Tommies to win, which may be the same thing. I can see why you and your friends resent the Tommies but if we're going to have any chance of ever seeing the back of these Boche, then it's going to be with their help. That's what I think. And Ghislaine too, though she'd probably be for getting on with killing the Boche now.'

He considered what she had said, observing her over his spectacles. 'But we have to deal with reality: half of France is occupied, the Boche are systematically looting us and the army's locked up in Germany. Until we get our young men back, there's nothing we can do. That's why the Maréchal needs our support. We have to help ourselves; but if that silly girl thinks that blowing up a few Boche on their way out of a café is going to make any real difference, then she's even stupider than I thought.'

Marie-Louise felt the usual anger rising in her. This was a familiar battleground pocked with shell-holes where the conflict had moved back and forth over the years with no resolution. She stood up, pushing down her anger so that all that showed was a flushing of her cheeks. Her father turned back again to his newspaper, pretending to ignore the banging of plates and savouring his little victory of sorts. Why had she allowed herself to be drawn? Why the antagonism between him and Ghislaine? Neither would explain. Had he listened to what she had said? Often he would appear to dismiss her and then, later, she would hear him expressing her views as if they were his own, sometimes with a conspiratorial wink, at other times, with no acknowledgement at all. She knew he was proud of her intellect and she had overheard him boasting of it to his friends – but he rarely paid her the compliment of the conversation of equals.

He was still reading the newspaper when she left, waving to her without looking up in response to her parting salutation that had not quite lost the anger she still felt as she wheeled her bicycle into the street. It was Saturday and there was no school. The market was bustling in the lower square, the Grand Place, that was washed by an autumnal sunshine that dappled the medley of stalls and barrows with dabs of colour as it broke its way through the early-morning fog. Horses stood patiently, eyes in blinkers and mouths in nosebags, occasionally shaking their manes against the damp. Simple barrows with a paucity of dirt-covered root vegetables, eggs and mushrooms were threaded among more permanent canvas-covered stalls that sold knives, baskets and the iron tools of peasant agriculture. Men and women, principally women, straight from a Millet or Courbet painting, pushed and railed at rival stallholders or in loud barter. Children, mostly her pupils, played around the pump, waving to her as she passed, one coming up to her with an apple as a present, one side half-eaten. The odour of horse dung, drains, unwashed clothes, goat's cheese and decaying, discarded vegetables flecked the air. Two Germans, off duty, wearing forage caps, picked their way through the crowd, the colour of their grey-green uniforms, with their white and black flashes, contrasting with the earth-tones of the crowd. Marie-Louise looked firmly ahead as, in her peripheral vision, she saw one nudge the other and point in her direction. An ancient lorry, belching black smoke, backed up one of the streets radiating from the square to a chorus of curses from peasants pushing barrows into position. She waited for the altercation to die down and the street to clear before mounting her bicycle, weaving her way though the thinning traffic and leaving the square behind her.

Ghislaine's house lay on the outskirts of the town. Its ground floor was given over to a surgery and dispensary. Its waiting room, during weekdays, was a repository for all of rural life: Ghislaine had told her that, on top of some gargoyle-like humans, she had once been confronted with a bestiary that included chickens, a pig, a calf and a cage of vocal geese. Today it smelt only of disinfectant as she let herself in and climbed the stairs to the apartment above, knocking as she entered. Ghislaine leant out of the kitchen into the narrow corridor. She was wearing a dressing-gown and greeted her friend warmly.

'Come and have some coffee, darling; Jacques and Stephan are here.'

She exchanged kisses with the two men whom she had known since childhood but who were Ghislaine's friends rather than hers. Their greeting was friendly but she noticed a glance between them that suggested concern rather than the usual male conspiracy of sexual interest. The small table was covered in books. Coffee cups and an overflowing ashtray fought for position with elbows and a slab of bread. Marie-Louise lit her own cigarette with contentment, enjoying the contrast with her own domestic situation, and indeed her own nature, which was congenitally tidy. With Ghislaine nothing was sacred – and her impromptu *salon* was a magnet for wild ideas, heated political discussion and music, awash with wine and quarrels that sometimes spilt violently on to the street. Though her husband was respectable and beyond reproach, Ghislaine was strong meat for the burghers of Montreuil – and their wives – whose provincial conservatism looked askance at her friends and views that veered substantively to the left. None were overtly Communist – but they might as well have been for all the nuances accorded to their views in the more establishment households, or indeed from the pulpit of the church that they never attended. Marie-Louise loved the company of Ghislaine and her circle – enjoying the frisson of the radical without having to bang its drum in public and bear the odium of her father's disapproval. This timidity was misinterpreted by many – most – on both sides of the fence, with her being judged a bad influence on the young by one side and a bourgeois Pétainist on the other.

The conversation ranged initially over the mundane: the black market; news, or lack of it, from icons of the left now on the run; the day-to-day irritations of an occupation now settling into its grinding stride. The subject of prisoners arose, a guaranteed catalyst for passion and anger. Everyone had a stake in this quarrel, whether it was a husband, son, brother or friend. With the armistice of July, signed in the same railway carriage in Compiègne that had hosted the defeat of Germany in November 1918, hostilities had ceased but the war had not ended. France had been divided with the north occupied as the hinterland for the invasion of England

and the south left under the leadership of Marshal Pétain in Vichy, a nondescript spa town in central France. The 'Maréchal' enjoyed an almost reverential reputation among the veterans of the Great War and among the conservative and Catholic. Others were prepared to give him the benefit of the doubt if he was able, first, to secure the release of prisoners of war and, secondly, to negotiate the withdrawal of the German army from French soil. Neither had happened.

'The old boy's gaga,' said Jacques dismissively. 'He's just a puppet for Laval: you can almost see that crook moving the old man's lips. No wonder the Boche are just laughing at him – and all of us.'

'If he was gaga,' said Stephan, 'that would be all right. He's more dangerous than that. He's a vain old fox who's trying to lay the blame for the debacle on anyone who wasn't in favour of universal conscription and military law – and on any general that isn't him. He thinks he's got enough prestige to get the Boche to take him seriously – but that's enough to make him a laughing stock even if he isn't the idiot you think he is.'

'So what do you think we should do?'

Marie-Louise's question was intended as a quest for enlightenment, but in her customary gauche way it came out as a challenge, one with unwitting barbs that had the two men glancing at each other again, this time with annoyance.

'I think what Marie-Louise means,' Ghislaine leant over the table and forcefully stubbed her cigarette while looking carefully at each man, 'is that there is an alternative to sitting back and letting the Boche walk all over us. Yes?'

Both men sat back. There was irritation there still – but also deference to Ghislaine's authority.

'Listen; Marie-Louise is an old friend of mine and she doesn't think like her father, if that's what's going through your minds. And she's discreet; unlike someone I know.'

Stephan blinked in acknowledgement of a past misdemeanour.

'So what can we do?' She held up a finger. 'We can do nothing; as we have done since the summer: you two missed the call-up and we all sat here and waited for the Boche to come, rather than heading west, which would at least have given us some options.' She held up another finger. 'We could make contact with someone – God knows where – who could get us to England to join this General de Gaulle, who may be a bit crazy, but at least he isn't licking the Boche's arse and getting shat on for the privilege. Or,' she held up a third finger, 'we can start something here to make the Boche want to go home to their *bratwurst* and *sauerkraut* . . . ' She looked around the kitchen with three elegant fingers in the air and a raised eyebrow. 'Have I missed anything? Marie-Louise?'

There was a challenge in her look that had the timidity and caution of Marie-Louise's nature welling to the surface. There was weight in her friend's question that she sensed was seminal. The momentum of a childhood friendship had carried them thus far but her answer to this question might decide the rest. She baulked. And the two men sensed it as she replied.

'There is another way, I think: to wait, to see how Pétain gets on . . . ' She heard her father speaking; hating it.' . . . if he can get the prisoners back . . . ' Ghislaine lit another cigarette, watching her. 'But if that doesn't work . . . by next spring, perhaps. Well, maybe then we look at other . . . things. I don't know. I need to think about it as we have to consider the consequences . . . hostages.'

She looked up at the others. Only Ghislaine held her eye.

'I agree,' said Ghislaine evenly. 'We have to think of everything. What the consequences are if we do something . . . or nothing. But we know what the consequences might be. Of course we do. It's the same in any war – people get killed. What's different here is that instead of young men being killed, it may be some of the high-ups in the town; or women; maybe even children. But that's what happens anyway when armies start fighting it out in towns or the Boche decide to bomb cities: look at Rotterdam or London. So if they take reprisals, the net result's the same. It's war. The question is: does what we can do make it worth it? Well?'

Marie-Louise felt, rather than saw, them staring at her. She grasped at the practical.

'But what weapons have we got? Some farmer's shotgun? I know my father keeps a pistol at home – but we'll need more than that to do any good. Explosives. Proper weapons surely? Where do we get those?'

'We can get them.'

'But how do we use them? Stephan is a *notaire* and Jacques a mechanic. Who will train us?'

'We know someone.'

She felt the cords tightening.

'What we want to know, *chérie*, is whether you'll help us. I've no idea yet how, but in whatever way you can. It will . . . might . . . be difficult for you . . . with your father. But he could be vital for us through his connections with the Boche. You might have to spy a bit. Pass on information that could be useful – you know the sort of thing. And something else: we – and I mean you and me and any girls who get involved – are going to have to use any means we can to get close to the Boche. You won't have to fuck them – but it's going to make life pretty uncomfortable with stupid cows like Adèle Carpentier gossiping and pointing fingers. Not much fun.'

Marie-Louise tried to drink some coffee but her hands were trembling so much she had to put the cup down. To steady them, she crossed her arms putting each hand under its opposite armpit. The room felt close and her usually ordered thought-train would only lurch from one incoherent notion to another confused image.

'Darling, we don't need an answer now.' She felt Ghislaine's hand on her shoulder, cool and steady. 'It's a lot to take in, we know.'

She nodded and raised her eyes. The two men were looking at her. What were they thinking? Was it scepticism that she saw through the tobacco smoke? Sympathetic or hostile? She couldn't tell. Staying in the room any longer was not an option. Neither gossip nor general conversation would be possible in the charged atmosphere and any enjoyment out of the question with the weight of the issue lying so heavily.

She stood up awkwardly, jogging the table and sending slops of coffee on to its crowded surface that no one made any effort to clear. She pushed her cigarettes into her bag and stood for a moment with the back of her hand pressed against her mouth.

'I'll think about it. *Au revoir.*'

She kissed her friend and waved to the two men. Ghislaine stood at the top of the stairs and watched her descend. As she opened the door, she turned and they looked at each other.

'I'm sorry.'

Marie-Louise nodded an acknowledgement and waved as she closed the door behind her. She stepped into the cold antiseptic of the waiting-room and out into the watery sunshine of an autumnal day that now held warmth as well as light. She sat on the steps to gather her thoughts, lit a cigarette and closed her eyes, allowing the sun to create fiery yellow pulses in her vision. The street was quiet except for the fluttering of plane-tree leaves as they moved to puffs of breeze that stirred and swirled the remnants of the morning fog.

Stephan's voice was just audible. 'Never. Not a hope. She's her father's daughter . . . '

*   *   *

Two weeks later the cold of winter set in, damp and dark. Marie-Louise left the school early with a satchel of exam papers to mark at home. The streets were still and greasy with light rain, the only sounds the bubbling of emptying gutters. As she approached her house the incongruous sound of ragtime piano, muffled by closed doors, filtered down the street.

She took off her coat in the hall, listening to the jangle of sound redolent of smoke-filled cellars and the clink of glasses. She hesitated. Her hand was on the newel post of the stairs, ahead was the parlour. She quietly opened the door and stood watching the back of his head and his fingers twinkling over the keys, flicking in irritation with each strike on the mute D sharp. She felt that she had to let him know she was there and gave the faintest of coughs – at which he started in shock, spinning on his stool. For a half-second he looked at her in open-mouthed astonishment – and she at him in wide-eyed shock – before he started laughing; again.

She found herself, unreasonably in the circumstances, as he was later to say to her, getting angry with him. Why was he always laughing at her? She knew it was ridiculous but persisted. He stood up, all mock concern, his arms reaching out to hold her forearms as if to steady her.

'*Madame!* Once again I have to beg your pardon – for startling you so badly. You must excuse my laughter . . . but you did look very funny. You really did.'

75

Not able to resist the good nature of his teasing, she too began to laugh.

'Come, *madame*, you must sit down.'

Holding on to her elbow he guided her into a chair and sat down opposite her, handing her a clean starched handkerchief. They looked at each other shyly. Suddenly, she remembered herself and stood up to close the curtains – shutting out any prying eyes. Facing him once again she spoke as an amused smile played over his face.

'I should introduce myself properly. My name is Marie-Louise Annecy – Annecy is my maiden name – but it might be better if you carried on calling me "*madame*" in public.'

'Of course, *madame*. And my name is Adam, though I have no objection to your calling me anything in public. Bloody Boche will do just fine. By the way, neither your maid nor your father is in the house.'

She knew that it was Bernadette's day off and her father never came home until seven.

'I know. Are you . . . flying tonight?'

'Not a chance. The weather has closed things down – and the forecast is awful for the next three days – so I will be "home",' he made parentheses with his fingers, 'instead. Which I hope won't be too trying. I'll make sure that no one is here before I inflict my playing on you or your father – or Bernadette, for that matter.'

'No. No, I love your playing. The piano has hardly been used since my mother died. It gives a different atmosphere to the house. My father may find it painful for the same reasons but . . . ' She shrugged.

'I'm sorry . . . about your mother. When did she die?'

'Four years ago. Of cancer.'

'I'm lucky. Both of my parents are still alive. Though – I have this theory – I'm not sure any of us becomes truly ourselves until our parents die.'

She found this idea slightly shocking. There must have been something, the faintest shake of her head, that showed it.

'I'm not saying that I don't love my parents. I don't know your father but mine is . . . how should I put it . . . he has firm ideas about things. And while I don't share them, I don't want to break with him, which means that I probably act out part of them in order to make him happy. But it's not me. Is that very complicated?'

'Quite. But I think I know what you mean. My father is also . . . rather dominating. Yes. I think I agree – even with my mother.'

There was a gentle hiatus in the conversation, filled again by the tick of the clock.

'May I smoke?'

'Of course. You'll be lonely in this house if you don't.'

The irony of this remark struck her. He was a Boche; the enemy, not a guest. Again he seemed to spot the cloud as it passed over her. He offered her a cigarette, which she took. He exhaled as he spoke, leaning forward.

'Thank you for speaking with me. I do appreciate it. I really do. I'm not cut out for military life: lots of men sharing uncomfortable barracks and the endless chat about sport and girls – not my thing.'

'So what is?'

He thought for a moment. 'Books. Music. I'd like to say travel – but that's rather difficult these days. I wouldn't count what I'm doing at the moment as the sort of travelling I had in mind: not at all.'

Until now there had been a playfulness about him, a boyishness. The levity was gone.

'Are you in bombers?'

'I don't think it would be giving away too many military secrets to confirm that. Nights, thank God. My squadron was decimated during the daylight raids in the summer, especially over London, which was just too far for the fighter escorts. The poor devils had about half an hour when they were on their own – and the Tommies made mincemeat of them. Luckily I was still training at the time, so I missed the worst. But it's not much fun being over England at night either – especially now that the weather has deteriorated.' He paused for a moment's thought. 'In the circumstances I suppose I can't expect you to feel too sorry for them – or me. If you are going to feel sorry for anyone, it should be the poor people being bombed, shouldn't it?'

'It's just the war.'

He considered this carefully. 'Yes. It is the war. But we all say that to justify just about anything: your husband locked up in some camp; me dropping bombs on women and children; me being foisted on you uninvited. They used to say, *"Deus vult"*, "God wills it", as if to say "I don't have any responsibility for this – it's nothing to do with me." I'm just not sure that's good enough, that's all. You can see why I'm not cut out for all this, can't you? Soldiers need a less complicated way of looking at things.'

He was no longer looking at her but at the piano, his thumbnail between his teeth. She tried to gauge his age: younger than her, but not much; not a boy. There was much that reminded her of her husband but, where he would have been angry, railing at the stupidity and injustice of it all, this man seemed puzzled by it. Not a man of action.

'Your French is excellent.'

'Thank you. It comes from being brought up in a complicated part of the world – the Rhineland. You – well the French army – spent rather a long time in occupation there. My mother's half French. What about you?'

'Born here. Only child. Married a local boy. I teach. Hence all these.' She pointed at her satchel of exam papers. 'It has its moments but there's only so much you can teach a peasant boy whose only interest is in becoming a man by taking on the family farm. I do get some bright ones. One went to the Sorbonne last year and another made it to the École Nationale two years ago. Better than being killed or rotting in a prisoner-of-war camp – like most of the men here. You're not a regular?'

'Me? God no! A student; rather an old student. I was in the middle of my doctorate on doctrinal differences in the Byzantine Orthodox Church during the sixth century. Not, unfortunately, considered to be vital war work among the powers that be in Germany. I can't imagine why not. I decided that it was better to join up early so that I didn't have to go into the army. I'm allergic to walking. I had the romantic idea that being a fighter pilot was the answer – but ended up in bombers. Bad decision. There's no other part of the great German war machine that's getting as many bullets fired at it at the moment. It's what happens when you try to be too clever.' He hesitated. 'I can see that this might appear as rather . . . tactless – but have you had news of your husband? Was he wounded?'

'No. He was captured in the first week of the invasion, near Sedan. He was lucky, from what I can gather. They were caught in the epicentre of things and about half of the men from the town were killed or wounded, but he and Robert, my friend Ghislaine's husband, got cut off and surrounded. They're in a camp near Darmstadt, bored and frustrated but otherwise healthy. I don't think it'll suit him at all – though he reads a lot. At least I can now send him books.'

She too was looking at the piano, thoughts drifting, absently twisting her long hair between the fingers of one hand, while the other stroked the bow of her top lip. He stole a glance at her, conscious that too long a stare could be misinterpreted, but captured a mental snapshot of her still renaissance beauty – features and expression in repose. In more normal moments, thoughts passed over her face, pursing her lips or wrinkling her forehead in quick succession, like the shadow of clouds over rippling barley. Her smile was always quick – almost a tic – that could be, and often was, interpreted as insincere – but was only the visible register of a tumble of thoughts and calculations. He savoured this sense of her being the incarnation of a Raphael madonna.

'*Madame* . . . Marie-Louise – if I may really call you that – you must be careful not to be seen to speak to me. I will always extend courtesies to you – but I don't expect any in return. But if we might, circumstances permitting, talk about things that are not the war – books perhaps, or paintings – it would make this winter bearable. If we are surprised, then maybe you could say that you were dealing with some domestic matter. You could even be angry with me. You seem to be quite good at it after all . . . '

She looked up at him to see amusement on his open face and smiled in return.

'I would like that too. I didn't realise how much I would miss masculine company. My father isn't really a substitute – he tends to tell me things rather than discuss them. And I find women's conversation – most of it, that is – a bit limiting. There aren't too many educated people in a provincial town like this and gossip only goes so far. But I wouldn't like you to misinterpret – misconstrue – any such conversation.' She felt herself blushing.

He held his hands up. 'Of course not.'

'I'm happily married.'

'There's no question.'

'I know Frenchwomen have a certain reputation.'

'And I am a Rhinelander – so I am, perhaps, in a better position than most of my compatriots to know the truth. Please don't concern yourself on this score. I was brought up in a family of many cousins, where friendships held no boundaries of gender. Please. Trust me.'

She nodded awkwardly, and stood up even more so, not sure where to put her hands.

'*Bonsoir*, then. And please carry on playing. I'll enjoy hearing it in my room.'

'I'm a soldier, so must always obey orders. This one won't be a burden. *Bonsoir, madame* . . . and *au revoir* only, I hope.'

He stood up as she left the room and closed the door behind her. She picked up her satchel and stood at the foot of the stairs, listening as the sound of a Scott Joplin melody lapped its way under the door, before slowly mounting the treads towards her room with her fingers tapping out the rhythm on the banisters.

*   *   *

The next day Ghislaine found Marie-Louise in the café that looked obliquely over the Grand Place. Unconsciously, Marie-Louise had avoided her friend since their conversation in the apartment above the doctor's surgery. As she glimpsed Ghislaine walking through the door, she realised that, until the unresolved question had insinuated itself into the interstices between them, there had barely been a day in their lives when they had not seen each other, often sitting together for an hour without speaking, comfortable in each other's company, then speaking at the same time to express a common thought that had grown in the silence.

There was a brittle brightness in their kissed greeting. Their initial conversation danced a minuet around the issue between them, enquiries and gobbets of gossip providing the music. The two women at the next table rose and left them alone across a corner table with only the *patron* behind the counter scraping the detritus of lunch from a recalcitrant saucepan. Smoke trickled from her nostrils as Ghislaine eyed her friend and leant closer.

'So?'

Marie-Louise didn't immediately answer but pushed the last of her soup around the bowl with a piece of rough bread. Her reluctance to answer furrowed familiar lines on her forehead. 'I want to help.'

'Good.'

'But I'm not sure how. How I can, that is. I'm not like you. You love being frightened, taking risks. I don't. I'm worried that I'll give you away by saying something stupid.'

'You don't have to do anything – yet. And don't worry, darling, the one thing you aren't is stupid. I wouldn't have asked you if you were.'

'Who else is . . . involved?'

Ghislaine looked at her steadily. 'I'll tell you anything you need to know, but you may not want to know even that one day.'

The implication of her remark sank in and Marie-Louise's face paled. 'I . . . I hadn't thought of that.'

'So what have you been thinking of? For two weeks!' Ghislaine rolled her eyes in exasperation. 'It's not a game. It's war. It's dangerous. Very dangerous.' She dropped her voice but the *patron* continued his scraping, oblivious of them. 'Why have you been avoiding me? Well, of course, I know why. And, darling, I under-stand why, I really do. I'm not going to be asking you to throw bombs at anyone – you'd probably kill everyone but the Boche you were aiming at. I just want to know that I can get help from you if we need it. Information. Stuff that the Boche you have living with you might let drop if he was drunk. Or your father. Things that they might tell him about troop movements or plans that, if we feed them to the right people, might be useful. It's not much, but if this goes on all over France, things might start to happen.' She noticed that Marie-Louise was far away, tugging absently at her lip. She reached over and clasped her hand. Her voice took on a new tone, gentler, less imperious. 'It's fine to be afraid. Right. If you weren't, you'd be too dangerous to trust. *Chérie*, everyone is scared; me included. There's nothing wrong in that, I promise. And your papa: you're not spying on him – only on the Boche by proxy. So don't feel guilty as well. You're the one that's doing the right thing.'

Marie-Louise pulled her hand away in anger.

'Stop all this insinuation about papa! He's doing what he thinks is right. Do you know something, I'm not sure that he is wrong – about Pétain. Or about the stupidity of doing something that ends up with indiscriminate reprisals. For what? To make a point: to pretend that we haven't been beaten. You always sneer at him, as if he's a coward. But he's the one that has the *Croix de Guerre*. I listen to him, then to you. You're both right. Or neither of you is wrong. He's as much of a patriot as you – but he just thinks there's another way. What is it between you two anyway? It's not just about this, is it? This has gone on for years. What is it? Tell me.'

Ghislaine looked at her with a mixture of irritation – and surprise at her uncharacteristic assertiveness. 'I . . . I just don't like him. I'm sorry.'

Marie-Louise knew there was more to it than dislike. Her friend's evasiveness was at odds with her normal openness. 'It's more than that. There's something else, isn't there? Something when we were much younger? What was it?'

Ghislaine's jaw clenched and she avoided eye contact. 'It's his attitude. To me, to you – to most women actually: patronising, arrogant and supercilious. Is that enough? He may have won the *Croix de Guerre* but that was in the last war. Maybe age doesn't suit him. And . . . that's all. Look, I don't want to do this – fight about your father. I'd rather fight the Boche. It's less complicated, it really is.'

Marie-Louise hesitated. Should she probe? What would she get from it? She sensed that whatever it was would be painful. The nagging tooth may be better left untouched – for the time being anyway. 'Yes. Let's leave it there. But there is something else, I know there is.'

Still no eye contact. And awkward silence.

'So what do you want me to do; to help?'

The relief at the change of subject was palpable.

'Nothing for the time being. Nothing. Keep your eyes and ears open. Make friends with the Boche in your house.'

'How? How am I going to do that?'

'Darling, you're a woman . . . and a rather nice-looking one at that. Pleasant chat at the foot of the stairs – not when your father is around for certain – the weather, food shortages, is he comfortable? You know the sort of thing – ordinary stuff. He's miles away from home and scared witless – so he isn't exactly going to be running away from you, is he? The opposite, I suspect. And anything else: stuff that you might see when you're bicycling round or if you go to Amiens or visit your grandmother in Honfleur. It might not make sense to us – but we have to think of it as a jigsaw for which we can provide the pieces even if the whole doesn't make much sense. Is that too bad? Nothing too scary?'

'No. I'm sure it'll be fine. I'll just have to think differently. Learn to be a spy. I never really thought of myself like that, that's all.'

'None of us did. It's the war.'

Marie-Louise smiled at her friend. 'That's not true – and you know it. You love this. The secrecy. The excitement. And being the leader. You do love that, don't you? You're good at it. I watched Jacques and Stephan the other day. They look up to you.'

Ghislaine was about to protest but instead nodded wryly. 'I do, I suppose. It suits me better than cutting off a geriatric's bunion – or telling some idiot peasant that rubbing cow muck on a wound isn't going to make it better; though, God knows, I seem to spend enough time doing that. But I know you don't feel the same – and that's fine, *chérie*, it really is.' Her hand reached across the table and held her arm. 'It really is.

7

Montreuil. Winter 1940–1

The first winter of the occupation settled into its plodding stride with slate skies and raw winds funnelling down the Channel to insinuate needle draughts into houses starved of coal. Long evenings of rattling windows and lonely women cloaked Montreuil in melancholy, with only the sound of a barking dog or banging shutter as a *leitmotif.* Men gathered in cafés, shuffling dominoes and sipping raw brandy, turning over the staples of provincial life – food, always food, the slow draining of the local economy, restrictions, shortages and gossip.

With the gloom of darkening evenings, the Annecy household settled into an eccentric routine. Bernadette left for her parents' farm at four – on foot (unless she managed to borrow her brother's ancient bicycle), the three-kilometre walk there and back being part of her daily routine. She left the fire in the parlour banked up and the curtains drawn over both the doors and the windows to contain the heat. Marie-Louise would return at half-past four, with homework to mark, and install herself at the writing desk in the corner of the parlour, taking off her coat for the first time after a damp, stone-cold day in snuffling, huddled classrooms. The German would start moving at about five. She would hear his barefoot padding on the ceiling above; follow his hurried visit to the bathroom at the end of the corridor, the muffled clink of a tapped razor on the edge of a china bowl, the hurried dressing and the clump of boots as a finale. As she heard him close the door and the stairs squeaking to each compression, a frisson of pleasurable anticipation would bring a smile to her face that she composed into a frown of concentration as his hand fell on the door handle. At first she was shocked at this. He was the Boche, the enemy. But as days passed she saw his uniform less and the man more, until, after a few weeks their exchanges took on such a domestic regularity that they could have been any long-married couple giving each other a preoccupied greeting at the end of a working day. She could tell that he was not someone who woke easily. Despite shaving in cold water and the ordeal of dressing in a swirl of Scandinavian draughts, his eyes were blurred and his manner distracted. He would go into the kitchen and she would hear the sound of coffee being poured and the rattling of the tray prepared by Bernadette that he would bring into the parlour and place on the table facing away from her. She would watch his back as he ate and drank, pretending to work, flicking the pages of exercise books to maintain the fiction but enjoying his silent presence – a quiet balm to loneliness. He would finish his nightly breakfast and turn round to her. She would be looking down in concentration and he would cough to get her attention. She would look at him in polite enquiry and he would ask her if she would mind if he smoked. She would indicate polite acquiescence and he would offer her a cigarette – which she would take. He would offer her a light and they would share a nicotine silence, broken only by the hiss of the coal fire, the ticking of the clock and the rattling of shutters. This became their ritual, a daily rite that seldom varied. They would read and talk intermittently. Sometimes, as an intermezzo, he would go to the piano, now tuned and repaired by him, and play happy tunes that were thousands of miles and a civilisation away, at odds with the cold dreariness outside.

One evening her father arrived home early, with his routine and *sang-froid* disturbed by a forgotten trifle. They heard the front door opening as Adam's right hand was working an intricate shuffle among the sharps and flats of the ancient piano. Without missing a note he nodded to Marie-Louise, indicating the kitchen door towards which she moved silently, her eyes dancing a nervous jitterbug of concern. She closed the door behind her and pretended industry around the stove with a clash of plate and cup. She heard the opening of the door into the parlour and the sudden silence from the piano; her mind's eye matched a formal and polite neck-bow with the click of heels just audible under the door. She hesitated. She knew that subterfuge was not her strong suit. She felt the colour rising over her face and her hands clenching. She fought down the inclination to remain silent where she was and gamble on her father's disconnection with all matters domestic – but she realised that her coat was on the peg and her books on the writing table. She leant the door open with her back, tray in hand. Her father was standing by the opposite door, still wearing his coat. She smiled brightly at him but could feel the heat in her face and a shaking of her hands on the tray.

'Papa! *Bonsoir*. You're home early. I've made some coffee for the leutnant who has just woken. Would you like some too; or some cognac?' She sensed he was between surprise and annoyance, acceptance and embarrassment. 'Bernadette has prepared a tray for Leutnant Kohl and I was making myself some hot milk to take to my room, so I can easily make some more for you if you would like. Maybe you should get warm in front of the fire before you go upstairs.'

'*Madame*, allow me, please.'

The German reached over and took the tray from her, avoiding eye contact, a model of polite formality. She was certain she could feel the heat of his hands through the tray. They watched him place the tray on the table. She could sense her father's indecision without looking at him.

'Papa?'

'Cognac. Thank you. That would be nice. On this . . . miserable evening. Please.'

He gestured towards one of the upright chairs, acknowledged by a bow from the German. She turned towards the cupboard containing the drinks in relief that her face was away from them both, but her pulse was beating a tatoo within her temples. She fumbled the lock and clumsily poured a large measure, which she took to her father who sat stiffly with his coat and hat on his knees. They waited for him to speak in respectful silence with only the sucking sound of lips testing hot liquid against the ticking of the clock, the hiss of the fire and the rattle of shutters.

'You're flying tonight, leutnant?'

'No, *monsieur*. The weather is keeping us earthbound for the time being . . . I'm pleased to say.'

'What do you fly, leutnant?'

'A Heinkel. Three crew.'

'You must get quite close to them, sharing the danger together. I did with my men when I was in the army; a very special relationship; one of the closest you'll ever have. I was at Verdun in the . . . last war. Was your father in the army?'

'He was at Verdun too; and in Russia. He said the same thing about his men. I suppose some things don't change whoever you're fighting for.'

'Yes. We don't seem to learn much, do we? Only twenty years since I was trying to kill your father and now our children are doing the same.'

There did not seem to be any response to this statement – but Marie-Louise felt an urge to fill the silence.

'Leutnant Kohl is from the Rhineland, papa; which is why his French is so good.'

'Yes. Excellent French, leutnant. You two have obviously had a good chat.'

She felt herself blushing under the accusation. But was that what it was? She glanced up at her father who was looking towards the clock. Probably not. The German picked up the ball.

'Not as much as I would like, *monsieur*. We only pass on the stairs or as I am collecting my tray from the kitchen. As I said to your daughter, sir, I am very conscious of the delicacy of my situation in your house and would like to try and make my unwelcome presence as painless as possible.'

Her father looked at the German as he swirled the cognac round his glass. 'Leutnant, let me put it this way: I hate your country, your leaders and your army's presence here. I hate your uniform; but I don't hate you personally. Why should I? You're sensitive and polite – educated. I don't see a contradiction here; so let us try and separate the two, shall we? If we are to be living together, we can attempt to do personally what we seem incapable of doing as nations.' He swallowed the cognac in one gulp. 'I must go now, as my game of whist is waiting for me to find my spectacles. And one other thing, leutnant: my daughter has her reputation to consider; so I would ask that you do nothing that might compromise her. I know that you are a gentleman and would do nothing untoward – but tongues wag. So whatever conversations that we have – you,

87

me and my daughter – must be kept very formal, most particularly in public. Do I make myself clear?'

A formal bow again.

'Of course.'

'Good-evening to you then. I would rather be here in the warm than battling my way to Monsieur Duchamp's house – but I've made a commitment.'

He kissed his daughter absent-mindedly and they stood formally as he left. They both carried on standing, in silence, listening to the strike of his metallic heels on the cobbles outside.

'Would you like some cognac?'

'I could think of nothing nicer.'

She filled a glass from the cupboard, put it in front of him and poured out more hot milk into her cup.

'He's a gentleman, your father.'

'Yes, he is. Not easy, though; to live with. He makes up his mind quickly and doesn't change it. He obviously likes you but he was . . . is . . . much more difficult with my husband.'

'Why?'

She looked up at him to gauge the tenor of his question. His wide face reflected sincerity and genuine interest. 'Why indeed? Jerome's hard working – he was an editor on the local paper. He's cultivated – he reads books and loves music. Not a businessman though: my father despises him for that. But perhaps they're too alike; both with firm views and intolerant of others' opinions. Political mainly: my father's conservative and my husband's of the left. My father says he's a Communist.'

'Is he?'

'No. He's a Socialist – though he has many friends who are Communists. He's too much of his own man to take orders from Moscow. He – my father – blames the Communists for everything. It's a difficult one to argue against after the Molotov-Ribbentrop pact, isn't it? The Russians and the Germans hand-in-glove, with orders from Moscow to the Communists in France not to resist the Germans? Which comes first? France or the party? I'm glad I don't have to make that sort of choice.'

They contemplated the fire for a few moments.

'Where did you live; you and your husband?'

'Here, in this house, with my father. We didn't have enough money for our own house. No. That's not really true. We could have rented a flat, but my mother had only just died and I felt I couldn't leave my father on his own. So we both moved in here. A mistake. They ended up like two dogs circling each other: snarling, with hackles up and neither ready to compromise. My stupid fault. But I'm not good at reading these things. I always think the world is logical and that people will behave rationally. But they don't, do they?'

Again there was an unspoken acknowledgement of a universal truth.

'And your politics?'

'I don't know: left I suppose. That's the problem, isn't it? You can't sit in the centre today can you? Everything's so polarised; Fascist or Communist; Catholic or atheist. Why can't you just be an agnostic; or someone who doesn't think anyone has all the answers. That's my problem, and it drives everyone mad – my father, my husband and my best friend, Ghislaine. They're all so certain – but I seem to see around the sides of every issue; see the shading, the areas that are grey rather than black or white; see the human being rather than a superman. Look at Pétain: my father worships him; thinks he can do no wrong and is the only man who can save France. And Ghislaine? She thinks he's a Fascist who'll take France back to the days of Dreyfus.'

'At least it's politics.'

Marie-Louise frowned in puzzlement. 'What do you mean?'

'In Germany there are no politics, no choices.' She looked up at him and for once there was no levity in his expression. 'I couldn't have this conversation in Germany; it would be too dangerous; or in Russia for that matter. There's no law; no opinion – other than that of the Nazis. We're a nation that's infantilised itself and handed itself over to one man to do with as he wishes in the belief that he's a genius. It's been like a trap shutting behind you. You go in so far, thinking you can go back – but once you've given over the levers of power, you have to go through with your Faustian pact as there's no means of getting those levers back. My parents can't – won't – see that. They only see the "miracle" that Hitler has conjured up for them, without seeing the price. So far it's been a price that hasn't been too heavy: a few Jews and Communists locked up. "Good riddance," my father says. No voting. Who needs that when everyone has a job and a full stomach? War: but victory everywhere, so who cares? You French are abasing yourselves, wallowing in self-recrimination and shame at a defeat. We are the ones who should be ashamed. We are the real cowards; moral cowards.'

She looked at him in astonishment. He was staring at the fire, as serious as she had ever seen him. This view of the enemy, the hated Boche, was radical for her. She felt that a light had been shone for her into the corner of a national psyche, illuminating something which she had always found inexplicable.

'Have you said this to anyone else before?'

'As I said, this conversation is not one I can have in Germany, other than with my greatest friend from university. Not with my family certainly. Even my sister goes along with it; though I'm not so sure now that the war is here. It's a strange thing to live in a country where you despise so many people – but for reasons that they would simply not understand. That's why I admire your country for all the things you despise in yourselves. You can see why I don't make a great soldier.' He grinned ruefully as he ran his hand through his hair, shaking his head in gentle disbelief. 'There's a Chinese curse . . . "May you live in interesting times." It's pretty interesting to have to risk your life every day for someone or something you find repugnant, don't you think?'

'I . . . I can't imagine such a thing. I had no idea. We only see uniforms that make everyone seem alike. I just assumed that an army is a solid thing. But it's a collection of individuals with different thoughts and motives. Just like our army; like Jerome and Robert. But I can see why they're the lucky ones even though they're in a prison camp. They've very different views – both of them – but neither is questioning whether France is a good thing or whether the war's right. Even the Communists think that in their heart of hearts, surely?'

'You'd think so. But people's capacity for self-delusion always amazes me. They can argue black into white whatever their eyes, ears and brain are telling them. Believe me, I know: I've watched it for years now. Nothing new about that either: I read about it every day when I was studying for my doctorate. Byzantine theologians could give Marxists a run for their money in their ability to shoehorn any human experience into an orthodoxy. It's quite impressive.'

'And depressing.'

He looked at her profile as she stared at the fire. She had the poker in one hand, prodding a piece of coal, while two fingers of the other hand twisted strands of hair around each other. In the soft firelight, backlit by the light of a single shaded lamp, she again reminded him of a Renaissance madonna, with her rounded features that had no sharp planes. This softness of contour and complexion gave her a luminosity that drew the eye but he was again struck by the contrast between the suggested stillness and the flickering frowns and mouth movements that reflected the tides of thoughts below.

'How long have you been married?'

'Four years. And you?'

'Not married. I was engaged though. Not for very long – a month or so. She was lovely but . . . it was the war. I knew – it was obvious – that it was coming and that I'd be called up and probably killed. So what would be the point of leaving her a widow, perhaps with a child? She married someone else.'

'I'm sorry.'

'Don't be. I'm not. Well, I'm not sorry I made the decision: it was the right one. But I do miss our friendship. We were very good friends. What is your French expression, *une amitié amoureuse?* Maybe that's not the same thing as it implies that you're lovers before it turns to friendship. We were actually more like brother and sister – so maybe it was better we didn't marry. It might have felt a touch incestuous.'

'Do you still see her?'

'No. It wouldn't be right. Apparently her husband's very jealous, so it really isn't an option. Though why he should be jealous of me I can't imagine. You'd have thought that I'd be the last person who'd be a threat, wouldn't you, in the circumstances?'

'You . . . might change your minds though.'

'No, I don't think so. I think it's just about possession, isn't it? He might not say so, but he probably feels that he owns her – and her him, for all I know. Isn't jealousy only insecurity of ownership after all?'

She hesitated, forming her words carefully. 'But if you met again, and it – what you had – rekindled, why shouldn't he be jealous. I feel jealousy. And so does Jerome. Doesn't everyone? Isn't it normal?'

'If something happened and he lost his wife to me, then yes, he'd be right to feel jealous. But we're not talking about that, are we? Just suspicion. Maybe it needs another word – the unjustified suspicion, I mean.'

'But isn't it normal to want to feel that you're the one, the special one, the love of someone's life.'

'Of course. But I don't see a contradiction – unless you feel you own someone. As I said, we were friends. And why shouldn't a friend have another friend?'

'It's different.'

'Why?'

'Because love's involved.'

'And you can't love more than one person at a time?'

'No. Well, not without jealousy anyway. It's too difficult.'

'And I thought you French were supposed to be good at that. In Germany we even call it "the French way".'

She looked up with annoyance, to find him again smiling teasingly at her. There was a smidgen of irritation in her reply. 'I know that. Everyone thinks French women are loose. It may be the case in Paris – but I can tell you it's not here. Talk with another man and the whole town's tut-tutting.'

He put his finger to his lips. 'I am not implying anything – certainly nothing insulting – the opposite in fact. I was only suggesting that your compatriots have a more sensible – adult, perhaps – way of looking at things. All I'm saying is that love doesn't have to be about possession. In fact, if it's not about possession but about letting go, about being a refuge not a straight-jacket, then no one needs to be jealous because you're gaining – not losing – something.'

'So you don't believe in marriage, in the vows; that you're "forsaking all others" when you make them?'

'I just think it's bit stultifying to interpret that as not being allowed to find anyone else attractive; or to have friendships – or more – that are enriching and rewarding.'

'Free love, then?'

'No, not at all. That'd imply a free-for-all, with no commitment or responsibility. That can't happen with children. All I'm suggesting is that two adults can love and treasure each other and make a lifelong commitment to each other without excluding others. Once you stop seeing love as about possession, then surely anything's possible?'

'But it's risky, very risky.'

'Any more risky than promising the impossible – or at least the very difficult? Aren't you setting yourself up to fail if you set the bar too high? I'd guess that more misery has come about through suspicion and recrimination than any act of infidelity ever warranted. But I grant you that if you're unhappy together, then it'd be disastrous. It's a paradox.'

'I don't believe it. It can't be done. People don't behave like that, do they? They get jealous. It's human nature.'

'Is it? Or is it cultural? I don't think men and women in the Middle Ages saw marriage the way we do, as a sort of fusion of souls where you "become one". It was a property contract – and patriarchal. Women were possessions for procreation. Love – romantic love – was for outside marriage. We seem to have gone to a different extreme, that's all; or a mixture, where we're trying to have the best of both at the same time – but tend to get the worst.'

'Why the worst? I don't feel hard done by.'

'Please, I'm not making any personal comments. I barely know you and have never met your husband – so how could I? I'm just interested in how things have changed. Then it was about property. Something changed in the eighteenth century – the Romantics it must have been – this idea that there is a soul-mate out there with whom one can merge oneself. We seem to have taken that on board and attached the property bit to it; tried to link the ecstasy of romantic love to the more prosaic matters of procreation and property. It's a tricky one to pull off, that's all.'

She considered a moment, working the poker into a crevice between pieces of coal.

'But isn't it better to marry for love and have at least a chance that you'll be happy, rather than it being just a contract between parents to safeguard property? It must be better, surely? I think that's progress. Would you want to go back to those days? Was the world a better or a worse place? I know which I'd prefer, as a woman anyway.'

'Romantic love? Champagne! How could you not prefer it – when it's happening to you? My problem is that it doesn't last that long. Like champagne, it loses its fizz and all too often goes flat and sour and ends with two people who can't conceive what it was that could have got them into their present situation. It's an intoxication – wonderful, unforgettable, life-changing – but it doesn't last a lifetime. Maybe there's a better way, where the question between two people who've been together for a lifetime is not "Are you still obsessed by me?" but "Do I still interest you and do you care for me as an equal?" – and "Are we worth more together than apart?" If I could get to that I'd be the happiest man alive.'

Marie-Louise stopped her prodding and turned over this idea, moved by it.

'That's very beautiful.'

She glanced up at him and he glimpsed a glistening in the corner of her eyes. She looked away, embarrassed. They sat in silence looking at the fire, both of them feeling a warmth that was more than physical. There was no awkwardness in the stillness of the moment, a contentment with each other's space that occurred to them separately.

Neither wanted to chime the end of the enchantment, to break the spell.

8

GERMANY

Silesia, Eastern Germany. 12 January 1945

The Russian offensive broke with a rumble in the east. Like summer thunder over distant mountains rattling windows and raising dogs' hackles, the percussion of artillery and bombs announced the long-awaited offensive. Flashes, rippling across the dawn sky, strobe-like in their frequency, brought blanket-swaddled forms to doors and children to tears. A miasma of foreboding and fearful exchanged glances settled over the countryside.

As the last cows were milked and plodded back to their winter barns in bovine placidity, snow began to fall, a grey-white blanket of deadened sound and foreshortened horizons. And on it went for two days, limiting the world to a few hundred metres, the normal bush-telegraph of country life cut off, leaving dependence on the wireless and its deluded version of reality, calm with the facts, talking of offensive operations and counter-attacks but divorced from the *actualité*, which was that of an engineless boat, drifting inexorably towards the roar of a waterfall, heard and seen in rainbow-hued spray, helpless, doomed. Two days; then clearing skies, needle winds and the first of the flotsam.

The arrival was announced by a baying of farm dogs, wolf-like shepherds, snapping the heels of an exhausted pony pulling a hay cart, barely moving through the drifts that lined the road to the house. The cart's driver, sex indeterminate under mummifying layers, knelt on a rolled mat, reins slack in hand, whip moving in automated motion unnoticed by the pony. Piled on the cart were the remnants of some lifetimes, even a rusted hand-pump, like a ship's figurehead, next to the driver. As Remmer caught the reins, the pony stopped but the whip kept rising and falling until Mimi stilled the driver's arm. A thin woman's voice came from under the layers – hoarse.

'Milk. For the baby. *Grüs Gott.*'

They lifted the canvas, brittle and stiff, revealing a nest of cow skins and blankets, dusted with snow and crusty with rime-ice, underneath which was a sleeping girl, breast exposed to an infant of only a few days. As Mimi reached for the baby, her hand brushed the breast, hard and cold. She recoiled from the touch, before gently pulling the bundle away from its mother, drawing it under the folds of her cloak, its imported chill sucking the warmth from her own breast. She exchanged glances with Remmer, indicating with a nod that he should ease the woman from her frozen supplications and bring her inside.

In the cellar's warmth they gently unpeeled the layers of swaddling from their tiny visitor, exposing the cold skin of a baby boy to the flickering orange balm of the fire, his crying now ominously reduced, his limbs still, then jerking into a spasm before twitching back into stillness. The dry twig of the remains of the umbilical cord stood proud of a distended belly button.

'Goat's milk, Frau Remmer; I think it's supposed to be like human milk – not too rich. Remmer: fill that big pan with warm water from the kettle. Quick. He's so cold. We have to get warmth back into him.'

As they rushed to their tasks, Mimi pulled up her smock and woollen vest, exposing the bare skin of her stomach and lower chest. She clasped the writhing nakedness against her. Gently, when the makeshift bath was ready, she lowered him in with his mouth shouting wordlessly, eyes shut and limbs moving convulsively. Slowly, very slowly, the thrashing became more constant, the skin more pink than grey, and the breaths and crying more loud and insistent: hungrier. The other childless woman took the infant, wrapped him in a rough kitchen towel and placed him on her lap where she dribbled warm milk from a spoon down her little finger and on to gums which gnawed insistently on its tip, gulping, sucking and crying intermittently. The strange, unsmiling woman nuzzled the dark hair of the child.

Mimi turned her attention to the old woman who was rocking back and forth to a rhythm of her own, wrapped in a blanket, with seemingly sightless eyes staring into the middle distance beyond the back of the fire. Her head was now bare, grey hair tied tight and her face just visible above a scarf of hessian sacking, a toothless peasant face of lines and the colouring of wood-smoke, sweat and limited access to warm water; an aged face of hardship rather than years. Gradually the fire's heat and the spooning of steaming broth focused her eyes and loosened her tongue.

'Cold, so cold.'

Mimi held her arm which she massaged against no resistance.

'Never been so cold.'

She raised an interrogative eyebrow towards the baby.

Mimi spoke. 'Fine: he's going to be fine. I don't know much about babies though. He's drinking goat's milk. Frau Remmer's doing a good job.'

'No good without a mother though.' It was a flat, matter-of-fact death sentence; a peasant familiarity with birth and death in all its forms – an intimacy with the tenuous life-thread of the orphan lamb. 'We won't get enough milk, any milk, on the road. Poor child.' Her gaze was dispassionate, as over a closed coffin.

The other two women glanced at each other, knowing the truth was being spoken and the war flooded into their house in all its dislocation and misery.

'The mother . . . she's your daughter?'

A nod.

'She's dead.'

Another nod.

'She had the fever. Two days after he was born. No chance in the cart. But what could I do?' This last was delivered without angst, only fatalism.

'Where have you come from? How long have you been travelling?'

'About eighty kilometres the other side of Breslau. No shelter. Every barn full. Houses locked. Pitchfork in my face once. Just kept going. No bombers, thank God; too much snow. Very cold. Three days, I think.' She reached out to stroke the baby's head, a calloused hand on silk hair, looking at the fire as she did so, distracted by memories, white memories. 'We can't stay. Ivan's not far behind us. You must go too. No time to lose.'

Mimi was aware of Remmer and his wife looking at her. What

was there? An accusation? They looked away but there was a finger pointing at her in their silence and from this huddled messenger from the outside world – a world that was now irredeemably hostile. She gave instructions to the two servants in a voice that no longer seemed her own and made her way through the freezing hall and landing to the refuge of her bedroom. She sat on the bed facing the fire and took in the kernel of what was left: the books, the elegant writing table and the chaise longue, where so many thoughts and words had been ingested; the familiar softness of the eiderdown with the faint sound of crushed feathers; photographs of other lives, of childhood – the threads that held the past to the present which were about to be snapped. Guilt and self-pity overwhelmed her. She had had months to prepare for this. Friends and relatives had warned her but she had done nothing. She should have gone in September, or sent the servants and farm workers ahead. She should have prepared the landau, shod the horses, preserved meats and stockpiled tents and blankets. The Remmers had looked to her for leadership and responsibility – assuming that both were her birthright – and she had failed them. She knew why – and the reason was in the cow barn.

Wrapping herself in a greatcoat and with a fur hat over her ears, she stumbled downstairs and through the snowdrift that filled the porch, leaning into the stabbing wind of deep winter towards the barn with its soft pungent scent of manure. She opened the door to the warm, damp breath of cattle and climbed the ladder to the loft not knowing what she was going to say, what reasoning she was going to employ with her lover, his companions and their guard. How could she persuade them to take their chances with the *Feldgendamerie*, the brutal sheepdogs of a beaten army?

Top rung. No one. Straw. No blankets. Only a blackened pot, too heavy to carry. Cold. Silence.

An emptiness engulfed her. The remains of the fire still dribbled whiskers of smoke. It was only a few hours ago that he had been there, teasing out its heat. He had left her without notice or farewell. In self-pity and loneliness, she lay alongside the pot, weeping the anger of abandonment, and fear; fear of failing in the responsibilities that now weighed on her like a grinding stone, fear of the cold and of the rumbling thunder over the horizon. At first she didn't hear the voice through her sobs, its definition lost in the rattle of wind-scraped timbers and shuffling cows. It was a man's voice, old, thin with tiredness – familiar but out of place.

'Mimi, my dear. Is that you? Are you all right? It is you, isn't it? Come down, my dear. Please. I can't make the steps.'

First the flotsam. Now the jetsam.

Facing forward and almost falling off the ladder in the rush to get to the bottom, she fell into the arms of Herr Reinhart, into the mothball-smelling astrakhan collar of his paternal hug, allowing him for a few moments to take the weight from her, to let her be a child again and weep a child's tears. His tender stroking of her back massaged the strength back into her, reasserting in her the right balance of care and dependence, returning her to adulthood, gently and bearably. With his arms around her she was able to rationalise again and remember that her lover was a prisoner, not a free agent. She took the handkerchief Reinhart offered, wiped her face and took him by his arm back towards the house, feeling his exhaustion through their ill-matched steps, easing the knapsack from his camel-rounded shoulders, guiding him over the doorstep and down to the womb of the cellar and its collage of humanity that was now her burden.

*   *   *

The next day, in a dawn pregnant with snow, the little convoy of Mimi, Herr Reinhart, the two Remmers, the peasant woman and the baby set sail. The peasant woman's cart and the landau were each overlaid with a delta of canvas forming a makeshift tent, leaving only the drivers exposed to the steady, freezing wind, mercifully at their backs in its passage from Siberia. Remmer and the peasant woman rode the cart, most of its load having been removed without protest. Mimi and Frau Remmer took it in turns to drive the landau and, with the help of Herr Reinhart, protect and warm the baby as best they could in their improvised shelter. Hay and forage for the horses filled the corners not packed with clothes and food. Only survival was now contemplated. As they left the gates, Mimi looked back. She knew that this part of her life was over, and that this would be her final view of the house. The house might survive – but the way of life was over as finally as death itself. Unlike Lot's wife, she did not look again. Her thoughts were on Herr Reinhart's story.

He had sat wearily by the fire, like the peasant woman before him, absorbing the soothing warmth and sipping turnip soup, a dribble running unnoticed down one of his many chins. He held Mimi's hand in his huge paw, squeezing it for emphasis as he talked.

They had left each other tearfully on New Year's Day, both still in shock from the brutality of Gauleiter Hanke, the laughter of his jackals hanging in the air – certain that this was a final farewell.

'Everything changed that morning, my dear. My café no longer felt like home, no longer safe. Of course I'd known what men like Hanke were capable of – but somehow by laughing at them they'd always seemed more ridiculous than dangerous. But when I realised that whether or not he'd had a live round in that gun of his was a matter of utter indifference to him, I became very afraid. And fear, my dear, is a horrible thing. Not the sort of fear you have when you slip near a precipice, when your guts turn to water, but the terrible feeling of loneliness, of being adrift in a malevolent sea. I missed you, my daughters, my past life; it was a terrible feeling that surrounded me at night – and I no longer had anything to do during the day, as my café had become a leper house – I was on my own – without even that silly girl who used to help me. Horrible.' Like a lugubrious bloodhound, he had stared at the fire. 'The offensive started. Two days of mixed news from the front. Then panic: stupid, irresponsible panic from Hanke and his band of butchers. They'd had months to evacuate civilians, instead of which they'd strutted up and down, talking of beating the Americans in the Ardennes, wonder weapons, London being raised to the ground by flying bombs and Ivan being too extended to launch an offensive. Fantasies. Did Hanke believe it? I don't know. Maybe the alternative of having to admit that the game was up was too much to contemplate. Anyway, panic: loudspeakers in the streets telling civilians to make their way west. Every train was engulfed by screaming women and children; hundreds were crushed in the station. Finally, the police drove families away from the trains and on to the road; in this cold. No food prepared. No shelter. Prams. Carts. Sledges. A nightmare.'

Mimi had listened without comment, the Remmers and the peasant woman looking at the fire, all unwilling to trespass into this world that was about to become theirs.

'I was packing a rucksack and loading a little wood-cart when I heard a crack – like a stick breaking – from next door: my neighbour, your friend in the bookshop, my dear – Herr Weisbaden, a gentleman in all senses of that word. I pushed the door open and found him. Dead. Blown out his brains. I nearly took the pistol to do the same. Finish it then. Couldn't do it. I remembered Hanke's gun against my temple . . . ' He had stopped, the memory of that tiptoe to the edge of eternity constricting his vocal chords. Mimi had stroked the back of his hand, reversing their roles in the barn. 'So I headed out on the road west. And what a Via Dolorosa it was. My little cart was a Mercedes among the prams and makeshift sledges made from trays that were carrying children too small to walk. There were nursing mothers huddled under the shelter of trees and barns trying to feed their little ones – too cold for either of them. And those pigs from the *Feldgendamerie,* pulling off scarves and balaclavas to check for deserters; not even doing it out of sight of the children; putting a bullet in the back of the neck or hanging the poor devils they winkled out on any nearby tree or lamp-post. I left the main road to come here – not expecting to find you, but at least knowing there was a house and some shelter. I'm so pleased to see you, my dear. So pleased.'

'And me you, Herr Reinhart. So pleased.'

She had lied. Not because she did not love this father figure, this friend and confidant, but because the task of nurturing three generations and a cripple out of the maw of danger now seemed Herculean. The peasant woman had given her a glimpse, but Reinhart the full preview, of the horrors awaiting them. Shelter, food and a beast of burden able to pull them through were the only things that now counted. She knew that a hard heart and a clear head would be needed: not something for which Flaubert and the gentler arts of conversation had prepared her.

All this was going through her mind as the main road came in sight, revealing a wagon-train without end, stretching to the horizon ahead and behind into a dawn of snow flurries and frigid wind. There was little noise as they joined the snow-deadened westward progress other than the jingle of horse bridles, the squeaking of axels and the occasional shout of alarm as horse or bullock lost its footing, threatening to drag its burden down with it. The steam of horse breath blew as a fine mist over mummified figures clutching reins or huddled among piled possessions.

The first test of her hardened heart appeared all too soon, a little group of statues petrified by the roadside, a mother and two children whose heads were just apparent from the blanket that was swathing them, its windward side white from driven snow; supplicants Mimi realised, looking for the salvation of transport. The exodus that Reinhart had described had already metamorphosed into a stark cull of those dependent on their feet alone. Would her fragile party survive if they took them on? Was there enough room or food for them all in the makeshift wigwams on their carts?

No.

Mimi watched the living milestone reach out an arm as the cart passed, attempting to shape some form of woollen igloo with the blanket. What did they look like, this family? What would they look like in a few hours? A still mound of snow, unnoticed, unmourned.

Within an hour the temperature, many degrees below freezing, began to take its toll, and the lassitude, the dullness of movement that Mimi had noticed around her, began to leave her stupefied, driving but not in control, her mind beginning to wander until, recognising the danger, she gratefully gave way to Frau Remmer and lowered herself into their makeshift caravan. Its tiny cargo, swathed in blankets, just a speck of a nose visible, was crying the same listless note of their first meeting. The churn of goats' milk was there – but already frozen solid, part of the survival plan but dependent on a fire to make it drinkable. The hunger would have to continue until darkness halted their progress and a fire was lit. And quickly it did come, in the foreshortened day of midwinter, greying the snow further, reducing the horizons to the width of the surrounding fields, their boundary lines of poplars tapering into the ground-kissing cloud. As the last light leached away, the wagon-train slowed to a halt with a collective hive-mind. Exhausted animals stood stock-still in their shafts and stiff wagoners stumbled to build fires that were soon ringed by exhausted huddles.

The peasant woman, inured to discomfort and accustomed to outdoor life, had an energy not shared by her fellow trekkers. She broke chunks of frozen stew into the single iron pot, ladling its steaming contents into shared bowls. It thawed them from the inside outwards, loosening limbs, sharpening wits. Herr Reinhart, Mimi noticed with concern, could hardly get down from the cart, all his years and more showing in every movement. Though the food had the same effect, it took longer, and, despite the cold at his back, she could see the enervating effect of the fire as he began to doze. She cajoled her charges into the landau and they prepared for the night, nesting as best they could, clutching each other for warmth, the sour smell of the peasant woman the overpowering companion of every lungful of air. A night followed of fitful snatches of sleep, jolted into wakefulness with every turn and dream; endless hours of dark thoughts. The pink dawn, when it came at long last, promised even lower temperatures but the expectation, at least, of later sunshine.

All the time, traffic pushed relentlessly in the other direction. Carts filled with ammunition, small arms and huddled soldiery: battered *Schutzenpanzerwagen*, half-track, semi-armoured personnel-carriers, their contents indistinguishable from the huddled forms heading in the opposite direction, spewing diesel smoke and a sheet of deafening sound in their passing, ruthlessly smashing aside any cart or person that meandered into their way. As the road wound closer to the arterial railway, trains in both directions clattered past, the heat of the steam blackening the engines in contrast to the snow-caked trucks behind, the open anti-aircraft wagons manned by hunched soldiers trying to reduce their surface area so as to be less exposed to the slicing wind. The trains moving west looked very different, with families hanging on to the boarding plates, clinging to any flat surface, even the roof, the crush of the insides of the carriages and cattle trucks unbearable to contemplate. Occasionally, a limpet would lose its grip and, with no more than a weak flutter of a frozen arm, like a dropped marionette, crumple into the drifts by the side of the tracks.

And with the clear skies came new danger in the first limb-numbed hour of the morning, with little warning other than a noise of engines, distant but building fast.

'*Jabos!*'

The shout went up and was repeated along the convoy. Figures fell out of carts, dragging children behind them. The newcomers, uncertain as to how this new threat would manifest itself, merely looked on as a pair of twin-engined fighter-bombers flashed over the top of a stand of trees in a side-slipping turn that brought them running the length of the road, sweeping over their heads with only feet to spare. Their passage was deafening, the backwash stripping the canvas off their makeshift tents, so close that Mimi caught the eye of the bomb-aimer through the perspex porthole in the fuselage. As the pony reared in panic, the smell of aviation fuel, metallic, mixed with a gale of exhaust fumes, overlaid frantic screams as carts overturned and animals evacuated themselves in terror. Bringing the pony under control, Mimi watched the rapidly receding silhouettes nose up slightly and twin bombs arch their way into the tangled convoy, the shock wave of the explosions rippling its way back towards them, thumping their ears, a pall of smoke and screaming emerging out of the receding engine ululations that faded as quickly as they had arrived.

Her small party stared stunned towards the pillar of smoke that was already shredded by the relentless wind. The ponies, whinnying in fear with foam-flecked mouths and prancing gait, twisted in their shafts, forcing Remmer and Mimi on to their feet to calm them with their own adrenalin-trembling hands barely able to grasp the bridles. Only just in control of themselves and the ponies, they were aware that the column was moving again. Like migrating wildebeest fording a crocodile-infested river, inured to the attrition of predators, the collective will of the column asserted itself, ignoring the carnage behind it in a surge westward, accepting its losses with a communal shrug. Woodenly accepting the collective decision, the party joined the flow, leaving the tombstone of smoke behind.

That evening, the wind mercifully abated and a star-vaulted sky roofed their camp. Mimi and Herr Reinhart shared a blanket and the luxury of a mink coat, still faintly smelling of perfume and cigars, bringing with it Proustian memories of a vanished life. They talked gently, with long pauses: of happy times, of friends, the predation of the war on both; about Max and the horror of their last meeting, the remembrance of which reduced them both to contemplative silence. She nursed her grief and he relived the terror of the pistol barrel against his temple. With the trust of this intimacy they gently probed personal spaces, culminating in the question that had been hovering between them.

'Why did you stay, my dear?'

She considered this carefully, an intense sense of privacy fighting with a closeness that was more than physical – an intimacy of a mutual acknowledgement that the mortal coil was at full stretch – and that there were no secrets in a hospice. 'A man. A prisoner of war. French. You'd like him.'

She felt his hand reach for hers under the fur, enveloping it, his thumb gently caressing the back of her hand. She leant her head on his shoulder as she had with Max all those months ago.

'Would you like to tell me about him? I won't be jealous, I promise.'

She hesitated before replying. 'It was new for me, this thing, whatever it is. He was the first man . . . he made me . . . it changed things for me. It sort of existed separately, in a little bubble, not about now . . . yet all about now. Not full of secrets, I think. Just no questions, not normal man-woman questions; or what I thought were normal. It sounds rather strange when I describe it; but it didn't feel strange then. Very natural: like when you're dancing with someone who's caught your rhythm, and you allow yourself to fold into them; separate but joined. A cocoon; a stupid, silly cocoon; which is why we're here. Irresponsible. I'm sorry.'

'Don't be sorry, Mimi dear; not for me anyway. Nor for the baby – nor its grandmother. Without you we'd be dead – so I think that balances out the Remmers, don't you? Or even if you don't think it, you have to put it behind you. Guilt is like jealousy: it takes up energy and gives nothing back. Not worth it. I found that out in the war, the last one that is; in the trenches. I made a mistake. I launched a mortar attack too early and killed half of my platoon who were on a raid to get prisoners. Two of them were family men. Did I kill them and orphan their children? Yes. Did I feel guilty? Yes, for years. Then one day I realised that all I'd done was make a mistake. Normal. Human. Irresponsible even. And as I didn't . . . don't . . . believe that God is either looking at me, or judging me, I suddenly realised I didn't need to cannibalise myself to feed that guilt any more. A liberation. Nurse yourself: don't hurt yourself, my dear; it's very important.'

'Maybe I'll get to that. But I do feel guilty. Guilty about Eric: guilty about the Remmers – even about my Frenchman. I think he's married, maybe with a family; I don't know. How could I love someone I don't know? Isn't that irresponsible; like some silly girl?'

The huge, gentle man considered this, treasuring this moment of intimacy, luxuriating in its physical closeness, a tender cocktail of the paternal and the amicable, with faint echoes of the sexual that tinge all friendships between men and women.

'As you know, my dear, I've squandered a lot of my life on frivolity. I haven't got much to show for it other than some friendships and my daughters. I've had much happiness – and much sadness – but the sadness was only the obverse of the happiness, the price you pay, so to speak. That's love too; twinned with hurt, grief and jealousy – but none the worse for that in all its forms. I was not entirely faithful to my wife; but do I regret it? Any pain to her, yes; but I have to balance that against the joys, what I learnt about life, the experiences that I can pass on. And I think . . . I know . . . it was positive, because I don't regret it in aggregate. Your problem, my dear, is that your face is pressed up against the canvas of the moment. All you can feel is the roughness of the paint, the craters of the palette knife. I see the whole, the frame, the composition, how it all fits together. The compensations of impotent old age, I suppose.'

They gazed upwards at the star-filled roof spanning their world, hearing snatches of muffled conversation near by, the hiss of the pine-fed fire and the occasional whinny of a horse answered by a distant dog bark from an isolated farmhouse.

'So you don't think I . . . we . . . have to answer for this: to someone, now; in another life, to God?'

'Mimi, who's questioning? Only you. If you feel that you've let yourself down, then it's only you who has the power to do better. Just don't set the bar too high – for your own sake. If God is setting the bar, then let's just hope he deals more in mercy than justice. I don't know about him, but I do know about me; and I hold you very high, my dear – very high.'

'What about Eric?'

'Eric only knows what he knows. If he knows anything now, he knows you've been a good wife to him. Because you've found something else, another compartment in your life, is that such a negative thing?'

'Depending on the choices I make.'

He considered this, the rumbling of his breath a refrain for his thoughts.

'Depending on the choices? Yes. I suppose so. But are you sure of your choices? Are you in control of your life now, Mimi? Not really. Did you have a choice to stay? No. Will you have the choice to go back? I doubt it. If someone has a pistol at your head, you have choices, but they aren't balanced choices – not choices at all. It seems to me that life is like a river in that it only flows one way. It has bits that are like rapids and wider sweeps where the little boat you're in turns gently in circles, giving you a view of the river all around, ahead and behind. But just when you think you've got your bearings, another set of rapids gets hold of you and it's all you can do to stay afloat, to avoid a shipwreck. Only in the wide sweeps do choices come in – and even then we make them on imperfect information, with defective scales. Take it as it comes, my dear: keep only the positive and throw away the rest. Not exactly the theology of a good Catholic – but it's worked for me . . . so far.'

She got up quietly, went to the fire and ladled some soup into a tin mug, bringing it back for them to share, the steam misting his spectacles, the heat bringing life back into their fingertips.

'You're very dear to try and make me feel better, but to me it feels foolish at best. How can I love a man I only half know? Perhaps what he showed me was that I was living half a life myself – which I knew – but only half knew. What I'm saying is that selfishly, for myself – not for anyone else – I'm bidding for the whole of me. What that will entail, I don't know – assuming I survive to bid for it. It's a choice, my dear friend, an eyes-open choice that I'll have to answer for to someone, maybe only to myself. And I'm happy with it. No. Not happy – that's the wrong word – committed to it; certain about it; for better or worse. Those words again: wedding words. How ironic.'

She stopped and in the gleam of the fire her friend saw a pair of tears rolling down her face, past her mouth, unchecked, her eyes unblinking, staring past the warmth and into another place, a place where he could not go. He put his arm around her, drawing her into his walrus vastness, wrapping the fur and blanket around them, swaddling them. A cocoon.

9

The road west from Breslau. Two days later

The baby died during the night. In the frigid dawn the refugees hobbled from their makeshift tents, limbs straightening with difficulty after a contorted night, joints welded into immobility by the cold, fingertips nipped by frost, circulation needing to be restored by pained movement.

The body lay in the snow, on the edge of the forest that now contained their world. The pink trunks of the pine trees were the only colour in the gloom of the darkened woods. The snow baffled the sound but, compacted under the tramp of thousands of feet into a hard surface, it squeaked with each compression. The peasant woman went about her business without explanation, the tiny bundle a hanging question that the others were loath to explore, with only exchanged glances between them. Gradually the truth began to dawn along with the first shards of a brittle sun, the slow realisation that the baby had been alive when it had been placed on the snow; that cold, rather than hunger, had administered the *coup de grâce*. As old as man himself, the relentless logic of survival dictated that helpless, superfluous mouths be abandoned on mountainsides, a practice giving rise to legends of she-wolf mothers and fox-whelped foundlings. Without mother's milk, without the warmth of a suckled breast and, more importantly, the will to self-sacrifice that only a mother's love can rationalise, his claim on life was cobweb thin and liable to be shredded by the merest draft – let alone the gale of a desperate trek.

No comment was made as the convoy heaved itself forward again, greaseless axels squealing against the crack of whips, every sting needed to push reluctant, hungry animals forward. No attempt was made at burial – out of the question in the bone-hard earth; the tiny bundle remained as just another signpost of suffering along the road. The same ground that was unable to accept the tiny body was beginning to claim other victims, starting with the cloven-hoofed beasts of burden: oxen, cows, and even, improbably, a reindeer – loot of sorts from the Baltic campaigns that had found its way into the zoo in Breslau. Without the protection of steel shoes, the frozen road relentlessly wore away at their hooves, filing down the cartilage until all that was left was a stump that smeared the track with blood as they stumbled pathetically to their knees, bellowing in the dual pain of their stumps and the cut of whips that frantically tried to keep them upright and moving. In their staggering falls they overturned carts, writhing in the shafts as their owners desperately tried to cut the traces and save their possessions. Cut free, they lay by the side of the road, flanks still heaving, as butchers descended on them to hack and saw steaks to provide the calories that might mean survival.

Families could be seen taking the place of their oxen, straining between the shafts, determined to keep their possessions no matter how useless they were in the circumstances – heirlooms of a past, settled life, such as chairs and tables, a hip bath or baby's cot. After a few hundred yards, exhaustion set in and they gave way to the angry shouts of the wagon train behind them, clustering around their pathetic carts and all that remained of home, reluctant to make the terrible choices of abandonment, not only of possessions but also of those too sick or too old to walk or be carried. So carts became catafalques, stationary tents silent with the dead or the nearly so. Butchered animals littered the road with their blood freezing in brown puddles licked by feral dogs that had either been left behind on local farms or separated from their owners on the road. Catholic of taste and lacking discrimination, they could be seen stripping human arms, crunching fingers, gnawing for the marrow within the bones.

The country had moved from the open fields of the Polish plain to the undulating forests approaching the River Neisse, the border between Silesia and Saxony and the place that conventional military wisdom, as it filtered along the file of humanity, held that the Russian advance would be halted. Get to the Neisse and there you could rest, take stock, find food, a cart, get warm. Survive. Rumours swept along from the east: tales of tanks pulverising columns of stragglers, grinding families in their tracks; fighter-bombers strafing civilians and military without discrimination; *Katyushas*, terrifying rockets, screaming overhead, churning and burning their way through the densely packed column. And wholesale rape, no protection offered by extreme youth or age.

For Mimi, the Neisse held another goal, the estate of the old Count von Pullendorf, Eric's godfather. The old man had proposed the toast at their wedding and stood as trustee and wise adviser when his friend, Eric's father, had descended into madness and an early death, haunted by his time in the charnel-house of Verdun. He had treated her as a daughter, letting slip one day that he found her an almost unbearable reminder of the child he had lost in her early twenties to the influenza that had swept Europe in the wake of war. Huge, with the appearance and manner of a *Junker*, his hobby was sewing tapestry and his first love the operas of Verdi. He ruled his estate firmly, feudally and fairly, loved by the few that knew him well and respected by those that didn't. Mimi had no doubt that he would still be there, impossible to imagine him not rooted to the place whose name he carried, a welcome in a journey of closed doors and locked barns.

The detour was gruelling. Pullendorf lay ten kilometres from the main road, drifts and knee-deep snow requiring everyone to shoulder the carts out of the snow's grip a dozen times an hour. They were exhausted by the time the walled town of the Middle Ages with its adjoined eighteenth-century schloss came into view – Muscovite in appearance, with a suggestion of onion domes – the count's ancestor's rococo homage to Catherine the Great, at whose court he had served as Saxon ambassador. They were not the only guests. Orange light from the stables and barns, abandoned carts and prams outside, showed that others had had similar thoughts, relying on the Count's famous hospitality: relatives, acquaintances or simply the indigent who had washed up on his shore by accident. His butler opened the door of the main house and stared at Mimi without recognition, making her aware for the first time of the marks that the journey had left on them. She caught a glimpse in an ornate mirror of the dirty, grey, peasant woman she had become, wrapped in an outsized greatcoat, which swamped the mink coat that she used as a liner, her dark curls lank and greasy under a fur hat that had seen better days. As the butler was apologising for his lack of recognition, the count appeared.

'My dear child, thank God you're here. I've been worrying about you ceaselessly since I managed to get a message from your parents that you were still at home when the offensive broke. Come in! Come in! Halder, quick, tell the countess that the Grafin von Hedow is here and that she must have a bath and a meal immediately. Immediately. And her friends: bring them in and find them some hot food. Get them warm. By the fire. Come. Ladies, gentlemen, please make way for our new guests.'

As they were ushered into the baroque glories of the hall, with its delicate gold leaf and pastoral murals of the *ancien régime*, they realised that the house was already packed with humanity. A crowd ranged around a fire, newer arrivals pressing as close as they could to absorb the heat. Those that had already done so were lying on the floor in family heaps, unconscious in the sleep of physical exhaustion. Her little party had not even the energy to fight for a place by the fire but lay down where they stood, not even bothering to find pillows of sorts for their heads before their eyes closed. Mimi would have joined them, for sleep as much as duty, but she was escorted by the butler to the countess's boudoir despite her protests. Fastidious and disapproving, the butler picked his way through piles of possessions that he clearly felt had no place in his master's domain. The countess was ministering to a pair of sick children in her dressing-room bed, sponging their heads with a wet flannel in an attempt to douse the fever that gripped them. She put her bowl aside when she saw Mimi, her powdered face radiating delight, relief and affection: she shared her husband's recognition of her dead daughter in the woman in front of her and her welcome was correspondingly maternal. Mimi found herself being undressed, bathed and put to bed, unable and unwilling to resist in her state of mental and physical depletion.

It was twenty-four hours before she woke again, hungry and cotton-headed with sleep but restored. Wearing the countess's dressing-gown over a medley of mothball-scented clothes, she picked her way back through hallways of bodies and possessions, past clumps of slumped families and into the hall where an expectant crowd was gathered around the fireplace where a spit was turning two impaled pigs, fat dribbling into the fire which flared to each drop. Eyes devoured the sizzling flesh, nostrils twitching with each eddy of roasting that drifted outwards into the room. Soup was being dispensed from a huge vat and consumed in all corners, the recipients staring into the middle distance as the restoring balm seeped into their core, making them feel human again, dignity restored; not merely animals obsessed only with warmth and food. Her own party had nested under the stairs, with Herr Reinhart already asleep again, still holding an enamel cup half-filled with soup; the Remmers were watching the fire with famished intensity, while the peasant woman obsessively reordered what remained of her worldly possessions.

When Mimi found the count, she saw with concern the tiredness in his old face and realised that the task of caring for this multitude was taking its toll, the strained eyes showing that he had not slept for days. He was wearing an old-fashioned uniform, the like of which she had never seen him wear before. Despite a physical resemblance to Bismarck, he was resolutely civilian, normally wearing a frock coat and high collar, summer and winter. He led her to his study, an oasis of privacy in what was now a communal house, placed her in a chair and went in search of food and his wife.

They both watched as Mimi wolfed down sausage and pickled cabbage, rocking gently, eyes closing in relief. They ate a little too, restoring themselves before they talked. Mimi told of her journey, of Max von Sheilditz, of Breslau and of Eric. They listened in silence, reflecting on the imminent end of the world as they knew it, with the countess holding Mimi's hand as she told of the horrors of the road. As she spoke she realised that this had become a familiar story to them and that their hospitality had brought down upon them countless similar tales of suffering and dislocation. Too polite to show this, they listened, but, as Mimi talked, she became aware that the count's attention was elsewhere: he was mulling something over, searching for an elusive answer to a dilemma. Mimi concluded her tale and turned her attention to the old man who was twisting his wedding ring as if it were a worry-bead. She leant over and addressed him as 'uncle', a family familiarity, staying his twisting hands with her expression of concern.

'You're probably wondering about this uniform, my dear. I haven't worn it other than at my regimental reunion for many years: it's a bit tighter than it should be now,' he smiled ruefully, 'but it's the only one available to us poor old men in the *Volkssturm*. "People's Army". What an absurd name for a bunch of cripples, children and men so old that they can hardly lift a rifle. Because I reached the giddy rank of captain and had the great misfortune to fight the Russians at Tannenburg in the last war, they've made me the local *Volkssturm* commander for the town – and my orders have just come through. We have to join the regular army, or what's left of it, in defending the main rail-bridge over the Neisse. With what, I asked them? Two Panzerfaust anti-tank weapons, some Mauser rifles that were out of date in the Kaiser's time and only a few dozen rounds of ammunition. We have been promised machine pistols and some mortars – but no sign of those yet. My second-in-command has cancer and two of my so-called men are only fourteen – twins who still sing treble in the church choir. Training? Marching and giving Nazi salutes – that's all. It'll be murder if we go and the officious little pig who is the *kreisleiter* for the area will murder us if we don't. I'm an old man and if I get killed it will not be that I haven't had a fine life . . . ' – he reached over and took his wife's hand – ' . . . but those boys? I don't think I can do it. It can't be my duty, can it, to get them all killed? For what? To keep the war going for another minute perhaps? How can I protect them? I'm too tired to think straight; too old; too scared if I'm honest. What should I do?'

Mimi looked up at him in surprise, realising that the old count was deferring to her. He had always been a father figure of decision, wisdom and authority, but she realised that he was handing over the baton of responsibility in an acceptance of old age. This was, she realised, growing up – and the lives of these men and boys were in her hands. She considered for a moment, thinking back to the road that had led them to Pullendorf, to the sepulchral darkness of the moss-floored forest, silent, still and impenetrable. She surprised herself with her own certainty, realising that over the last two weeks she had already made many life and death choices and this was but one more – with more to come. She took the baton firmly, the mettle in her voice arousing proud interest in the elderly couple.

'You have to go. Staying here isn't an option – I've seen what the *Feldgendamerie* do to deserters – or to any poor wretch who has mislaid his papers or his unit. They love their work and, believe me, pity isn't in their lexicon. It's what you do then that's important. I'm not a soldier but even I can see that the forest either side of the road is somewhere that no vehicle can negotiate and I would think the Russians will avoid moving off the road if they can. You'll stand a chance if you can drag your feet until their vanguard has gone through – up the main road and railway line – and then melt into the forest, keeping together to fight off any rear units until you can make your way back here and into civilian clothes again. You must have someone in your unit who has knowledge of the forest. I'm making it sound simple, aren't I? What do I know about war?'

She shrugged her shoulders, but the old count patted her leg with a smile.

'Too much, clearly, my dear. Enough for me to appreciate your help as I can't think of any better plan – one that at least gives us some chance – even if we do have to deal with the Russians in civilian clothes later. You mustn't be here when they arrive. And you must take my wife with you as I fear what will follow.'

The countess spoke. 'No. I'm staying here to wait for you. I'm too old for moving now. We both are. We'll take our chances here. But you, Mimi, must go now. We can give you a mule – the only one the army failed to requisition – to replace that worn-out old pony; and you must go soon as the Neisse is not going to hold them up long – it's not much of a river – not like the Elbe. We belong here; you don't. So take your friends and leave as soon as possible; maybe not tonight as it's snowing, but certainly tomorrow at dawn. You must put as many miles, and as much time, between you and the Russians as possible. And don't try to persuade us to come with you. We're too old to be moving and we have responsibilities that we can't abandon now. Just look after yourself, child. Please do that.'

Mimi stayed her thoughts: that this pair of aristocrats would be the first to feel the bitter knife of Beria's killing machine – even if they survived the first onslaught of the Red Army; that this house, they and their possessions would be a magnet for all the pent-up vengeance rolling over the horizon. She knew that they knew this too and didn't need a painful reminder to poison their last moments together, least of all from her, the last incarnate memory of their beloved daughter, who now held their hands in hers. They sat for what seemed like minutes, eyes damp but drawing strength from each other, wordlessly saying important things over which mere words would have choked and stumbled. The only sound was the rumbling of the human herd the other side of the door and the spit and click of a pine-wood fire in the close warmth of the study.

Suddenly, like a wasp nest excited by a stick, the noise outside swelled to an angry hum, with louder shouts audible. The count snapped out of his meditation, revived and concerned. Mimi and the countess followed him as he parted the crowd that was craning its collective neck the better to see the disturbance in the hall that was flare-lit by the fat-fuelled surges from the pigs roasting on the fire. In the hearth stood a thin man in a brown uniform, pistol in one gloved hand, the other on his hip. A slight tic betrayed that he was more nervous than his stance was meant to indicate. His whole demeanour and appearance suggested a clerk rather than a soldier. Four other men were struggling with the spitted pigs, trying to manhandle the rod ends with sacks wrapped around their hands to protect them from the heat in the metal. There was a palpable fury in the crowd, kept at bay by a combination of the pistol and an innate and ingrained deference to the uniform the man was wearing. One in the crowd refused to be intimidated.

'We haven't eaten properly for weeks, you bastard. What are you doing?'

The uniformed man held up his free hand and the hum subsided to a grumbling growl.

'I'm confiscating these illegally slaughtered animals under Sub-section 4 of the military regulations that now apply in Saxony and Silesia. I . . . '

'You want to eat them yourself, you greedy sod!'

The laughter contained more menace than humour and the first pair of pork carriers was jostled as the crowd surged towards the official whose light-brown shirt-collar was beginning to darken with sweat. His voice went up an octave as he sensed he was losing control of the situation; the pistol unconsciously raised itself with his voice.

'The penalty for the illegal killing of livestock is death. The severest penalties will apply to anyone who abets this sabotaging of the war effort. Clear a way immediately . . . immediately do you hear . . . now!'

Unconsciously, he stepped back under pressure from the crowd. A hurled bottle shattered against the fireside spattering his arm with shards of glass. In shock, he stepped sideways and tripped backwards, putting out his free arm to break his fall but instead plunging it into the bowels of the fire, his pistol discharging as he fell. The shriek as his arm erupted stilled the crowd, who watched horrified as he fell forward with flames running around his chest. His acolytes stared stupidly, still holding the sizzling pigs as he rolled on the floor beating the flames with his pistol hand.

The count barged forward, grabbing a blanket from the shoulders of a watching woman, smothering the rolling, screaming figure on the floor while another onlooker beat him with a leather coat. Once the flames were doused, the official sat on the floor singed and shocked. Still the four men holding the pigs did nothing except stare, hemmed in by the crowd and uncertain what they should now do. The count stood on the raised step and pointed to the fire. 'They will need a bit more cooking, gentlemen. Please be so good as to place the spits back on their stands. Thank you.'

The four men shuffled back towards the fireplace. As they were struggling to balance their burdens on the turning frame, the dazed figure on the floor recovered himself and, ignoring the indignity of his smouldering hair and singed uniform, started to wave his pistol in the air and shout in a voice that betrayed shock, pain and anger.

'No you don't. Take those carcases out to the vehicle immediately. Now! Now!'

The four men hesitated.

The count turned towards the official who appeared drunk – eyes watering and peering through the smoke that was coming off his clothes, swaying from foot to foot. The count's roar conceded nothing to his age. 'How dare you come into my house and give orders without consulting me. Get out! Get out now, before I roast you on that fire. And if you come back again I'll set my hunting dogs on you. Out!'

The four assistants simply dropped their load and scuttled for the door, running the gauntlet of the crowd from which an occasional cuff or kick hurried them on their way. The official stood his ground for a few seconds, his pistol tracing an uncertain pattern but remaining pointed towards the floor.

'You'll suffer for this. Yes, you will. Do you hear?'

His voice betrayed him by slithering into a falsetto and the indignity of laughter finished him off, his authority in the same state as his uniform as he stumbled his way to the door.

Far from triumphant, the count took Mimi's arm and led her towards the stairs where her party was encamped. He knew it was only a Pyrrhic victory.

'You must go first thing. He'll be back tomorrow with cohorts of his Nazi friends, riddled with class hatred and dying to cut me down to size. I suppose I should be grateful that it's taken this long for them to find a good enough excuse to get me. They'll come in force and will want everyone's papers. Yours will cause you trouble – so you must leave before they get here, before first light. I'll have the mule organised for you now.'

It was still dark as the landau and cart set off into the foggy wreaths of a steady thaw. The recently fallen snow was wet and sticky, balling up in the animals' hooves, the sides of the forest only just visible even on that narrow road, silent and dripping. At least the road was clear and the snow fresh, with the old hardened snow acting as tracks underneath to keep their tyre-less wheels from sliding sideways into the rough-cut ditches on either side. All this changed as they reached the bridges over the Neisse. The rail-bridge, a girdered structure, had a narrow footbridge on one side. It was clad with a fur of foot-bound refugees, bowed beneath slings and packs containing what remained of their possessions, enveloped alternately in surges of steam from a grinding loco-motive and curtains of fog. The old stone road-bridge was chaotic. The westbound wagon train was stationary with some trekkers remonstrating with the military policemen guarding the approaches; others, seated on driving plates rocked in exhaustion, their draft animals asleep on their feet. The bridge was clearly too narrow to take opposing streams. The traffic the other way was constant: lorries and carts filled with ordnance and men; columns of marching soldiers, weighed down by packs and rifles, trying to maintain their footing in the compacted slush; half-track wagons and menacing panzers pouring black diesel smoke that mingled with the fog and steam to create an infernal cocktail of sound and fumes.

Mimi spotted a staff car by the side of the road with its bonnet up and its driver absorbed in something mechanical. A *Wehrmacht* officer was sitting in the back, greatcoat pulled high round his ears and smoking. She removed her hat, allowing her now clean curls to fall over her shoulders as she approached the car. Surprised and disconcerted, the man threw away his cigarette and straightened. As he removed his cap, she could see an iron cross at his throat and tiredness in his eyes. He neck-bowed but said nothing.

'*Oberst,*' she guessed his rank, 'could you let us know what's happening? We're trying to get to Bautzen. How long has the bridge been closed? Do you think we'll be able to get across soon? I hope that you'll be able to help as I don't think we'll get much information there.' She gestured towards the *Feldgendamerie.*

He considered for a moment, leant over and opened the door of the car. 'Please, *fraülein*; join me for some coffee – ersatz, I'm afraid, but hot at least. Please.'

She hesitantly joined him and accepted an offered rug and a cup that he filled from a thermos.

'Where have you come from?'

He listened attentively as she briefly told her tale. Occasionally, his focus drifted towards the bridge or back to her companions. Two days' stubble and dark rings under his eyes told his story. When she had finished he offered her a cigarette, which she gladly accepted and they smoked in silence for a time.

'I am afraid, *fraülein*, that you'll have to abandon your carts. My task, probably my final task,' he smiled a thin smile, 'is to make sure that this bridge remains clear. At the moment it has to be open for traffic going to the front, but soon, very soon, I suspect, it will have to be open for traffic going the other way: a retreat. More like a rout probably. And when that happens, I have to make sure that it is blown up to stop the Ivans using it. The only certainty is that civilians won't be using it. I'm sorry.'

'Where is the front now?'

He shrugged. 'I heard that they've crossed the Oder – but who knows. It's chaos. Information gets fed up to headquarters and then disseminated to the likes of me – but it's normally at least a day old by then and the Russians' tanks are blowing a hole in the side of the house you're sleeping in when you thought they were sixty kilometres away. My guess? Two days away from here. Which is why you have to get going. May I make a suggestion?'

'Of course.'

'Leave your carts and load a tent and as much food as you can on to the ponies. The river is still frozen – just – and there's a path that will take you down to it about half a kilometre to the right of the bridge. If you use your horses as pack animals, I think you and your companions,' he glanced at the two old, stooped figures and the one-armed man, 'may have a good chance. I'm sorry I cannot offer you more. Truly sorry.'

She saw in him shadows of her friend Max von Seilditz, and without thinking, she reached across and placed her hand on his.

'Thank you. That's more than helpful.'

He gently withdrew his hand and, without looking at her, he reached into his breast pocket and handed her a letter.

'May I ask you a favour, please. Could you post this when you get to somewhere away from the front? It's a letter to my wife and my two sons whom I . . . I don't think I'll be seeing again. I'm sure that you'll do your best to do this; and if you would do me this favour it will make what has to be . . . a bit more bearable. Goodbye. And thank you, *fraülein*. I would have liked to have met you in happier circumstances. But there it is.'

He reached across to open the door. She turned round once before setting off towards her companions and he bowed from the neck again before sinking back into the folds of his greatcoat.

Her companions listened without comment. The scene in front of them told them there was no alternative. Using the driving harnesses as frames, they decanted only the essentials on to the pony and the mule, who twisted and backed away in protest at the unaccustomed weight. The track had been well used, horse droppings and the skid marks of sliding hooves showing that others had been there before in similar circumstances. Ice and snow still covered the river, but instead of a featureless white carpet, the expanse was pockmarked with holes showing the black swirls of the river running below. Spreading out to lessen the weight, they started to cross, almost every step accompanied by groaning creaks. Whether it was the noises themselves, or the nervousness that they engendered in the party, the animals began to pull back and it needed the peasant woman, wielding a cutting whip behind, to force them forward, their forelegs tapping out a tattoo of reluctant fright.

Without warning the mule lashed out, both rear legs extending parallel and catching the peasant woman full in the chest, cannoning her backwards towards a large hole into which she slid head first, fingers vainly clawing at the smooth blue ice of the rim before the current caught her torso and flipped her flailing legs into a parody of a somersault. One foot caught the rim and, for a second or two, a shoe remained in view before disappearing.

Where a few seconds before there had been a vital, cursing and flogging life, all that remained was the gurgle of blue-black water and an indentation in the snow.

10

Saxony. Ten days later. 13 February 1945

An air-raid siren woke her.

The blackness of the room was absolute, the air still and stuffy –
but cold. She was warm in bed – but hungry; the sort of hunger that
allows no other thoughts and which tyrannises the consciousness
and invades the unconsciousness of dreams: dreams of feasts just
out of reach; the torture of Tantalus. Where was she? The door
opened and a woman was silhouetted against a single lamp in the
next room. She was wearing a coat and woollen scarf against the
interior chill.

'Mimi, wake up. The siren's gone. What do you want to do? It's
been nothing but false alarms for days, so I'm buggered if I'm
going to sit in some stinking shelter surrounded by screaming
children and geriatrics wetting themselves. Well?'

Mimi struggled back into the present, woollenly trying to place
herself in time and space, struggling to separate dreams of the past
from the solidly temporal. Yes. Of course. Eva. Dear Eva. Thank
God for Eva.

'No. Let's stay here. Definitely. You're right.'

'Of course I'm right. I always am. Stay there and get yourself
together and I'll make you some coffee and heat some bread. Not
much to go with it though, except some potato soup. OK?'

Mimi nodded and smiled gratefully at her friend, whose shadow
she watched through the door as it busied itself in the narrow
kitchenette, its owner being just out of her line of sight: Eva, with
her big bosom and bigger heart, her sharp wit and her coarse
sense of humour – and even coarser appetites. Thank God she was
still here, a rock to cling to in a cold and bitter river. Her bladder
told her she needed to leave the warmth of the bed and she braced
herself against the metallic cold as she felt her way along the
blackness of the outside corridor to the rankness of the communal

privy. Her feet frozen, but her bladder relieved, she returned to the bedroom, gently pulling the door shut to exclude light from the kitchenette before easing a corner of the blackout blind and pushing open a crack in the high casement window. Outside, sabres of light sparred against the clear black sky, crisscrossing each other as they probed the void above, refracting every now and then through a puff of cloud. The noise – or lack of it – was promising: she knew, from the experience of staying with her parents in Baden Baden, the rumbling cadence of massed bomber fleets as they passed overhead, rattling windows and causing dogs to cower. Aeroplanes there were, but individuals; impossible to tell if they were friend or foe – but an unconscious calculation told her that any bomb or bullet was aimed generally and not specifically. Low odds.

She climbed back into the cooling bed and curled into the foetal position with the blankets over her head to rebuild warmth; a womb-like nest; safe. The clonk of enamel plates told her that the food was ready and she anticipated the brutality of the single central bulb by reaching for the shaded bedside lamp for a mellower light. Her friend backed into the room with a steaming tray and placed it on the side of the bed, displaying what Mimi knew to be a goodly proportion of her weekly rations. There was only one set of utensils on the tray. Through her hunger she felt a surge of affection for this old friend, a friend who had weathered the disapproving pomposity of her husband who had distained the earthy humour and frowned on her promiscuity – a promiscuity she had made little effort to hide and which she relayed to Mimi in outlandish stories that had Mimi, in her relative innocence, shocked and wide-eyed, but both of them giggling like schoolgirls. Mimi knew that the brass on the surface hid a softer centre that was easily hurt; hers was a nature more romantic than she would ever have acknowledged and it frequently collided with her urgent physicality.

Mimi fell on the black bread, hardly noticing the grittiness of its texture as she dunked hunks into the potato broth. Guiltily, she saw Eva's eyes flicking down to the tray and her throat working, piston-like. She forced herself to stop eating and pushed the tray towards her friend who acknowledged the gesture with a glance and a smile before spooning the grey thick liquid into her own mouth. They alternated until the tray was denuded of the last trace of food. Still fully clothed, with a scarf, coat and beret, Eva climbed into the double bed next to her friend and they lay beside each other, with just their heads above the covers, luxuriating in the shared warmth and the leaden comfort of full stomachs. Outside the siren sounded again and the drone of an aero engine lapped against the window. A lorry passed below, its driver shouting something that was lost in the clatter of a diesel engine. They lay in a bubble of companionship, not speaking, but happy, as Mimi quietly acknowledged to herself, for a bomb to finish it there and then, to deliver them from cold, hunger and loneliness. Feeding off each other's sense of security they dozed with chastely touching fingers and the feathers of their breaths warming the air around each other's faces.

It was the All Clear that roused them. Both lay awake, but not moving, until Eva rolled on to her stomach and with one cheek on the pillow gazed at her friend's profile as she had done many times before, enjoying the way that her smile created a pair of dimples either side of her mouth. She prodded her to get the effect and was not disappointed.

'Why did you have to wake me?'

'I didn't. The siren did: so don't make me feel guilty.'

Mimi rolled on her side and they faced each other.

'God, this is nice.' The pleasure was mutual and no acknowledgement was needed. 'Thank you for being here. I don't know what I'd have done otherwise. I wasn't sure . . . I didn't know what to expect . . . about Stefan . . . whether they'd got you too. It was too dangerous to write. You do know that, don't you. It wasn't that I didn't care.'

Eva squeezed her hand and smiled – but tears floated on her eyelashes. 'I know that. Of course I knew that. It's just been so lonely. There's been no one, really no one, to talk to about it. It's been horrible. Horrible. I haven't been able to sleep for more than a few minutes at a time since he was picked up. I seem to have developed a super-sensitivity to cars or vans in the night. If they slow down outside, I'm upright in bed with a knot in my stomach that has me being sick, actually sick. That's why that bucket is by the bed – not so that I can pee in it rather than make the trek to that ghastly room down the corridor.' They both made faces.

Stefan had been her lover: a gentle, cultivated man unlike the usual run of her admirers who tended to the athletic rather than the intellectual. While not religious, he was steeped in the Greek philosophic tradition of the virtuous life, an innocent caught up in the violence of a totalitarian state. Whether or not he had been involved in the July Plot to kill Hitler the previous year hadn't really mattered, as his choice of friends and accident of family had been ill-starred: Helmut von Moltke had been his friend from university and Adam von Trott a cousin by marriage. Both had died lonely, agonising deaths in Plötzensee Prison, slowly garrotted by piano wires, naked, under arc lights, to the clickering of a movie-camera recording their twisting extinction for the vengeful entertainment of their intended victim. Picked up as a fellow traveller in the secondary purge of the following months, Stefan had vanished into the maw of the camps, gone as surely as if he had been obliterated by a bomb or shell: no sight, sound or mention of him; any association with him lethal if the net were widened further.

'In some ways it's been worse than the bombing in Berlin. It doesn't stop. Ever. All day, every day. And night. Sometimes I wish they'd just come and get me – get it over with. Then at least you're dealing with something that surely can't be worse than you imagine. Surely?' Quietly, they pondered that question. It could be. Mimi knew it could be. 'I don't think he had a clue what was going on. It just wasn't like him to be making bombs or plotting. He'd have blown himself up. You know how impractical and sweet he was: he was a hopeless liar and couldn't even mend a bicycle puncture. Useless.'

Mimi realised that they were talking about him in the past tense. The passage to the world of the camps was as unidirectional as the voyage over the River Styx. No one returned and no word came out. Below the window, the hollow sound of horse-steps could be heard again and the echoing bells of empty milk churns chiming against each other, pealing to the chattering pattern of wheel-struck cobbles.

Eva propped herself on her elbow. Mimi ran her fingers over her friend's face, worrying her little finger around the bags under her eyes, tracing new lines spidering outwards in skin that had lost its alluring bloom: tired, malnourished.

'The bombing gets to you, Mimi. It's got to me. The first time's terrifying, no matter where you are. It's not just the noise, but also the way the ground trembles as each explosion melds into the next so that it seems to come out of the ground – like an earthquake. You can't believe that any building could be standing afterwards. Most aren't. But the worst thing is what's happened to the people. You know what we Germans are like – very polite, very clean – tidy people. Everyone in Berlin – and I suppose it must be similar in every other smashed-up city – is so tired, so exhausted. Never a good night's sleep. Day after day covered in dust, freezing in offices and trams without windows. No proper food. And then the raids: shelters filled with screaming children and the smell of shit – you can't get to any toilet it's so crowded. And everyone is rude, hysterical; so angry – especially if it looks as though you might be a bit privileged. Don't ever wear that old fur coat of yours anywhere unless you want to be jostled and shouted at. I actually saw one woman being spat on. Why? She was wearing make-up. Difficult place for an old tart like me.' She laughed a mirthless laugh.

'It was the last night there that was the worst, just before I was able to come back here. I was walking across the Tiergarten when the siren went off, not far from the Zoo, quite close to a huge flak tower that looks like it's been dropped to earth by aliens. You don't fuck around in Berlin when that happens, I can tell you. I managed to get to the tower, which sits on top of one of the biggest shelters in Berlin, just as the first bombs started falling and they were closing the metal doors. It was packed: so packed that it was standing room only, with your arms pinned to your sides and a feeling of claustrophobia the like of which I can't even bear to remember. There was the usual heaving and shaking and dimming of lights: sometimes they went off completely and all that was left was this weird light from the luminous paint on the walls. Oh, and the walls are so damp from condensation that they stream water. There was one warden nearby with a candle held up above his head. It kept on going out. He relit it lower; and again lower until it got to face height – when I realised what he was doing: monitoring the oxygen as it was used up. There was no getting any lower as there was no room to even kneel, let alone sit or lie. So do you know what they did? They opened the doors: they didn't have any choice as we would all have been asphyxiated. The shock waves from the blast almost knocked everyone over but, thank God, being in the middle of a park, we weren't the main target area. I think the fact that we were groggy from lack of oxygen probably stopped a mad panic. We were lucky: we must have been at the end of a stray stick of bombs as we fell out of the shelter into the park. There was the odd explosion but nothing too close and nothing burning, except some trees that had phosphorous sticks caught in their branches. The rest of Berlin, all around, was a sea of flames with a towering pillar of fire coming from towards the Unter der Linden, casting everything in a hellish orange glow. It was like one of those Hieronymus Bosch paintings with animals tearing past us: a lion with its guts trailing behind it, a zebra mad with fear and an elephant falling over a mangled leg. Bombs must have hit the Zoo and blown holes in the enclosures. Poor things.' She looked haunted and tired, her natural *joie de vivre* drained away. 'Don't you feel as if everyone's trying to do you harm? I feel like a rat in a barrel and it's getting smaller and smaller. Soon there'll be nowhere to run or move to; no quiet city where the Americans aren't going to bomb you or where some Cossack isn't going to rape you and cut your throat. Why haven't they bombed us here? Perhaps they're planning to leave one city that isn't a pile of rubble for the Russians to enjoy.'

They lay in silence listening to the tinkling of a horse bridle that was suddenly drowned by the sound of falling milk churns and the tip-tap of alarmed hooves on cobbles, accompanied by cursing in a Saxon patois. Eva got out of bed and eased open a crack in the blackout curtain.

'Do you know, it's so nice to hear that sort of sound after Berlin. It's gone there completely. It's another world. Not one any human should have to live in, I can tell you. I'm so glad to be away from it, Mimi; so glad to be back in boring old Saxony. I never thought I'd say that.' She climbed back into bed and sat upright, arms folded. 'So tell me the rest, from where you fell asleep on me. What happened after the woman was kicked by the mule into the river? Did you have to walk the whole way here? I'm listening.'

Mimi's jaw took on a firmer set and her gaze moved to a point behind her friend, who reached for her hand under the bedcovers, palm on palm with the other hand gently stroking the back of her hand; coaxing; comforting.

'It was so shocking; so violent. One moment she was there – and then gone. We hadn't really got to know her – she spoke little, and then only about practical things. Very tough. She understood about draft animals in a way that none of us did. She was the one who checked the horses' feet every time we stopped – and shod them if they threw a shoe. I treated them as pets but she saw them as engines, nothing more – which was why she was the one flogging them across the ice, which needed to be done, but why she got kicked. It sounds rather silly, but we all kept looking at the downstream holes in the ice expecting to see her pop out like a seal on to an ice floe – and then carry on as if nothing had happened, dry and healthy. Don't ask me why – I can't imagine myself now. Maybe it's a coping mechanism that allows you to deal with such a shock. Funny, even the horses picked up on this and seemed to calm down – though I suppose that Remmer's way with them might have been better. He always led them rather than pushed them, speaking to them rather than beating them. He coaxed them to the other side and we all stood stupidly on the bank somehow thinking that she might reappear.

'Reinhart took it worse than the rest of us. Perhaps it was because the peasant woman had been his unconscious prop, her practicality something that he needed as a bolster, an armour of sorts. The Remmers and I were still young and fit compared with him, even though Remmer suffered from his wounds. We'd all been doing physical work around the house or farm. He wasn't exactly old – but fat and sedentary: I doubt he'd ever walked farther than he had from Breslau to our schloss – and that had nearly killed him. It's small things that make the difference, Eva: his boots, for instance. They'd belonged to his brother, who was a keen mountaineer – but were half a size too small. He didn't complain – but I know that every step became a nightmare for him. In the landau he had been fine, as he'd always managed to nest himself out of the wind and swathe himself in blankets – he slept most of the time. But when we started walking, I think he realised that he just didn't have it in him – physically or mentally – especially after that first night in our makeshift tent. It wasn't nearly as cold as it had been after we left Breslau but the thaw was in many ways worse. We were lying on a piece of canvas over slush and mud. Sodden. Right through everything. Have you ever worn a fur coat that's got really wet – wet for a few days? It's disgusting. It starts to rot as the skin rehydrates – a stinking, slimy, disintegrating thing. But I knew I had to hang on to it for warmth. I can't get the smell out of my mind. Ugh.'

She paused at the memory, her face screwed up in disgust.

'Couldn't you find any shelter – a barn? A house? There are hotels on that road. Surely there was somewhere?'

'Almost everywhere was abandoned. But boarded up and locked. I'm sure we could have broken in, but we really didn't have the energy. There were barns, it's true, but they were packed. You've never seen such misery in one place, Eva, really: frozen, wet, hungry, lost. No one really knew where they were going – the next village or town – Bautzen in our case. And the humans weren't the only ones. On almost every farm there were cows wandering to and fro with full udders, as hungry as we were. They kept coming up to us, butting us, begging to be milked. We were more than glad to oblige, to have some warm milk. Occasionally, if there was a hay-stack, we were able to feed them and take some for our animals. All the time that we were walking, it was with a specific goal in sight: Bautzen. You've been there, haven't you? We spent a lovely night there on the way to our honeymoon. I'll always remember walking down those pretty narrow streets on a hot August night with the smell of wild herbs wafting up from the rough ground near the city walls. It was funny, because all of us had similar memories of it – for some reason we'd all been there before in summer. It became something of an oasis for us all as we counted off the kilometres on the signposts. It was going to be the place where we could rest and recuperate. But as we got closer, rumours came back down the column that they had closed the town and were making it into a *festung,* like Breslau, and that no civilians were to be allowed in. None of us wanted to believe it, but when we finally rounded the last bend in the valley and could see the town on its hill, it was clear that it was true. We had to keep going.

'That was when dear Reinhart died. Not there physically, but in spirit. We all saw it. It was like someone turning off a switch. You saw it in the way he walked. In order to keep the pain of his blisters down he had developed a sort of goose-step that meant he walked on the flats rather than the heels of his boots. As we were turned away, it became a round-shouldered shuffle, as if the pain no longer registered. You remember his face, don't you? Those double chins? And his eyes, those alert little eyes that were always sweeping his café for an empty cup or an interesting conversation? They all collapsed. It was as if he was folding himself inside himself, consuming himself from the inside, reducing like a deflating bladder. I suggested that he rode the mule, but he'd have none of it. We rested for longer and longer. It took him for ever to get up, his legs stiffening so much that we had to massage them for minutes before he could flex them. He would hold the mule's mane and be half dragged along. I could sense, and I think he could too, that the Remmers were for cutting him off: leaving him; lightening the load so to speak. They didn't say it, but I could feel it in the way they never looked at him and withdrew into each other. They helped him, but with no goodwill. Cold comfort.' Mimi engaged the gaze of her friend and paused, the memory raw enough to choke her. She bit her lip before continuing. 'He said he needed to stop to relieve himself, so we pulled off the road near a barn behind which he hobbled. We waited. And waited. The Remmers were actually getting angry, when we heard a crack – like a breaking branch. I went to see what was happening and there he was, sitting upright on a pile of logs with his head back and his blood and brains splattering the side of the barn. His eyes were still open. What was he looking at? He looked astonished. What was he thinking about as he pulled the trigger of Herr Weisbaden's pistol? I kept it. Here it is.'

She reached below the bed and pulled up a long leather cross-shoulder bag. She rummaged inside before teasing out a small low-calibre, lightly decorated pistol: a lady's gun. She put it on the eiderdown between them. She cradled her cheek in her palm, staring at it. Eva held her other hand.

'There are four bullets left in it. Maybe one's for me if . . . no . . . don't worry . . . not now. But perhaps some time. If I didn't have any hope left. Like Reinhart. Nothing to look forward to. I can understand that, can't you? Just one terrible instant of violence – then nothing. But that last split second? What do you think about in that last moment of being, that last little fingernail clinging to existence? What do you think about before thinking's over? This stayed in my mind for days afterwards. I couldn't shake it off as we walked. I used to feel that pistol in my bag, stroke it even. I got to love the contrast of the cold barrel with the wooden warmth of the grip. I used to take out the remaining bullets and finger the two empty shell cases and imagine their missing heads; where they were now. Not good thoughts when you're a refugee, frozen, filthy, exhausted and lonely. I wanted to mourn him – but I couldn't. That's what cold and hunger does. It numbs you: makes you – allows you – to count him as a burden rather than a friend. The Remmers could barely conceal their relief when they saw what he'd done. I shouldn't blame them really, but they repelled me. But then I was repelled by myself.'

She picked up the pistol and carefully placed it in her bag before getting out of bed to go to the window. As she eased open the blackout blind, Eva switched off the light to save an angry visit from an air-raid warden and a stinging fine. The milk cart was loaded again and the horses settled. The night was clear with only threads of cloud matching the swathe of the Milky Way clearly visible above a darkened city.

Mimi turned without closing the curtain. 'I missed him dreadfully. I miss him now. But the awful thing is that I shared some of the Remmers' relief. I had begun to wonder if we could make it with him in tow. You get to think like that after a while; when you've been hungry, cold and tired for weeks. And frightened. Reinhart was right. The attrition of fear is worse than the shock. It wears down your mental resources as surely as the cold gets to the physical. And you have the guilt of secretly wanting him . . . you know . . . .' She halted with her hand still on the curtain. 'I need to check on the Remmers down at the encampment. I know they're with their friends but I feel I ought to check. I got them into this by not leaving earlier, so I feel responsible. Will you come with me? I know it's late. Not for long; just down to the park and back.'

'Just to the park. But we come back here as soon as possible – agreed?'

'Agreed.'

By the time they reached the street, the milk cart had turned the corner, leaving behind only the soft smell of horse manure. They could see the curved roof of the Hauptbahnof, the railway station, and struck out in that direction. There were occasional huddled forms in doorways, wedged among sacks and suitcases. Mimi was expecting more refugees and remarked on it to her friend.

'They're moving them on as quickly as they arrive by simply not giving them ration cards. But most are by the station in a huge encampment. Don't worry. There'll be plenty of Silesians for you to chat with about the old days.'

Sure enough, as they turned the corner they were confronted with a sea of carts and canvas. The hum of thousands of voices melded into one and a mixture of wood smoke and the steam of massed breath meeting cold air formed a thin fog. Figures wrapped in scarves and blankets moved among the chaos. A pig stared at them before scurrying behind a cart; the scratching cry of a small baby rose above the din.

Suddenly, the metallic muezzin of an air-raid siren ripped the air, dipping and howling. As in a speeded-up film, the square leapt to life, canvas trembling to invisible panic within. Two police vans converged, disgorging men in high black helmets. A disembodied voice hacked its way over the siren's insistent clamour.

'Attention, attention! Air attack! Air attack! Make your way to the station. There is shelter on the lower level. Attention. Enemy bomber forces have changed course and are now approaching the city area. Air attack. Make your way to shelter. Air attack!'

Mimi looked at Eva, a veteran. The casual carelessness of her reaction to the previous alarm was absent, replaced by a hunted look as she assessed the situation. There was a brief lull in the siren's wail and they could hear the distinctive grumbling drone of aero engines out there in the darkness, a darkness that suddenly flickered white and green in a gentle firework display of magnesium light, a hundred softly descending stars that created hard shadows and trailed tails of iridescent sparks. Yet more erupted, springing to life in a waterfall of glistening beauty. Mimi gazed on, transfixed. Out of the white light, came a more insistent red, clustering towards the river.

Eva grabbed her arm and started running towards the station. 'Shit! It's Christmas trees. For God's sake run!'

11

Dresden. 10 p.m., 13 February 1945

The phosphorous light of massed flares threw the steel of the station into strident relief, every girder casting an oily shadow on to the reflecting gleam of the glass. As Mimi and Eva ran through the arch of the entrance, the same light was bathing the concourse and the platforms beyond, illuminating the swirls of steam from the waiting trains into a sinister chiaroscuro as the light waxed and waned in flickering intensity.

'Down the stairs – on the left – quick!'

Despite their head start, the top of the stairs was already a press of human-tide, funnelling with a dangerous intensity. As fresh bodies joined the crush, screams rose above the drumming of a thousand feet. The first detonation was some way off, but with it any sense of rationality gave way to raw fear and the crowd only pressed harder into the choked neck of the stairs. Three more explosions in quick succession – escalating.

Eva grabbed Mimi's hand. 'No. Too late. Where can we go? Where? Where?'

She scanned the station as she pulled Mimi towards a side wall, both of them almost bowled over by a crowd that had now only one thought – or rather one instinct. There was no rationality in the lemming-like plunge into the packed stairwell.

Both saw the tunnel entrance at almost the same instant. A *Verboten* sign crowned the arch but ghostly light could be seen at the far end: shelter of sorts – but what was at the end? They ran towards the light, just visible over what looked like a concrete wall, not quite hard against the tunnel's end, but too tight to accept any adult around the side and too high to climb. Sheer concrete. They ran back towards the station and into a flash and shockwave that slammed them against the side wall. The noise of shattered glass ricocheting off a myriad of surfaces and the belly-flopping smash of intact plate-glass on to waiting locomotives filled every aural space, echoing and intensified in their tunnel. Stunned, they crawled back towards the end wall as incandescent bursts now drowned the flares' glittering light. They clung to each other as the odd fragment ricocheted off the tunnel's sides and the flashes increased in intensity until it was impossible to tell where one stopped and another started. Patterns emerged with each stick of bombs. A distant detonation heralded either a relaxation of the grip of terror or an escalation as the bomb-load hop-scotched its way across the target, each split second a building crescendo that seemed to lead to an inevitable direct hit close by, the pressure wave compressing internal organs, torturing the inner ear, numbing the ability to trace the Doppler effect of the receding footfall of explosions.

There was a local pause. Elsewhere the sounds of destruction continued, the rippling flashes throwing strobe-like illumination at either end of the tunnel. The women relaxed their grip on each other, unable to believe that the battering concussions and the spattering of fragments had left them unscathed. Dust-filled air and steam from what they realised were the boilers of shattered locomotives constricted their breathing and dulled the continuing flashes into indistinct sheet lightning. Again they made their way to the entrance on to the station where curtains of steam-spawned fog eddied and parted to give glimpses of spectacular destruction. Huge holes in the roof were venting the infernal concoction to a sky that had metamorphosed from the white on black of a photographic negative to flame orange, punctuated by multiple flashes that were now so frequent that the effect was occlusive – more light than dark. A locomotive was spread-eagled over two crushed carriages that were pouring smoke and flames. Its whistle was jammed open and a banshee blast mercifully drowning out the screams of the crushed and burned, or the merely maimed and wounded who lay among those standing in bemused shock. The main entrance had collapsed and flames and smoke were issuing from the stairway to the lower area. Against a wall was a mound of still-moving bodies, brushed together by a carriage on its side that had been blown across the platform like a diabolic snowplough to sweep all before it. Dense smoke was pouring from its bowels. A child, still wearing her school beret and with a satchel over her shoulder stood, unreachable behind a barrier, looking at the remains of an arm that was hanging on by a piece of gristle, an artery pumping a hose of blood on to the platform.

The two women looked at each other wildly. There was no possible exit except over the wall at the other end of the tunnel. But how? It was too tall to scale without a ladder. Or something. A length of partially twisted railing, a shoe of concrete attached to one limb, lay against the wall. Wordlessly – words were useless in the cacophony that seemed to saturate every fibre – they dragged it towards the sheer wall with billows of steam-soaked smoke choking every heave and darkening their exertions. Lungs rebelling and Eva vomiting, they hauled their makeshift ladder into place. Mimi climbed, slipped, felt a ragged iron edge gouge her leg. Blindly she felt for the rim of the wall, sobbing and choking as she heaved herself into the clearer air, retching as she felt Eva struggling beside her, gurgling and half choked. Together, like rag dolls, they hung over the wall, smoke avalanching over the backs of their heads, temporarily blinded, unable to open their smoke-plagued eyes, their retinas, through tight-closed lids, registering the red and yellow illuminations, their arms and hair the impact of spent fragments.

As they blinked open their streaming eyes, they found themselves level with a sheet of water reflecting tongues of star-licking fire that roared in between detonations which rippled shock waves of water over their arms and soaked them with freezing water. Eva put her mouth close to Mimi's ear to have some chance of being heard through the din and over the tinnitus that seemed to come from the middle of their heads.

'It's a fire-fighting water tank.' She coughed and dry-retched as a billow curled over from the tunnel behind them. 'Let's stay here. Stay here.' Her chest heaved again and her head fell forward.

In between billows, when she closed her eyes and held her breath, Mimi became conscious that there was a palpable slackening of the number of explosions – but a corresponding building of the sound and sight of fire, huge fire running like an avalanche through the tented encampment the other side of the tank. Wagons, their canvas coverings burning with the suddenness and intensity of co-joined matches, displayed in seconds their ribs and iron links, their wooden bodywork catching in the next instant to flare eagerly before they collapsed in on themselves as their frames buckled and curled. In one, as if in submission to the demands of *suttee*, the silhouette of a kneeling woman, hair ablaze, weaved in the flames before crumpling into the tentacles of her pyre. Another billowed blast from the tunnel behind them obscured the scene, grit-filled smoke blanketing outlines, grey-black streaks filtering the light that was now white and orange and infused with an intense radiated heat.

Mimi pushed her mouth against her friend's ear, at first coughing so hard that she thought she must be sick. 'We have to get away from here. Into the water. Hold the side.'

Even with the oven heat of the air, the frigid water tightened their lungs, an involuntary intake of breath setting off coughing that took in water as well. Heaving, choking, they dragged themselves around the tank's perimeter, increasingly sheltered from the full intensity of the fire by the six inches of concrete between the surface of the water and the top of the wall. The air they breathed, now nearly free from the smoke of the tunnel, scorched their nostrils like an overheated sauna. The intense radiated heat toasted each hand in turn as it grasped the rim of the wall, lengthy exposure an impossibility as the fire intensified, creating surging, blistering williwaws that churned the surface and forced their heads under the water for protection.

They cowered in their watery refuge while the fire played itself out, ripping through the encampment, the very inflammability of the tented wagons giving it a short-lived intensity that matured swiftly from white to the glowing orange of superheated metal, buckling and sagging among trees that burned like giant candelabra. Cautiously they peeped over the parapet of the tank. A pair of bodies, mother and child, holding charred hands, lay in the foreground, obscenely blackened on one side, clothes smouldering. Black billows continued to pour from the tunnel behind them and towering flames corkscrewed with paired smoke from the roof of the station. In every direction the light of countless fires, some merely flickering in windows of buildings, others blazing with fierce white flames, illuminated the scene. The air was thick with sparks. An artificial wind veered and backed without pattern, then twisted into a sudden tornado's funnel to spin like a befuddled belly dancer. As the encampment settled into smouldering embers, the women pulled closer together, the wounds of smoke scraping their lungs with every breath.

Mimi was the first to shout over the whistling roar of fire. 'Is it over? Have the bombs stopped? Please say they have.'

Though the heat was still intense and the noise from hundreds of fires cracked and whistled, there were no further explosions. Eva, her blonde hair darkened by the water and burnt away in one place by a cinder that had left a smoking wound, wiped her streaming face, pulling herself together in between retching coughs.

'The All Clear hasn't sounded. Wait. Unless there's a direct hit, we're safe here.'

*   *   *

No warning of the second wave. The first bombs were very close, announcing themselves with a whistling roar that came out of a sky free of the sound of sirens but dense with the crackling of a thousand fires. The percussion and the shock waves that succeeded each other reverberated around the tank, shaking the women's hands from the lip, and creating upsurges that sloshed over them and smashed them against the walls. Desperately they grasped for the lip, their clothes a leaden handicap in their attempts to swim if they lost their grip. Debris rained down upon them; a curbstone shattered on the station wall, fragments stinging the back of Mimi's head. Acting like a huge drum, the water amplified the vibrations that seemed to lift the tank, punching them in their stomachs and chests, compressing their lungs. Again the agonising tramp of explosions that escalated to a crescendo that seemed guaranteed to be a direct hit – but miraculously expended itself in a blast that deafened and spattered but left them alive. Eva had been right: the tank was a serendipitous shelter.

Suddenly it ceased. Two isolated explosions; then the roar of the fire. No longer the sound of a thousand bonfires but the howl of hell. Eva, her face glistening with water and red from the infernal light, scanned the square, its tented encampment now glowing ash, twisted trees, smashed and burning.

'The river. We must go to the river. We'll have to see which streets we can get down. God knows which ones are blocked. Come on!'

She pulled herself over the lip of the tank, hung by her hands with her feet two metres above the hard cobbles, then let go, crumpling into a heap with her back to the wall. Mimi followed, but felt her friend's hands supporting her feet as she let go, cushioning her fall as they both rolled uninjured on to stones too hot to touch with unprotected hands. Mimi felt her friend untying the soaked woollen scarf that had been wound around her neck and passively stood while she bound her head with it, leaving only a slit for sight. Thank God for Eva. Mimi did the same for her friend, who pointed towards the street that led to their apartment – and on to the Elbe beyond.

Both were aware of an increase in the wind, an artificial tempest that was beginning to tug at them, a sirocco that relentlessly attempted to drag them back, away from where they wanted to go, but was thereby signalling the route to safety, away from the inferno that was inexorably sucking in air to feed its frenzy. They shouldered their way against a hurricane of sparks that pressed them back, the hot wind moaning like an organ with its stops open in a long subhuman howl. Into the canyon of their street they pushed on, as fistfuls of flame grasped outwards from red-eyed windows, plucking at chimneys or diving down like animated tongues to lick at ant-like humans struggling between termite mounds of rubble.

Others, their arms attempting to shelter their heads from the twisting tendrils of fire, were fighting their way in the same direction, blinded by the sparks, their clothing erupting in patches of flame, fanned and doused in turn by the buffeting wind. One woman, a demented Medusa with flaming snake-tails of hair, screams unheard, stood as if attached to the ground, rocking to and fro, her mind gone. Mimi felt her friend grab her arm, half, she felt instinctively, to help, but half to make sure that the horrors were shared – too much to bear alone as they plunged on, melting asphalt pulling at the soles of the calf-length boots that had seen her through ice and now fire. She allowed Eva to guide her, trusting to her knowledge of her native city, as they groped instinctively for the open spaces – and the Elbe, the antidote to the flames that towered around them. Through the slit in the soaked woollen scarf that she realised had saved them from the fate of the screaming Medusa, she absorbed a fountain filled with a Bosch-like vision of hell, a twisting heap of bodies desperately searching for the balm and shelter of water. On they pushed, the intensity of the wind threatening to pluck them off their feet, one blast forcing them to their knees to grasp the curb as a child and a bench bowled past them, sucked towards the heart of the fire. But out of their peripheral vision wider spaces, less hemmed in by canyons of heat, became apparent, not dark but less filled with flames. Still the wind intensified, forcing them to their knees to present a smaller profile as they crawled towards the river and salvation; but before long it was all they could do to cower against the curb as lethal debris hurtled past – bicycles, burning branches, even a horse, legs flailing, terror in the whites of its eyes.

Shelter came in the unlikely guise of a *pissoir*, a solid metallic tombstone of a structure rising out of the cobbles, a rock in what now resembled a sea of fire as the melting asphalt took on the reflective qualities of a pitch lake, a lake that rippled in thick oily undulations to the tempest that rampaged over its surface. They scrambled into its lee, shivering despite the heat that was evaporating the water from their clothes so that wisps of steam blinded them as they pressed themselves against their shelter. The hurricane battered on, hurling debris against the *pissoir*, one impact sounding it like a drum, shaking it on its foundations. The heat rose still further as the heart of the fire widened, the second wave of bombs doing its work as intended. The option of cowering on behind their refuge was no longer possible as the temperature inexorably climbed. Signing to her friend to follow, Eva shouldered her way into the tempest again, off the cobbles and into the pitch lake, paddling towards the embankment of the river a few hundred yards away. Immediately the cloying tar gripped their boots, sucking at them, anchoring them to the ground. Each step became a struggle against the down-pull of the bitumen and the tempest that had them in a wind tunnel filled with flying debris that they could not see, let alone dodge. Ahead of them were two women wearing shoes that slipped off at any attempt take a step. One of them, hit by an airborne branch, was spun sideways leaving her shoe behind, her stockinged foot now deep in the black maw of melted tar, as locked in hell as any manacled slave. Step by embogged step, Mimi and Eva leant their way to the river's embankment and the staircase that led to its winter waters.

As they grasped the wall, they looked back at a fire that had now swollen into a monstrous self-feeding fireball that towered so high that they could barely see its crown against a sky that was glowing a pulsating orange as the thin cloud reflected the inferno below. The Baroque towers of the Frauenkirche jutted out of the flames, providing some definition against the flaming caldron in which it was floating. The river, usually black with only the reflection of an occasional moon or pale streetlamp to give it a night-time lustre, now glowed the sheen of reflected fire, a rippling orange blanket mantling its winter flood and spark-laden spray driven across its surface by the fire-feeding tempest. The bridge was so densely packed, the crowd pressing so hard at either end, that specks in ones, twos or family groups dropped into the river to take their chances in the icy waters, the probability of drowning preferred to the certainty of being crushed or burned. Now sheltered by the embankment wall, Mimi and Eva grasped the iron handrail as they followed others down the narrow stairs to the river's edge. On the mud were huddled the scorched and shocked remnants of a city that had travelled from proud history to immolation within two hours. Some were in the water, seeking relief from burns; others pressed themselves against the embankment wall that afforded shelter of sorts from the eruption above them; yet others lay outstretched: asleep or dead, it was hard to tell.

The two women's knees buckled in sudden exhaustion. They lay together on the steaming mud with water flowing over their burned and tar-covered feet, spray spattering their steaming coats and above them a blooming canopy of fire.

Despite the noise, a tenor howl that rose and fell in whistling ululations, they slept.

12

FRANCE

Montreuil. Spring 1941

The lengthening days brought changes with them. The weather improved and the flying increased. Sometimes every night for a week, Adam Kohl would don his padded flying suit and head for England's industrial heartland; occasionally in squadron strength, but often alone, flying along one radio beam to an intersection with another, where he would unload his bombs; on to factories and warehouses in theory, but the accuracy of such bombing methods made it just as likely that his cargo would fall on a residential area. The darkened cities gave nothing away. Only the fires caused by a previous raid gave an illuminated target to bomb – but with that came night fighters, anti-aircraft fire and increased casualties.

When the weather, or duty roster, allowed him a free evening, the light put paid to the domestic routine that he and Marie-Louise had established: drawn curtains would have been cause for comment and a window open to the world was not conducive to the fireside intimacy that they had both come to anticipate with pleasure. Awkwardly – it was not discussed openly between them – they met instead on the stairs. Marie-Louise would sit on the fourth step and the German on a chair facing her at the foot. He would eat his breakfast as they spoke – mostly in French but increasingly in German; hers had been rudimentary but it became a gentle joke between them as she practised. She had a natural faculty for languages and soon their conversation weaved between the two languages without them noticing it. It was the search for the German word for bluebell that prompted him.

'I would like to go walking in the woods to see them; maybe this weekend, as the weather's promising. I have some leave. I . . . I was wondering if you would be able to come with me.'

She looked up at him, startled. He continued hurriedly.

'Not here, of course. It would be impossible and I would never suggest such a thing. I was planning to go to Rouen for two days and if you would consider coming – we would stay in different hotels of course – well, it would give me great pleasure.'

She felt herself reddening and he watched her twisting her wedding ring in her agitation. 'Impossible. You know that. Any Frenchwoman seen with a German would be . . . would be spat at probably . . . worse perhaps. Impossible. Don't suggest it. Please.'

He watched her as the turbulence in her mind reflected itself on her face. He noted with amused affection that she would be physically unable to lie. 'You're right. And I wouldn't suggest it. But what if it was a Frenchman and Frenchwoman? Or a German man and woman? Would that be a problem?'

She looked at him blankly.

'I don't always wear this uniform, you know; and your German's good – good enough for no Frenchman to know the difference anyway. Please. I don't see any harm, I really don't.'

She looked at him, trying to read his mind. She sensed a dangerous double step into new territory, but also a frisson of excitement that was foreign to her, a risk with pleasure at the end of it.

'But what if I were seen?'

'By whom? And if you were, all they would see would be you having a drink with a friend, a cousin perhaps. Yes, that would do nicely: a cousin from Alsace; or a fellow teacher. After all, I'm only proposing the odd walk, a bit of sightseeing and perhaps lunch or dinner if you will join me. I . . . I miss our talks. I won't pretend that I don't. I wasn't expecting a friendship like this in the middle of a war. Is that so bad?'

She smiled at him uncertainly. 'No. Not at all. But I can guarantee that no one else would see it the same way. Would they? Anyone?' She hesitated with two fingers tapping pursed lips, studying the floor. Without looking up, she stroked her skirt-covered legs away from her, massaging out a decision. 'When?'

'My leave is this weekend. And the weather forecast is good.'

'And the bluebells will be at their best?'

'They certainly will.'

'Then I'd like you to show them to me.'

*   *   *

As he had promised, the late April sunshine was warm – but the air was still cool under the morning shade of the west front of Rouen cathedral as she craned her neck towards the rose window, marvelling at its intricate tracery and the glow of the glass. A faint breeze stirred the canvas of a card-seller's cart by the monumental west door. She did not recognise him as he approached, seeing only a man in a suit and felt hat – which he removed with a flourish, kissing her hand in the same bowing movement.

'*Enchanté, mademoiselle.* Have you been to Rouen before?'

His grin was infectious.

'Once. But you would never tire of that, would you?'

She looked up at the Gothic waterfall of stone, haloed by the mid-morning sun. As they stood like pilgrims, awed by man's work to the glory of God and drinking in the nectar of the morning, a skirl of pigeons dipped though the aurora of light to pepper the stonework and bob into the crevices behind the raised arms of saints petrified in the act of benediction.

'Richard the Lionheart is buried here; at least that is what I read in my guidebook. And over there,' he turned and pointed to a spot behind them, 'was where Joan of Arc was burned.'

The familiar shadow darkened her smile. 'What a horrible death.'

He offered her his arm. 'A drink, *mademoiselle*?'

Arm in arm they strolled across the square to a café in its summer colours of jaunty parasols and checked tablecloths. The only hint that this was not a peacetime spring was three soldiers, tourists too, self-consciously ordering smoky Pernod, observed with the traditional disdain of the French waiter. As if relieved from the weight of concealment, both felt an intoxication that had little to do with the champagne they drank. For Marie-Louise this was a new world, the first time that she had shed the leaden blanket of Montreuil and the provincial tyranny under which she had always lived. She had married the boy next door, lived with her father and taught at the school where she had herself spent her childhood;

her life had been observed and judged. Here she was anonymous, wanted for an inner self that was unrelated to the past or her family by a man whose view of the world was through a different prism. As the bubbles released by the opening of the bottle rushed to the surface, so, in the sunlight, her spirits manifested themselves in laughter and a glowing radiance that he observed in stolen glances, imbibing from the same cup. Their conversation lost the gravity of their winter tête-à-têtes and took on the rococo hues of spring, frivolous and teasing.

They wandered through the narrow streets of the old city, dipping into book and antique shops. At his insistence, they spent an hour in a milliner's, she trying on hats and matching scarves and gloves with him in stern-faced judgement. Heavy with a lunch bulked out by a bribe to the chef to surmount the prevailing shortages, they sat opposite each other by the window of a small restaurant and watched the slow afternoon pass outside: couples promenading; Germans in uniform *flâneuring* between shops that were huddled under the eves of old timber houses; children in search of weekend amusement out of school in cheerful squabbling gangs. They enjoyed the seeping languor of the wine that oiled a conversation that needed little prompting, freed from its previous constraints. He asked about her husband, how they had met and what had made her love him.

She told him. She told how he had caught her attention at school by his skill as a cartoonist; how he had read in the corner of the playground, deep in Balzac while his contemporaries bet on games of *pétanque* or fought over football. He had been popular but eccentric, inspiring not a little fear with the sharpness of his tongue when provoked. As a gauche pubescent while he was entertaining adulthood, she had nursed a crush on him that went unnoticed until he returned from his military service. He had found her metamorphosed from a cygnet into a swan, but shy, and an awkward mix of intellectual acuity and clumsy intuitiveness that attracted and rebuffed in equal measure. She had been aware of her father's wealth – though they lived modestly, in bourgeois style, in a house that stood on the street rather than behind gates – and the effect that that had on the boys and men paying court to her. Her mother, a gentle, religious woman with the shrewdness of the Norman *bourgeoise* that she was, had steered her through this minefield, subtly indicating her endorsement or displeasure with respectively vocal diplomacy or a smiling silence that spoke louder than words.

As she talked of her mother, her eyes filled and she had to stop. He reached across the table and put his hand on hers, withdrawing it gently as she dabbed the tears away with her napkin.

Jerome's courtship had none of the clichéd rituals – neither flowers nor elaborate compliments. He had sent her books and magazine articles with notes that contained neither endearments nor flattery but cartoons of their contemporaries or articles that he had written for the newspaper on which he worked. He had treated her as an intellectual equal and friend, as he did Ghislaine, with whom he sparred in verbal dogfights that they both enjoyed. It many times occurred to Marie-Louise that they could have been brother and sister, being so alike in their lithe physiques and in their energy. So comfortable were they with each other that Marie-Louise sometimes felt the worm of jealousy twisting in her gut – an experience that was new to her and had shocked with its power.

He had kissed her for the first time in the garden of the Citadelle on a hot August evening. They had strolled along the walls of the fortified town, looking over the river valley that bled away to the north into the water meadows and marshes between Le Touquet and Étaples. Stands of poplars, normally trembling at the slightest breeze, stood motionless in the humidity of a thunder-charged evening, flicked by bats and the dipping and twisting of swifts. He had held her hand as they picked their way past huddles of youths escaping the heat, with feet hanging over the wall and cigarettes glowing. As they walked, she was certain that he must have been able to hear the sound of her heart, since it boomed so in her own ears. At the highest point of the walls, looking back over the château from which Field Marshal Haig had directed the slaughter on the sanguineous plain of Picardy, he had put his hand in her hair and gently pulled her towards him till she could feel his contours through her light dress and his lips pressing gently against hers. Not knowing whether to open her mouth to his kiss, she froze, feeling his tongue running along her lips. He pulled back slightly so that she could see the shadowed silhouette of his head but only the hint of features so close was he. He had stroked her cheeks with his fingers and to the fore came the memories of girlish discussions of kissing techniques and the erotic gradations that were allowed. He felt her relax in his arms, and at the second attempt, she softened herself, marvelling through the pounding of her heart at the sensuality of the experience. The sliding of a cat against her leg broke the spell and wordlessly they had strolled on into the gloaming, drops of warm rain heightening the night scent of summer.

They had married that autumn in the Abbatiale St Saulve. She had persuaded him to take the sacrament at the nuptial mass; his earlier refusal had nearly caused a withdrawal of reluctant parental consent to the marriage. Her father had no time for intellectuals and little for a journalist whose father was only a clerk to the town *notaire*: an atheist was a bridge too far. Jerome had bowed to her logic that if the bread and wine were only that – then what did it matter? It was hardly a human sacrifice after all. They had spent their honeymoon in Le Touquet; a long walk along the bleak post-season beach had been the prelude to their wedding night in a hotel that was modelled on a *stube* in the Black Forest. She had sensed that his nervousness matched her own and both had been preoccupied as they retired to bed after dinner. He had lit a candle in the bedroom and they undressed each other with a fumbling unfamiliarity with each other's clothes and embarrassment at every revelation. As he stroked her, she knew she should relax, but a trembling took hold of her, her legs shivering to such an extent that she had to lie on the bed, her back towards him. He had lain beside her and enveloped her in his arms, a hand on each breast and his hardness pressed against her buttocks. He had caressed her neck, until her trembling subsided and a soporific languor overcame her – the symptoms almost of shock. He turned her to face him and she could feel him kissing her lips, her breasts, her stomach – and his fingers between her legs – but almost as a disembodied experience. The pain of him entering her elicited a sharp cry of pain that froze them both. They had looked at each other in bewilderment, both unsure what should happen next, knowing the theory but nonplussed by the actuality. He moved – but again a sharp outcry. She had felt hot tears running on to the pillow, half of pain, half of humiliation. She felt him withdraw and they lay beside each other with only their fingers interlocked.

They tried twice more that night – with similar results. They finally slept but each woke intermittently to turbulent thoughts of disappointment and failure. Neither spoke about it the next day as they walked along the beach at low tide; the sand and shallow foreshore melded into the sea mist that formed the conjunction between sea and sky. They held hands but she could sense a concern that had not been there the day before. Filled with dread, they went to bed again in the failing autumn light. She was touched by his gentleness as he caressed her everywhere and she began to relax into him, feeling for the first time the stirring of stimulation as his tongue flicked between her legs. With the help of some oil he penetrated her, this time with no pain, and they held each other in gratefulness as she felt him move inside her with growing intensity, his orgasm releasing the tensions of the previous day.

All these memories rose out of her subconscious as she told the German about her husband. She smiled and frowned as each vivid recollection occurred to her, often dissociated from the vignette that she was describing to him. As she spoke, she was aware of the paradox of the attraction she felt for the man she was with when she realised she missed her husband so intensely. She surprised herself with her acceptance of both – and the comfort with which she described one to the other. She asked him more about his family and allowed him to talk without interruption, with her chin resting on her hand, enjoying the chance to look at him without fear of misinterpretation. He told her about his eccentric Italian grandmother, from whom his dark looks had clearly come. She could see that he would always struggle to hold his weight in check, judging by a fleshiness that rounded his face and doubled his chin as he looked down. There was a femininity about him that was not effeminate. He spoke to her with no trace of the masculine condescension that she had learnt to treat as normal from men.

They rented bicycles and rode them out of town in the fullness of a spring afternoon to the edge of a wood where the still skeletal trees threw shadows of indigo over the bluebell carpet that he had promised. They walked along a stream and sat against a fallen tree to doze in the late-afternoon sun until driven home by the early chill as the sun lost its battle with the deepening shade. Dinner was followed by a chaste kiss of her hand.

Their rendezvous the next day was at the café in the square. As he approached, she felt a wave of pleasure that startled her. He felt to her like a comfortable coat, soft and loose-fitting with no constriction. Soft. That was it. Jerome was sharp: interesting, edged and unpredictable. This man enveloped her and unscrambled the muddled thoughts that milled inside. With Jerome she was stimulated; with him she was safe.

He leant back in his chair smoking and sipping coffee, smiling at her. 'What a lovely weekend. One of the nicest I've ever had. Thank you.'

She chewed the inside of her cheek and looked at the remains of their breakfast rather than at him. 'I should be thanking you.'

'Let's just be thankful that we've been able to do this during a war when by rights we should be trying to kill each other. How could such a thing happen? Madness.' He looked up from under the brim of his hat at the sun-drenched side of the cathedral. 'Almost every night, I take off in my aeroplane to destroy something as beautiful as that – not to mention kill and maim human beings. Of course, I'm trying to bomb a factory or a ship – but I'm smashing up centuries of civilisation when I miss – which happens all the time. And yet we're sitting here as if that's not going on, as if we don't have to go back to the craziness of me being *un sale boche* and you treating me like an unwelcome stranger.'

She blinked in surprise as she had quite forgotten he was a German: she now saw only the man. With a sense of dread she recalled the reality, the future prospect of incidental conversation on the stairs and snatched moments in the kitchen; also the danger that he lived under and fragility of their existence. She found she could not look at him or speak. She felt his hand on hers and made no move to withdraw it.

'May we do this again?' she heard him say. 'Please.'

She nodded – and knew that she had crossed her Rubicon.

*   *   *

A note was waiting for her on her return. She recognised Ghislaine's handwriting, but instead of the usual pleasure that it elicited, she felt an up-welling of trepidation. The message was short: an invitation to meet with some friends at her flat on Thursday evening; a joke about the food that she could expect and an exhortation to bring some of her father's wine; an unexceptional letter between friends. But she had never had a note like it before.

It festered in her handbag during the week, its curled edges a chiding reminder a dozen times a day. What did they want her to do? Would she be able to do it? She found herself unable to concentrate on her teaching – looking at upheld hands, but forgetting the question that she had asked and apologising to puzzled children.

Ghislaine's flat was tidier than she remembered, but only superficially so, with piles of paper and books on the floor rather than in their customary place on every raised horizontal surface. The dining-room table, normally an office of sorts, was laid for six she noticed, as she left her rain-soaked coat on the stand and made her way towards the warmth and light of the sitting room from where the sound of voices reached her. She smoothed back her hair and composed her features in anticipation. As she stood at the door the conversation petered out and Ghislaine turned round with a smile of welcome.

'*Bonsoir, chérie.*' She touched her ear affectionately after kissing her on both cheeks. 'I need to introduce you – Stephan and Jacques you know, of course. Victor and Janette are from Calais: friends who are staying for a few days. Wine?'

Janette nodded a cool greeting; Victor advanced two steps towards her, took her hand and kissed it formally. She sensed an energy in the man as the stubble of a burgeoning beard brushed the top of her hand. The greeting felt out of place in the company and she found herself rubbing the back of her hand as if to scrub away the imprint of his lips.

'Ghislaine has told us a lot about you. You're very old friends, no?'

'As long as I can remember. And you? How long have you known Ghislaine?'

'A short time. But sweet; she's very *sympathique*.'

She could not think of a reply and was glad when Ghislaine arrived with a glass, allowing her to talk about the wine and anticipate the food.

Victor stood his ground and, as soon as Ghislaine's back was turned, he resumed. 'You're a teacher, I understand. And Ghislaine tells me that your father's the mayor here. Difficult in wartime, I'd guess?'

'Ghislaine's probably also told you that he's a collaborator. She and he have never seen eye to eye, so I'd take what she says with a pinch of salt.'

He nodded. 'So what would you call him?'

She felt anger rising. 'A patriot. A patriot who's doing a job he'd rather not do because he thinks that it's his duty. Is that good enough for you?'

Victor looked at her with interest and raised his hands in mock surrender. 'I'm sorry. That was rude. But I admire your filial piety.'

'It's not filial piety! It's what I think; what I genuinely think. He's a good man but not an easy man; someone who's proved himself a patriot by risking his life for France – unlike some people.'

She was aware that her voice was above its normal pitch and that the conversation around her was petering out. She stopped, confused and angry: angry at the implied insult to her father; at having to defend him; at their condescension and at herself for rising to the bait. She felt a hand on her arm. It was Janette.

'I apologise, Marie-Louise – for Victor's rudeness. He likes to challenge people and he rates them by how well they stand up to him. I think he'll hold you high on that score, is that not right, Victor?'

There was a brittle silence.

'Yes. Indeed. And your riposte was well aimed. I apologise. Please. Can we now be friends? Perhaps some wine and dinner will help the healing process.'

Marie-Louise nodded and gulped some wine. 'I think I'll go and help Ghislaine in the kitchen.'

As she walked down the passage, with Ghislaine behind her, she could hear the resumption of some whispered conversation – an indistinct angry hiss from Janette. The two women faced each other in the kitchen.

'*Chérie* . . . '

'Don't *chérie* me, Ghislaine. Don't. Not if you're going to treat me like this. Why? Why have you asked me here? To insult my father? Again. Why?'

'Because Victor and Janette wanted to meet you. That's why.'

'Well, I don't like your new friends.'

They looked at each other.

'They aren't my friends. And Victor and Janette aren't their real names. And they don't come from Calais; at least I assume they don't. I've no idea where they live.'

Marie-Louise blinked. 'You've never met them before?'

'No.'

Ghislaine offered her a cigarette, which she took. Her hand was shaking as she leant over to accept a light.

'So . . . who are they?'

'Organisers. The people who'll be our link to de Gaulle in London. I presume they're local. Difficult to tell. I get the feeling they're in charge – but that's a guess too. I had half an hour with them before you came. He's worried about you; but he's more worried about the Communists.'

'Why?'

'They have their own agenda. Officially Moscow is friends with Berlin – at least according to Molotov and Ribbentrop – though the whole world knows that they hate each other's guts. He says he'd rather have to deal with a collaborator's daughter than a Communist.'

'Thanks.'

There was bitter irony in her voice but no apology from Ghislaine whose own words were harder.

'Look, *chérie*, it's not just me. Believe me. It's how most people see him. It's not personal. Really. Now will you help me get some food on the table so that we can eat? Maybe we'll all be more civilised with something inside us.'

Nothing more was said between them as they cut bread and poured soup into bowls.

The conversation was about the war, the German invasion of Yugoslavia and Greece and the battles in North Africa between the Italians and the British. It was difficult to be optimistic in the circumstances, as every little ray of sunshine began to seem smothered by black clouds. At one point their talk was drowned by the rumbling roar of aircraft: bombers gathering in formation overhead for a sortie over the Channel to the north. In the lull in the conversation, while the glasses and cutlery vibrated and the mechanism of the wall-clock rattled in discord, Marie-Louise thought of Adam, almost certainly above them, focused on the glowing dials of his instruments and avoiding collisions with the aircraft around him. The ambivalence of the circumstances made her almost dizzy and she forced herself to look at the others around her. She focused on Victor who was opposite, smoking and blowing rings towards the central light, rings that stalled, hung and dissolved as they sank back towards the table. He was dark, made darker by the three-day stubble that was the same length and consistency as the cropped hair on his head. He wore a suit and waistcoat that were well tailored and a stiff collar and tie, in contrast to the collarless shirts and rolled-up sleeves of the other men. Professional, she thought: a *notaire* perhaps, or an engineer. His contributions to the conversation were sharp, realistic and astute. He observed, and spoke little, but all the time his eyes flicked around the table. A cold man, she suspected, but capable and competent. The thunder of the bombers abated and the crockery stilled itself.

He cleared his throat. 'Ghislaine, would you mind seeing that the windows are fully shut and check the street outside. A bit of paranoia is a good thing – no – essential. Some cognac?'

They smoked silently until she returned and the cognac splashed into beakers. He looked slowly round the table before resuming.

'You four know each other – obviously. But you will only be able to contact anyone else in the organisation through me, or Janette.

I'm sure I don't have to spell out why. We'll operate a method of drops to communicate. We'll have an agreed spot, moved regularly, where you can leave messages. It works. Never, never use the telephone or the post. Let me tell you something. It's not the Boche you have to fear. It's each other: someone doing something stupid and putting all the rest of us in danger. And traitors. They come in all shapes: venal, stupid, black marketeers and fascists. Look out for them everywhere: in each other – in fact, that's where they always are, by definition. War and shortages don't bring out the best in people, I'm afraid. You all know how few of us there are. You won't find many friends outside these four walls. Most are hostile to what we're trying to do: they don't see the point and think any killing of the Boche will only bring down reprisals on their heads. Many remember what the Boche did in occupied France in the last war and know what they are capable of. So don't expect support or sympathy. Any questions so far?'

Around the table, eyes were downcast, discomfort in the air. Marie-Louise raised her hand. 'What . . . what do you want us to do?'

Victor considered for a moment. 'Information at the moment. About the Boche. You have one in your house. What time does he leave the house? Where does he go? Stuff that your father might talk about that the Boche have told him – like units being moved. Billets. Counting bombers out and back so that we have some idea about the losses they're suffering. Visiting bigwigs. Who are they? Are they vulnerable?'

'Vulnerable to what?'

He looked at Marie-Louise in surprise. 'Assassination, of course. The aim is to kill Germans. It's only if we can kill more of them than they can kill of us that we are going to win the war. It's just a question of when we start. I can't say when – as I don't know. I'm awaiting instructions. And until I get those instructions, no one is to do anything. Understood?'

Ghislaine spoke. 'What about training? And supplies of weapons?'

'It's happening. Soon. Within the next month we should be able to start – with the objective of commencing the first operations in late summer. Probably bomb attacks.'

'What about reprisals?'

'Inevitable.'

There was silence

'And that doesn't bother you?'

Eyes turned to Marie-Louise. Victor looked at her and drew on his cigarette before replying.

'This town was Field Marshal Haig's headquarters in the Great War, wasn't it?'

She nodded.

'Do you think that, every day, Haig got up and said, "Today, I'm going to kill or maim thousands of young men and the same number of civilians"? No. I don't think he did. When he said his prayers – and he was a religious man, by all accounts – I suspect he said to his God, "Please help me to win this war so that we can get this aggressive country back within its borders, in order that millions of peaceful people can get on with their normal lives – and forgive me the terrible cost of undertaking this task." Does it bother me that innocent people get killed in wars? Of course. I'm not Hitler. It's the cost, the inevitable cost, of using force. Unfortunately we aren't going to get rid of the Boche by negotiation. Pétain thinks he can – but where's that got him? He's had a year and what has he achieved? The Boche only understand force. Nothing else is going to move them; which is why we're here now. So to answer your question: yes, it does bother me. But I'm quite clear about cause and effect. The Boche started this war and they'll be the ones killing innocents – not me, nor you, nor the Tommy bomber pilot who drops his bombs on a school rather than a gun emplacement.' He stubbed out his cigarette slowly and contemplated the cognac. 'Am I prepared to be ruthless? Yes. I am. Because once we're in this thing – and we are in it whether we like it or not – then the quickest way to end it is to do what has to be done as hard and efficiently as possible. What did someone, Clauswitz I think, say? "Moderation in war is imbecility." I agree with him. Wringing my hands isn't going to finish it; strangling a Boche might.'

There was something shockingly brutal about the final phrase. A bomb or bullet had a sense of proxy about it. The tactility of strangling, the visualisation of choking, the pressure needed to throttle, brought the inhumanity of what was being proposed into glaring relief. Marie-Louise could not stop herself imagining the gurgling death rattle of Adam under her hands, his face purple and his spit spattering her own. She put out a hand to steady herself, her knuckles whitening as she grasped the table's edge.

She felt Ghislaine's hand holding her arm.

'Are you all right, *chérie*?'

She nodded and forced herself to breathe deeply, feeling the hazing of her vision hardening into focus again. 'Fine. Thank you. Stuffy in here. I'm sorry.' She shook her head to clear it and smiled unconvincingly. 'Sorry.'

'There's nothing to be sorry about.' Victor's voice was concerned. 'Here. Have some water.'

She drank gratefully and accepted a cigarette, the nicotine's calming effects seeping through her.

'OK?'

She nodded at him. He sat back and considered her. 'I think we might leave guns and bombs to others, don't you?' He was smiling. 'There'll be plenty of ways in which you can help without having to kill anyone. Really. Does that make you feel better?'

She nodded and swallowed hard.

'Good. Let's start then.'

13

The cold spring rain that fell in late April faded with the daffodils and, with the advent of May, a premature summer yielded the first crop of hay that shimmered through drifts of pollen. Shutters were thrown open and rooms that had been damp with mildew were drenched in sunshine. The town turned itself inside out, moving on to the street, the better to suck in the sunshine after the long dearth of light. Old women sat on chairs at diagonals to the street, toothlessly gossiping as they observed the business of youth passing by. Neighbours, usually on nodding terms only, leant on door-frames and exchanged stories, enjoying the sun on shoulders that had only weeks before been hunched against the biting winds of winter.

In the secrecy of the hall and staircase, a visit to Paris was plotted. Twice they had heard the approach of Michel Annecy in the coaching entrance beside the house and without a word they had turned and gone in their different directions: to a bedroom for the one on the stairs, or the parlour for the one seated on the chair at the foot. There was something childish about it that had them giggling afterwards, seeing themselves as naughty children scampering away from trouble.

Paris had been a childhood dream for Marie-Louise, enticing but also frightening. One side of her longed to be rid of the provincialism of her upbringing but her innate timidity held her back from grasping the alternative. This visit presented a similar dichotomy. She wanted to explore the Paris of her imagination with this man but knew that there might – would – be other things that she desired but dreaded in the same thought. She had always imagined that such musings were for the unhappily married, that sadness and lack of fulfilment were the route to adultery. She was sure that she was happy – certain. Jerome was intriguing and had loved her from timid virginity to mutual satisfaction. He could be moody and angry but that was no punishable offence in the balance sheet that she tried to construct in her mind. So why was she here, looking at another man in this way? She had to conclude that there was no reason other than the man himself. In a very different way he intrigued her too, valued her and coaxed out the best in her femininity. Unlike Jerome, he had an ease about him that relaxed her, allowing a respite from the complex thought processes that so often exhausted her. He was less competitive than her husband – neither worse nor better – but different. It was this failure to establish a qualitative gap between them that so disturbed her: such a gap could have justified her musings and fantasies. She was forced to the conclusion that she loved both men for their own merits, a deduction that did little to assuage the guilt that swept over her as she tossed and turned in the small hours of the night.

Despite this conflict, she found herself on a train heading south to Paris with flecks of ash and the smell of steaming coal blowing though a window that was wide open to combat the unseasonable heat. The door into the corridor was ajar, creating a through draft. Two German soldiers stood outside smoking and glancing surreptitiously at her. A mother and child sat opposite, story exhausted, looking out of the window as the downland of northern France rolled by, obscured by the occasional spiral of smoke from the labouring locomotive. There was a mustiness about the ancient turn-of-the-century carriage that was enervating, but also evocative of childhood journeys to visit her grandmother in Honfleur, whose house, with its tightly sealed windows, smelt of leather and old age. She allowed herself to daydream. She imagined a café in Montmartre, with views across mansard roofs forested with chimney pots to a distant Eiffel Tower. She dreamed in the black and white of contemporary film with the backlighting of a studio-set in all its oily texture that had formed her picture of a Paris so often idealised but never visited. She imagined a hotel of elegant sophistication. He was there, gently touching her face, kissing her. She imagined his smell, masculine, the feel of the roughness of his cheek against hers and the pressure of his body. The surge of desire jolted her back to the present and she looked guiltily across the carriage, certain that her arousal must have drawn all eyes to her. The child was still asleep and the woman almost, her eyelids heavy as she nodded to the rhythm of the rails. The Germans were engaged in a guessing game with playing cards. She sank back into the realm of the imagination, admitting to herself that she wanted him and that she would not only accept an advance from him but desired it with an urgency that had her shaking her head in disbelief. She allowed herself to drift again, playing with erotic threads that formed and dissolved as her conscious and unconscious sparred with each other, conjuring images that had her breathing heavily and her heart beating wildly with desire, while intermittently she scanned the carriage in guilt and fear of discovery. The woman's head remained lolled forward in the limbo between sleep and wakefulness and the soldiers carried on smoking with the inherent boredom of their profession.

There must have been an afterglow to her musings, as Adam was conscious of something different about her when he met her by the barrier at the Gare du Nord. As he kissed her on both cheeks, his smell and texture were as she had fantasised, carrying with them the shreds of her daydreams and their disturbing sensuality. He took her suitcase and she his arm and she leant against him as they walked across the concourse with the shape of her breast discernable against his biceps. Neither said anything but both knew that there was a charge to this assignation that had not been there in Rouen.

They walked into the street and Paris absorbed them. As with the German uniforms when she had first seen them, the colours startled her in their greens and browns after the monochrome of her imagination. And the smell. Wartime shortages of fuel had brought horses once again on to the streets along with the odour of their sweat and dung. The *pissoirs*, with their ornate ironwork, reeked of stale urine and the drains of worse. The familiar fragrance of tobacco smoke mixed with perfume of a headier kind that trailed elegant women whose dogs added to the olfactory cocktail.

They paused for a while at a crowded café that had spread itself over the pavement flanking a boulevard and watched the metropolitan world pass them by. German uniforms were out in force, some officers with proud wives, but most in groups of two or three, relaxing in the arrogance of victory. The natives ignored them, one woman walking past a bowing officer, who was attempting gallantry, as if he didn't exist. Adam, a seeming Frenchman now, did the same but almost gave himself away before checking himself as he was rising to his feet to salute a senior officer.

A bicycle taxi delivered them to the Tuilleries gardens and they strolled, arm in arm, as had innumerable tourists before them, along the banks of the Seine, to the Île-de-la-Cité. The open boulevards gave way to medieval Paris, the ancient crooked streets cooler in the evening shade and comparatively deserted. The hotel was tall and narrow, more a rickety tenement than the *fin-de-siècle* elegance that she had spun in her imagination, with two rooms on each floor threaded together by winding stairs; her room was on the first floor, his in the attic. They registered separately, treating each other as strangers as they passed on the stairs.

Their twilight rendezvous was in front of Notre Dame, its stone figures – saints, gargoyles and devils – merged into a rough-textured, smoke-blackened crag. The sun was below the horizon but a last shaft of orange light caught the pinnacles of the spires causing them to glow against the darkness below. Bats jigged against the cobalt sky as the damp chill of the night settled upon the river. They strolled around the cathedral, glad of their coats as they leant over the parapet of the embankment wall and looked up the Seine to where the iconic tower was silhouetted against the gloaming. Urchins were playing on the mud below, skipping stones into the darkness where the splashes flashed white in tightening steps to shouts of competitive excitement. She felt his hand around hers, warm against the chilled air around. He raised it reverentially and kissed it, holding it for a brief moment against his cheek before taking it to his chest, the movement bringing her to face him. They stood there, so close that she could feel his breath on her forehead for what seemed like minutes, their radiated heat warming the air between them. His hand disengaged from hers and she felt its touch against her cheek, her nerve endings so sensitive that she could discern each hair on the soft backs of his fingers as he drew a delicate circular pattern along her jaw line. Gently he pulled her face towards him and his lips brushed hers before lingering softly with the feathers of their breath inter-mingling. She reached up and put her hand behind his head, her fingers raking his hair and tracing their own patterns on his scalp. She drew him towards her, pulling his lips on to hers, nuzzling into their softness and letting her tongue trickle along their profile. She laid her head against his chest, feeling the soft beat of his heart; her own heartbeat was steady in synchrony, with none of the pounding of the past, calmed and steadied by the bear-hug enveloping her. They remained like this for some time before they silently unwound and, leaning against each other, strolled along the embankment, matching step for step, both keenly aware of the rhythm as they traced their path back into the narrow chasms of the old city with the etoilated sky a shimmering roof to the darkened streets below.

Still without words they entered a restaurant – a shock of light and a blanket of merged conversation, tinkling with glass and cutlery and rushed with waiters. Settled at their table, they ordered aperitifs and took in the scene, not looking at each other but each content in the other's company – to the extent that a stranger observing them might have guessed the indifference of a burned-out marriage. He held his glass to her and she reciprocated, looking him in the eye as they drank. His hand reached across and covered the back of hers.

'How did this thing happen?'

She gazed across the room as she considered his question. 'I don't know. And I don't really know what "it" is. Do you?'

'I can guess. But I don't have much experience of it. Not like this anyway.'

She smiled and shook her head. 'Nor me. But it's wrong isn't it? Surely? It just doesn't feel it. That's what I find confusing.'

She swirled the liquid round her glass and studied it intently, as if for the runes it might contain.

'It's the war,' he replied. 'I know I don't believe in that as a justification, but it's all right as an explanation. There's no other reason for us being here, so maybe there is some good in it after all.'

'It's different for you.'

'Yes. It is.' He nodded slowly. 'I'm sorry.'

She looked back at him with great tenderness. 'No. Not sorry. Please don't say that. This isn't some seduction. I know. I'm just having to readjust my compass – if that makes any sense. I always imagined that such a thing would be an "or"; that if you felt like this for someone else you would have to have stopped loving the other. That's what I'm trying to get used to. It doesn't appear to be like that. So I feel a bit confused. Guilty. But happy too. Really. Can you understand that?'

He didn't answer immediately, but reached out and with the back of his middle finger traced a serpentine pattern along the back of her hand while his eyes savoured her, halting momentarily on each feature before holding the grey-blue of her eyes with his own.

'Yes. Of course I can. If you didn't feel like that, you wouldn't be you. It's what I love about you: all that confusion, all that doubt, all that worrying. I've watched it all winter; treasured it. Each evening, when I climbed into my car to go to the airfield, I used to laugh to myself as I replayed our time together, turning over the snippets of conversation, enjoying over again the thought of you worrying, working things to and fro in your mind. You probably aren't aware of how you spin things to yourself – what comes out verbally is just the end of the thought trail. My favourite game was to try and pick up the thread before you said anything. I've got quite good at it. Not perfect yet. But practice does perfection make, they say. But then I love the surprises. I haven't had a bad one yet.'

'Neither have I.' She looked back at her glass, slowly chewing her bottom lip. 'But I don't think I'm ever going to be able to settle it. It's too difficult. Is that hurtful for you?'

'Remember what I said to you about possession? I don't want to possess you. I can't. I just want to share a bit of you. Is that so bad?'

'No. Put like that, no. But I can't make it that simple. I try, but it just gets complicated and I don't think I'll ever be able to compartmentalise in the way that you can.'

'Compartmentalise? Maybe. Yes. I suppose that's as good a way of describing it as any. I was trying to work out how I feel about Alix, my fiancé – my ex-fiancée. I still love her. Of course I do. It isn't something I can switch off just because I decided not to marry her. It just seems to me that that was then – and this is now. They're separate experiences. They build up into the big experience that makes me, me. Perhaps it's one of those strange paradoxes: you don't have a defined amount of love that's used up bit by bit, leaving the metaphorical box a little emptier each time. Perhaps whenever you use it, with lovers, children, friends, it actually gets fuller. Maybe that's why this is making me happy; very happy; and you perhaps a little sad.'

'No. No, not sad. Not sad at all, I promise. But maybe a bit unhappy. Now that's a paradox, isn't it?'

'No better or worse than mine.'

He held her eye, his glass towards her. 'To paradoxes. And all who sail in them.'

They were still smiling as the waiter appeared with the limited wartime menu. They ate and drank with the tyranny of the curfew hanging over them, the restaurant emptying as the ordained hour approached. When the *patron* bolted the door behind them, the streets were deserted apart from a solitary gendarme, and the only sound, other than the strike of their shoes on the ancient cobbles, was that of domestic strife emanating from an opened upper window. The concierge handed them their keys without a glance and they made their way up the stairs. She opened the door of her room and turned to face him.

They looked at each other without speaking. She turned and went into the room and he followed, quietly closing the door behind him. Milky shafts of moonlight through the half-closed slatted shutters illuminated the bed in a chequered chiaroscuro leached of colour. He led her out of the shadow and into the moon-shafts. In their striped light they kissed with a new intensity. They undressed slowly and faced each other again. She was struck by the contrast between her lover and her husband. Where her husband was lean, all sharp angles, with almost no body hair, taut and spare, her lover was softly hirsute, not fat but rounded, the dark hair on his chest extending down across his stomach. As he kissed her again, the bulk of his arousal pressed against her, erect, but again with a softness that contrasted with the insistent hardness of her previous experience.

Under the slatted moonlight they made comfortable love, lingering with an unlearned intimacy that held no surprises or embarrassments. His body held for her a sensuality into which she wanted to nestle and bury herself. She had a sensation of absorbing him into her rather than being penetrated as they worked themselves to a comfortable completion rather than an abandoned climax. Afterwards she lay against him, running her fingers through the luxuriance of his chest hair, burying her nose in its novel scent. And so it went on through the night – a tranquil succession of sleep, lovemaking and gentle talk flavoured by cigarettes – until the morning sun threw its own strips of light where the moon's had been, dazzling them into heavy-eyed wakefulness.

Still groggy with sleep, they dressed and left the hotel in search of breakfast. Still on the Île-de-la-Cité, they found a café and ordered brioche and the *ersatz* coffee that was now so familiar that it was hard to remember the taste of the real thing. They sat outside, as they had in Rouen, but under a parasol as the direct sun was too intense for comfort at this late hour. Neither said anything but occasionally they would shift their gaze from the world passing by to each other and smile conspiratorially and reach out and touch each other's hands, wrapped in the cotton wool of contentment. Suddenly, there was a soft slap on the ground next to them. They both turned to see a pigeon squab, nascent feathers sprouting from ugly pink skin, struggling to raise its head and move its unformed wings, its legs jerking in piteous spasms. Its parent, flapping and cooing over the umbrellas in hovering panic, got so close that they could feel the stirring of the air caused by its beating wings. Above them, on a balcony's edge, the nest trembled with the movement of hungry siblings. A man at the next table put down his newspaper, stood up and ground his heel on the struggling chick, its legs stretching as its spine was crushed, blood squirting either side of the shoe. As he sat down again, the remains twitched and settled to become just one more scrap of detritus on a Parisian pavement.

Marie-Louise found that her face was wet with tears. Adam shifted his chair round so that he was facing her with his legs overlapping hers. He took her face in his hand and kissed her forehead in an attempt to comfort her. She took his proffered handkerchief, but still the tears ran down her face. He whispered consoling words until, eyes red and mouth twisted in the attempt to control herself, she sat back and looked at him. Her words, when they came, were full of anguish.

'You're going to be killed, aren't you?'

He looked away from her, down the street that was vital with the lifeblood of Paris, dogs, street vendors and the swoop of waiters.

'Yes. I think so.'

14

The summer held no joy for her. Each evening they would meet on the stairs as before – but now he would hold her briefly in his arms and they would rock against each other. He still had his breakfast tray balanced on his knee at the bottom of the stairs and she still sat on the fourth step with her chin in her hands and her eyes meandering over him – now desperate to fix each detail in her memory. Until Paris she had seen him as the man at the foot of the stairs or laughing in front of the fire in the parlour. Now she visualised him trapped in a burning aeroplane; or as a charred skeleton such as had sat in the pilot's seat of the Heinkel that had crashed below the town's walls until the fuselage had cooled sufficiently for the remains to be carted away; or floating lifeless in the cold waters of the English Channel. He tried to coax her out of this morbidity, made light of the dangers, lied that he was on training missions. She pretended to be persuaded, but her inability to dissimulate gave her away when he caught her glancing at him with premature grief etched on her face. The instantly recognisable note of the German aero-engines, with their unmatched timing that set up an undulating harmonic, became a funeral fugue in her imagination. As June wore on, and the nights shortened to only six hours, she encountered him in the early hours on the landing outside his room with the marks of his flying goggles still framing his dark ringed eyes. At these times there was a distance between them, as if he was still inhabiting a foreign world. They would nod to each other before he disappeared into his room; no endearments, just exhaustion.

However, as it does for grief itself, time weaved its healing magic and brought him back into the realms of the vital rather than the dead, so that when she thought of him she could imagine the hotel room in Paris rather than the wastes of the Channel or the flame-shrouded plunge of a stricken bomber.

One day, it was 22 June, under the pleasant sun of an afternoon of cumulus clouds and strong breezes, she cycled round the corner into the Place Vert, the small square in front of their house, to see him pacing up and down the lines of trees with his tunic undone and smoking with a distracted intensity. There was no one else in sight but she could feel eyes on her from the surrounding windows. He saw her coming towards him as he turned at the far end of his line of march. She dismounted as he strode towards her, not knowing what to do. He stopped a yard from her, threw the cigarette away and gave a half-bow. He was unshaven and unsteady. She realised, as he straightened, that he was drunk. She glanced either side of him, looking for an escape route.

'Good-afternoon, *madame*. A good day I hope?'

He bowed again. She nodded back and made a line for the gate into the coach entrance next to her house. He put out a hand to stop her bicycle. While this irritated her, she was aware that, for watching eyes, this was a bullying Boche accosting an unwilling Frenchwoman.

'Have you heard the news?'

'No. What news?' Her heartbeat increased. What was it? Were the prisoners being released?

'We've invaded Russia. I heard the Führer's speech. A war of annihilation. No room on this earth for both Slavs and Germans, apparently.' His voice was slightly slurred and louder than usual. He was running his fingers through his hair distractedly. 'It's madness. Complete fucking madness.' She had never heard him swear before, nor seen him drunk – beyond the smiling intoxication of a shared bottle of wine. 'Do you understand what this means? Do you?'

She had avoided eye contact until now, antennae quivering in the knowledge of the eyes and ears around her. She reached out and took his wrist, firmly pushing his hand away from the handlebars of her bicycle while looking him in the eye.

'Leutnant, please let me go into my house. I understand your . . . unhappiness. If you like, I will ask Bernadette to prepare some coffee and food for you.' She could see her alarm registering with him.

He blinked and let go, pulling himself together, becoming a Luftwaffe officer once again. He clicked his heals. 'Apologies, *madame*. I am sorry. Truly sorry. Coffee would be most welcome. A necessity. Thank you. May I take your bicycle for you?'

'No. No thank you, Leutnant. I will manage myself. Good-evening.'

Despite his intoxication, he caught the glance of concern that she gave him as she left him standing under the trees and made her way through the side door to the house. As on the first day that the Germans had arrived, she closed the door behind her and ran to the top of the stairs to look down on to the small square where she could see him pacing and smoking once again.

'What's happening?'

She spun round in alarm. Her father was standing outside his room. She looked at him in shock with her hand over her mouth. 'Papa! You surprised me.'

He said nothing but raised an eyebrow and nodded towards the window. They both looked out and watched the German.

'Well?'

'He's drunk.'

He watched for a few more seconds.

'Unusual.'

'He's very upset. Apparently the Boche have invaded Russia.'

'I just heard myself. But why's he drunk? You'd think he'd be delighted to be dealing finally with the Bolsheviks. How do you know this, anyway?'

'He stopped me in the street, on my way back from school. He was pacing up and down, like he is now, when I got back.'

'Was he making a nuisance of himself?'

She sensed the danger in the question. 'No. No . . . he just wanted to tell someone. Share it, I suppose. And I was the first person he recognised.' She shrugged.

'Not improper, I hope?'

'No.' She looked out of the window again to avoid eye contact. 'Just upset. I can see why.'

'I don't see why.'

There was a bellicosity in his tone that she recognised of old and the smell of brandy on his breath. That was why he was home early.

'It's the first decent thing the Boche have done in years. Thank God someone's doing it – dealing with the Reds once and for all. Now, perhaps, the Maréchal can sign a peace treaty and we can join them in dealing with Moscow.'

She knew the futility of such a debate and turned back to the stairs. 'Papa, I'm going to ask Bernadette to make some coffee for the leutnant. Would you like some?'

'Why?'

'Because he's drunk.'

'Are you suggesting I am?'

'No, papa. Of course not. If you want some coffee, then there'll be some downstairs when you're ready.'

He hesitated, balancing.

'I'll come down when I've changed.'

She heard him go back into his room as she reached the bottom of the stairs. She could hear Bernadette bustling in the kitchen and could imagine Adam still pacing outside. She sat on the chair at the stair's foot and tried to compose herself. She rubbed her face and breathed deeply before she made her way to the kitchen to give Bernadette her instructions.

She was sitting on the edge of a stool in the parlour, strategically placed between the two chairs, when she heard Adam come into the hall. There was a short hiatus when she could visualise him buttoning his tunic and smoothing back his hair in front of the looking-glass opposite the door. When he entered he looked passable – though the dark shadow of his unshaven beard gave the game away.

He nodded to her. 'I'm sorry.'

She looked at him with an expression that had nothing to do with the form of her words.

'Your apology is accepted, leutnant. Please sit down. Bernadette is making you some coffee and my father is joining us in a few minutes.'

He sat on the chair opposite her. Their eyes met and they reached across and silently squeezed each other's hands. When Michel

Annecy entered the room, Adam stood formally and bowed. There was a sardonic twist in the older man's lip. The younger spoke first.

'*Monsieur*, I owe you and your daughter an apology. It won't happen again. There's no excuse.'

She noticed that the slur was now almost imperceptible.

'I accept your apology, leutnant. It's not yet a crime to get drunk, not here anyway – though what you might do or say when you're drunk is another matter. I hope that you didn't compromise my daughter in any way. You do understand what I am telling you?'

'Papa, there was no question of that. The leutnant was perfectly correct.'

He held up his hand to his daughter without looking at her, his gaze steady on the German. There was a tone to this gesture that was insulting and Marie-Louise found herself pursing her lips to stop herself replying.

'Please, leutnant, sit down. Marie-Louise, will you ask Bernadette to bring us coffee – real, not ersatz.'

As he said this, the door to the kitchen opened and the tiny Bernadette, holding a tray that overwhelmed her, bobbed her way into the room, bird-like, and placed the tray on the stool, her eyes flicking furtively around the room. There was silence as she poured each cup before scuttling back to the kitchen, leaving behind the telltale reminder of her presence – the smell of infrequent contact with soap and water.

Michel Annecy sat back and eyed the German over his spectacles. 'My daughter tells me you're upset by today's news. I'm interested. Why?'

Adam took a sip from his cup and contemplated his boots before replying.

'Personal, *monsieur*. What I do now is dangerous enough. War with Russia will be long and brutal and I reckon that my chances of making it through are limited, to say the least. It was self-pity, I'm afraid. I'm not a hero.'

'No man who's fought in a war and done his duty should say that. Fear is a natural emotion – unless you're an idiot; and I don't think you are. From what my daughter has told me, you're being, I think, a little economical with me. I understand that the turn the war has taken upsets you; that this move on the Reds is not to your liking, apparently. I'm interested in that. Surely us French and you Germans can agree that the elimination of the Bolsheviks is a good thing? Surely?'

Adam contemplated his coffee, running his finger round the rim of his cup before replying. 'Only if we win, whoever "we" are. What happens if we don't?'

Michel Annecy looked at him with astonishment that bordered on incredulity. 'If the German army can beat us and the British and every other army in Europe in six weeks, surely they, and we if we join them, can sort out the Red Army in a few months? Surely? Especially as Stalin has decimated his own officer corps in the purges of the last few years.'

'Napoleon made a similar calculation – and lost.'

'Things were different then. Armies walked everywhere: no tanks, no aeroplanes.'

'But if we do lose, then the consequences won't just be an armistice, with a Marshal Pétain figure promising life as usual – but the destruction of everything we know. Stalin and Beria will rule the whole of Europe. That seems to be beyond gambling to me – more like Russian roulette.'

Michel Annecy made a dismissive gesture with his hand. 'Russia will fall apart like a house of cards in a few weeks. Anywhere that is held together by terror will simply collapse once defeat is in the air.'

'Like Germany?'

The older man looked at Adam in amazement.

'And,' Adam went on, 'if Russia is defeated what happens then? I don't think the Führer has in his mind a crusade of brother countries sharing the glory of the defeat of a common infidel. You have heard the expression *Deutschland uber alles . . . ?*'

The sound of the German language grated, its meaning emphasised by the tone.

'You surprise me, leutnant.'

'I surprise myself – though I wouldn't have chosen to have this conversation. I would be grateful, *monsieur*, if it could remain between these four walls.'

Michel Annecy acknowledged him with a nod. 'Of course. And

my daughter agrees also.' He failed to look at her as he spoke and, once again, Marie-Louise found herself biting her lip in irritation. 'Tell me, leutnant, are your views typical? I mean among your comrades.'

Adam shrugged. 'I've no idea. It's not the sort of thing that we talk about in the mess – or anywhere for that matter. We gave up our ability to debate these things some time ago. I suspect there are many who share your views – as there are in France: Communism is a convincing enemy – better than Britain; and victory is an addictive drug – dangerously so.'

In the hiatus, the clink of cup on saucer became intrusive.

'I won't pretend that I'm not disappointed by what you've told me, leutnant. I had hoped that at least we could agree that Communism is the real threat of our time, the one thing that we could all make common cause against. That cause could be the catalyst that stops France and Germany tearing away at each other every generation.'

'*Monsieur*, I dislike Communism as much as you do. What I don't think you understand is that there's a difference, a huge difference, between Germany and Nazi Germany. Remember it's National Socialism we're talking about, Germany as the master race. Your crusade could never be a partnership of equals. It would be Germany and its subjects against Russia, not just to get rid of the Reds, but to get what Hitler calls *Lebensraum* – living space; not for the French, nor anyone else; only Germans. I read his *Mein Kampf* – it's all there for anyone to read. There shouldn't be any surprises. I just believe that for you and me, and for anyone who wants peace rather than war, the outcome of this will be disastrous. Which is why I couldn't sleep when I heard the news and decided on drinking rather than eating at lunchtime – for which I apologise to you both again. It was a one-off, not a habit, I assure you. As I haven't had much sleep, and I'm flying tonight, I hope you'll excuse me if I go upstairs now and try and repair some of the damage I've done to myself.' He stood. '*Madame*; *monsieur*; *bon-soir* – and thank you for the coffee.'

They stayed seated as he left the room with nothing said between them as they listened to him climb the stairs and close the door of his room.

'An interesting man.' Michel Annecy shook a cigarette into his fingers and lit it without reference to his daughter. 'But wrong. He underestimates how much we French and the British, and everyone in Europe, hate the Reds. This is the day that things will start to happen, mark my words. Hitler needs us all to help him crush Stalin and this will be the event that gives the Maréchal the leverage he needs to force through a peace treaty that gets our boys back from Germany.'

'It also means that every Communist in France, and all over Europe, will now be fighting the Boche.'

He looked up at her in surprise. She realised that he had almost forgotten that she was in the room – as a partner in conversation rather than a pourer of coffee.

'So? What can they do against an army like Hitler's, the best the world has ever seen? It's one thing to street-fight with Fascist bully boys, or throw the odd bomb at a magistrate, but rather more difficult to take on a panzer with a pistol.'

'Papa, the Boche are now fighting on two fronts, three if you count North Africa. This will be another front, tying down weapons and troops in garrisons all over Europe. I agree that they won't make a difference on their own . . . but cumulatively . . . '

They both looked up at the mechanical bell above the window that chimed to the strike of a hammer connected to a cable that led to the outside door.

Her father looked at her with a raised eyebrow. 'Are you expecting someone?'

She shook her head. He opened the front door to Ghislaine, whose smile wilted as she saw him. With no word of greeting, he stood back with one hand on the door handle and the other indicating his daughter's presence in the doorway of the parlour. Ghislaine recovered herself and walked haughtily past him with only a nod of acknowledgement. He followed her into the parlour where an awkward silence reigned. He looked at Ghislaine with a look of sardonic triumph.

'Not a good day for you and your friends.'

Not to be outdone in mutual contempt, Ghislaine held his eye. 'What friends?'

'The Reds, the Bolsheviks, the Communists – whatever you want to call those scum.'

'Not my friends. I'm a Socialist – which is a bit different. But on the basis that my enemy's enemy is my friend – then maybe they could be my friends. I prefer them to collaborators.'

He blinked as the imputation struck home. Marie-Louise could see the colour rising in his face and his fists clenching. Visibly he was fighting with himself, his hands working into themselves and his jaw clenched. He glanced at his daughter and in his face she read fury, hurt and pride. Without saying anything and looking straight ahead, he walked stiffly out and up the stairs, taking each tread carefully, only his hands still clenching, betraying the inner tension.

The two women looked at the threadbare rug until the door closed upstairs. Ghislaine reached into her bag for her cigarettes, and as she rasped the flint on her lighter, Marie-Louise noticed that her hands were shaking.

'I thought I'd overdone it that time.'

Marie-Louise didn't answer at first but picked up the cups and saucers and carefully put them on the tray. She lent on the edge of the table facing her friend.

'I know why you're here. Things are getting going now that Russia is in the war, aren't they? Already?'

Ghislaine nodded. 'Yes, they are. Victor wants to meet tomorrow. I know he doesn't trust the Communists; he thinks they are going to hijack the movement for their own ends, so I suspect he'll want to stamp his authority while he can. Nothing's ever simple in France,' she laughed bitterly, 'even fighting the Boche.'

'Where?'

'My apartment; at six tomorrow. And I'm sorry, *chérie*. Really. I didn't come round to have a fight with him. You know that, don't you?'

Marie-Louise nodded. 'Yes. I do know that.'

*   *   *

She saw neither Adam nor her father the next day. She heard the pilot's weary steps on the stairs in the cool of the early morning and his familiar routine through the joists that vibrated to his movements. She visualised him collapsing on to the bed and then the stillness of exhausted sleep stealing over him. Unable to sleep again herself, and keen to avoid meeting her father, she rose earlier than usual and set out for the school in the still hours before even the first peasant farmers' carts rattled their way to the market square. She sat outside her classroom with her shawl wrapped around her against the morning chill, her eyes gritty from lack of sleep. As the sun came over the top of the wall opposite, she allowed the fireflies of eyelid-refracted sun to dance in her vision and the pleasure of momentary dozing to envelop her. On each return to wakefulness the turmoil of the night returned.

She could not escape the sensation of being pulled apart by conflicting forces – loyalty and love, filial duty and patriotism – but none of them clear-cut; all of them ambivalent, at variance with themselves and with each other. She yearned for the certainties of a crusader, or the single-minded obsession of the adolescent – anything rather than the rack of ambivalence on which she was now stretched. The only people she could talk to were, themselves, the very cords that were tugging her in different directions.

Fitfully, she dozed and worried until she was gently shaken awake by the headmaster, a kindly man whose face had been wrecked by shrapnel in the previous war and left with only one eye, half a nose and an inability to smile. The shock of this awakening jarred. The burden of unresolved worries now mixed with a disturbing image of disfigurement that intermittently floated in from her subconscious. Throughout the day she felt unbalanced, as if she had not properly woken. Her lessons seemed to be conducted by someone else that she was observing from close by, her voice a disembodied sound that was separate from her thoughts. She kept glancing at her class to see their reaction to her strange behaviour, but all she saw were the familiar lines of faces, the usual suspects showing their habitual *ennui*, none looking at her as the outsider she felt herself to be. During lunch she went for a walk – but the disembodied sensation persisted throughout the afternoon until she found herself at six o'clock at the foot of Ghislaine's stairs. She could hear voices, and hesitated, stretching her features and breathing heavily in an attempt to restore a sense of physical, if not mental, normality before mounting the stairs.

The main room was fuller than she had anticipated. As well as Victor and Janette, and the others that she knew, there were two unknown men, both in suits but physically contrasted: one huge, with rounded shoulders and a simian posture; the other thin, ascetic, with rimless glasses and the querulous expression of an exasperated academic. They introduced themselves respectively as Felix and Étienne. Victor only nodded a welcome to Marie-Louise, smiling but businesslike. He took up a position by the fireplace, checked the time by his fob-watch with one hand and held up the other to emphasise his wish for silence. He looked carefully at each person in the room before speaking.

'I don't have to tell you what yesterday means. I won't pretend that I like the Communists – or admire their slavish obedience to Moscow. But now that Russia is in the war, much changes here in France. We now have on our side the natural enemies of Fascism, those who perhaps should have been better patriots over the last two years of the disgusting Ribbentrop-Molotov pact. But let's leave that be now and focus on the future. By chance, Felix and Étienne are here with us on a rather auspicious day. Felix is an explosives expert and Étienne is going to teach us about radios – and assassination. Étienne has orders from General de Gaulle – directions might be a better description – as much is being left to individual units to improvise. All I can tell you is that we are opening another front here in France. We will beat the Boche, no matter how many years it takes. *Vive la France!*'

They looked at each other, moved. Cautious of the circumstance, their reply was ragged and slightly embarrassed.

'*Vive la France!*'

'Étienne, perhaps you could tell us what the general has ordered?'

Étienne nodded in acknowledgement and took two steps that placed him alongside Victor. He sat on the edge of the table, lips pursed with a slight twitch in them that could have suggested distaste in other circumstances, his fingers like spider's legs, splayed, with their tips on the table top.

'The general has said that you and others like you are the true heart of France – still beating bravely even though our country is in chains. He and the Free French forces in England are the key to the lock of those chains and they will do all in their power to free our country when they can. But, in the meantime, the heart must continue to beat in order to keep France alive and free, in mind if not in body. Our soldiers are imprisoned in Germany and cannot shoulder the task, so it is down to you to show the Nazis that, though they may occupy our country, they will never feel safe here: never feel that they can sit in our cafés without the nagging fear that a bomb or gun may be their welcome. I have come to give you the training and tools to fight them with.'

He raised an eyebrow towards Victor, who continued. 'We have isolated two targets: the barracks in Étaples and the airfield at Le Touquet. The barracks hold a garrison and troops that may be used for another attempt at invading England – though that looks rather unlikely now that Hitler has attacked Russia – and Le Touquet is obviously on the front line as a bomber station. Anything that we can do there will help the general with the war that he is waging across the Channel. The barracks are currently an open target for a bomb – which is where Felix here will be vital.' Felix acknowledged him with a nod and a smile. 'The airfield is more difficult. The hangars are heavily guarded and the perimeter fence aggressively patrolled. No civilians are allowed within the fence. There is an Achilles heel, however . . . '

Marie-Louise felt a dread sense of anticipation, sensing where the logic of Victor's analysis was going, willing it not to be so and hoping against hope that she was wrong. His voice seemed to echo in a space outside her head, disembodied, as he continued.

' . . . in the personnel, the pilots, who are billeted in the town. These aren't cannon fodder but highly trained men whose loss will make a real difference. There's one billeted with Marie-Louise and her father – he'll be an easy target as he travels daily between Montreuil and Le Touquet. There's an ideal ambush place where the road goes under the railway. We have a choice of nailing him on his way to the airfield in the evening, or in the early morning as he returns. Étienne will be in charge of this operation – Étienne?'

The baton was handed back.

'My preference would be for the early morning. I would favour a bomb detonated under the bridge; it would not only collapse on top of the target making sure of him but also seriously disrupt the rail traffic back and forth from the coast for a couple of weeks at least. The early morning would give us plenty of time to plant the explosives under cover of darkness. The disadvantage is that it makes getting away after the operation more difficult: anyone moving around the countryside or on the roads is very obvious, whereas in the evening they would attract no attention.'

There was a pause. Ghislaine spoke. 'When?'

'There's no moon tomorrow night. It won't be much help in getting away afterwards but it will allow us to place the explosives without any danger of discovery.'

'Who?'

'Felix. Me obviously. We need someone who knows the area well. Not Marie-Louise as the first enquiries will be on her doorstep. So you – and Stephan or Jacques. I would like it to be you and . . . Stephan – thank you.' Stephan's hand was raised. 'We need to reconnoitre the bridge and the escape routes well, so we'll want a pair of bicycles and a cart which we will "repair" by the side of the road in order to get the explosives hidden on site. We don't want to be walking around during the night carrying them with us. Timing? They take off at about ten and are normally back on the ground by two at the latest – depending on the target and how far away it is. They have a debrief and something to eat, so it's nearly always light by the time they head back to Montreuil, either in a lorry together – which would be ideal as we could get half a dozen in one go – or in a staff car if it's an officer alone. We don't want to be heading back down the main road after a bang that's going to wake up every Boche within ten kilometres, so we need a safe-house that we can get to within two kilometres. Ghislaine has found somewhere that will be ideal; just for the day, and then we can make it away the following night under cover of darkness. Any questions?'

The sense of out-of-body amplified itself as the discussion continued. The details floated by her like echoes in a cavern, toffee-thick noise that made no sense. The figures, both standing and seated, blurred into shapes that refused to define themselves. She swallowed and breathed deeply and both sound and shape came back into focus but made little sense in the scramble of thoughts that crowded in on every side.

'Marie-Louise?'

She managed to shake her head.

'No.'

*   *   *

She returned home barely able to think coherently. Rather than confront her father again, she took a pack of cigarettes and walked into the Place Gambetta that lay obliquely to the left of her house, one side dominated by the maire and another by the Gothic buttresses of the Abbatiale. She sat on a ledge by the door of the church, shivering slightly and hugging herself to keep warm as the cool of the evening established itself. A mule, in the shafts of a cart, stood placidly nearby and contemplated her with only a blink and the occasional swish of its tail. She stared back, envying it its stolidity and calmness, its only concerns those of hunger, thirst and tiredness – no responsibilities, no anticipation, no desperate contortions to avoid the snapping jaws of fate that now seemed to menace her from every direction.

She pictured the scene: the weary tramp towards a waiting lorry; exhausted men smoking as they contemplated their boots, all talk expended. She saw him by the tailgate, head cushioned on his flying jacket, lolling and jolted into wakefulness by the shock of the worst potholes, the lorry fumes polluting the purity of the early morning. She could see the bend in the road as it dipped and twisted under the railway and the brief roaring echo of the diesel engine as the bridge amplified the sound; the explosion; the crumpling of the chassis, the shredding of the canvas roof; the collapse of the bridge on to the shattered remains of bodies and machinery. She felt her hands to have been on the plunger as starkly as she had felt them around her lover's throat in Ghislaine's apartment. She could see her handiwork's torn and scorched results as clearly as she had then felt the flecks of phlegm on her face from his throttled gasps. Anyone but him. Others would just be the sinister generality of field grey and coal-scuttle helmets. She

179

could feel the softness of his body hair and smell his musk-scent under the moon-stripes of a Paris hotel room. Impossible.

As this was playing in her imagination, her eyes were focused on the middle-distance, the centre of the square, where there was no movement other than the staccato progress of a foraging rat. From the direction of her father's house, a woman was walking with a firmness and spring that could only belong to Ghislaine. Marie-Louise raised her hand in greeting, and her friend sat down beside her, saying nothing. They smoked; Ghislaine's warmth, both physical and companionable, was a welcome change from the chilled loneliness of terrible imaginings.

'Are you all right?' Ghislaine's eyes were following the rat.

'No. Not really.'

'Do you like him?'

She breathed deeply. The urge to tell Ghislaine everything, to unburden herself, was overpowering. 'He's lived in our house for a year.'

'He's a Boche.'

'I know.'

Marie-Louise looked sideways at her friend's Attic profile, her gaze still on the rat. She noticed that her fingers were drumming on her knee, a measure of the latent energy confined within. There was a hard alertness as Ghislaine turned to face her, resting her chin on her palm.

'Are you going to warn him?'

Marie-Louise turned back towards the rat, which was standing on its hind-legs and sniffing the air for danger. She drew on the cigarette before answering. 'No.'

Ghislaine nodded slowly. 'Good. I was worried. Listen, *chérie*, I know how difficult this is for you. I do. Really. It's the war. Just the fucking war.' Ghislaine put her arm around her shoulder and edged closer. Again the urge to tell rose in a surge that she had to fight with a physical effort that manifested itself in a trembling that shook her body.

'You're cold, *chérie*. Home?'

'My father's there.'

'I don't think I'd be very welcome.'

They smiled at each other, Marie-Louise still shivering.

'No.'

'Take my jacket then. You can give it back to me tomorrow.'

'Thanks.'

Ghislaine draped the woollen jacket over her friend's shoulders and moved in front of her, kneeling down to her level. She put an affectionate hand against her friend's cheek. 'Courage, *chérie*. I admire you. Very much.'

'Well, I don't admire myself. Why should I?'

Ghislaine took her hand. 'Because it's always difficult for you. Too much thinking. Decisions are easy for me – but I know they aren't for you. Now this. For me – he's a Boche. For you – a man. I know that. But it's got to be done. By the end of this war, if we are going to win it, he'll almost certainly be dead anyway. If we don't kill him, someone else will. You're in it now – whether you like it or not. Maybe I shouldn't have . . . but it's done. We do what we have to do.' She stared at the ground for a couple of seconds. A hardness returned as she looked up. 'If you warn him . . . you'll probably kill me – and the others. You know that, don't you?' Marie-Louise nodded without meeting her gaze. 'Think of Jerome and Robert. They faced tanks and Stukas. This is our war. Just as nasty probably, maybe worse.' She stood up and looked down on her friend. 'Don't get too cold.'

As Ghislaine walked away, the loneliness and indecision returned with redoubled shivering. She stood with difficulty as her chilled limbs straightened. The mule was eying her with the wariness of a draft animal that equates humans with the pain of blows. She reached out slowly to pat it – but it craned its neck away. Wise, she thought; not to trust. The rat also saw her and skittered its way back to the drain that was its oubliette.

As she reached the door of her house, she heard the sound of boots on the stairs. She hesitated but before she could make a decision the door was opened by Adam, flying jacket slung over one shoulder. He smiled at her and, like Ghislaine, reached out and touched her cheek – before speaking in a louder voice than was natural, raising his eyes to indicate her father's presence upstairs.

'Good-evening, *madame*. A good day I hope. I must be on my way. May I wish you a pleasant evening.'

As he stepped past her into the narrow privacy of the gated coach entrance, she took his hand and kissed it. The gate closed behind him and she touched her cheek, wondering about the kiss that Judas had bestowed on Jesus.

*　　*　　*

The following evening, she made her decision.

The sound of him made up her mind for her. She heard the clink of his razor through his bedroom door and it brought back the etched memory of his naked back in the Parisian hotel room as he was shaving, one hand stretching tight his skin and the other fingering the open razor around the contours of his face. She could visualise the concentration reflected in the shaving mirror and smell the uniquely masculine scent of shaving soap and the dregs of sex.

She waited for him in the parlour where he greeted her with surprise and an anxious look that relaxed when she told him that neither her father nor Bernadette were in the house. She brought him his customary tray and they sat, as they had done many times before, at the foot of the stairs in their little carapace of privacy. Neither spoke much, Marie-Louise still not knowing how to tell him and he picking up on her distractedness.

Finally she steeled herself. 'At the airfield . . . do you have somewhere you could sleep . . . if you didn't come back here?' He looked at her with surprise. 'Tonight . . . just tonight.'

She forced herself to look at him, willing him simply to accept her hint without asking any further questions. She found she could not look him in the eye as he slowly put down his tray and offered her a cigarette.

He blew a mushroom of smoke over her head as he leant back and considered her. 'Just tonight?'

She nodded. She was aware that he was staring at her intently even though she could not look at him.

'Tell me: if for some reason I do decide to stay at the airfield, what will happen? To you, I mean.'

As in all moments of stress, she was twisting her hair around her fingers.

'Nothing. I don't know. I'll think of something.'

'They'll know it's you, won't they. Why else would I change my routine?'

'You've stayed there before.'

'Twice. And not in the last three months.'

'It could be chance. A training flight. Something like that.'

'It could be. But unlikely. In the circumstances.'

He reached out for her hands, which he enveloped in his. 'Look at me.'

She complied. Tears were running down her face.

'Listen. I have virtually no chance of surviving this war. It's not about skill, just odds. And if I did, what then? You've a husband whom you love. What we have is truly special but it's about now. It has a past – but no future. Has it? I'm so happy with that, I promise you. It's been a year that I managed to . . . salvage from the fire. A bonus, a wonderful bonus. If not this, then what? Drowning in the Channel? Russian flak? Now I know something is happening, I may be able to avoid it; but if I change my routine, whoever it is will know that you warned me, won't they? Won't they?'

She nodded.

'Thank you, *chérie*, for this. For everything. You've done what you could. Really.' He cupped her face in his hands and kissed her gently on her lips. '*Au revoir, chérie*. Only *au revoir*, I'm sure.'

He gathered his flying suit, turned to the door, and was gone.

*   *   *

The night was interminable. Unable to tame her fears, Marie-Louise left her house and walked to the Citadelle where Jerome had kissed her for the first time in that far-off summer of peacetime. The long twilight of midsummer left a cobalt tinge to the night sky long after the sun had finally dipped below the horizon. It was still there when the sound of aeroplane engines, a distant drone, reached her ears. In the total blackout of wartime, darkness lay heavily on the countryside below, with only a strip of light along the western horizon and the first stars illuminating the thin band of the Milky Way. Away to the north the throbbing of the heavily laden bombers fighting gravity in their quest for height oscillated in tone as they circled and grouped invisibly above the coast. Occasionally a signal-lamp flashed, pinpointing the source of the sound that seemed diffused across the faint join between ground and sky. Slowly, as the last light faded, the roar became a hum and the pricks of light disappeared leaving only pitch darkness and the sound of a dog barking somewhere in the valley.

Marie-Louise stared into the blackness which slowly surrendered the form of woods as her eyes became accustomed to the dark. She imagined her friend down there now, warily making her rendezvous with Étienne and the others, crouched in the ditch by the side of the road or in the old barn abutting the railway line from where the entrance to the bridge was visible. Would they risk smoking? Had they placed the explosives? She could imagine the tension of the wait, the impossibility of sleep and the hiss of whispered exchanges as all eventualities were rehearsed once again. She stared hard into the blackness – but it gave up no clues. She walked back down the cobbled streets that were now deserted, apart from the darting of a cat. She heard the rattle of dominoes from an open window and masculine voices as she reached the small square outside her house where Adam had accosted her. She paced up and down as he had done, the sky above framed by the espaliered limes. Her only companion was the chiming of the church clock on the quarter, the gap between each chime seeming longer and longer until, finally, some time after the symphony of bells had heralded the new day, she went inside and resumed her pacing in the parlour to the metronome of a different clock. Outside the window, the eastern sky eventually paled and she sat down, physically exhausted from the distance she had covered to and fro.

She woke with a start. Sun was refracting though the panes of the half-open window casting a dusty spectrum on the tobacco-stained paint of the wall opposite. A starling, tail bobbing, was observing her from a cherry-tree branch that waved slowly to an imperceptible breeze. The sun was high. She looked in panic at the clock. Quarter to seven. Her eyes were gritty and unfocused. She rubbed them and looked again as the long hand jerked on another minute. She stood up quickly and went back out into the lime-shaded square. A peasant was pushing a barrow up the hill towards her and a dog was raising its leg against the fence that protected the war memorial. A normal morning. No heads craning out of windows, no pall of smoke drifting over the rooftops. Relief swept over her, an exaltation almost, banishing her tiredness. She sat on the bench in the early sun with her head in her hands and her fingers massaging her eyelids, feeling the heat of the sun penetrate her cardigan. Over the sound of birdsong, she was aware of the strike of shoes on cobbles, not the slow percussion of emburdened clogs, but fast and purposeful. The sun was in her eyes and she shaded them with one hand, allowing the fireballs in her vision to subside. The silhouette of a woman in a skirt and beret, but indistinct in the aurora of light, cast a shadow over her. Ghislaine.

'You told him, didn't you?'

Marie-Louise shifted herself along the bench, still shading her eyes but now able to see Ghislaine's face, hard with fury.

'You bloody told him. A fucking Boche. You nearly killed us all. For him. And you promised me. You stupid, stupid bitch!'

All this was delivered in a terrible hiss.

'No . . .'

'Then why didn't he turn up? Regular as clockwork for months, then nothing. We managed to get the explosives off the bridge. Just. But we so nearly got caught by a lorry-load of Boche soldiers heading south from Étaples. A whisker. That's all it was. That close.' She pinched her fingers almost together in illustration, her mouth pursed in fury. 'Don't bother to lie. You're useless at it. I know you too well. Too bloody well.' The last was said with real bitterness, setting the seal on the ruins of a friendship. 'Well?'

Marie-Louise nodded but could only look at the cobbles and not at the figure standing over her.

'Well?'

The second question was accompanied by a brutal shove to Marie-Louise's shoulder, causing her neck to whiplash painfully.

'Look at me! Bloody look at me!'

Her eyes remained fixed on the cobbles.

'Stephan was right. You are your father's daughter. Worse. Not just a collaborator – but a fucking traitor!'

There was a hiatus in the heavy breathing, a cleared throat; then hawking and the damp flop of expectorate on her hair, trickling over her ear and dripping on to her shoulder. Her eyes were still fixed on Ghislaine's shoes. She saw them pivot about and the first stride took them out of the perimeter of her self-imposed circle of sight. Still she stared down. A globule of spit, like an extended stalactite, wobbled to the breeze in her peripheral vision before breaking off to stain blue the corner of a dusty cobblestone.

She sat for some time, in shock, with a roaring in her ears and a battered sense of detachment, knowing that if she stayed as she was, then there was a certain anaesthetic at work that would protect her and allow her to stay numbed with her thoughts and emotions disengaged. Slowly, both returned as the sun's heat penetrated the hair on the crown of her bowed head, bringing with them nausea but also the familiar out-of-body sensation. Slowly she stood, and unsteadily walked towards her house, into the shade of trees that allowed her to see down the now empty street without being blinded by the glare of harsh sunlight. Shutters remained closed; no eyes were gazing on her shame.

She could still feel the sticky weight of the coagulating spit above her ear as she mounted the stairs to her room. She made no effort to clean it off. Slowly, with infinite weariness, she sank on to her bed. She lay like the wife of a pious crusader, petrified in eternal prayer atop her tomb, with her fingers entwined and her eyes shut as if in profound sleep or contemplation.

If she had dreamt, no memory lingered as she started awake to a banging sound from down the corridor. She felt her hair. It was matted and hardened. Another bang. Her heart leapt, and without attempting to repair the damage to her fine hair or crumpled skirt, she hurried to the door, longing to see his familiar face, slack with exhaustion but there and alive.

Two bareheaded German soldiers looked at her, startled. They were carrying a metal trunk.

'What are you doing?' she asked in German.

The two men looked at each other before the older man answered.

'We're picking up the leutnant's kit. We're sorry to have disturbed you, *madame*.'

'Is he leaving us then . . . to sleep at the airfield?'

The relief flooded through her.

'No, *madame*. The leutnant was shot down last night. His aircraft blew up. No survivors.'

15

GERMANY

Dresden. Ash Wednesday, 14 February 1945

The breaking dawn was barely discernable. The two women woke in a huddle of hundreds that stirred and twitched in pain or shock, murmuring with a descant of coughing and moans of grief. Gone were the tempest and the hellish illumination. Instead, a leaden twilight of brown and grey lay like a pall over the cremated corpse of the city. Fires were still burning, furiously in places, but individual now, blobs of orange on a mat canvas, the colour of smoke having become the dominant hue and human pain the prevailing sound. There was the growl of an aero-engine. Low, over the river, just below the worst of the smoke, flew a Fieseler Storch spotter plane – an explorer from the land of the living reporting on that of the dead.

They looked at each other as strangers. Eva's blonde hair was burnt away on one side, her scalp scorched, and the other side was matted with blood from an open wound. Both women's faces were blackened – their wrappings in tatters with livid flay-marks of burnt skin from flying cinders and eyes blood red from smoke. Mimi grasped her friend's hand as she dry-retched. Billows of smoke drifted over the embankment wall, obscuring for moments the pewter-coloured river and isolating their huddle of suffering in a sinister fog that glowed like an eerie sunset. Mimi's leg ached above the speckled scorching of her face and the blistering agony of her feet. She remembered their ladder to the salvation of the water tank and lifted her long skirt to inspect the damage. Her woollen stocking was ripped and a jagged mouth of splayed flesh and skin oozed coagulating blood. Her feet were burned but saved, she knew, by the boots that had done her such service on the icy trek from Breslau: out of the freezer and into the fire, she thought bitterly.

'Can you walk?'

Without answering, Mimi grasped her friend's shoulder and heaved herself up. The pain in her feet was acute, but she stood without assistance. Mimi glanced at her watch. Ten o'clock. The unseen sun had been up for two hours at least in this terrible twilight. They picked their way through the human detritus – some asleep, others staring sightlessly and silently and yet others keening gently in shock – towards the steps up the embankment wall. Bodies occupied each step, some not reacting even as they accidentally stood on a burned hand or stumbled over a rounded back.

They breasted the top of the wall and surveyed what was left of the city through the febble dawn. Beside the river, over the centuries, the inhabitants of one of the finest cities of Europe had idled away many a pleasant hour, their aesthetic sensibilities massaged by the gentle curve of the Elbe and its famous Baroque skyline of palaces, churches and theatres. Only the Frauenkirche now remained, with its cupola just visible in between the drifts of smoke, haloed by the fires of the Altstadt behind. Gone was the Zwinger Palace of the cultivated and priapic Augustus the Strong, consumed by fires that were now played out, leaving only the jagged silhouettes of collapsed windows like upended extracted molars. Single walls teetered at impossible angles: one collapsed as they watched, contributing an avalanche of dust to thicken the smoke yet further. Two bodies lay in the open space surrounding a statue, the now-hardened asphalt holding them partly submerged in an implacable grip.

Neither woman said anything: it was too much for words. Instinctively they both started to walk, hobble rather, in the direction of Eva's flat near the station, the atavistic need for home outweighing any realistic possibility of it still being there. As in the immediate vicinity of a geyser, an intense stored heat leached out of the ground, plaguing their already broiled feet, and as they approached smouldering buildings, this was twinned with a radiated heat that caused their damp clothes to steam. All landmarks had gone, buildings hollowed out and roofless and trees splintered or collapsed. Individual bodies, in every permutation of contortion, lay in blackened stiffness. Fountains of marble dolphins and carefree cherubs, holding pitchers that usually sprayed jets of crystal water, now presided over heaped corpses that intertwined in an orgy of death, co-joined in a last desperate search for the balm of water to salve a plague of burns.

As the open public spaces gave way to streets, the full extent of the destruction revealed itself. What remained of the upright walls contained still-burning fires that were now reduced to consuming the roots of floor joists or fragments of wood that were stirred into the rubble of brick and stone that filled every street so chaotically as to make them impassable to any vehicle – or even a horse. They stumbled on through the blasted landscape, narrowly avoiding annihilation as the side of a building collapsed behind them, wrapping them in a blanket of dust that had them coughing uncontrollably for minutes. As it cleared, they were aware of movement at the base of the heap of rubble on which they were resting. An adolescent in the uniform of the Hitler Youth, his face blackened like theirs, was tearing at stones and hurling aside pieces of mortar. They scrambled down to him. There was something miraculous in finding something living in this desolation. He started as Mimi touched his back, reddened and swollen eyes wide in fright, staring at them as he backed away.

'What are you doing?' Mimi asked gently.

He pointed at his ears and shook his head. 'Can't hear, *fraülein*. I'm sorry. My parents. And my sister. They're in the cellar. There's an entrance through the coal hatch.' His shoulders drooped in sudden exhaustion. 'It's somewhere here.' A bloody hand traced out a patch of rubble that was indistinguishable from that next to it. 'Somewhere here.'

He leant down once more and continued to tear at the stones with raw fingers.

The women looked at each other and, without speaking, bent over beside him and dug alongside, the sound of their collective breathing coming out in sobs and coughs, human sounds competing with the occasional crack of heat-split stone or the muffled roar of collapsing masonry around them. They too worked until their hands bled and black beads of sweat blinded them.

'There! There it is!' he choked, dropping to his knees the better to scrabble at the hole that was now opening up. They could see wood, a trapdoor perhaps, and they redoubled their efforts to clear its full area so that they could work it open. Loose spoil kept rolling back to frustrate them, but eventually they were able to grasp the metal handle with a bundle of rags and heave the hatch open. They recoiled from the oven-like heat that was released, staggering back from the blackness of the hole. The boy dived towards it but Eva grabbed him and pulled him away. They fought for some seconds before he collapsed like the child that he was into her arms.

'Wait. Wait. It's too hot,' she struggled to say through a coughing fit, before realising that in his deafened state he could not hear her and settling instead for a rocking embrace that seemed to quiet him. Feeling him relax, Eva loosened her grip. He scrambled up the spoil to his bag from which he produced a hurricane lamp; his shredded hands trembled as they trimmed the wick but the flame settled to reveal a coal-chute and a metal ladder. Heat was still exhaled from the blackness but now more that of a sauna than an oven. Bearable. Just. The boy held the lantern as Eva descended the ladder. He handed it down to her before descending himself, followed by Mimi who found them standing on a pile of coal and staring at a door that connected with a cellar beyond. The boy gently pushed the door open and darkness crept up behind them as the lamp entered the next room and another wave of baked air funnelled towards the open hatch.

A domestic scene confronted them. A man in the uniform of a stationmaster sat in a canvas chair. A woman half lay, half sat, on a camp bed with a young girl's head on her lap. They looked asleep except for a pink brownness. Cooked. The boy held out his hand, as if blind, as he approached his mother. He touched her face and recoiled, looking down at his fingers in shock. He looked at Eva, eyes wide and questioning. She tentatively did the same, pulling her hand away from the heated corpse after the briefest of touches. She took his hand and led him back into the relative cool of the coalhole where they crouched in the faint light of the phantom day. They could see tears streaking the black of his cheeks.

'Carbon monoxide,' Eva mouthed at him.

He looked at her without comprehension. She pointed to her

mouth and breathed heavily, coughed, recovered and made the motions of going to sleep. 'No pain.' She mouthed the words again. 'Like going to sleep.'

He made no sign that he understood but his tears redoubled. Eva took his hand again and pointed upwards. The heat was becoming unbearable. They climbed out and scrambled up the sides of the spoil that slipped in chunks down the hole that steadily exuded baked air and the smell of cooked meat. They sat in exhaustion and parched with thirst among the mounds of debris that smoked and rumbled as they settled; dust and sweat plagued their eyes. The boy just stared at the ruins with smutty rivulets coursing down his cheeks.

A new sound insinuated itself. Neither woman was sure when she first heard it but it began as a background trembling that was more felt than heard, a tremor that could have been distant thunder on a summer night – familiar. Quickly, sound twinned with the vibration into a hideous déjà-vu that had the three of them looking at each other in incredulity. There were no sirens – but there didn't need to be. Eva articulated their hunted despair. 'It's another raid for God's sake. Another! What are they trying to do to us? The bastards!'

Red flares once again burst around them; this time their harsh light was filtered by smoke but bright enough as they neared the ground to cast a hard shadow. The rumbling was now all around, shaking the devastated ground underneath them, settling the rubble further, kindling small fires that flared once more and collapsing walls that had managed to remain vertical. All veterans now, they searched around them in a desperate quest for shelter. Only the black hole adjacent to the catacomb they had just left yawned temptingly. They hesitated: the memory of the heat, the clawing dark and the smell of baked meat held them back, reddened eyes hunting for an alternative. It was only when the first concussions shook the ground again, that they abandoned their futile search and scrambled for the beckoning blackness.

The three of them cowered on the pile of coal below the open hatch as the detonations began their familiar crushing strides towards them, each shock-wave merging into the next until it seemed that the subsequent must surely pound them under its obliterating heel. One landed so close that the blast hurled them against the wall, pelting them with rubble from above and even coal from below that ricocheted off the walls before partially burying them as they curled into balls with their hands over eardrums that no longer functioned. Dust and smoke tore their lungs. Darkness descended like a shroud.

The earth continued to shake after the detonations had ceased. The sound of walls collapsing and the movement of unstable rubble kept Mimi with her face buried in her scarf, huddled against the metal ladder in their potential tomb. A patter of bricks and cement avalanched over her back. As the ground settled, she raised her head and opened her eyes to a Stygian darkness. Swirls of dust and smoke filled her eyes and nose and abraded her already tortured lungs. She felt, and glimpsed through agonising blinks, the coughing form of the boy, doubled up on his knees and dry-retching – but no Eva. By touch more than by sight she located an arm, then a shoulder, before grazing her knuckles against a rush of rubble that she realised was covering her friend's head. She screamed at the boy to help and, with hands that were already raw, they burrowed once more. Rid of the layers of masonry, they rolled her over and, in the clearing eddies of light, Mimi felt desperately for a sign of life. Her own pulse drowned out any trace of another and the after-tremors and deafness made a search for breathing impossible. In desperation, in between coughing fits that she was sure would rupture her lungs, she forced air between slack lips that refused to respond. She cursed and pummelled the inert body in a fury of impotent grief. Just as she had given up, and had slumped against the wall of the coal-hole, Eva stirred. She blinked and then she too began coughing, bending double in a spluttering heap, before crawling towards them and lying against them, lungs heaving and another head-wound streaming blood over her eyes.

When they finally climbed the ladder and crawled through wreckage knitted together by a spaghetti of domestic wiring, some of the dust and much of the smoke had cleared. Phosphorous incendiaries, designed to nestle in the attics of buildings whose roofs had been peeled by high explosive, flared redundantly among the already demolished houses. Newly exposed timbers flamed and smoked as isolated flares. No one spoke – they had been deafened by the cacophony – as they picked their way down streets that barely had that definition, stumbling over the detritus of wholesale destruction – cisterns, sinks, contorted pipes, a shattered piano, metal bedsteads and blackened bodies. Thirst now tortured them as they made for the river once more, halting intermittently as eddies of smoke enveloped them and reduced them to choking huddles unable to move while the fits lasted.

Farther downstream from their night-time refuge, they again descended steps to the mud bank and threw themselves into the shallows, drinking out of cupped hands before dragging themselves half ashore, trailing their scorched feet in the water. Two corpses bumped together next to them, caught on a tree branch – one was that of a woman whose skirt was pulled up to her neck, doubling the indignity of death. They lay there until the February chill roused them and they began to shiver, half from shock, half from cold. Through chattering teeth and coughing fits they consulted. The boy pointed over the river towards the high ground to the north-west. 'My grandfather lives there. My parents and my sister . . . ' he hesitated, ' . . . agreed that if there was bombing and we got separated, we would meet there. Will you come with me?'

It took two attempts before the women understood what he was saying and nodded their agreement. Standing unsteadily, Mimi was agonisingly aware of the raw wound to her leg. They joined others shuffling away from the smoking pyre behind them. No one spoke. One man was bare to the waist with a boiled lobster of a burn bubbling along the line of his spine. A woman held the hand of a girl whose other arm hung by her side in a useless mess of dislocation and multiple fractures. Another child nursed a tiny dog, denuded of hair, pink with burns – dead. Only the occasional whimper broke the silence. They crossed the bridge towards the Neustadt and followed the line of the river downstream, every step taking them back into a world of standing buildings and normality. How long it took them to get to their refuge neither woman could remember. How the kindly grandfather greeted them and how he took the news of his daughter and grand-daughter's deaths was lost in an exhaustion that claimed them for two days.

*   *   *

Mimi woke in full daylight. Her leg ached. She raised the bed covers to see that it was cleanly bandaged, before sinking back to try and master her heaving lungs. A collage of memories rushed back on her as she took in the neat bedroom and the once-white sheets that were streaked with soot and mud. She felt around her face where the wounds of flying cinders were pin-stabs of pain. She pulled herself upright and tested her legs on the floor, glimpsing herself as she did so in the wall mirror. Her hair, in places, was singed to the scalp; her eyes were bloodshot and her face smeared as if with camouflage paint. The window looked out over the city. Smoke rose off it, not now in the billows of a grotesque bonfire, but rising from the smouldering ruins and settling horizontally like mist in an autumnal valley.

She found the boy and his grandfather sitting silently across the table from each other in the small sitting room. Blotches on the laundered lace tablecloth in front of them spoke of their grief. The boy was clean and wearing a suit that engulfed him. His hands were bandaged and he too had livid facial blisters. The man had Wilhelmine whiskers and puffy eyes – but red with tears rather than smoke.

He nursed them for a week, dressing the women's wounds and dabbing antiseptic on their burns. At times, he disappeared on his bicycle to return with black bread and a bucket of soup from an emergency food station. His dead wife's clothes became theirs: at night they heard him scrubbing away the smoke and repairing the scorch holes in their own. After two days and rain, the smouldering of the city reduced. As it did, the Frauenkirke's dome, the only recognisable landmark that remained, collapsed. The rumble of its demise echoed through the valley, leaving only an ascending column of dust to mark where it had stood for over two hundred years. New fires started in what had been squares, parks and gardens. The smell of roasting meat filled the house. The old man returned on his bicycle with hesitant stories of steaming mounds of bodies and details of corpse-miners combing cellars. Sometimes their task was impossible and flame-throwers were used to immolate decomposing family groups where they had suffocated or baked to death in their shelters.

He also bought news from the front. At night the eastern horizon flashed with unnatural lightning. The rumour-mill was mixed. Most credible were anecdotes from wounded soldiers in transit through what remained of the city. East Prussia, most of Silesia and nearly all of Pomerania were lost – their populations either in full flight to the west or submerged under a savagery that had last been seen in the time of Genghis Khan. There were too many tales of indiscriminate rape and murder, too many sober eyewitness accounts for them to be brushed aside as propaganda. The last vestiges of paternalism still nagged at Mimi as she fretted about the Remmers, who had been encamped by the station on the eve of the raid. In all likelihood they were dead – either incinerated in the area surrounding the water-tank that had saved the two women, or crushed and buried in the subterranean areas below the Haufbahnhoff.

Eva was pragmatic and cynical. 'From what you told me, if they are alive, they won't be thinking about you. And if they're dead . . . ' She looked over the city where the pyres were smoking balefully. 'We have to go. You know that. Stop playing the lady of the manor. That's over. We need to get as near to the Americans as we can; away from here; however we can, as soon as we can.'

The grandfather, Herr Ferzen, gazed over the remains of the city of his birth and subsequent life. 'We'll come too. There's nothing for us here any more. For me, something, maybe. For Tomas,' he nodded towards the boy who had sat in a corner for the previous days without speaking, 'nothing. Trains are going west again.'

Mimi bowed to the logic and the next day, in cold rain, Herr Ferzen locked the front door, carefully placed the key under a flowerpot, and left his home behind. Their destination was Nuremburg: far enough to the west, in the American line of advance and home to Eva's sister. They queued for hours at the makeshift station on the north bank of the Elbe with survivors from the raid and more refugees from Silesia and Saxony, as well as wounded soldiers returning from the front. The carriages were packed, so they elbowed their way into a *viehwagon* – a freight car for cattle – where the only upholstery was straw and the latrine an oil drum. To one side of them was a woman who was tenderly nursed by her son – no more than ten. He stroked her back as she keened quietly during her waking hours over a small suitcase that she grasped to her chest; she defecated without embarrassment, still clutching the case. She was only quiet when she slept – though the screams from her occasional nightmares woke the entire wagon. On the other side of them was a young girl, beautiful in one profile – but the other encased in a dressing that protected a savage burn. Her whimperings of pain rarely stopped. By the end of the first day the straw was sodden: the rotten timbers of the roof let in steady drips of water despite their efforts to caulk the holes with straw and rags. Food and water were in short supply. Buckets of soup, gritty bread and *grutze* were handed up in provincial stations and the noisome oil drum poured out of the open door during the interminable waits in sidings for the end of an air raid or the repair of tracks ahead. Through cracks in the boarded sides they glimpsed the bare winter countryside passing – little changed from peacetime, with tidy prosperous farms and rococo churches seen through driving sleet. There was silence in the wagon as they transited devastated cities, Chemnitz being the first. There was no distinction between the concentric rings of industry and the old city centres. All were merged into a continuum of nondescript rubble – flattened, eyeless ruins. Occasionally something distinct survived, miraculously un-touched – a chimney or a church. Bayreuth was passed at night. The train halted for some minutes in the ruins of the station where Winifred Wagner had so often greeted Hitler on his annual pilgrimage to the festival. A single lamp illuminated a huge eagle surmounting a broken swastika of only three arms. One of its wings sagged down over the upper limb, waving in the wind that swept the rubble-strewn platform. The familiar sour smell of saturated burnt wood and putrefaction seeped into the freight car.

The same odour told them they were in Nuremburg. It was eight days after they had left Dresden on a journey that, in more normal times, would have taken as many hours. At midday police-men marched along the platform hammering on the doors with truncheons. The woman with the suitcase seemed oblivious to their peremptory orders to disembark. She stood in the doorway, alone, with her son holding out his hand, beckoning to her from the platform. Mimi moved forward to help, gently adding her entreaties to those of the boy. Still she cowered in the doorway. Two men in uniform appeared and brusquely shouted at her to step down. She remained where she was. Without further ado, they jumped up and manhandled her to the step, forcing the suitcase out of her grasp. It struck the ground and burst open, strewing underwear and the decomposing corpse of a baby, still in its swaddling clothes, on to the platform. The woman's screams, and the son's small hands tugging at the hem of her skirt against the brute force of her escorts, shook them all to silence.

From the steps to the station they could see only devastation – streets clear of rubble but almost nothing whole and entire; a clock, on what had been a civic building, disgorged its innards down the canine tooth of the remains of a tower. Though it was noon, there was an eerie quietness, made more sinister by a spring sun that had the effect of accentuating the absence of colour – everything a dusty grey. No birdsong – only the caw of a solitary crow hooking his beak into a crevice in a window that had long ago lost its glazing. A woman appeared from some subterranean shelter and crossed what had conceivably once been a street to disappear again into a warren of rubble. They searched uncertainly for clues to orientate themselves: the distant view of a church spire that still stood; street signs that were now painted boards rather than iron-work; a façade that still claimed to adorn the finest emporium in Nuremburg, a ruined void behind.

Eva's sister's house was two kilometres from the station. It had once been a substantial town house, the home of a prosperous lawyer, detached from its neighbours, with plane trees shading the pavement. Now only a side-wall remained. A bath hung by its plumbing from what had been the first floor. The trees were charred skeletons with no hope of spring.

Eva's sister, Irma, was hanging some clothes on an improvised washing line as they approached. Mimi remembered her as sharing Eva's pre-war bloom – but she now had the same grubby chalkiness as the washing she was trying to dry. The sisters hugged each other with tears streaking their faces. As Eva introduced her companions, Mimi could see the apprehension in Irma's face. She knew the thoughts going through her mind – children to feed, no ration cards, no house, nothing to offer. They hesitated on the street. Eva took her sister's hand and they walked out of earshot. Mimi saw Irma wipe a tear away as they returned. She nodded towards a side door, the entrance to the cellar.

In the semi-darkness, viscous with damp, they were greeted by two girls – five and seven respectively. Blonde like their mother, they scratched at the lice in their hair and the impetigo that disfigured their forearms with weeping sores. Light came from a half-submerged window that had, miraculously, kept its glass. More light filtered in from the door, opened, they realised, for the first time in many months, allowing light and air into the fungal staleness. A crude sump in a corner drained damp from the walls. In the shadows beyond, two rats were cleaning themselves. There were two pairs of metal bunks in a corner and, in the room adjoining, Mimi spied the post of a brass bed.

'The girls can share my bed with me and you can have the bunks.' Irma held the back of her hand against her forehead in a gesture of exhaustion. 'It's filthy, shitty, horrible. I'm sorry. This is what we're reduced to. There's no toilet – we use the bomb crater at the end of the garden. No water. We get that from the standpipe at the end of the road.' She shook her head. 'Let's sit outside in the sun.'

Already the noxious atmosphere of the cellar was oppressing them all. Gratefully they sat on what had been the steps to the front door looking out over the ruins. Occasionally someone would appear, as if out of nowhere, from the underworld and then disappear into some other subterranean refuge. Everywhere were rats, sunning themselves like the humans, foraging, sniffing the air and even mating: it was spring after all. The warm air carried the smell of decomposition. And there were the flies – green, and bigger than any they had seen before. No one said as much, but it occurred to them all that they were sitting in the midst of a necropolis. Under the ruins were countless rotting cadavers – rat food. This spring warmth, that seemed like a blessing, was also a curse, resurrecting the dead in a stinking miasma flecked with flies.

Three nights of dank hospitality were enough. The coughing, the skittering of rats, the drip of condensation and the scratching of the children forced the guests into a private huddle. They had other options: Mimi, her parents in Baden-Baden, and Herr Ferzen, his brother in Munich. Even if they had enough food, which they did not, none could bear to contemplate this Stygian degradation any longer. The sun was shining still as they said goodbye to one another on what remained of the station. The sisters hugged each other long and hard, while Herr Ferzen and his grandson bowed a formal farewell; Herr Ferzen handed Mimi a note but all were conscious that the etiquette of an exchange of addresses was absurd between homeless refugees. Mimi noticed that Tomas was not in control of a lip that trembled with barely disguised emotion. She quietly folded him in her arms and she felt the hotness of his breathing and the damp of his tears though her shirt.

The cattle car they joined was little different from the one they had left – the same stinking oil drum and saturated straw. The passengers were an encapsulation of the greater Reich, now imploding like a deflating bladder. There were Germans, Sudatens from Bohemia and Silesians, as well as Lithuanians and Poles fleeing from their so-called liberators. Despite their hunger and thirst there were no complaints: all were grateful to be heading west with some form of roof over their heads. Moans and screams accompanied them from the cars in front, where wounded soldiers lay in the agony of gangrene without penicillin or anaesthetic. They began to lose track of the days: endless unexplained waits in sidings; less and less food: potatoes, turnips in a thin gruel and bread so coarse that it was questionable if the grains of flour outnumbered the specks of grit; lice they picked off each other like grooming baboons; water with a provenance that resulted in desperate queues for the oil drum and hanging outside the moving train held by two others braced against the doors.

At last they found themselves stationary for nearly a day, near Munich – that much they knew. There was the sound of artillery ahead. The Americans. No one moved. Where should they go? Inertia held them where they were, squinting out of air vents and crowding round the door as jeeps and Sherman tanks – insubstantial compared with the familiar panzers – churned past. The soldiers were preoccupied, eyes sweeping the track ahead. A crack. The driver of a jeep screamed and held his neck. A tank's gun elevated. The crash of the gun was almost instantaneously followed by the collapse of a water-tower that spilled water and the field-grey figure of a sniper on to the ground below.

Mimi observed the Americans with curiosity. She watched them relax as they realised the sniper had been alone. They were bigger than she had expected – not fat, but with large behinds. Their uniforms were worn carelessly, with chinstraps flapping and belts of ammunition slung as casual sashes. Their jaws worked constantly on gum. Cigarettes dribbled smoke from the edges of mouths, spreading the exotic smell of unfamiliar Virginia tobacco. They glanced at the train and its cargo of privation with limited interest, as at the commonplace. They were men, she realised, who had survived and were now on what everyone knew was the last furlong. Days of heroism were over. Survival was everything. They seemed oblivious to the hundreds of hungry eyes watching them from the train as they traded candy-bars and worked dirty fingers into cans of rations, exchanging banter while still scanning their surroundings for danger. One man leaning on a jeep caught her eye. He looked at her in a way that was unfamiliar, with neither pity nor sexual interest. She recognised, in her filth and malnutrition, that she was only a curiosity; theoretically human, but separated by a chasm of deprivation from his world.

Orders came through on a radio and the soldiers moved on, leaving the train in a limbo of uncertainty. Low-level aircraft in pairs criss-crossed the marshalling yard and in the distance there was the crackle of small-arms fire. A jeep appeared driven by a soldier and bearing a railway official in uniform who dismounted to speak to the train driver. The train began to reverse and tendrils of smoke from the locomotive kept pace with the wagons as it backed alongside a fortified barbed-wire fence. The familiar smell of death mixed with the coal-smoke. Through the haze of steam and smoke, the outline of a mound of rags and limbs defined itself, half as tall as the fence itself: shaven skulls, legs with swollen joints and emaciated thighs, torsos of projecting ribs and buttocks of sagging skin. Some were clothed in stripped pyjamas; most were naked. One man, or was it a woman, stared at them, head thrown back, eyes wide open and mouth stretched into a rictus. The stench was all-enveloping, an almost tangible thing that provoked dry retching from empty stomachs. Three more mounds, one half as high again, stretched parallel to the train behind the fence. Another two jeeps appeared. These soldiers had none of the casual indifference of those they had encountered earlier. An officer, a burly man with a crew cut and a limp, jumped out and shouted at the open doors of the train in graceless German that spat hard fury. They could make out scatological references to Hitler and Germans. He repeated himself along the train, followed by others whose expressions contained the same fury and disgust, boys from small-town America who now knew what they had been fighting against. Mimi overheard one of them speaking German and as he passed the step of the wagon she raised her arm to get his attention. His carbine was pointed at her as she asked where they were. He looked her up and down. 'Dachau,' he answered and spat on her arm.

16

Baden-Baden, Western Germany. May 1945

The wireless hummed into life and martial music, a solemn dirge, crackled into the room.

The man, thin of face and mouth with a faint moustache dusting his upper lip, sat upright in a writing chair staring at the gauze covering the speaker. Neatness was his dominant characteristic, from the narrow stiff collar and black tie, down to the two-tone shoes that were used to care and attention. His thin grey hair was cut short at the sides and parted in the middle giving a boyish caste to an expression that was anything but: a professional man without doubt, in need of the certainties and order that a profession imposed. He was expressionless – except for a working of the mouth that was followed by a compression of the lips every thirty seconds or so. He was unconscious of this facial quirk. His wife was cut from different cloth. Dark, with no grey in hair that was tied up in a bun, she was rounded – but not with the fleshiness of a peacetime diet; rather, there was a hollowness to her. Grief may have played a part. It was doing so now as she held a handkerchief to her mouth. There had been beauty there once – but it was lost now in pouches and empty folds of flesh. The warmth in her had struggled to survive in a cold climate.

Mimi sat in a velvet-covered armchair with her head back against a white lace antimacassar. Her hands were on her lap and her legs crossed. One leg was bandaged. Her face showed malnutrition and scorch scars that were pink-white. She knew the precise place of each object in the room: indeed, if she had returned blind she would have been able to lay her hand on everything, without hesitation. The room was wood, velvet, leather and brown; clean, antiseptically so; smelling of polish – and unchanged since the prosperity of the antebellum empire: a museum, a shrine even, to those days of *haute bourgeois* certainty. No books intruded.

Mimi stared out of the window where tendrils of wisteria were knocking against the panes, driven by the stirrings of a spring shower that was already clearing to allow through brittle splinters of sun. This had once been her home. It provided security now: a refuge from being a refugee. But the cost was high. It suffocated her. She observed her parents almost as if she was seeing them for the first time, as an adult without the filter of childhood. She saw the interdependence of cold and hot. She saw a love of order at the expense of right. She saw mourning for the lost security of their youth and their son. She saw bewilderment and fear at the new unknown; guilt well buried; love imperfectly shown. She saw their vulnerability and felt the affection of understanding rather than the imperative of filial obligation.

The music stopped. A fizzle of interference and then the voice of the announcer: 'The Führer.'

There was a rustle of paper. How many times had they sat like this awaiting the metallic Austrian tones of the magician? She remembered the excitement that carried you along with it, the vision he conjured up and the sense of belonging.

'Grand Admiral Doenitz.'

'My people . . . ' the voice was military, from the north. 'My task today is a heavy one' . . . he coughed . . . ' I have today signed the instrument of surrender of all German forces, sea, land and air. Orders have gone to all . . . '

As the details came out in brusque sentences, clipped, in control, Mimi watched her parents. Her father blinked but betrayed no emotion. Her mother stared at the wireless as at a malevolent messenger, her hand and handkerchief against her mouth. There was a pause. Interference. The next words were lost in a crashing wave. ' . . . courage and resilience. We are now in the hands of the victors. May they show magnanimity. Long live Germany!' There was a knock of a hand against a microphone. Music. The last bars faded and they carried on staring. Her mother sobbed. Her father stood. He swayed slightly before reaching out to the off-dial. There was silence, except for the smack of flowers on a pane and the splatter of rain.

'Twice.' There was a catch in his voice. 'Twice in a lifetime.' He sat down again and turned his face away.

Mimi had never seen him cry before. She felt an anger stirring in her; anger at his self-pity. She spoke with its traces in her voice. 'Thank God it's over. At long last.'

His shoulders straightened but he didn't turn round to face his daughter. 'Once maybe . . . but twice. We don't deserve this. After all we've sacrificed!'

Mimi stood up. She wanted to give him time to tend his pride and dry his eyes; and herself time to force down the ire inside her. She walked to the window and stood in the sudden harsh sunlight. There was still anger in her voice. 'After all we've sacrificed?'

'What do you mean?'

'You know what I mean, papa.'

'Stop this. Stop, please.'

Mimi turned towards her mother who was holding an imploring hand towards her. She hesitated, chewed her lip and shook her head. 'No, mama, I won't. No. How can papa say that we deserve anything other than what's happened.'

'It was war!'

'And who started it?'

Father and daughter stared at each other. Both their voices were raised: a new and shocking thing. Both shifted their gaze away from the other.

He answered. 'If you're threatened, then you have the right to self-defence.'

Mimi shook her head. 'Papa. Who attacked whom? Did Poland, or France, or England, or Greece, or Russia attack us?'

'The Comintern would have: the Bolsheviks made no secret of their aim of world domination. Now it looks like they've got it.'

Mimi stared at him, shaking her head again in disbelief. 'You're a lawyer, papa. If you heard that logic in court, you'd tear it apart. They have us at their mercy because we attacked them . . . and lost . . . '

'If we hadn't declared war on America . . . '

'Yes, it was the Americans . . . ' Her mother looked triumphant.

Mimi turned back to the window. She longed for a cigarette but breathed deeply instead. Part of her just wanted to go back to bed, to leave this for another day. The exhaustion she felt was all-enveloping. But after three months of suffering and pondering, lonely self-searching thoughts stirred inside and seeped out. 'And the camps?'

'Propaganda!'

'No.'

'Child, truth is the first victim of war.'

'No!' She turned back to face him. 'So was I lying about Dachau?'

'It was the end of hostilities. It happened after the last war – no food, malnutrition. My sister died then. She was skin and bone, too.'

'Can't you see the difference?'

'No. No, I can't. It's war. Everything broken down; no food, no medicine. You should blame the bombing.'

She hobbled back to her chair. Her leg ached. She sat back and stretched it out, settling her gaze on the window, anywhere but on her parents. Her father continued to stand and his wife to wipe her reddened eyes. There was a weary resignation in Mimi's voice. 'You know where I've been, don't you? Well? Over the last three months I have seen terrible things . . . terrible, terrible things; things you might understand, papa: you were at Verdun. I've told you about Dachau, but I haven't told you about the Polish woman on the train.'

He stared at her. 'And what lies did she tell you.'

Mimi forced herself to ignore his taunt. 'It was after we had seen Dachau. We had assumed she was German; she seemed to understand what we were saying, though she never spoke. She was unaffected by what we'd seen, unlike the rest of us. I asked her why. She turned out to be Polish; a simple woman – she kept us awake with the endless rattling of her rosary. She'd survived the occupation by doing laundry for the SS in a camp that they'd set up in the countryside nearby. She said it was called Treblinka. It wasn't a huge camp, because it wasn't a prison. It was a place where they killed people; not in hundreds, but hundreds of thousands; Jews mainly; from the ghettos of the occupied territories; whole families.'

Her mother shook her head with her handkerchief once again pressed against her mouth. 'It's not possible.'

'Apparently it wasn't so efficient at first. They started by shooting them. She said they could hear the sound of gunshots all day long. And they buried them. But there were too many, and the decomposing bodies created so much methane that the earth moved and the smell became intolerable. So they started to burn them instead, on griddles above fires in massive pits. They dug up all the ones they'd tried to bury and burned them as well.'

'Did she see this?' Her father's tone was that of the cross-examining lawyer.

'No. It was carefully disguised behind trees and hedges with a little station decorated with flowers. But the SS men would boast to her about it. They told her about the change of killing method. Gas. She saw a new building go up and the sound of shooting stopped; but the flames and the smoke and, Mama, the smell, continued. It was a killing factory where old people, women, children and babies were stripped, killed and burned and their possessions stolen within a couple of hours of their arrival. That's what she told me.'

'She was lying, of course. What do you expect of a Pole? You're naïve.' Her father's mouth was pursing and twisting more than usual.

'Why should she? Why shouldn't I believe her after what I'd just seen at Dachau? And after what I'd heard from Max about Russia; about what he'd seen in Poland and the Ukraine? There'll be more, papa, much more. So much that I dread what'll happen to us. I really do.'

'But why us? We – and you – haven't killed anyone, have we? We're not responsible for something like that. We had nothing to do with it.'

'You did, papa. You were a member of the Party. You went to rallies in the early days. You, a lawyer, welcomed the Nuremburg laws that reduced Jews to nothing in Germany. You both welcomed the war.'

'So did you.'

Mimi looked at her parents, and then away. She nodded wearily. 'Yes. I did. No. That's not quite true. I cheered the *Anschluss*. I loved the idea of a greater Germany and the union with Austria – and bringing the Sudetenland back. But the rest of Czechoslovakia? Poland? The others? No.'

'But you were a Party member . . . you were a Nazi too.'

There was a pause, filled by the sweep of another shower.

'Yes. Yes, I was. Still am, I suppose. I never resigned.'

She felt the catch in her voice and despised it for the self-pity there. She sensed her mother moving forward in her chair and felt her hand on her hair. Comforting. Or was it a complicitous attempt to fold her back into a *faux*-collective innocence? Not wanting to hurt her, Mimi moved her head forward slowly enough not to suggest spurning, but firmly enough to establish a rejection.

She turned to face them both. They looked old to her. She asked them. 'How did we get from there . . . to here? I could – but I'm not going to – claim youth. I was young – and really didn't know anything else. But I do now. But you? Why do you still believe in him?'

Her father did not answer immediately. He looked down at the backs of his hands as if he was inspecting his fingernails. 'What had democracy given us – except poverty and humiliation?'

'But, papa, the violence? The Jews? You're a lawyer . . . '

'I know. I've thought about that. Often. But it was a revolution. And revolutions are violent. And we were dealing with violent people.'

'But the Jews?'

'He was much too extreme on that, I agree. But there was some sense in what he said. We could see them every day flaunting their wealth when . . . when I had to sell your mother's engagement ring . . . to feed the family. And so many of the really dangerous Communists were Jews. But we always felt uncomfortable about that, didn't we, dear?'

His wife nodded and added: 'Yes; that was always difficult for us. We had many Jewish friends. My best friend at school was Jewish. But she and her husband emigrated in 1935 – as did nearly all the Jews we knew. I suppose they were the ones who could afford to. Kristallnacht was shocking. Horrible. We never felt badly towards them. But by that time there was nothing we could do about it. We were powerless. We would have been beaten up ourselves if we had said anything. It was too late by then.'

There was a hiatus. Mimi felt the need to move. The room was becoming oppressive and was darkening once more as black shower-clouds swept past the glittering spring sun. She stood to switch on the electric light but remembered that there was no power, and that while her parents' house was superficially un-damaged and unchanged, the world outside had slipped into the Dark Ages. She limped to the window again. She spoke while looking out on to the garden where the neat beds were now given over to vegetables.

'Wasn't that inevitable? Once you took away all laws, all restraint and handed power over to one man, with the police and the army there to do his bidding, weren't the camps and everything that has happened inevitable?'

Neither answered for a few seconds. Then her mother spoke. 'Yes. Yes, perhaps. But at the time, how could we know? We had no means of knowing.'

'So if you handed a child a loaded gun, you wouldn't be responsible for someone being shot?'

'It wouldn't be murder.'

'No, papa, but it'd be manslaughter at the very least.'

'Your analogy's a distortion. He was a genius. He cured the unemployment. He cleared the streets of the Communists. He gave us back the Rhineland – and brought about the *Anschluss*: you know how wonderful that was even if you were too young to remember what he'd saved us from. We gave him the power to make a difference and he did – beyond our wildest dreams. He gave us hope. Identity. Pride. And victory – there's nothing wrong with that. He gave us back what we'd lost in the last war; restored us to our rightful place.'

'So this is our rightful place?'

'Of course not.'

'But, papa, can't you see that all those victories, aggressive victories over just about every country in Europe, led to this . . . this utter disaster? Can't you see? Mama? What about you?'

In contrast to her father, whose carapace of self-justification displayed neither chink nor crack, her mother's was softening – albeit mottled by the tumours of self-pity. 'Disaster? Yes, it is a disaster. Mimi's right, dear. Worse. A catastrophe. At least in the last war, we had an armistice; we were never invaded; or bombed. Now everything's gone – including our son. We're occupied and have no food, no power. Nothing. She's right.' Though she was still holding her handkerchief, she was dry-eyed and staring towards her daughter by the window.

Mimi felt the righteous anger rising again. 'But what about the millions killed and maimed: orphaned children who've seen things that no human should ever see? All those ruined lives that we – yes, we – are responsible for? Don't you feel any disgrace? Don't you think that when you appear in front of the Almighty he might just hold you accountable for some bit of it? It's no good pointing at the SS. It's us too.'

They were silent. Mimi felt a weight of tiredness and sadness. Perhaps it was age. Perhaps the capacity to absorb these body blows to both a personal and national self-worth wasn't possible with age. Age blunted other faculties – so why not self-knowledge? She had hoped that there might be something there that would heal the fissure, bridge the chasm between them. Perhaps time might do it – but time was against them. She could feel disgust welling up and overwhelming filial love. Duty would be there, a duty of care – but only the unleavened chore of obligation.

'Where's your friend?' asked her mother.

'Still asleep. She's very weak. I don't think she'll will be up to much for at least a fortnight.'

'So how long will she be staying here?'

'We'll leave when she's well enough to move.'

'If Eric's a prisoner, he'll probably be home soon – and you must be there to welcome him.'

Mimi shook her head wearily. 'In Breslau? What do you think I would be going back to, mama? There won't be many Germans in Silesia now. If he's alive, he's probably in a camp in Siberia. There's nothing there for me.'

'So where will you go?'

Mimi sighed. 'I don't know. I've . . . No. I need to think it through.'

'As you wish.'

'But how are we going to feed . . . your friend?'

Mimi had almost forgotten her father was in the room. 'You've got food, papa.'

'If we are careful it will last us, but not if . . . '

'. . . if you give too much to your daughter and the friend who saved her life?'

Lines of definition blurred around the room as if through the skin of a bubble. The rush of rain on the window rattled the frame. She turned and faced him. She was expecting to see wounded pride behind the iron self-control. Instead she saw the muscles in his face relax and a tear rolling down his face.

'Forgive me. How could I say such a thing? My dear, please; please forgive me.'

Mimi went up to him. They put a hand on each other's shoulders and lent towards one another with their heads just touching, ear to ear. She felt a tear on her arm. This was more emotion than he had ever shown with her – but intimacy takes time and practice: formality held them apart.

They disengaged awkwardly as he dabbed his eyes. 'You, and Eva, must stay as long as you like. We'll find food. I have cigarettes – no, my dear, I haven't taken up smoking – which we can barter for food. And summer's near – so there'll be vegetables. We have our house – which is more than many can say. There it is.'

He glanced at his fob watch, fully recovered now. Mimi recognised the gesture. She was sure he used it with his clients to signify that their time was up and that he needed to move on to other matters. The emotion was forgotten and the uncomfortable questions filed away. If there had been a newspaper, he would now be reading it with the focus and exclusion of a tidy mind. A part of Mimi envied this coping mechanism that enabled him to glimpse his part in an all-embracing evil and, ten minutes later, armour himself so completely against the consequences. She felt her own rawness the more for it. Her leg hurt. There was nowhere further to go.

'I'm going up to see Eva.'

'There'll be some soup for lunch. Potato.'

'Thank you, mama.'

As she left the room she glanced back. They were both looking at the rain that was running in rivulets down the casements. Her mother reached out and put her hand on her father's arm. His mouth pursed but he made no acknowledgement, his carapace intact.

The rain was still beating on the windows and the roof as she opened the door of Eva's attic room. The bare parquet, with only a single bed and a mahogany armoire to baffle the sound, made it difficult to enter softly. It was cold, spartan and drab, except for the blonde of Eva's hair on the pillow. She was asleep. Mimi sat carefully on the bed and watched her. The last year had left its marks: burns – now healing; hair – flat and lifeless; skin – looser and lined; dark patches under the eyes. In sleep, the vitality that was her calling card evaporated and left her with the face of a woman twice her age, wilted and drained. She opened her eyes without waking, closed them again and tilted her head the other way to display a livid and still-scabbed scar above her ear.

Mimi waited. She sat for half an hour, happy to be next to her sleeping friend and away from the strained ambivalence below. Despite the low ceilings of the attic and the tunnelled narrowness of the dormer window, an oppressiveness was lifted from her and she sat patiently, attuned to every domestic sound and allowing her mind to settle. She stirred and Eva woke. They smiled at each other as Eva levered herself against the pillows.

'It's over. Doenitz was on the wireless.'

Eva struggled a hand from under the eiderdown and placed it on her friend's arm. 'I didn't think we'd make it.'

'Nor me.'

'Why us?'

'I don't know. Just luck, I think.'

Eva raised her head off the pillow but sank back. 'I feel so weak I can't imagine ever being strong again. You?'

Mimi's eyes meandered along the wall behind the bed. 'I think so. Yes. No. My parents . . . I don't like them. Is that a terrible thing to say?' Eva squeezed her arm. 'After Doenitz had finished, I told them about what the Polish woman told us. What was I expecting? Shock? Horror? I got a bit of those. Denial? I certainly got that. Acknowledgement? Nothing. I think I was prepared, but . . . it was disappointing. No. Worse than that. What I realise is that they're just two among millions: regretful to be sure. But mistakes: that's what they regret; the fact that they didn't win. Even knowing what they know now, they would be amnesiac about it if we were still on top. They, and all those millions, don't have any shame because they just don't think it's got anything to do with them. Maybe it's a coping mechanism. How do you take on board that you've been party to mass-murder in your old age? Maybe acknowledging requires time you don't have; time to change things; about yourself; to give yourself a new moral compass.' Mimi drew a circle with her finger on the starched sheets. 'The problem is that I don't think it is about old age: I think that if you went around all the stinking cellars in Germany's bombed-out cities – or you spent some time in the prisoner-of-war camps – they'd say the same thing . . . "if only". The truth is just too squalid. Is that right?'

Eva chewed the inside of her mouth. 'I think it's too early. And you're too harsh. There's only so much you can cope with. And dealing with the fact that all this suffering and sacrifice was for something monstrously criminal is too much – for now. They'll have to confront it at some point – but I can see why people like your parents can't do it now. I'm not sure I can.'

Mimi placed her other hand on her friend's arm. She was not smiling as she replied, 'But you don't have anything to be ashamed of. You always saw him for what he was. You did something about it – what you could anyway. Me? I worshipped him.'

'You were a child then.'

'But I carried on. I was like my parents. I ignored the violence. I talked about means and ends and didn't have the sense to see where that awful phrase leads. And when I did realise, I didn't do anything except shut myself off in Silesia as a lady of the manor. Just reading; that's all I did. What did Thomas à Kempis say? Something like: "When it comes to judgement day, we'll be asked what we did . . . not what we read." '

'What could you have done?'

'More. Much more. Or certainly less – I didn't even have the guts to resign from the Party. You didn't know I was a member did you? I joined on my sixteenth birthday. A nasty little secret that'll come and bite me soon, I'm sure. Even when I knew what we'd got ourselves into, I did nothing. Did you ever meet Missie Vassiltchikov? She is . . . was probably – she must be dead – a White Russian settled in Germany. Her sister is Princess Tatiana Metternich whose husband,

Paul, has . . . had . . . a huge estate not too far from us, in the Sudetanland. Eric knew him well and they both came to stay for a weekend early in the war. Missie's a wonderful person: beautiful inside and out. Her great friend was Adam von Trott, and even then they were plotting, trying to do something. I can't believe she's survived as she must have been up to her neck in the bomb plot. That weekend she asked me to help. I refused – or rather I didn't do anything. Why? I was scared. I just talked about it to those I could trust and shook my head . . . but did nothing. Nothing. I'm so ashamed.'

A silence descended. Mimi was aware of the steady weight of her friend's hand on her arm and was grateful for it.

'So what will you do now?' Eva asked.

'Over the next few weeks? Stay here with you until you're better . . . then . . . I don't know. Maybe . . . no. What about you?'

'Neither of us has got a home to go back to. I don't know. Anywhere where there'll be Americans rather than Russians – the British will be too correct – and too poor for an old tart like me. And the French too angry. Maybe I'll get myself a handsome GI and make babies in New Jersey.' She laughed but it turned to coughing. Mimi handed her a glass of water, over which she spluttered, before falling back on the pillows once again, breathing heavily, fighting the scarring of her lungs. She contemplated her friend. 'You want to try and find him, don't you?'

Mimi nodded.

'What do . . . ?'

'What do I think I'll find? I don't know. I can guess. I've been guessing for months. I've played out every scenario. Wife. Wife alive. Wife dead. Children. Him dead. Him missing. Quite reprehensively careless that one – both a husband and a lover missing. Him welcoming me. Him ignoring me. Cold. Hot. Guilt. Explanations. Lynched maybe. It's mad – but if I don't do it, I think I'll go mad. It's funny, isn't it? I really didn't think this happened – this obsession thing. I can't get him out of my head. Have you ever had that?'

'No. Not like that. I've been crazy about a couple of them – but then they treated me like shit . . . and I realised that they were . . . shits. I just want one who'll be nice to me. Cook for me when I feel like this. Be my friend.'

'I had just that: a husband who was my friend; someone who cared for me, loved me; kind and gentle. But I want more; you want less. I dream and daydream about him, about the sex. It's like an ache. Even when we were so cold, hungry and ill on the train, I was thinking about him. The fucking. It'll go – I'm sure these things do. But it almost hurts it's so strong. And yet I hardly know him – at least, some of the more important things – other than where he lives and his name. We ignored all that; just left it to one side. Does that sound strange? It is strange. But it didn't seem so then. I suppose it allowed us to be irresponsible. It was like a bath in forgetfulness – guiltless. Of course there's a wife. Maybe. Though I hope not. I have to keep thinking that. Talk about self-delusion.'

She gave a wry smile and squeezed Eva's hand. 'I certainly give old tarts a run for their money, don't I?'

'If it's a numbers' game, you're not even in it.'

They laughed. Eva shifted sideways allowing Mimi to lie next to her with her legs on the bed. They stared at the ceiling where a spider was elaborating its web.

Eva spoke. 'So you'll just turn up and say, "Here I am"?'

'I suppose so. I don't know.'

'How will you get there? What will you survive on?'

'I picked the diamonds out of my jewellery: Reichmarks aren't going to count for much now. I want you to have some.' Eva squeezed her hand. 'As for travelling . . . the whole of Europe's going to be on the move over the next months: labourers going home, prisoners, Jews that survived. I'll just be one more destitute – without papers or possessions. I could be Jewish, couldn't I? Dark enough. A French Jew. A Nazi French Jew. How about that?'

There was no humour in her laugh.

'Is your French good enough?'

'I think so. I have an Alsatian accent – which the French make fun of. But if I'm Jewish too . . . .'

'And Eric?'

'I don't know. I just don't know. I've got to do this, even if I get there and find Jerome curled up with his wife. At least I'll know . . . know that it isn't an option. Then what? God knows.'

'Eric's dead. No word for nearly a year: he must be.'

'So I won't feel guilty?'

'Yes.'

'It doesn't work like that. You know it doesn't.'

'I know. But there's only so much you can blame yourself for. We're weak – both of us. You know that. It's like waking up in the early hours and trying to work through a problem: it's too black. But in the morning it feels solvable. Look at us: burned; starved; me with dysentery – neither of us has had a period for months. We both look a hundred and fifty. You need to get yourself well, get that bloom back. When you do, you'll be able to cope, make better decisions and see the wood for the trees. Don't rush this, darling. Please.'

There was silence in the room filled by the distant calling voice of Mimi's mother. Neither woman moved as they watched the spider escalading a gossamer thread that trembled to an imperceptible draft.

'Two weeks. You'll be better then. Then I'll go. I have to. You know that, don't you?' The pressure of affirmation again on her arm. 'I'll get you some soup.'

17

FRANCE

Montreuil. Three and a half years earlier. August 1941

When she missed her second period, Marie-Louise knew that she was pregnant. The first she put down to the trauma of Adam's death. It dealt her a blow that manifested itself in a physical collapse, a nervous breakdown so complete that she was unable to leave the house for nearly three weeks. The doctor was called to investigate the symptoms but was only able to mutter about fever and, like some medieval apothecary, prescribe herbal remedies, substitutes for the drugs that were now in such short supply. Her father, with surprising tenderness and devotion, was always at her bedside and nursed her selflessly. She was aware of his presence in the deep of the night and the gentleness of his kiss on her forehead as he slipped away to sleep.

When she had recovered enough to leave her bedroom and the weather permitted, she sat outside in the garden, opting for a cane chair under the spread of an apple tree, where the dappled light through half-closed eyes soothed her and the branches protected her from the prying eyes that she felt were accusing her on every side. With no society other than her father and Bernadette, she lacked any sense of perspective and her fears multiplied in the vacuum. She was sick in the mornings and there was an unfamiliar tenderness in her breasts. At first, she recognised neither of these symptoms for what they were as she simply lacked the basic knowledge of physiology to draw the correct conclusions: her mother had never been the sort of woman to discuss such things, and her only intimate friend, Ghislaine, was both childless and now estranged from her. As the heights of summer were scaled, the realisation slowly dawned on her, nearly tipping her once more into the state of nervous collapse that had become a refuge from her inner conflicts. But the knowledge also provided a counteracting balm to the grief that she had had to shoulder alone. She began to nurture the quickening being inside her as a sort of compensation for what she had lost. So, while the practical realities increasingly filled her with horror, the desolation of loss was softened. For her there would be no seeking out of a woman in Boulogne, rumours of whose services she had heard whispered among the more risqué female elements of Montreuil.

The apples were fully formed on the tree and some were scattered on the ground around her chair when she decided to tell her father. There was no one else. He had formed the habit of joining her in her private bower between noon and lunchtime. He would bring another chair and sit opposite her in a collarless shirt; having kissed her good-morning, he would read his newspaper and smoke – mainly in silence, though occasionally he would remark on something in the news and invite her opinion. She noticed that there was a subtle change in the way he now engaged with her. Instead of a brusque statement of fact, he would phrase it as an opinion that invited a dialogue. She realised that this was a conscious effort. When she looked up and caught him staring at her with the fear of loss in his eyes, she realised that he loved her, however imperfectly, and was moved by it. Even so, she dreaded the moment of telling him. He was staring into the middle distance with his newspaper on his knee when she spoke.

'Papa, I have something to tell you. Something very difficult.' He looked at her, his expression unchanged. 'Papa, I think I'm pregnant.'

'The German?'

She started in surprise and swallowed hard. 'Yes.'

He nodded thoughtfully. 'I should have guessed. Are you sure?'

'Yes.'

'I knew it was connected – your illness – and his death. Too much of a coincidence.' He lit a cigarette and looked away again. 'Where?'

'Paris.'

He nodded again. 'So what are we going to do?' The 'we' caught Marie-Louise wrong footed. She had been expecting anger at the least; certainly scorn and perhaps worse, a cold bleakness. 'He was an exceptional young man. I can see that. I would have been happy to have had him as my son-in-law . . . in other circumstances. But we have some thinking to do . . . in these circumstances. Does anyone else know? That friend of yours?' She shook her head. 'Good. That's good. She's a gossip.'

Marie-Louise knew this was a calumny – but held her peace.

'You won't . . . ?'

'No, papa. Never.'

'It would be a mortal sin. You know that, don't you?'

She nodded.

'Let me think about it. Lunch will probably help us both. I'll get Bernadette to bring it out here; we must enjoy the summer while it lasts.'

He shook his head as he walked towards the house, leaving his daughter watching his back – the characteristic limp an eloquent reminder of his *Croix de Guerre*. Not for the first time he had surprised her, showing her a side of himself that she had never glimpsed before. Experience told her that such a revelation was often followed by a comment or observation of such insensitivity and cruelty that it was better to stay on the defensive than let down one's guard. But she sensed that this was different, that something had changed; that fear had crept into his soul: not the fear of pain or of what another human could do, but the fear of the barren heart of loneliness. She felt a soothing sense of fatality. The burden was shared and, for the first time in weeks, she relaxed and allowed herself to be caressed by the late summer sun as she waited for her father to return. When he did, he remained standing but leant against the tree, nursing a cigarette that he neglected to light, looking at her thoughtfully.

'Your grandmother. I'll write to your grandmother. She'll help.'

'But papa . . . '

'I know what you're thinking. How can a bedridden old lady help? A rather religious old lady.' Her grandmother had mass said in her bedroom daily and Marie-Louise had never spoken to her without the background tic-tac of a rosary. Her mantilla was worn more often than her hat. 'You're old enough to know something about her, something that your mother only found out about a few years ago when she was nursing her through one of her illnesses.

You wouldn't know that she and your grandfather weren't happy: he wasn't an easy man, and she was often ill – psychosomatic, probably. Over some years she formed an attachment to her doctor. They saw each other every day – and one thing led to another. In due course a child was born – a half-sister to your mother – much younger. Your grandfather, as you know, was killed in the trenches – when she was only three months pregnant. Appearances were kept up – but the child died when she was only three, of influenza, after the war. She always took that as being God's punishment for her adultery. She's never ceased mourning that child. I suspect that the chance to assist you would be an atonement of sorts – a replacement perhaps. What do you think?'

His daughter was looking at him in astonishment. He smiled wryly at her. 'It's . . . a bit surprising, I agree. But there it is. Life.'

'What are you suggesting, papa?'

'I'm suggesting that you go and stay with your grandmother in Honfleur until the baby's born. You obviously can't stay here. No one, no one must know that the father was a Boche – certainly not her. We can think of some story – this won't be the first or last time that this sort of thing has happened in wartime. When the baby's born, we can arrange for it to be looked after – if we give it a dowry, so to speak. There'll certainly be some peasant family who'll be delighted to take it on. You can then come back to Montreuil, fully recovered from your "illness", and no one – not Jerome, not anyone – need ever know.'

Marie-Louise stroked the back of her hand as she listened, with her eyes on the moss-covered roots of the tree.

'Thank you, papa.'

At that moment Bernadette's bustle insinuated itself. They both watched as she laid a small table between them and placed ham and bread alongside a jug of water. Michel Annecy's contacts still protected them from the food shortages that were now the common lot of France. As they ate, Marie-Louise thought calmly for the first time in weeks. She knew her father's plan was the only sensible one – logical and practical. What else could she do? But deep inside, physically and figuratively, she couldn't tidy away the end, the entity that was part of her and of the gentle human being that was no more. Her father could never understand that – certainly not now – so she quietly finished her lunch without raising the subject again.

Three weeks later she boarded the train for Honfleur. Movement within the occupied zone was severely restricted and permission to move to a port required military papers that even the mayor of Montreuil found a challenge. The headmaster, teachers and numerous friends had sent messages enquiring after her health. This, and the chattering gossip of Bernadette, gradually allayed her fears. She realised that no one in the town, other than Ghislaine, had any idea of the truth. Whatever her fears for the future, the present was safe enough in the taciturn hands of her father. She walked to the station on his arm, with him carrying her suitcase. Though her illness had been mental, its legacy was physical: thin and weak, she asked him to wait while she sat and rested half a dozen times during the downhill walk from their house. Those who saw them stopped, raised their hats and wished her well, their expressions of disquiet reflecting concern, not disapproval.

The station was a marshalling yard for poultry and portable livestock as much as for humankind. The lack of fuel for transport meant that every carriage was a clucking, squawking, squealing bestiary, the luggage racks shedding feathers, fur-balls and the occasional squirt of something worse. Unwashed clothes and bodies meant that travel was not for the squeamish. Her father found her a corner next to a window and remonstrated with a leathery woman displaying a single brown tooth to move a basket containing a goose from the bench to the floor. He kissed her goodbye without emotion, though, as Marie-Louise watched him walk away, she noticed him remove a handkerchief from his pocket, move it to his face and return it before she lost sight of him.

The journey through the Normandy countryside lasted most of the day, stops at each small town involving a loading and dis-charging that took up to half an hour. The slatted seat became unbearable, and no position was comfortable by the time the churning locomotive ground along the Seine estuary and into Honfleur. Marie-Louise was faint with exhaustion when she was met by her grandmother's housekeeper on the platform and ushered into a pony-drawn trap for the final kilometres to the house that stood in its own demesne on the edge of the town. The good-natured woman talked incessantly, but Marie-Louise only half took in her prattling through the light-headedness that she could feel creeping up on her; so much so that, by the time they were outside the house, she had to be helped inside and put to bed before seeing her grandmother.

It was nearly noon the next day when she woke. Even after washing in the cold water of the washstand and breathing in the cool sea air of early autumn through an open window, she still felt the heaviness of sleep. The sugar from a madelaine, left on a tray by her bed, restored her but she was still not herself as she approached her grandmother's bedroom door.

Isabelle Gurlaine was not that old – barely sixty-five – but illness had scarred her; and nearly a quarter of a century of solitary living had nurtured her eccentricity. Michel Annecy insisted that, even before her extended convalescence, she had never been entirely conventional. Like many people of independent means – her parents had died young leaving her rich by provincial standards – she had been able to cultivate a hobby to the point of obsession, hers being parrots and parakeets. As Marie-Louise knocked on the door, there was a storm of squawking that would have terrified the uninitiated. With the benefit of experience, she eased the door ajar and felt the downdraft from beating wings as birds that habitually roosted on the door-frame bestirred themselves and hovered in panic over her head. The avian smell hit her as she stepped smartly in, closing the door behind her to avoid the fury of the old lady if one of her beloved flock slipped into the corridor.

Her grandmother was sitting upright, in the bedclothes that she always wore – a *belle époque* lace nightdress and a black silk shawl. Her hair was piled high on her head in the style of the *faubourg* during the period before the Great War, powdered and pinned with combs, its texture and colour that of straw. Over it, in the style of a Velázquez grandee, she wore the mantilla she assumed for the daily mass that was celebrated by a long-suffering priest who put up with the swoop and chatter of dozens of parrots in return for a stipend that was more than generous. His cassock needed a weekly clean to rid it of the streaks of excreta that were the curious cross he had to bear.

The old lady held out her arms and smiled a smile of gappy yellowed gums: she was not good at remembering to put in her false teeth. 'My poor dear. Come here and kiss me.'

Marie-Louise held her breath as she was pulled into a sickly embrace of perfume and powder, conscious of the dry crêpiness of the cheek as it touched hers. Her grandmother held her hands as she examined her.

'You look terrible, my dear – much too thin and pale. I was the same in your condition though. It never agreed with me; couldn't eat a thing; sick all the time. Now sit down and I'll ask Francine to bring us some coffee – and something delicious to tempt you; and something for all the darlings here.' She made a gesture that might have been a benediction in other circumstances. 'Sit yourself down,' she patted the bed next to her, 'and *raconte, chérie*. I want to hear all about Montreuil. The last time I was there was for your wedding. So beautiful: you, the church, the whole day. I don't think I'll be visiting again though – my doctor would never allow it. So you must tell me everything. Not everything. Your father has explained, and I won't pry. But it's what happens when you marry an atheist, you know. Don't get me wrong, my dear, I like your husband, but I disapprove of him. Come. Sit down.'

Marie-Louise sat on the edge of the bed as her grandmother reached for the handbell beside her and rang it with a vigour that set off a chorus of protests around the room. She then opened the drawer beside her bed and extracted a jar of corn, the contents of which she scattered over a tray on the floor, whistling through her few remaining teeth and calling down a skirl of wings and snapping beaks. Marie-Louise watched this familiar scene from her child-hood fondly: the visits to this kindly but alarming woman were a child's delight – but disconcerting as her attention weaved between some perceived imperfection or misdemeanour and suffocating affection. After she had fussed with further crumbs and instructed the maid, whose status as a neophyte in her current employment was demonstrated by her wide-eyed panic at the parrot settling on her shoulder and nibbling her ear, she focused again on her granddaughter. There was shrewdness in her gaze.

'Do you love this man?'

Marie-Louise found that she could not hold her grandmother's eye.

'Yes. I did. But he's dead.'

'Ah! Your father didn't mention that. My darling child, I'm so sorry. War: it's a terrible thing. Do we never learn? You'd have thought that after the terrible suffering last time things might change. But men like to fight – leaving us women to pick up the pieces. And your husband – my dear, what's his name? – thank you – knows nothing, I presume?'

'No. Only you and papa. No one else.'

'Good. I've spoken to Father Pierre about the situation. I put him under the oath of the confessional so that I can use his contacts in the orphanage to find a suitable family. Madame Verdin and Francine have been told that you are to stay with me for your confinement and then will go back to join your father with the baby – which is, of course, your husband's – once you're well enough to go. I'll look after you properly, my dear; don't you worry.'

Marie-Louise gave her a fragile smile that was halfway to tears – tears of gratitude and of sadness that was only just below the surface.

Her grandmother squeezed her hand. 'We have some months to talk, my dear. There's no hurry and you must only tell me what you want to tell me. I won't pry, I promise you. I have to say that when I got the letter from your father, I was delighted. Not for you, of course, but selfishly for me as I don't have much company – educated company that is. Sermons only go so far. I'm looking forward to getting to know you better now that you're no longer a child. But you must eat. Where is that silly girl?'

The old lady reached once again for her bell and rang it with an added fury that set off a cacophony of bird-squeals.

Over the following months, as the baby grew inside her, they spent hours every day in each other's company. The old lady insisted that Marie-Louise attended the daily mass that took place at eleven in the morning. To the uninitiated there was a surreal quality to the proceedings. A handsome macaw made it his business to sit on the edge of the small table that doubled as an altar and mimic random Latin words. His *pièce de résistance* was an almost word-perfect first line of the Ave Maria – and a wolf-whistle at the solemn moment of consecration. Neither the priest nor Isabelle Gurlaine seemed to notice, but the whistle gave Marie-Louise the giggles, bringing down on her head a daily lecture on the sanctity of the moment of transubstantiation from her grandmother – who then promptly forgot what she had been cross about until the next day. They would talk and her granddaughter would read to her until lunch, after which they would part until the hour before dinner that became their time for more intimate exchanges, accompanied by a bottle of local cider as an aperitif.

Marie-Louise told her about Adam – but not that he was German. This was a surprisingly easy fact to omit: she was vague about detail and expansive on his character and the subjects of their hours of discussions. Her grandmother would watch her as she spoke, like many before her captivated by the Renaissance beauty now glowing in the bloom of pregnancy. She was a sympathetic listener, sipping cider and dipping dry bread into her glass as she nodded agreement or waved a finger of interjection or contra-diction – a disconcerting mixture of Proustian grandeur and *haute paysanne*, conservative Catholic of the nineteenth century and earthy pragmatist. One day she fixed her granddaughter with a beady eye and a raised eyebrow.

'You love your husband, don't you? And this other man too? Will this other man and this baby destroy what you have with your husband – even if he never finds out about either of them? Most men are very stupid about these things and are utterly blind until they have it spelt out to them. But there can be a silent poison at work that sours relationships. I've seen it many times. Do you think you can avoid it?'

Marie-Louise looked down at her hands resting on her swelling stomach. 'I don't know, grandmama. I think about it all the time; about Jerome and how he will be when he comes back. He'll be different. War and prison change people – they must. When? Next year. In ten years? Who knows how long this war will go on for? We'll both be different people, don't you think? And we won't have shared these years. I'm frightened that we may have drifted apart anyway. He can be a harsh man and I can't imagine that whatever he's been through will make him softer.'

'Prayer helps with these things, child. You need to pray more. God's grace can make things better. He can repair things between you.'

Marie-Louise looked up. 'But, grandmamma, there's nothing wrong between us. That's the point. This . . . ' she pointed at her belly . . . 'has nothing to do with Jerome. It happened on its own, a thing in its own right. Loneliness and circumstance played their part; of course they did. It was the war. But there was nothing wrong with what Jerome and I had together, I promise you.'

The old lady gave her a sceptical look. 'Love two men at the same time? I don't think so. You must have been unhappy to contemplate . . . well . . . what you did.'

'That's what I always thought would be the case, grandmamma. But Adam . . . he showed me I was wrong; and so are you, I think: not about the guilt – I feel that every day. But everyone has their own take on these things, grandmamma – it doesn't fit into a catechism, because everyone and every circumstance is different. You've had a different life from me, so you've developed different views perhaps.'

'Dangerous thoughts, child. You're saying that there's no right or wrong – only what's good for you. Look where that sort of godless talk's got us. Look!'

Her finger and a cider-sodden piece of bread were raised in emphasis, but Marie-Louise, in a way that she would never have done in the past, stood her ground.

'Papa would say that too, grandmamma; and so would mama if she were still alive. But Adam, and Jerome too, would say that we are where we are because everyone is too certain that they're right. Look at the Communists. Who could be more certain? Father Pierre perhaps? Or Hitler? All I see around me are certainties. And the only certainty, grandmamma, is that they can't all be right, can they?'

'Father Pierre . . . no . . . not him . . . he's a fool . . . a good man, but a fool. No. Father Vincent – a Jesuit – he would say that that was Satan talking. Easy talk. Relative. We're all fallen and in sin, and what you've done is a sin no matter what you say. Your love of your husband is right and blessed by the church and your love for this other man is adultery. Simple. Don't make it more complicated than it is, child. We all sin – that's our nature. We can get forgiveness – which is why we have confession and the Eucharist. But there are rights and wrongs, absolutes, certainties if you like.' She was now warming to her theme, slopping crumb-filled cider on to a bird-stained eiderdown. She stopped to gather her thoughts, waving away a parakeet that was trying to steal the bread in her hand.

'You're right, grandmamma. There are certainties for some people. Maybe your certainties are the right ones. But I'm so surrounded by certainties that they've driven me nearly to madness. I feel overwhelmed by them. I feel guilt for what I may have done to Jerome, to papa and to you. But do I feel that Adam was bad and that our friendship – a deep, deep friendship – was evil; that this baby's a curse? No . . . never. Maybe this is the road to hell. Maybe. But I think that all of us have inside a sort of moral gyroscope that keeps us upright. Father Pierre might say that there are only absolutes – but I just don't believe him. How can I, when what I know in my heart, and what I see with my eyes, says no. He's a good man; but neither he, you, the Pope, nor me, can know everything. We're just humans doing the best we can.'

'Exactly, my dear, exactly. We are humans; fallen angels. That's why it's the eternal teachings of the church, not any human ideas, that are right and proper and the only basis on which to live our lives.'

'But they're human too, aren't they, interpreted and changed by cardinals and popes?'

'But graced by the Holy Spirit; Jesus's words explained and expanded: God's words.'

Marie-Louise shook her head. 'So if the church believes that heretics should be burned at the stake, that witches should be tortured or Jews persecuted, then that's right? Would you do these things if Father Pierre or Father Vincent told you to? Of course you wouldn't! You have your gyroscope – as I do, as does everyone.'

'Those things were a long time ago, in a different age. Then, they really thought that the heretic's body was being burned to save his soul from eternal fire. Maybe they were right. We don't know – and we won't know until we're at God's right hand or in hell – with or without them. Witches? They lived in a time when most things were unexplained. Now science – a gift from God – gives us answers and frightened humans don't have to blame strange old ladies like me for the things that scare them. What you're talking about is fallen human nature being mistaken for God's word. Were the Borgia popes bad men? Of course they were. But that doesn't mean that the teachings of Jesus are bad – only that men don't hear them properly – or choose not to hear them at all. Don't forget that for every heretic burner, there was a St Francis.'

The old lady gummed noisily on a soggy chunk of cider-soaked bread and contemplated her granddaughter who, forehead furrowed in concentration, was gazing at the fire and twisting her fair hair round her fingers. Neither spoke for a few seconds. The younger woman put her cider glass on the side table and gazed at the coal fire that fought the alabaster cold of midwinter outside.

'For every heretic burner, a St Francis? Isn't that just a picture of human nature? For every Beria, there's a Communist idealist; for every Himmler a gentle boy who loves his country. Don't worry, grandmamma, I'm not an atheist. But I'm not Torquemada either. I think I feel God around me – but the noise makes him difficult to hear sometimes. Not the bad noise but the good noise – that's the problem: bad noise would throw him into relief, make him easier to see. It's the good noise – the gentle atheist, the agnostic St Francis – that makes him hard to see. I just don't know. That's my problem – not knowing.'

'So you need to pray, my dear, pray for the grace of faith. It's a gift.'

'But what happens if it isn't given?'

'Just pray for it. It's all you can do.'

'But who to? I need faith; but to get faith I have to pray to someone who I'm not sure is listening, who perhaps isn't there. How long do I have to do that for?'

'Perhaps all your life. The fact that you are questing for it is redemption in itself. Not everyone is given revelation but it's there for everyone to ask for and by asking for it you're in a state of grace. Just keep praying.'

Marie-Louise looked up at her grandmother with a rueful smile and a shake of her head. 'I'll try, grandmamma. But a lifetime seems a long time to spend trying to contact someone who may not be there; and a long time to follow the teachings of a Church that may be God's work on earth but hasn't, in the past, always done good things. Even now it seems lined up behind the Maréchal and against the British. Can that be right? I was given a brain and a gyroscope – wouldn't it be a sin not to use both?'

'That, my dear, could be the sin of pride – thinking that you know better than God; that you don't need God.'

'But if the gyroscope and the brain are in conflict with the Church?'

'Then you must have the humility to submit and acknowledge you're only one person against the revealed word of God and the accumulated wisdom of the fathers of the Church.'

The younger woman furrowed her brow before replying. 'If I have to choose, grandmamma, then I have to follow my gyroscope and my reason. If I have a soul, then that's it – and I would be betraying it unless I did. I'll try praying. Nothing to lose, I suppose. Maybe faith will come and I'll find the true path. All I know now is that there's a lot of bad in the world – and a lot of good. But they all seem muddled up. Like me. I'll just try and do the best I can. What else can I do?'

'Pray, child, pray. That's what you can do.'

Marie-Louise reached out to the bed and took her grandmother's hand in hers, conscious of the bones, veins and the parchment quality of the skin to the touch. A cockatoo on the bed-head fluffed his feathers and both women stared at the glowing coals.

18

Montreuil. Three years later. 4 September 1944

The percussion of artillery echoed from the valley floor, smacking off the walls of the town in a secondary tremor. Anxious eyes peered from shuttered windows of taped glass, fearful and anticipatory. Children pushed up behind the skirts of anxious mothers, eager to look out but pulled back into the shade of rooms prepared for war, with mattresses and tables upended in expectation.

The streets were empty apart from the occasional dash by a young man holding a pistol or rifle that had spent five years in greased hiding under a damp floor. Doors were ajar with alert heads craning towards the Place Gambetta and the *mairie*, where lorries idled and grey uniforms busied themselves. Boxes were being loaded by perspiring men with rolled-up sleeves to the nagging barks of NCOs to speed them on. An older man, tunic wide to the heat of the day, staggered slightly and leant against a pilaster, choleric in colour and breathing with difficulty. He rocked on his heels with his hands on his knees as his comrades pushed by him, one almost knocking him over as he breasted the top step with a pile of files that obscured his view forward. The red-faced man caught himself against the iron guardrail and pushed himself upright with his face to the square.

Marie-Louise could never say whether she saw his neck snap back before she heard the report of a rifle as the man's brains bespattered the peeling render of the wall behind him. He fell backwards against the rails, slumped, with his legs bent and head forward, showing his crudely trepanned cranium to the world. Instantly boxes were dropped and uniforms wriggled under lorries or weaved their way into the shaded hallway of the *mairie*. Gun barrels appeared out of windows above the door and the chatter of machine pistols and the whine of ricochets filled the square.

A channel gouged itself in the side of the shutter next to Marie-

Louise's head. Splintered wood, blue paint and a lead fragment clipped off the wall within the room behind her. She sprang back with her heart pounding. Collecting herself, she moved to the door and on to the landing where her father was standing phlegmatically by the window looking at the same scene.

He spoke without looking at her. 'OK?'

She breathed deeply before replying. 'Yes, but that was close.'

He shrugged the shrug of a veteran and carried on looking obliquely from the window into the chaos of the square. She edged alongside him. The firing had died down to intermittent single shots from two rifle barrels pointing out of the first-floor window above the door. Either honour had been satisfied by the lethal single shot, or the marksman had been killed by the return volley, as no further shots were coming from the windows opposite the *mairie* – out of sight of the Annecys' house. Activity redoubled under the swastika that rippled to the breeze. Now wearing coalscuttle helmets, men hauled the body inside, and more boxes, crates of wine, suitcases and files were slung on to the tailboards of lorries and into the half-track personnel carrier that stood like a squat armadillo alongside the steps. As a refrain, the rumble of artillery rolled again over the town, provoking anxious glances from the scurrying soldiers. Finally, with machine pistols covering his exit, an officer appeared in the doorway. Self-consciously, he stood on the top step adjusting his cuffs for longer than was necessary. He looked deliberately ahead as he descended and returned the salute of the soldier who opened the door into the personnel carrier. Behind him there was no such dignity. Soldiers, and some civilians, dashed for the lorries, pulled inside by outstretched hands, the NCOs shepherding the stragglers and waving down the two marksmen from the upstairs window. One appeared with a cat under his arm. Soldiers, with guns pointing up at the buildings around them, sat on the sills of the lorries, with others hanging on to the canvas frames at the rear and yet more bristling the armoured sides of the carrier. In a cacophony that almost drowned the increasing sound of artillery, the convoy ground its way out of the square in a blue cloud that was mixed and churned into a cocktail of noise and dust that almost obscured individual vehicles.

Marie-Louise and her father looked down on the column from their vantage point: the helmets and guns were now going in the opposite direction from those of that summer of defeat four years before when they had stood by the same window. Anxious eyes scanned buildings and roofs once again – but older, much older, than those of the boys of 1940 whose bones were now scattered over the Russian steppe. They watched the vehicles reach the corner and turn up the hill, leaving behind only a disembodied roar and the gritty smell and taste of diesel fumes. Windows and doors opened. A young man stood on the front step of the house opposite the Annecys' and fired a pistol into the air. A girl appeared behind him and, pushing him out of the way, unfurled a tricolour the size of a bed-sheet on to the cobbles. They took a corner each and the flag rippled out horizontally behind them as they ran towards the square. It sagged as they hesitated on the edge of the open space, uncertain if there might still be rifles concealed in the darkness of the *mairie*'s interior. More figures appeared on the street, still timid, glancing at the point where the receding din of engines placed the retreating Germans, trying to ascertain if there might be a change of heart and a return – almost not believing that the long-awaited hour of liberation was at hand. Now ignoring the sound of artillery, yet more ventured out, some holding pistols, one an ancient shotgun and others with nothing but a child by the hand. They followed the running couple with the tricolour who were now mounting the steps that rose towards the open door of the *mairie*. From somewhere came the first phrases of the Marseillaise in a powerful soprano that was picked up almost instantly by the laughing, smiling, hugging throng that now spilled on to the street. There was a collective catch in the throat at the climax and, when Marie-Louise glanced at her father, she saw tears streaming down his immobile face. The couple with the banner appeared, framed in the first-floor window of the *mairie*. The man stretched out to the flagpole to grasp the hoist and, after fumbling with a recalcitrant knot, tore down the hated swastika that bloomed for a last time as it billowed and sank to the ground. Instantly, it was seized and ripped to shreds by the swelling crowd. Cheers and broken snatches of the national anthem spurred on the couple as they struggled to attach their tricolour, erupting into a roar as it opened and filled.

Marie-Louise grabbed her father's arm. 'Papa, I'm going out to the square – will you come?' He shook his head and continued to stare at the scene below with tears trickling down his face.

She hesitated in the shade of the gateway before stepping out into the street that was now filled with fluttering reds, whites and blues, and the sounds of cheers and song that echoed in the tunnel-like cool where she stood. She had an instinctive fear of crowds, their moods and their potential for madness. This joy was close to hysteria she felt, and her hand lay for a few seconds on the cold iron of the gate before she cast herself into the human cascade that was flowing into the square. She crossed the torrent at an oblique angle, into the eddy of the espaliered area by the war memorial where Madame Acarier, from the house opposite, was standing, bemused, in the swirl. They made shy eye contact and the older woman, normally taciturn and unsmiling, opened her arms in invitation, tears staining the starched white of the apron she always wore. The two women, who had only ever exchanged a nodded greeting, embraced without a word. Still unspeaking, they held hands as they joined the flow again, for a while secure in each other's company. Marie-Louise glanced back to the house where the solitary figure of her father still stood in his private oubliette.

Tricolours of every shape, tone and material flicked, fluttered and blossomed around them. Some were flags, moth-eaten and faded; others were paper bannerettes that had last seen service on a wedding cake; yet more were the creation of children in crayoned reds and blues. Men, women and children were hugging each other spontaneously and indiscriminately in an infectious way that over-came both women's inhibitions – and within seconds Marie-Louise had been enveloped by the unwashed bear-hug of an ancient peasant and kissed on both cheeks by stubbled lips that smelt of wine and halitosis. Every permutation of joy suffused the singing, cheering multitude. From outside the square a new refrain arose.

'*Les Canadiens!* They're coming!'

Heads turned towards the shouting and away from the upper window of the *mairie* from where a woman was now leaning in front of a dozen conspicuously armed *résistants*, cupping her ear in a mock imitation of deafness to incite the crowd to new vocal heights. It was Ghislaine. Above the shouting was building the sound of engines once again, gearboxes engaging and the metallic clatter of tracks on cobbles. As the mechanical clamour rose, so did the human, rising like a slow wave marking the progress of vehicles that were still out of sight. A tank, dust-stained below its fleece of excited humanity, lurched into the square to a roar that swept everyone with it, lost in a collective ecstasy. The driver, fending off flowers and kisses from women and girls swarming up the sloping front of the Sherman, alternated between a grin and a frown of concern as he gunned the engine in warning, inching his way forward into the surging host that threatened to crush itself under his gingerly turning tracks. Behind were jeeps, all of them over-whelmed by children. One danced for joy on a bonnet with a raised handful of sweets – treasure beyond price after the privations of five long years of rationing. Almost invisible under the tide of boarders, were smiling bareheaded soldiers, handing out cigarettes and receiving in return outstretched bottles of champagne that had been squirrelled away years ago in anticipation of this moment, accompanied by passionate kisses from girls regardless of the recipient's age or physical desirability.

The column, with its happy cargo, inched its way forward into the middle of the square, pressed hard on all sides by the crowd – three tanks and a dozen jeeps. As it came to a halt, an officer, dis-tinguished by a pair of revolvers carried in cowboy-style holsters and a peaked cap, stood on the seat and swung himself on to the bonnet, where he stood with both arms in the air to rapturous applause and a diva's shower of flowers. To Marie-Louise, he appeared impossibly glamorous, with his Clark Gable moustache and white teeth that gleamed in contrast to his dusted bronzed face. Well fed and fit, with the confidence and power of the New World, now in such contrast to the drawn grey of the Old, he revelled in the elation, conducting surges of cheering with his arms. At length, he held his arms still for silence and slowly, like ebbing waves, the crowd settled from the centre, humming in anticipation. She noticed the maple-leaf red flash on one arm of his tunic as he twisted to the right and left, taking in the crowd that by now included the entire population of the town. He placed his hands on his hips before he spoke in the accent of *Français Québécois*.

'*Mes amis . . . c'est le jour de votre libération!*'

The roar of the crowd overwhelmed his subsequent words. He shook his head and, grasping the windshield with one hand, stretched down into the crowd, the waving corn of outstretched hands, and grabbed the neck of a proffered bottle of champagne. He held it high with one hand while signalling for silence again, then handed the bottle to a young boy who was sharing the bonnet with him, and, cupping his hands around his mouth, he bellowed, '*Vive la France! Vive la belle France!*'

The refrain that answered him echoed round the square, rising and falling in surges of sound that carried Marie-Louise with it in its delirium. She surrendered herself to the ecstasy, joining the chorus from the depths of her being – waving, shouting, weeping, hugging until she could feel her voice lapsing into hoarseness. She found herself carried by the press towards the jeep and reached out, as a supplicant to a healer, to touch the khaki serge of the officer's uniform. Though she was one of many – and he was waving in the other direction – he turned to her touch and caught her eye. Close up, the mud smears, the tiredness and the smell of sweat were there – but so were the vigour and the excitement. He leant down from the jeep and, cupping her head in his hands, he drew her to him and kissed her on the lips. She felt the snickering of his tongue touching hers and heard the crowd around her roaring its approval. The multitude surged again and she was swept away from him as another girl in a torn dress pulled her way over the footplate and grabbed his head towards hers. Marie-Louise allowed herself to be carried by the flow until the grip of the crowd loosened, depositing her like foam on a riverbank at the square's edge. She suddenly felt tired, cotton-mouthed and hot. Dust, stirred by a thousand feet, swirled above the throng, occasionally obscuring the tanks and their dancing, waving hitchhikers. It caught in her throat and she needed to sit, rest her legs and drink. By chance she again found herself facing a disorientated Madame Acarier, swaying slightly and rubbing her eyes with her forearm, which left a streak of grime in a line from an eye to an ear. Her apron was blotched by sprayed wine. Marie-Louise put an arm round her and together they dodged the dancers and the drunks until they were out of the Place Gambetta and back in the relative calm of the Place Vert, where a bottle of cider stood abandoned on the arm of a bench. The two women, comrades now, sat down gratefully and took turns in drinking from the bottle; for all their newfound companionship, neither woman had spoken a word to the other – but this did not seem to matter in the elevated atmosphere. Songs rose out of the space behind them, ragged at first, but building into full voice with familiar choruses: all sentimental, some of them *pouilu* marching songs during which more tears were added to the wine on Madame Acarier's apron. Giving way to her weariness, after escorting her now unsteady companion to her front door, Marie-Louise wound her way to her own house and sat quietly in the parlour, with the sound of the crowd and the footsteps of her father upstairs as the companions to her dozing.

She awoke suddenly. She lay for a while as her thoughts settled and the present reasserted itself. It was dusk, or at least the waning of the afternoon. She could hear the crowd, not singing now, but still a live collective thing that murmured over the roof of her house. She went into the kitchen and splashed water on her face to clear away the drowsiness, still feeling the effects of the cider that had been stronger than she had imagined. She considered going upstairs to see her father but thought better of it: the collective joy of the square was still with her and her father had no place in that. Wrapping herself in her mother's silk shawl, she left the house on her own and joined the now-thinned throng in the early autumn chill of evening.

Some boys had built a bonfire in front of the Abbatiale St Saulve. The Canadians had abandoned their vehicles where the crowd had halted them and joined the girls and adolescents around its warmth, accompanied by a seemingly inexhaustible supply of wine. They drank purposefully with no heed to the morning: one was already asleep between the tracks of his tank, another was kissing a girl, one hand on a thigh that was clothed in nylon – a gift that was likely to get its reward before the night was out. Shyly, Marie-Louise approached the fire, glad of its warmth but nervous of the atmosphere that she sensed had subtly changed from the joy of the late afternoon to something more febrile and unpredictable under the influence of alcohol. A couple, one half of whom she recognised as Stephan, were arguing under the lee of a tank. The sound of a piano fluttered out of an open window and there was the splash of broken glass nearby. The press of the afternoon had dissipated, but clusters of drinkers, some still singing, stood or squatted in fluid groups that occasionally erupted in laughter or ragged applause. The September dusk gave way to the orange of the bonfire and individual faces could only be discerned by the light of the fire. Marie-Louise spotted an ammunition box and sat on it, absorbing the singeing heat of the fire. A soldier edged up to her and squatted by her side. He swayed slightly on his heels and reached out a hand to the tank for support, three stripes visible on his steadying arm. He spoke to her in clumsy French that she could barely understand and which he repeated in the slur of deep drunkenness. Seemingly forgetting why he was there, he stood, reeled against a jeep and staggered into the crowd. Relieved, Marie-Louise shrugged her shawl further round her shoulders, cupped her chin in the palm of a hand, and leant forward to enjoy the heat.

A new sound – a chant – insinuated itself. It came from the street that led into the square alongside the *mairie*, ugly in tone. As it drew closer, the word defined itself as it was reiterated with a hard emphasis on the second syllable.

'*Putain! Putain!*'

The ripple of interest was visible and audible with seated groups standing and jostling for a better view. As the object of interest drew closer, the chant in all its ugliness was taken up by a new chorus, so that by the time it was illuminated by the fire, the crowd's voice had the flaying rhythm of the bastinado. Marie-Louise retreated behind the tracks of the Sherman. The firelight revealed a girl – that was all she was – barely out of her teens, with a bundle in her arms and trepidation in every disorientated step she took, pursued by mocking laughter, crude hand gestures and the insistent refrain. Marie-Louise recognised her as a former pupil, a simple girl whose father was the caretaker of the school. A woman walked forward into the path of the girl's terrified meandering and stood in her way with legs apart and hands on hips. The girl cringed, flinching as a glistening globule of spit spattered her cheek to an approving jeer. Others stepped forward and within seconds the arm upheld to protect herself had taken on a reflective sheen with the splatter of expectorate. She backed against the tank, only a metre from where Marie-Louise was standing. From that close the sound of a baby's mewing was audible and she had a glimpse of a nose and toothless mouth wide in unheeded distress.

A man kicked the ammunition box on which Marie-Louise had been sitting into the no man's land between the rim of the crowd and the maw of the fire, where it sat like an executioner's block, the first row of the crowd illuminated by weaving tongues of flame. Out of the parting crowd appeared a woman, arms raised like boxer entering the ring, one hand holding sheep shears – two crude knives attached by a metal fly-spring. She snapped them together to a sporadic cheer. It was the same Adèle Carpentier who had insinuated *collaboration horizontale* to Marie-Louise on the very first day of the occupation.

The girl seemed to shrink at the snicker-snack of the shears, backing herself like an embayed deer into the space between the tank tracks, cowering away from her nemesis who was wearing the sneer of the self-righteous. Adèle grabbed a handful of hair. The girl resisted, squirming and twisting as she was dragged stumbling to the box. She sat bowed in the forlornness of fear and shame, staring at the ground, blinking and shivering as the shears dug into her long hair, auburn in the firelight. She winced and cried out in pain as the blades overlapped and slabs of hair were stretched and torn. Each cut handful was held up to applause before being tossed towards the fire. The girl leant forward to comfort the baby, only to be wrenched back by a harsh tug on a remaining tuft that elicited a scream that silenced the crowd. Leaving straggling tendrils of twisted hair over tussocks of scalp-stubble, the executioner stood back to admire her handiwork. She tossed aside the shears and moved contemptuously to face her victim, who now had her baby clutched hard to her chest and was rocking back and forth, keening piteously. She grasped a shoulder with one hand and placed the palm of the other on the girl's forehead, forcing her head back till the skin of her brow was stretched tight, forcing open her eyes so that the whites framed the pupils. From a few inches away, Adèle spat into her face and pushed at the same moment so that the girl fell backwards, still clutching the baby as she rolled on to the cobbles.

The push galvanised her, and in an instant she was standing and charging blindly towards the spectators who parted with the instinctive fear of the berserk, gaps opening to each wild lunge. She hesitated in a newly opened space, despairingly searching for a way out. The mob was quiet now, no longer jeering but wary, atavistically sensing that the girl was teetering on the brink of insanity and capable of anything. She swayed and blinked as she re-orientated herself, seemingly unaware of the insistent screams of the baby in her arms. She rocked on the heels of bare feet that were raw and bleeding. Blood from a torn portion of scalp trickled in front of her ear and stained the rough cotton dress at the shoulder. She stared ahead as if the orange-hued horde no longer existed, limping and stumbling away from the fire, the white of her naked scalp the last trace to disappear as the shadows and crowd swallowed her.

Adèle Carpentier watched her go with a bottle in one hand and an elbow on the tank's tracks. She was wearing trousers and a beret – a form of uniform, Marie-Louise realised, of the *résistants*: she remembered Ghislaine, framed in the window of the *mairie*, similarly attired. She was laughing with two men and wiping the sweat of her exertions from her forehead with the sleeve of her shirt, enjoying her power and holding the stares from individuals in the throng so that they were forced to look away in nervous embarrassment. She was two years older than Marie-Louise and remembered by her classmates as an imperious bully who used her brittle prettiness and instinct for weakness to gather round her a coterie of those with a similar taste for casual cruelty. Ghislaine had been younger – but tough, both mentally and physically. She had always refused to be browbeaten, gathering around her friends, like Marie-Louise, whom she protected with a scorching tongue and fearless stare. As adults, the two women still circled each other with a barely suppressed dislike, both dominant but neither able to achieve the ascendancy.

She caught sight of Marie-Louise behind the tracks of the tank. She raised an eyebrow and smiled slyly as she held out the bottle. 'Have a drink.'

There was something complicit in the invitation: compliance would carry with it an acknowledgement or approval of what had just occurred. Without the steel of Ghislaine by her side, Marie-Louise's ingrained timidity had her stepping out from her quasi hiding-place and taking the proffered bottle. In her nervousness, some of the wine missed her mouth and red splotches appeared on her shawl. Adèle observed her with a feline coolness, accepting the bottle back and taking a pull on it herself.

'Where's your father?' she asked.

Marie-Louise found that she could not hold the other woman's eye. 'At home, I think. I haven't seen him since . . . a couple of hours ago.'

'Not out celebrating then?'

The implication within the question made the two men interrupt their conversation and listen in anticipation. She knew that she was a poor liar and could feel the colour rising in her face – but the light of the fire camouflaged it, she sensed.

'Of course he was. Everyone has.'

'Everyone? No, *chérie*, I don't think everyone has. She wasn't,' she nodded in the direction of where the shorn girl had been, 'was she?'

Marie-Louise felt herself swallowing as she twisted under the implication and the basilisk stare. She tried to look surprised. 'I saw him following the tanks into the square – a bit the worse for wear, I suspect.' She forced herself to smile with a levity she did not feel.

'I didn't. Did you boys? We were with the tanks. We rode on them into town. We saw you snog the Canadian though. Difficult, I'd have thought – kissing in the middle of the square and seeing your papa cheering the tanks on their way in.'

Marie-Louise shook her head, searching for a credible reply. 'I . . . I was quite drunk. I'm sure I saw him though. By the entrance to the Place Vert; near our house.'

'Cheering too? I'm sure he was. Good thing for him to do . . . in the circumstances. If I were a collaborator, that's what I'd do. Eh? Boys? Wouldn't you? Cheer for your life. Try to make out that the years I'd spent with my tongue up the Boche's arse was all a trick, and that really . . . really . . . all that time I'd been trying to shoot them. The trouble is, *chérie*, I don't believe it. Nor does anyone else. Would you?'

She spat on the ground. Something about the brutality of the woman sparked inside Marie-Louise an uncharacteristic fury at her own passivity and collaboration – collaboration in the cruelty she had observed and now in the verbal lynching of her father. She knew her tormenter of old and that knowledge fuelled her question.

'So how long have you been in the Resistance, Adèle?'

Her tone had the two men looking at her. Adèle's mouth tightened.

'What's that got to do with you?'

'Interest. That's all. Just wondered when you got involved.'

'From the beginning.'

'From when the Boche arrived?'

'No. Not straight away. Months after. I can't remember precisely. Anyway, what's that got to do with your bloody father? It's him we're talking about.' She had her arms crossed and her mouth set in a hard line.

'So 1940?'

'Yes. It must have been. Winter. Yes, it was winter.'

Normally Marie-Louise would have been unable to hold this woman's eye but the ire inside gave her a light-headed heedlessness and an abnormal boldness. She tried to imagine Ghislaine beside her and to draw on some of her fierceness and courage. There was the flare of a match as one of the men lit a cigarette.

'You were in contact with de Gaulle's people then? Or maybe you were a Communist?'

'I've never been a Communist!'

'Nor me. But I don't remember you being . . . involved . . . then. With Victor and Janette?'

A blink and swallowing showed her aim was true.

'I was . . . doing other things. Secret. I can't talk about it. Of course I can't: there's still a war going on.'

Her face was away from the fire and in shadow – but the imputation had registered in the amused smiles of the two men. It was Adèle who was now having difficulty holding a stare.

Marie-Louise's voice was quiet. 'None of us knows the whole story, do we? Let's just leave it there. There is a war going on; you're right . . . and it might be a bit early . . . for this sort of thing.' She pointed towards the hair and the shears

The other woman's jaw was working in anger. She faced the fire and swung the bottle by its neck towards the fire, letting go so that it arced towards the fire's edge where it pitched over before rolling into the embers without breaking. The noise drew glances from the milling crowd. She pushed her face closer so that Marie-Louise could feel her breath as she spoke in a hard whisper.

'Your father's a collaborator. I know that. Everyone knows it. That little tart fucked not one but two Boche – and that bastard she was hauling around . . . she doesn't even know who the father is. I don't care who sorts them out. Me. This lot. I couldn't give a shit. It's payback time, _chérie_. We're going to get them all. All the ones that ran away with the Boche – we'll get them too when it's all over. The Boche left half their files in the _mairie_ and they'll be interesting reading – bound to be. Four years' worth of records: who paid whom for what, that sort of thing. And I bet your papa was up to his neck in it, don't you? Him and all his friends. That Communist cell that the Gestapo rounded up: someone betrayed them – and you know how much he hated the Commies. As of today, he isn't mayor any more. We're in charge now . . . and don't forget it. He won't.' She carried on staring at Marie-Louise as she spat on the ground again. 'He won't. Nor will you.'

The weather changed the next day in sympathy with the hangover that lay over Montreuil. Just after dawn, in a fine drizzle, the noise of tanks starting woke all but those who had drunk themselves into insensibility. Those who had slept by the fire watched with sticky eyes, damp clothes and dishevelled hair as officers rounded up their men. The harsh discipline of the years of training was now replaced by a quiet word and a shake of the shoulder: three months of fighting had made them all veterans with the interplay of respect that was vital for survival. As they dragged themselves into their vehicles, few looked like conquerors: all were unshaven; one was sick on the front wheel of his jeep; another relieved himself against the wall of the Abbatiale before unsteadily mounting his tank, only to slip on the rain-greased surface of the turret, cursing in a Quebec patois. He blew a kiss towards a girl who sadly waved back as the tracks ground over the cobbles, drowning out the engines of the jeeps as they formed a convey in the wake of the Germans.

From her window Marie-Louise watched them pass. Her father's door had been closed when she had tiptoed past on waking and no sound came from behind it now. As the noise receded, voices could be heard outside and the familiar wartime clicker-clack of wooden articulated soles on stone. These had replaced the traditional leather that had slowly disappeared to feed the German war-machine. To the beat of these distinctive footsteps, a man and woman were singing the paean to that sound of clacking shoes by Maurice Chevalier – '*La symphonie des semelles de bois*' – a tune as redolent of occupied France as the brass of Glen Miller was of England at the same period. They skipped a half step at the end of each phrase, giggling at their dancing rhythm. Marie-Louise smiled at the sound, an overture of sorts for peace. She quietly made her way to the kitchen and set a coffee pot to boil, contemplating its acid smell, ersatz and acorn: even the black market for the genuine article had dried up months ago. The sweetness of honey made it drinkable as she sat on the stool contemplating the tree outside with its reddening apples glossed by fine rain and its leaves agglomerating what was almost mist into splashing drops.

She thought back to the day when she had sat in its shade almost exactly three years before and confided in her father. She tried to imagine, as she did every day, the waking of her child on a Norman farm. He would be talking now, calling another woman '*maman*'. What did he look like, this piece of her that felt like an amputated limb? She knew that to think of him brought with it a pain that made her almost sick with longing but, every day, sometimes many times a day, she took the thought from its storing place, a little corner of her consciousness, and held it in her hands to stroke and treasure, almost welcoming the exquisite agony that was its concomitant.

She heard her father move upstairs and the dread that had settled on her by the tank the previous evening elbowed its way back in. That there would be an *épuration sauvage* – an unofficial purge – was certain. Any servant of Vichy was in the firing line, whatever their motives. No matter that the government of the Maréchal had been supported by the vast majority of France in the wake of the debacle of 1940. Now everyone was a *résistant* – none more vengeful and self-righteous than the neophytes desperate to parade their credentials. It was her father's obduracy that would now be his undoing. Not for him the trimming of his friends and colleagues who had sniffed the way the tide of war was running and cut their ties with the sinking ship. Whatever his faults, anti-Semitism and cowardice were not among them. She knew that the craven cruelties of the dog days of the regime revolted him; that he detested the seedy expediency of Laval and the hounding of the Jews and *résistants* by the Milice, the vicious Fascist police. But he despised even more what he saw as the disloyalty to Pétain, whom he still held on a pedestal as the saviour of France, a man of integrity and greatness. His own stubborn integrity failed to recognise the vanity, slyness and conceit of the old man. The more his contemporaries deserted Vichy, the more loyal to the Maréchal he became. Marie-Louise knew that France had no greater patriot – but that patriotism was now going to be twisted into collaboration; unjust perhaps, but understandable in the zeitgeist.

She heard the door of his room opening and his steps descending the stairs. She stood to meet him in the parlour where he kissed her before sitting at the table, contemplating her as she returned to the stool next to the kitchen door. Was she imagining it, or had age leapfrogged on to him? The upright vigour was now replaced by something that resembled a stoop – and there was a thinness to his hair that surely had not been there before? What had always been a complex relationship now took on a further element, that of protection.

'What time did you get back last night?'

There was no hidden insinuation in the question.

'About ten, I think.' There was a pause before she continued. 'It was horrible. Horrible!'

He looked at her, visibly moved by the distress in her voice. 'I heard. I thought something like that would happen. What did they do to the poor girl?'

'Shaved her head. Spat on her. It was disgusting. And, papa, the worst thing is that I did nothing. I taught that girl. She wasn't much more than a child and I watched it without doing anything. Some liberation!' There was bitter anger in her voice.

He shook his head as he spoke. 'My dear, it's crowds. They're ugly things. Look what's happened throughout our history when crowds ruled the roost: the Terror, the Commune – savagery and butchery. Anonymous cruelty is easy to get away with; and people like cruelty. Lots of things are going to be done over the next few days and weeks by these . . . patriots.' There was contempt in every syllable of the last word. 'I'm bound to be a target. And maybe you. I'm sorry. You don't deserve it. Thank God you went to . . . '

He halted, embarrassed that he had almost brought up the subject that had never been alluded to again after their conversation under the tree three years earlier.

She had returned from Honfleur a month after her confinement. They had taken the baby away to a wet nurse after cutting the umbilical cord, barely allowing her to hold and smell him. She had lain for days in her bedroom, her breasts swollen and sore, leaking milk and fighting an overpowering longing. Her grandmother came to visit three or four times a day, their roles reversed – with the old lady at the side of the bed in her embroidered dressing-gown and her granddaughter staring at the ceiling with tears rolling down her face and unable to articulate the misery within. The older woman held her hand and often never said a word, for which the younger was grateful, her presence and unspoken sympathy enough. Some days she felt the cotton wool of a breakdown stealing up on her, an abnegation of the misery of consciousness, where she could float in a disembodied calm divorced from the nagging pain of grief. Slowly, as her body recovered from its hormonal assault, she was able to eat and with that came a gradual recovery into a new world of duality, one half of her able to return to her previous life, the other fighting a private battle with grief and guilt. She allowed her grandmother into this private realm, knowing that this was where she was able to be a guide of sorts, a navigator to steer her away from the reefs of insanity. It was she who taught her granddaughter to place her grief in a mental casket – only to be unlocked in careful solitude, its contents allowed free rein only when it was safe, when she could wallow in it without a shipwreck. With this intimacy, Marie-Louise grew to love this big-hearted and eccentric woman, a feeling that was reciprocated with the intensity of a last love on the older woman's part. On the day of her return to Montreuil, with the glad dancing of blossom outside the window and the scratching and chattering of parrots within, they had held on to each other silently and long, with neither attempting to muffle their sobs or staunch their tears.

She had returned to the school outwardly the same, but thinner – a change that went unremarked with the settling in of real food shortages and the cold introspection and meanness of spirit that was the companion of hunger. Some noticed a newfound stillness of expression that was in contrast to the mirror of her internal thoughts that had been so characteristic. She had never had intimate friends, other than Ghislaine. Some gossiped that they were no longer to be seen together but no one made any reference to the real reason – which Marie-Louise realised, gratefully, was the obligation of a past friendship being honoured. They saw each other – not to would have been impossible in a small town – but other than an exchange of pleasantries, each gave the other a wide berth. The relationship with her father was also changed. Gone were the sarcasm and the high-handed disdain. Replacing it was hardly an intimate gentleness, but a concern and a courtesy with her that she recognised as how he had treated her mother. She wondered about this change and realised that he too was increasingly isolated as the political tide turned. Soon after her return, the Germans had occupied the whole of France. Vichy's claim to be the voice of an independent France now chimed hollow, its failures and sordidness thrown into relief. Not only did the prisoners-of-war remain in Germany but also the need for labour in the factories of the Reich started to suck in young men and women as drafts to be deported as slave labour to cities that were beginning to be under devastating bombardment by the Allied bomber fleets. In the wilder, forested parts of France many took their chances with the Maquis, but in the more manicured and urban areas youngsters awaited with dread the monthly lists of those selected. Food became increasingly scarce and fuel hard to come by – and even those privileged with contacts and money got thinner and more thread-bare. Reserves of altruism were depleted and compassion became a rarity to be remarked on in a world preoccupied with necessities.

Communication with Jerome in Germany became more difficult. Letters and parcels with preserved foods and books went astray as he was moved to a camp in Pomerania, an eastern province, and then to Upper Silesia where he worked in a munitions factory at monotonous work with little food. She had created a fictional domestic world for him – of gossip and companionship. Of her inner guilt and misery she could, of course, mention nothing; nor of her loneliness which was assuaged only by occasional visits to her grandmother to whom she could unburden herself. From Jerome came letters that told of increased frustration and boredom and of the indignities and irritations of confinement in damp dormitories where quarrels festered and, on occasions, erupted violently. Mental illness took its toll. He wrote of the occupant of the bunk above him slashing his wrists in the middle of the night and his awaking to find himself drenched in the man's blood. Politics, as polarised as they were in France itself, poisoned the atmosphere, with Communists and Pétainists quarrelling and factionalising. He occupied the dreary breaks from work with learning poetry by rote and in studying psychology, burying himself in the works of Freud. He took particular pleasure in this as an antidote to the anti-Semitism that was rife, not only among Germans, but among his fellow prisoners. She began to sense in their correspondence what she had dreaded in the early days of his captivity – a gradual estrangement; nothing sudden but a divergence in their experiences that was opening up a gulley between them; not yet a ravine, but a distance that would take delicacy and care to bridge. Through the spiralling privations of 1943 and into the summer of 1944, she could feel a rankling in his increasingly infrequent letters that contrasted with her enforced replies of a false jollity and optimism. Now that the liberation had come, she realised that the tenuous link with him would be broken. There would be neither food parcels nor books to send. She would not know where he was, be able to support him or have any inkling of his mental state. He was also parlously close to the approaching Eastern Front where she knew he would be between the hammer and the anvil as the invasion of Germany itself loomed.

As she worried about her husband she still mourned her lover, another secret grief that she could not share. Her waking dream was often of him; on the stairs. She would be watching the crown of his head as he addressed his breakfast tray. Or she would see him sprawled over the first treads with his tunic unbuttoned, laughing at her. Time had helped. The initial collapse and all-enveloping grief had melded into a gentle longing that never left her. It had become a companion of sorts that was now part of her daily life

Her father coughed in embarrassment and stared at the steadily falling rain. Marie-Louise stood, hesitated for a moment, then took two steps towards where her father was sitting and placed her hand tentatively on his arm. He carried on looking outside.

'Thank you, papa. You've supported me more . . . more than I could ever have expected. I don't know what I would have done without you. Really. You know I haven't agreed with you about . . . politics . . . the Maréchal. But I'm with you whatever they do.'

For the second time in a day, a tear ran down his face. She had only ever seen him cry once before, when the doctor had told him that there was no hope for his wife. When she had died, at her funeral, on the anniversaries of her death, he had been impassive. He had thrown the first sod on to the dull drum of her coffin dispassionately, had allowed his daughter to grasp his arm in her own paroxysms of grief without tears to match. He wiped this one away with a starched handkerchief that he carefully refolded and pushed into the breast pocket of his jacket. He moved his hand across as if to place it on his daughter's, but checked himself with his fingers above hers. There was something seminal about the gesture that they both sensed. Withdrawal would return their relationship to the authoritarian interplay of father and child, but the fall of the hand would acknowledge need and dependence – age itself. His gaze was still over the sill of the window and hers obliquely down the slant of his shoulder as his hand brushed hers, trembling as it settled on her wrist. Neither moved for some seconds before she felt the briefest of pressures as the hand was withdrawn to fumble for a packet of cigarettes in his jacket pocket. Marie-Louise busied herself with the coffee pot. Both were embarrassed – but also moved. She sat down again with her hands on her lap and looked at him as he smoked.

'Papa . . . there were threats last night . . . against you. Adèle Carpentier . . . do you know her?' He nodded with no expression. 'She was . . . was saying something about you being . . . something about a Communist cell in the Resistance.'

He blinked. 'What did she say?'

'That you . . . that you had something to do with betraying them. Papa, is it true?'

He still looked outside rather than at her.

'No. No, I didn't betray them. I never would. But I know who did – and I won't betray him because he's a better patriot than any of those scum who only ever did anything for France when Stalin told them to.'

She bowed her head, enabling her to look at the floor and not into his eye. 'Papa, you must be careful. Very careful. These people are . . . vindictive. You mustn't be arrogant or even try too much self-justification. Everyone in France has had to collaborate in some form or another and everyone is now trying to put as much distance as they can between what they had to do to survive and where they are now. For every person that was in the Resistance in the early days, there are twenty now, all of them keen to denounce anyone else in order to deflect attention from what they did, or didn't, do. The Boche left a lot of papers behind. Is there anything there that might . . . ' she hesitated . . . 'cause you any . . . embarrassment.'

'Such as?'

She could sense exactly the arrogant anger in his voice that she was trying to warn him against. She persisted. 'Business deals. Anything to do with deportations for forced labour. Or Jews. Papa, don't hide anything from me. Please. I'm on your side; they aren't. I can only help you if I know what they might attack you with. Do you understand?'

His hands were clenching in anger. The colour was rising in his face, his temples pulsing. 'Of course I understand. And I have nothing . . . nothing to hide! Do you understand? Do you? I admire and follow the Maréchal but detest some of the men around him: that traitor Laval and that thug Darnard with his bullyboys in the Milice – no better than the Nazis; shameful apologies for Frenchmen. In my business I've done no more or less than anyone who's tried to keep his head above water for the last four years. Of course I've had to trade favours. I had no choice but to administer the deportations – for labour – not the Jews. As mayor, what could I do? I wasn't deporting them – it was the Boche. I may as well have lain down in the road for all the good it would have done . . . '

'I know that, papa, but it will be twisted by others. They will say that it was instigated by you . . . '

'Then they can say it!'

He banged the table with his fist. Coffee sloshed over the edge of the cup, puddling in the saucer. She looked up at him, feeling her own anger rising. She held his gaze, refusing to be browbeaten. She carefully placed her own cup on the table and paused before replying.

'Listen, papa, and listen carefully. You're in grave danger. More than that: mortal danger. This isn't politics where the worst that can happen is that you lose an election. They – whoever they are, all your old enemies plus a few more now – are going to be looking for a scapegoat with all the moral indignation of those with the grubbiest consciences. At best there'll be a trial. At worst you could be lynched. You're the face of Vichy. I know that everyone, well a good majority anyway, were behind you in 1940. I know that you saw it as your duty to cooperate in order to make the occupation bearable and I know that you could do nothing to protect those two Jewish families or the workers being deported. But you have to see that your enemies – and you have a few – will put the worst complexion on anything you've done. You'll be labelled a collaborator for certain. You may be shot. Do you understand that? Being arrogant and pig-headed will play into their hands; give them the rope they need. It'll be stupid, papa, stupid. Be brave by all means, but don't be stupid. You . . . we . . . are on the wrong side. You'll probably get away with the odd business deal, and having to administer Boche orders. But if you so much as hint that you sympathise with, or had anything to do with, the rounding up of any *résistants*, you're done for. Do you understand? Do you?'

He was now the one avoiding eye contact. He was breathing heavily through his nose with a set jaw. But he nodded. She continued: 'The next few days will be particularly dangerous. It's anarchy out there. Children with guns and moral indignation – and nothing to stop them doing pretty well what they want until some sort of government gets established. Any soldiers – Tommies, Canadians or Yankees – are just going to stand by and watch, like they did last night. They'll make sure any poor girl that slept with a Boche . . . ' she hesitated, swallowing the bile of embarrassment and fear that rose in her throat . . . 'gets a *tonte.*' She subconsciously fingered her fine hair. 'Then they'll come after anyone whom they can paint as a traitor . . . and they'll try it with you, papa; they're bound to. You're an obvious target. You must emphasise your *Croix de Guerre* and your loyalty to the Maréchal personally. Use him as your shield. There are enough out there who still think that he's been manipulated and used as a figurehead for it to cut some ice. Everyone hates and despises the likes of Laval – so blame everything bad on him and his cronies. And, papa, don't say anything about the Communists. Promise me. I know you hate everything they stand for, but, like it or not, they've been the backbone of the Resistance since the Boche invaded Russia – and they'll be out to settle some scores. What you said to me earlier will be enough to get you killed by them. Remember there's nothing to stop them at the moment. You have to tread carefully, very carefully.'

Silence followed, filled only with his muscular breathing. He stood and took two steps to the window, where he hesitated with one hand in his pocket and the other flicking over his silver cigarette-case to the rhythm of the clock. He turned back to his daughter and contemplated her for a couple of seconds. He nodded and strode towards the stairs and his room.

They came for him that afternoon. The sound of a small crowd, all talking at once, prefaced the hammering on the door. As Marie-Louise stepped on to the landing she saw her father at the top of the stairs in a suit with a stiff collar and tie. She had noticed him becoming slovenly of late – but now he was clean-shaven, with his hair carefully combed back. He smiled thinly.

'It looks as though they want me. I shouldn't disappoint my public, should I?' He looked down at his shoes. 'It'll be fine.'

She followed him down the stairs and saw him straighten as he opened the door. Through the doorway, in the shadowed carriage entrance outside, were berets, arms holding guns and pale faces, ill-defined. She heard Adèle's voice as the shouting quieted itself to a flutter of chatter.

'The committee want to see you, Annecy. Now. In the *mairie*.' The talking subsided into silence. 'Now, Annecy. Get moving.'

Marie-Louise could only see his back but could imagine the cold impassivity of his stare, one hand in his pocket and the other on the door handle.

'Who wants to see me? I'm not aware of any committee.'

There was a stirring.

'Well, you wouldn't be, would you – you fucking collaborator?' Adèle's voice was venomous, its owner still out of sight.

Still he didn't move. Then, slowly, he turned to the coat-stand and took his best hat and carefully put it on his head before stepping into the crowd that parted in front of him as he walked towards the gate with his daughter tailing behind, unnoticed. The rain had stopped but the afternoon was humid with low cloud that could almost be mist. The green of the trees' leaves had a saturated heaviness about them and the cobbles the slimy sheen of recent rain that no sun had evaporated. Marie-Louise was conscious of the steady strike of her father's metal-heeled pre-war shoes in contrast to the dragging of clogs around him. He strode his way through the detritus of the previous day's celebration: bottles, broken glass, an abandoned mattress. Two men were sitting on the steps of the *mairie*. They stood to let him pass as he took two steps at a time, placing himself ahead of the posse as he entered the door. Without pausing, he turned right into the chamber from where voices could be heard. They subsided to a whisper as he entered. The arrest party, joined by Marie-Louise, jostled behind him.

Four people were seated behind a table at the end of the room: she recognised Victor and Janette, and her father's Socialist rival for the post of mayor, Henri Labord. The other man was a stranger. Around the room were unshaven faces and drifting cigarette smoke, cotton dresses that had seen better days; familiar faces including those of children and adolescents she had taught, lean and sallow. An older man in front of her leant over and put a steadying hand over an ancient revolver that a boy of no more than fourteen was waving with the casualness of an index finger. There was a single chair in front of the table beside which her father was standing, with his hat still on and his hands behind his back. Marie-Louise pushed around the edges of the room so that she could see his face. There was a dignity in the formality of his dress that contrasted with the collarless shirts and patched jackets of the mob sitting on windowsills and on the benches and tables lining the walls. She was reminded of an illustration in one of her history textbooks of the trial of Robespierre, and the *tricoteuse* who knitted at the foot of the guillotine. Victor, thinner and greyer than when she had seen him last, motioned with his hand that her father should sit. The unfamiliar man rapped the table and the talking subsided. He nodded to Victor who cleared his throat and stubbed his cigarette.

'Michel Annecy?'

She saw her father's eyes move from the wall above the table, from which hung a crude reproduction of Delacroix's bare-chested Liberty breasting the barricades, to Victor.

'Yes. I am the mayor of Montreuil.'

'*Non, monsieur*, you were the mayor of Montreuil. No longer.'

They stared at each other.

'How strange. I was elected under the laws of the Third Republic and was not aware that there has been an election – which I appear to have lost. Have I missed something?'

'It seems so, *monsieur*. It's called the war.' A ripple of laughter. Victor continued. 'The provisional government of France is now headed by General de Gaulle in Paris. You may not have heard, *monsieur*, but Paris was liberated two weeks ago. You might also not have heard that the collaborationist Vichy government is now in Germany. Perhaps that might give you some understanding as to why Marshal Pétain and Monsieur Laval do not currently have much . . . how shall I put it . . . legitimacy in France. You are right that elections have not yet been held – but it is abundantly clear that the will of the people,' he waved his hand to indicate the packed room, 'is behind the General rather than the Maréchal at the moment. Would you not agree?'

'*Monsieur*, I would be grateful if you didn't patronise me. I am as disgusted as you are that Laval is in Germany at the moment. He's a traitor. The Maréchal, on the other hand, is a hero of France and the saviour of Verdun. I fought under him and received the *Croix de Guerre* from him personally on top of the ruins of the Fort Douaumont. You may have heard of that place, *monsieur*.' Fort Douaumont was the iconic epicentre of the slaughter at Verdun. 'I doubt that such a man is in Germany of his own free will, don't you?'

There was a stirring of talk and a voice from the back. 'He's a senile old fool.'

Victor held up his hand for silence. 'No one is questioning the Maréchal's heroism in the last war. He's going to be judged, as are others, *monsieur*, on what he's done during this war, on bringing disgrace on France by his collaboration with the Boche. That's why you're here too.'

Her father remained expressionless and the crowd silent other than shuffles and coughs. He looked to the right and left of him, slowly and carefully holding individuals' eyes until they looked away, before settling his gaze back on Victor.

'I was elected to serve Montreuil as mayor. I believe I've done that faithfully and well. Can I remind you, *monsieur*, that until yesterday this town was on the front line? We were under the direct rule of the German High Command in Brussels, in a heavily militarised area. Do you think that being mayor of Montreuil, in such circumstances, is something that I relished? Of course not. I was mayor before the war and I saw it as my duty to carry on and try to do my best to make the harsh conditions of such an occupation bearable. I could pretend that I was a *résistant* since 1940 . . . as many round here will do . . . but I don't. Talleyrand once said that treason is a question of dates. Well I'm not so old . . . or senile . . . ' he looked to where the voice from the crowd had come . . . 'that I've forgotten what it was like after the armistice was signed and the English had attacked and destroyed our fleet in the Mediterranean, killing nearly sixteen hundred French sailors. Everyone's now for de Gaulle – but perhaps we should remember that when he set himself up in London in '40 there were over a hundred thousand French soldiers in England who'd managed to get away with the Tommies at Dunkirk and Narvik. Nearly all of them came back to France within two weeks because the legal government in France, at that time, told them to do so. Things have changed and there's no one – no one – who is more delighted than me that the Boche are thrashed and the war might be over this year. But I, like most people in this room, *monsieur*, thought that we'd lost in 1940 – as we had in 1870 – and that there was no hope for the Tommies. I was wrong. But that doesn't make me a traitor . . . or a collaborator.'

There was a pregnant quiet in the room. Marie-Louise could sense a change in the mood in response to the power of his argument and the quiet strength of its delivery. There was anger too. He was speaking some uncomfortable truths that grated against the present self-image of heroic resistance that had only grains of truth in it. The truth was what France was trying to forget and Marie-Louise sensed that her father's efforts to resurrect it would not be welcome. Victor glanced at the fourth man at the table before continuing. Something about his calm demeanour made Marie-Louise realise that his profession was an *avocat*, and that cross-examination was bread and butter to him. What her father could not know, and what she was desperate to warn him about, was that sarcasm and a sardonic scepticism would play badly against a genuine *résistant* – more than that – a leader from the beginning.

'Monsieur Annecy, no one here's impugning your motives in staying on as mayor. Your courage isn't in question. Defeat's a terrible thing. Where do loyalties lie? You were one among millions, the majority I'm sure, who looked to the Maréchal for leadership amid the failures of the Republic. The peace of the armistice wasn't a perfect one. How could it be, from the barrel of a gun?' He paused and looked around the room. Marie-Louise could see where his line was running, and searched her father's face for signs that he could see the same. Victor's gaze settled back on her father. 'But that period isn't the one I'm talking about. Like you, most people thought the war was lost then and were prepared to give the Maréchal his chance to negotiate something with the Boche. We know now that he failed.'

'And I was supposed to know that then?' Michel Annecy sat forward with his elbows on his knees.

'No. Of course not. But later? After the Americans came into the war? And after the Boche occupied the whole of France? And when the likes of Laval made speeches saying that they hoped for a German victory? And when the Milice started fighting the Resistance – Frenchmen killing Frenchmen? And when the Boche started trawling France for able-bodied men to work in Germany? And when they started to loot anything of any value leaving us with nothing, only just enough food to survive? It's what you did then, Annecy, that we're interested in.'

'Like what?' He sat back in his chair. 'May I smoke?'

Victor nodded and also leant back and took a cigarette proffered by Janette. They observed each other through smoke plumes.

'Like what? Like giving away the hiding places of those *réfractaires* trying to avoid deportation. Like betraying a Resistance unit to the Gestapo. That's what.'

The knife was now out in all its glittering danger. The hive-like crowd hummed in anticipation.

'Why would I do such a thing? Why?'

'They were Communists. And you hate Communists.'

'Am I alone in that?'

Marie-Louise felt a tightening in her stomach as she willed him away from the trap opening up in front of him.

'I distrust their motives too. But I'd never betray a fellow French-man for that reason. You did.'

'When?'

'Before Christmas last year. Two of them died under torture and the other three . . . who knows? If they're alive, they're in prison somewhere.'

Her father shrugged his shoulders. 'It had nothing to do with me.'

The arrogance in the shrug and his insouciance raised a murmur of anger. The stranger beside Victor now spoke. He had a half-beard, broken teeth and fingers that drummed incessantly.

'I think it did, Annecy. You know who did betray them . . . and you encouraged him. We know that.'

Only her father's eyes moved to his new interlocutor. 'How do you know so much?'

'Because I'm a Communist and those four men and one woman were under my command. Only one person had the information to betray them and he, funnily enough, isn't here in Montreuil. Maybe he's with your precious Maréchal in Germany. Jacques Lamartine was your deputy, Annecy, and he didn't fart without asking you. You must have known what he was up to.'

A growl rose and fell round the room. Michel Annecy remained still. '*Monsieur*, you may have heard the expression, "I am not my brother's keeper." '

'He wasn't your brother; he was your poodle.'

Victor raised his finger to interject. 'I think the evidence is circumstantial at the moment. The papers that we've collected from the *mairie* will be interesting. What have got your fingerprints all over them, Annecy, are the deportations. All over them.'

The accused sat back in his chair again with a raised eyebrow indicating the final quarter of his cigarette. Victor pushed the wooden ashtray towards him and he carefully stubbed it out, ignoring a rising tide of talk in the room. He cleared his throat before replying.

'I had to administer the deportations. I don't deny it. Someone had to. We tried to make it fair and include only single people with no children or dependants. What would have been the alternative? The Boche sending out snatch-squads to pick up the first person they saw? Or smashing down random doors in the middle of the night? Perhaps you would have had a better solution, *monsieur*? I didn't deport them: the Boche did. Do you think that I enjoyed it?

'Yes, *monsieur*, in many cases we think you did. You simply packed the deportation quotas with your political enemies or their children. It wasn't fair at all, was it?' Coughs and a stirring of feet. The stranger picked up the thread. 'And the majority, the large majority were Communists, weren't they?' Her father shrugged again as if to say, 'So what?' More angry murmurs. 'And when they made a run for it, you did everything you could to make sure the Boche found them, didn't you? You tipped off the police and the Gestapo. Quite a few of those they captured didn't make it to Germany: two that I knew were beaten to death.'

'You bastard, Annecy!' A voice from the crowd and an eruption of jeers and threats; the deportations had affected every family.

Marie-Louise saw her father about to speak before holding back in deference to the verbal assault. She tried to catch his eye, willing him to stay silent as she could see where any justification would lead – straight back to the betrayal of the *résistants*. Victor held up his hand again but its effectiveness was distinctly diminished this time. The hostility was palpable. It was now a lynch mob. He took the ashtray and banged it hard on the table, its contents spilling. The shouting quietened to an intimidating mutter. He indicated with an open palm that the Communist should continue, which he was opening his mouth to do when a voice came from the crowd – a woman's voice – clear and steady.

'May I say something, please?'

Heads turned. Marie-Louise strained to see the speaker pushing her way to the front opposite her. It was Ghislaine. She was wearing trousers, a khaki shirt and a beret. Her military mien was emphasised by the pistol in a holster at her hip on which she laid a hand while resting the other on the edge of a table. Her eyes flicked around the room, pausing for a moment on Marie-Louise without a blink of recognition. She addressed herself to the room rather than to the figures behind the table or her old adversary in the chair. Marie-Louise felt a coffin lid of dread pressing down on her

'My name is Ghislaine Proux. I think nearly all of you know me.' Her status as the town's *de facto* doctor for the early part of the occupation meant that there were few in the room who had not consulted her. Whatever had happened over the war years had left an indelible mark on her. Always a commanding presence, she stood with the quiet authority of someone used to giving orders and being obeyed. 'What you may not know is that I've been the Resistance commander for Montreuil since late 1940. My superior has been Monsieur Rimbaud,' she nodded towards Victor, 'who had responsibility for all activity in the Pas de Calais area under the direct command of General de Gaulle in London. Monsieur Granèche,' she indicated the *soit-disant* Communist next to him, 'has been under my command since . . . ' she paused to make the point . . . 'Russia joined the war in 1941. Some of you may know that I've never seen eye to eye with Monsieur Annecy. This is personal and has nothing to do with his activities . . . ' she paused again . . . 'during the occupation. I can't say whether Monsieur Annecy's business activities were helpful to the Boche. That'll come out later when all the files upstairs are gone through in detail. What I can tell you is what Monsieur Annecy did with regard to the Resistance and the *réfractaires* trying to escape deportation.' Silence in anticipation of the executioner's blow. 'Monsieur Annecy did give away the hiding places of some *réfractaires.*'

Jeers from the crowd and a drumming on the tables that built into a din that drowned Ghislaine's voice. She waited calmly, allowing the rumble to subside, talking over the receding cacophony.

'This was on my orders.'

Shocked silence before an uproar again. She held up her hand for silence. Marie-Louise glanced at the main protagonists: the Communist and Victor were wearing expressions of astonishment; her father was as inscrutable as ever.

'I gave those orders so that Monsieur Annecy could continue feeding me vital information about the Boche and their plans. The Boche had to trust him: it was vital. I made the decision that it was more important for us to have the intelligence that only he could provide than to save a handful of workers from going to Germany. The Boche would only have taken others if the *réfractaires* hadn't been found . . . '

Michel Annecy, who had been staring, without expression, at the Delacroix reproduction, turned his head towards Ghislaine. If his face gave anything away, Marie-Louise was unable to detect it. The Communist held up his hand and spoke.

'We didn't know this! Why not?'

Ghislaine looked at him steadily. 'Because I didn't know whom to trust. If I told you – or even Victor Rimbaud,' she nodded towards Victor, 'and the Boche captured either of you, everything would have been lost. Neither of you needed to know – so I didn't tell you.'

The Communist threw up his hands in anger, shaking his head. Victor lit a cigarette and considered what she had just said through half-closed eyes, ignoring the ebb and flow of exclamations and questions within the crowd. Ghislaine indicated that she wished to speak again.

'So I'm telling you that Monsieur Annecy is no traitor. He's done his duty at some risk to himself. We aren't friends. I can't answer for what else he may have done over the last four years, but in this matter, at least, he's been a patriot.'

She nodded to the table before picking her way back through a crowd that parted in respectful silence to sit on a table that was pushed against the wall. She folded her arms and watched. Victor blew a thoughtful avalanche of smoke over the table before speaking.

'*Mes amis*, in the light of what Ghislaine Proux has just told us, we owe Monsieur Annecy an apology . . . ' he looked at Marie-Louise's father as he hesitated ' . . . in this matter anyway. There'll be other things, I suspect, *monsieur*, but in the meantime you're free to go.'

Michel Annecy stood slowly, buttoned his jacket and put on his hat. He nodded perfunctorily towards the committee and walked towards the door without a glance to the left or right, leaving a ferment of gesticulations and comment in his wake. Marie-Louise sat on the bench, leaning against the wall, as the rest stood to discuss the drama. At waist level she felt protected by the claustrophobic wall of bodies surrounding her, the smell of damp unwashed clothes, hangovers and tobacco, warm and comforting. She smoked unnoticed as the shield around her thinned, leaving groups of three or four between whom she could see Ghislaine, also sitting on her own, also smoking and watching. The Resistance commander swung her legs to the floor, walked across and sat next to Marie-Louise. There was a metre between them. They watched the room clearing until there remained only a handful gossiping in a corner, the sound of their voices echoing around the emptying space, bouncing off the hard reflective surfaces of the wooden furniture.

They were effectively alone. Neither looked at the other nor spoke for some time.

Marie-Louise swallowed hard before saying softly at last, 'Thank you. You saved him.'

Her erstwhile friend ground her cigarette into the floor with her shoe before replying, 'I've got something for you.'

She reached into the pocket of her trousers and handed Marie-Louise a folded piece of hard vellum. Marie-Louise took it uncertainly. She unfolded it to reveal that it had a torn edge. It was a page from a book of sorts, bearing a handwritten list of names and addresses covering both sides. She scanned one side without recognition. A third of the way down the other she saw her own name and below it, in distinctive letters, 'Leutnant Adam Kohl, Luftwaffe'. The jolt of recognition left a pounding in her temples. She shook her head in shock.

'It's a page from a hotel register in Paris. The date is May 1941. It found its way to me about a year ago; God knows how. Luckily for you it was me . . . or it would have been a *tonte* for you last night.'

Marie-Louise's hand was shaking and the vellum trembled. She could not look at the woman beside her, whose eyes she could feel on her and whose voice was so hard.

'Why did you do that? You? You of all people.'

Marie-Louise folded the sheet slowly and gripped it hard to stop the trembling. 'I . . . it . . . happened . . . ' She struggled to find the right words. 'It happened over a long time. A year. He . . . it crept up. It crept up so slowly that I didn't recognise what it was. He spoke nearly perfect French and we were both alone . . . lonely. We talked in the evening after I came back from school and before he went to the airfield. Just talked.'

'You fucked him in a Paris hotel!'

There was brutal hostility in Ghislaine's voice. It would have intimidated Marie-Louise in the past but the intervening years had changed her too. There was a flash of anger in her reply as she now turned to look at her former friend.

'Don't insult me! Do you think that I'd do such a thing lightly? Do you?'

Ghislaine's jaw was set hard. 'But you did, didn't you?'

'I made love to a man who loved me. An exceptional human being. Yes. I did.'

'You deserve a *tonte!*'

'Yes. I do. And I've spent three years expecting it. So let's get it over with. You and Adèle can take it in turns.'

Ghislaine sprang to her feet and faced Marie-Louise. 'Don't insult *me!* Don't put me in the same space as that cow! I'd never do such a thing – and you know it. Why do you think I've just given you the evidence that would have had that bitch taking every last hair off your head? Because I can't stand her and . . . *merde* . . . you were my friend.' She shook her head and looked up at the peeling paint around the cornice, her mouth working with emotion. She looked back at Marie-Louise. 'I saw you last night. Behind the tank. I couldn't do that to you, or watch them do it to you. Never.' The last loiterers had now left the room and they were alone. They had been speaking *sotto voce* but now they spoke without restraint. Ghislaine began to pace between the table and the wall. 'And I couldn't let them lynch your father. They'd have done it – Adèle and Granèche. He's a savage: I saw what he did to an informer. Victor's a decent man – but even he couldn't have stopped them if I hadn't given them all that . . . bullshit.' Marie-Louise looked up at her, non-plussed. Ghislaine laughed bitterly and derisively. 'Of course it was bullshit! Do you really think he was helping us? He's a collaborator through and through. I don't know whether he helped betray the Communists. On past form I'd say it was a certainty, wouldn't you. The *réfractaires?* He's been Pétain's poodle for years and would do anything the gaga old fool said without blinking. They'll get him later for something; but by then the bloodlust will be over and he'll just get the disgrace he deserves. That's fine by me. I've been involved in too much killing over the last few years to want any more – even that old bastard.'

'So why . . . ?'

' . . . why did I save his bacon here? For you, of course. I was angry, so angry about you warning the Boche. And when I received that page out of the hotel register, I should have been even angrier still. But somehow . . . well . . . it all fell into place. Your illness.' She stopped pacing and perched on the edge of a table. She sighed and her shoulders slumped. 'And me. I'd changed by then too, I suppose. Less bloodthirsty. Tired of killing. Less hatred. Enough lives ruined. I suppose I wanted it all to stop. But it couldn't, of course – until now. This was the first chance to say "enough is enough". And I don't know whether I regret it or not . . . yet.' She rubbed her eyes and observed Marie-Louise with her chin cupped in her palm. 'I've been so looking forward to this liberation: the chance to deal with all the collaborators and traitors. We talked about it every time we met. Nursed the hatred. It worked. But after I saw that girl being sheared last night, I realised that if we do that enough, we just become like the Boche. Don't get me wrong; there are plenty of real bastards who deserve a bullet . . . but that girl? No. If it was her . . . then it had to be you. No.' She considered her shoes for a moment. 'Any news from Jerome?'

Marie-Louise shook her head. 'The last I heard was that he was being moved from a munitions factory to a farm in Silesia. And Robert?'

'He's been ill: pneumonia. Managed to treat himself with some antibiotics. God knows where he got them. Lucky it wasn't winter. He's in a camp near Pforsheim. This will be the worst time – the next few months. No news. We'll just have to wait, won't we? And pray it may all be over this year. Then what? It'll be different. For all of us. I'm not sure I'm looking forward to it. The peace I mean. A lot's happened, hasn't it?'

Marie-Louise considered. 'Not too much, I hope.'

They looked at each other and then away, pondering the thought. They could hear the sound of voices outside, with Granèche's angry tones clearly audible. Ghislaine straightened and breathed deeply.

'We'll find out soon enough.'

19

Montreuil. Nine months later. Late May 1945

Every wild flower on the riverbank was in full bloom. Forget-me-nots, daisies and dandelions competed with bluebells and cowslips for the late spring sunshine that periodically hid itself behind sculptured clouds that marched across an azure sky faster than the wind in the shelter of the valley would have suggested. The tricolour above the Citadelle, two kilometres away, was stretched out, horizontal and stiff. The noise of the weir flushing through the mill-race overwhelmed the rattle of poplar leaves that trembled to the neutered breeze on the valley floor. Marie-Louise found the constant noise of water soothing. She sat back on the hard wooden kitchen chair under the mill-house wall and allowed the sun to warm her face and flood her closed eyes with its radiance. She had finished the laundry – hard physical work – and was tired. Sleep touched her momentarily. She allowed herself to drift in and out of consciousness, enjoying the particular sensuality of the sun on her bare feet that had not felt its touch for many months. The dog that had come with the house, a mongrel shepherd, stirred itself from panting inertia and growled at a foreign presence. She sat upright feeling faintly dizzy, awaiting the visitor's appearance as the faint sound of footsteps marked his progress round the house.

The dog's hackles were raised as a man wearing a beret, greatcoat and haversack rounded the corner. It was Jerome. She stood. He swung his burden from shoulder to floor. His hair had thinned and his face was pared by malnutrition. He walked towards her and put his arms around her shoulders, pulling her into the thin nap of his overcoat that smelt of wood-smoke, horses and ancient perspiration. Her hands joined behind him and they stood, rocking against each other, as the sun reappeared from behind a cloud, needling its heat through their clothes. She had imagined this differently; many times. He was to have been wearing the uniform

264

in which she had said goodbye to him, starched and smelling of soap. She was to have greeted him home wearing her best dress and shedding tears of joy. But here they stood, in each other's arms, in threadbare clothes that would have disgraced a tramp in more normal times, pale and pinched, outside a house that was not their own, dry of eye. She felt his embrace relax and they stood awkwardly, looking at each other.

'Let's sit down,' she said. 'I'll get a chair.'

He nodded and she left him, collecting his hat and haversack as she entered the twilight of the house whose walls still held the chill of winter. In the passageway she halted at the looking glass and unpinned her hair so that it fell over her shoulders. She massaged her cheeks before taking a chair out into the spring sunshine where her husband was standing. They sat at a diagonal to each other and he took her hand.

'I went to the house – but it was shuttered and locked. Madame Acarier told me you were down here. A lorry dropped me by the path. Lucky. I had to walk up the hill into the town and I was feeling very tired. I always seem to be tired these days.'

'Have you been ill?'

'No. Thank God. If I had, I don't think I'd have made it.' He looked at her carefully. 'And you? You look thin but . . . it's good to see you. So good.'

He touched her cheek. She held his hand against her, conscious of the callused texture of their fingers – fingers accustomed to physical work. They sat with his caressing her cheek and hers the back of his hand.

'Why are you here? Your father?'

She nodded.

'Is he here?'

'No. Not at the moment. He's up in the town. I . . . I hate him going there. There's always something that upsets him. Someone says something and he comes back in a fury. Every time. That's why we came here. So that he could go outside and walk without someone taunting him. It's not been easy.'

'What happened?'

'A trial. November last year. Anyone who had . . . cooperated . . .

with the Boche. He avoided a prison sentence but was given an *indignité nationale*, which means that he's excluded from running for any public office – a sort of official disgrace. For life. So he's nothing to do, not many friends and a lot of enemies who love kicking him now that he's down. He always rises to the bait. Maybe we should have moved farther away. But he wouldn't hear of it. This was the best I could do.'

They looked at the flower-strewn bank and the foaming water framed by poplars and willows in the full flush of spring.

'You did well. It's beautiful.'

He sat back in the chair and closed his eyes, basking in the sun. With his face in repose, she could see the lines of hunger that lack of soap and water accentuated, with dirt etching itself into the crevices. Exhausted. If he had been boyish when he went away, there were now premature marks of age, with dark rings under his eyes and many days of beard surrounding his faintly feminine mouth. He squinted against the sun. She could just see the pupils that were observing her – as blue as she remembered.

'Is there any food?'

'Bread and cheese. Some mutton.'

'Drink?'

'Wine. Or cider.'

'And a bath?'

'A hipbath only. But I can heat some water. It'll take about half an hour.'

'I've dreamt about it for five years: half-an-hour's nothing. Perhaps I could eat first? As much as I want? Then a shave and a bath? Then a sleep in a bed. That's been a long time too.'

His eyes closed again and they both sat in the restorative sunlight. Above the sound of the water came a child's cry, not distressed but requiring attention. Jerome opened his eyes and raised an interrogatory eyebrow.

'It's Philippe. He's my cousin's son. An orphan. He's been living with us for the last five months. Stay here while I put water on to boil and get you some food. You can meet Philippe when he's woken properly.'

She stood and hesitated. He rose slowly and took her head in his hands and kissed her on her forehead and then on her lips – gently and softly. His breath had the halitosis of hunger. There was an awkwardness in the way she disengaged that they both felt.

'I won't be long.'

She returned again to the dusk of the mill's kitchen with its damp granite walls. She threw some logs into the fuel reservoir of the cast-iron range and left open the door so that the flames cast light, as well as warmth, into the cave-like room. She worked the hand pump until she had filled three buckets and these she poured into a voluminous hissing pot. As she worked, she could hear her son in the room above moving around, crying listlessly. Her husband was framed by the open door, standing and looking at the river with his hands buried in his overcoat pockets. He bent down to pick up a pebble which he threw out of her view before sitting again as the sun came out once more. She peeled a damp cloth from over a cheese and placed the cheese on a tray with a pewter beaker, a jug of wine and all the bread remaining in the house; then she drew a chair next to the range and gathered her thoughts. She would have to tell him – but not now.

She had made up her mind about the child upstairs after the trial of the previous November with its acid slipstream of recrimination and shame. Force of law had returned with the autumn, along with *réfractaires* and members of the Maquis in search of revenge. The *épuration* became official rather than *sauvage* – but relentless none the less: her father was one of many whose dealings and actions over the previous four years were forensically picked apart, judged and condemned. Charity and mercy seemed to be as rationed as food during that last astringent winter of the war. Disgrace settled over the Annecy household, contaminating Marie-Louise, as well as her father, in spite of moral support from Ghislaine, who publicly took her arm in the face of Adèle and her coterie's cold persecution. A deep melancholy settled on her father who rarely left his room. On days when some of his old spirit returned, he would venture out to his customary haunts – only to return in impotent rage and frustration after some bruising encounter. When she suggested they move to the old mill in the valley below the town, he had grunted his acquiescence, having demurred at the initial suggestion of Boulogne or Amiens. When she told him of her decision to bring his grandson to live with them, he had merely shrugged his shoulders.

The Christmas of 1944, with Montreuil freezing in the same arctic blast that had dogged Hitler's last-gasp offensive in the Ardennes, had been the catalyst. Marie-Louise and her father had spent most of the feast-day itself in bed for warmth: there was barely enough fuel for the cooking of what little food was available, let alone for heating. During these dreary hours of virtual hibernation, she had unlocked her secret casket for longer than she usually allowed herself and cradled her child in her imagination, stroking his hair and burying her face in the soft folds of his dimpled body, feeling him squirm and settle in her grasp, imagining his gentle breathing as he slept beside her. She could smell him; hear him murmur in his sleep. With the New Year, as the skies cleared and the blizzards relented, she resolved to bring him back to live with her, adopted as the orphan child of relatives killed in the fighting in Normandy the previous year – a common enough story that would have elicited neither surprise nor questions. She had made her way to the farm that had been found by Father Pierre and saw him for the first time on a clear January morning as he chased chickens with a twig in one hand and a handful of snow in the other, seemingly oblivious to the cold. He was darker than she had imagined, black haired and eyed but with a tinge of reddish brown caught by the harsh winter sun. As she watched him play, she realised guiltily that his tough independence was the consequence of benign neglect by the couple who had fostered him. They had older children and, while kindly enough, they had looked on their charge as an income producer rather than an adopted son. He was well fed and healthy but had never known maternal intimacy. As they sat together in the freezing train carriage, she acknowledged to herself that this emotional starvation was why he had left the farm with only the briefest of tears and accepted her as a substitute without protest.

As she opened the door into his room, he raised his arms to be held by her, his eyes still bleary and a droop of snot clinging to his nose. She carried him downstairs, flopped over her shoulder with his finger and thumb massaging her earlobe. She managed to carry both the tray and him out to Jerome at the same time and he nestled on her knee as her husband assaulted the food without word or halt until even the crumbs had been swept up by a damp finger. He placed the tray on the ground and considered the child with the tentative smile of a man unused to children. He reached over to ruffle his hair – but the boy retreated back into the protection of the arc between his mother's chin and breast. There was a stiffness between the three of them that Marie-Louise tried to ignore by cradling the child as if he were a baby, swinging him so that he gave himself over to the sensation with an expression of bliss consumed. Jerome's thin smile, she realised, contained jealousy – and she inwardly kicked herself for her insensitivity. This time was for him and not the child. Why had she not thought this moment through? It had only required some imagination. She reached over to him and rested her hand on his arm.

'The water will be boiling now. I'll put the bath in the kitchen next to the range – it's the warmest place. And I'll get clean clothes and a razor.'

He did not reply but took her hand in his and looked over the river. A tear splashed on the lapel of his coat as he squeezed her hand. They stayed like this for some time with the child absent-mindedly fondling her chin and her husband staring at the river, swallowing to contain his emotion until she withdrew her hand in order to attend to the practicalities. When he came into the house, the hipbath was steaming and Philippe was absorbed in a game at the table. Marie-Louise stepped behind him and took his coat. He stood uncertainly as she undid the buttons on his grey flannel shirt with its tidemarks of sweat and peppering of holes to reveal the ivory white of his ribcage and arms of swollen joints and loose skin. Tenderly, she leant forward and kissed his chest, feeling his hand stroke the back of her head as she did so. He sat on a stool and undid his boots while she knelt on the floor in front of him with the vanilla and cheese smell of profoundly unwashed clothes assaulting her. Naked, with raw impetigo sores and the scars of his hungry imprisonment displayed, she observed him with a maternal anger. She had always before seen his body as a sexual thing – and as assertively vital – but this emaciated physique was something for compassion rather than desire. She held his arm as he stepped into the bath and lay back with his eyes closed and hot water lapping over him. She slowly poured a jug over his head and rubbed soap into his hair and loofahed his back, massaging him as she did so, feeling him relax under the pressure of her fingers. She lathered shaving soap and held a mirror for him as he carefully worked a razor through his beard to reveal the face that she remembered, hollow-cheeked and sabre-lined with tiredness – but her husband none the less, returned, against the odds, from his war. He stood passive and childlike as she worked an abrasive towel over him, running it around his groin with the touch of a nurse rather than a lover. She had imagined their reunion being a charged outpouring of the pent-up frustrations of five years, followed by a clinging together as he softened inside her. That would come later. She handed him clothes that he held up to his nose, breathing in the cleanliness, soap and camphor.

'Food. Bath. Now bed?'

She led him up the stairs, again like a nurse. Her room had the simplicity of a cell with only brushstrokes of femininity – a hat with a faded ribbon over the rosewood mirror, her mother's silk dressing-gown trailing from a wedge between stones, a stick of flowering blackthorn in a rough pot. Whitewashed walls. He allowed her to turn down the cover and lay down compliantly.

'Sit with me for a while. Please.'

She sat on the edge of the bed with his hand in hers – his callused thumb working over the veins on the back of her hand.

'There's a lot I need to tell you.'

'And me you. We've plenty of time. Sleep now – as long as you can.'

She felt his grip slacken and his pulse tapping against her index finger. His wet hair stained the pillow, a halo framing his familiar, but long absent, face. She noted the slackening of the edges of his mouth that she had observed on countless mornings. She could hear the bleat of Philippe from below – but ignored it, taking the opportunity to observe him without a questioning return of eye contact. In sleep some of the strain ebbed away from his face. The lines were less etched without the emphasis of engrained dirt, but the pinched cheeks and furrowed brow were immune to soap. He had been away for five years – but had returned ten years older. His hair had receded at the temples. The thinness took away some of the overt sensuality of his lips and rebalanced this mature face into something nobler than before. Memories stirred in her of kisses, and those lips working below her waist with her fingers entwined in his damp hair. A more insistent cry from below terminated her reverie and she quietly closed the door on his sleeping form.

As she absent-mindedly attended to her son's demands, she turned over the previous hours in her mind. What should she tell him? When? How? How would he react? This last closeness might have been just that – the final trusting moment between them before recriminations and the bitterness of betrayal set in. She had broached it with her father during the final days of the war, when the moment of Jerome's return was an imminent possibility. She had stammered over it, tongue-tripped and embarrassed.

He had considered her quandary for a few moments. 'Wait,' he had said. 'Wait until he's settled.'

'But it would be a lie, papa: a lie.'

'So? The world's built on lies. Imagine the carnage if everyone spoke the truth.'

She had thought he was being obtuse but, on consideration, she appreciated the wisdom in what he was saying.

'But later?'

'Maybe. That's for you to decide. If you don't, then what's lost? Everyone has little guilty secrets tucked away. I've always thought that truthfulness is an overrated virtue – unless it's handled carefully. It's a dish better served with sauce and spice to disguise the not-so-palatable raw materials. You'd risk everything by telling him – and you don't have to, do you?'

She had turned this over many times in her mind since, but now that he was home she felt the horns of the dilemma even more acutely. She had anticipated a change in him – but not the extent of his physical deterioration; if she was going to tell him, it would have to be later when he was stronger, when there was more chance of a balanced understanding and when she had shared something of his sufferings. Thinking of his recumbent form upstairs and of his ravaged nakedness in the bath, she felt a surge of love that surprised her. Her nagging doubt had been that what she still so keenly felt for Adam must, of necessity, deplete that available for her husband. To her relief, as she stoked the fire with Philippe tugging at her skirt, she realised that Adam Kohl had led her to an insight: that the love for one person did not negate love for another; that the curious vessel of the emotions had the miraculous capacity of expanding to contain whatever was added to it. Without jealousy, anything was possible. But there's the rub, she thought: without jealousy. Was that possible?

So buried was she in her thoughts that she did not hear her father enter the house and noticed him only when his shadow darkened the already gloomy kitchen. He took in the bath and the pile of clothes on the floor.

'He's back?'

She nodded.

'And?'

'He's thin. Very thin. And tired. I put him to bed. He'll sleep for a long time. But no injuries – physically, anyway. His mind? I don't know. He looks ten years older.'

He put his hand on her shoulder. 'My dear, you must expect him to be different. It's war. No one who's witnessed it is the same afterwards. He'll have seen things . . . things that humans aren't prepared for . . . terrible things probably. He'll recover, God willing, but it'll take time. And patience. Don't rush things. Anything.'

She reached up and placed her hand on his. Philippe had gone quiet and was watching the two adults with a thumb in his mouth and a twig swishing back and forth. Her father squeezed her shoulder.

'I'll take my things and stay in Pierre Duchamp's spare room for a few days while you two get used to each other again. I've already asked him in anticipation – and he and his wife have agreed. It'll be better for you both not having me around. You'll need time on your own.' She reached up to the hand on her shoulder and pressured it in grateful acknowledgement. 'But before I go, I think we should take this young man paddling in the river as we agreed this morning. And we might take some wine with us to celebrate your husband's return.'

Jerome slept for two days. Every few hours during the day, and at least once during the night, Marie-Louise would climb the stairs and open the door a crack. If he stirred, she would retreat, but if the eiderdown continued to rise and fall with each breath, she would sit on the chair and watch his sleeping face as his beard grew and he occasionally called out to someone in another place. Once he opened his eyes – but they were staring elsewhere, too, and they closed again without recognition.

He appeared in the kitchen, wearing his nightshirt and the confusion of long sleep, just as she and Philippe were finishing a bare breakfast of rough bread. Marie-Louise rose and kissed the stubble of his cheek, guiding him next to the child who offered him his hot milk as a gift. She could see from the way his eyes darted towards any possible depository of food that the void in his stomach was monopolising his thoughts. The previous day she had prepared a stew of snared rabbit and potatoes in anticipation of his awakening – so she set about warming the pot while stealing glances at him as he played awkwardly with the child. He ate with the urgency of someone who had long ago learnt to eat whenever the opportunity arose – feral eyes casting around for more even as his hands relentlessly shovelled food towards his mouth. She had prepared enough stew for three – but when it was finished he continued to glance greedily at anything edible, despite the discomfort that the sudden surfeit was inflicting on a constitution unused to such riches. Apart from the greeting that accompanied the kiss, the only words he spoke were of request and gratitude, with the child observing silently. He finished and eyed the daybed in the corner of the room.

'Do you mind if I lie down to digest all that. I haven't eaten so much since . . . I can't remember. You've no idea how good it feels.'

He was slightly crouched with indigestion as he edged his way on to the mahogany *bateau-lit* that had come with them from the town house. He arranged himself against the bolster and beckoned Philippe to join him. The child climbed up – but not without a questioning glance towards his mother, who drew her chair to the edge of the bed in reassurance. His deep-scarred lines were still shocking to her, but something of his previous vigour had returned along with its sharp edges. It was there in his movements: the way his eyes swept the room, taking in the raw stone shining with damp, the hand pump over the sink – the house of an artisan rather than a bourgeois. He reached over and took her hand.

'How are you? I never asked yesterday. Was it yesterday?'

'Two days ago.'

'Two days!' A thought insinuated itself. 'But where's your father?'

'Staying with a friend – just about the only one he still has – in town. He wanted us to have some time on our own.'

He nodded slowly with his eyebrows raised in surprise.

'That was . . . good of him.'

'He's changed. He's an old man now. The last year nearly killed him. He's gone from being mayor and war hero to a collaborator who was nearly lynched after the liberation. It's why we're here and not in our house in the town.'

'And Bernadette?'

'Her mother refused to allow her to work for us any more. We manage – though I miss the school. I had to resign. Not because of papa – but for Philippe. Victoire and her husband were killed in Normandy during the bombing of Caen.' She forced herself to look at the narrow defile into the wooden staircase as she delivered her lie. 'There was no one else to care for him.' She willed her eyes back towards her husband. 'I'm sorry I couldn't ask you or even let you know. It's a big shock, I know. An instant family. But I had to do something.'

His smile was stretched, clearly not entirely comfortable – but ingenuous. The paternal did not come naturally, she could see, but there was a largeness of spirit in the comforting pressure on her hand that triggered a resurgence of the feelings she had had as she had watched him sleep. He ruffled Philippe's hair in the way that those unused to children indicate affection and intimacy.

'I think we'll get on, won't we?'

The child looked at him, then at his mother, and pointed towards the *étranger* in the house.

'Mama, is that my papa?'

She nodded.

The child considered this and, with the abrupt acceptance that only children manage, returned to digging at the mattress with his stick. She squeezed Jerome's hand.

'Will you tell me what happened to you – since you moved to the farm from the factory? I don't know if you received any letters from me: I sent one every fortnight after the liberation in the hope that they might get through . . . . but I got nothing back. Nothing. Like dropping stones into a well and hearing no splash. We heard about the Russian offensive and about the big air raids. And the snow and cold. I thought about you every day – many times a day. Tell me. Please. I've done so much guessing.'

He did not answer immediately but watched the child who was absorbed in his excavations. He carried on looking at him as he spoke, slowly at first, then faster, with his voice rising with anger or stumbling occasionally with emotion as he described his experiences.

'The farm was a big improvement on the factory. That was in October, I think, just after the harvest. No *appel* at dawn and plenty of food: a chance to build ourselves up. I don't think any of us would have made it otherwise. It was about twenty kilometres from Breslau in Silesia: flat country, rich soil and peaceful. You wouldn't have known there was a war going on. There were only three of us – Pierre, Raphael and me. Pierre . . . . poor Pierre had TB. The coughing drove us mad but anything was better than those huge huts near the factory that had each held five hundred, at least half of them mad in one way or another after five years behind wire. The owner was a decent woman. Better than that. She found medicine for Pierre and let me have the run of the library in the schloss. That was almost as good as the food as there was a whole section of French literature; I wasn't feeling too keen on even the greatest writing in German at that point. The work was hard, but whatever I lost to the work, I gained back in the food. I've probably never been fitter.' He gave a mirthless laugh. 'We knew that this couldn't go on for ever: it was only a matter of time until the Russians invaded. We heard – how the news got to us, I've no idea – about the breakout from Normandy and the liberation of Paris. All I wanted to hear was news from the north, from Montreuil, or at least from Boulogne or Calais. If they were liberated then surely you would be in Montreuil as well. But nothing. During the autumn and winter it was just us three, so we didn't have the access to news that seemed to arrive almost instantaneously in a big camp. On the farm we had to guess from what the Germans told us – and all they had was propaganda. We were despondent when we heard that the Western offensive had petered out in the autumn. We had all hoped that the war would be over last year. We heard about the Boche offensive in the Ardennes – they were screaming it from the rooftops – but then silence. We could guess what had happened. There was a mood change at that point, after New Year. Even our old guard, a farmer from Bavaria – a nice, gentle man – became hard and difficult. We all – the guards and us – knew that this was the endgame and that we were in the worst place possible: as far as we could be from the Western Allies and right in the way of the Russians. The Germans dreaded them – and so did we. We'd shared a hut with some Poles and Lithuanians and the stories they told us about life under Stalin made us as anxious as the Germans to get as far west as we could. Rather ironic, isn't it – to be terrified of your liberators?'

'What about escape?'

'We thought about it; talked about it often. But we were hundreds of miles into eastern Germany and all the roads and railways were crawling with military police. Our guards were terrified of them. Any man in civilian clothes, or uniform, would have had his papers checked a dozen times a day and from what we heard – and saw hanging from trees – they didn't waste time with trials or inquiries. We reckoned that at some point the Boche would move us westwards and that we would be better off in a train with an armed guard than trying to make it on our own on foot. We could make a break when we were nearer France. From what we saw later, it was the right decision.' He hesitated, weighing up the retrospective probabilities. 'The offensive broke in mid-January. It was cold, as cold as I can ever remember. We were woken before dawn and marched about five kilometres to a small station where we were locked in the waiting room. It was just off the main road to the west that was choked with refugees: no men other than the very old; mothers and children mainly. As night fell, they let some join us in the shelter of the waiting room until there was no room to lie down, or even sit. The guards locked the door again. In the morning, when we went outside, there were whole families frozen on the platform in little huddles. And one woman – it's funny, I can't get her out of my mind, though I saw many other worse things – with a baby frozen to her nipple. She looked like my cousin, Simone.'

Philippe looked up at him, sensing the change in his voice. He swallowed to control his emotion.

'A train stopped the next day and they pushed us into a cattle truck that was full of other prisoners-of-war – packed in. We were lucky. There were a dozen Americans who had been captured in Normandy in the summer: tough, fit and well led by a colonel who organised a roster which circulated everyone around the truck so that some could lie while others stood around the edges. Without that, those on the edges would have frozen. There were some Tommies on board who wouldn't cooperate. The colonel simply threw the ringleader out of the train into a snowdrift. The others fell into line after that. We were on the train for two or three days. Endless waits in sidings as we stopped for trains going towards the front. No food – other than what we had taken with us from the farm – and the only water was melted snow. But anything was better than the horrors we could see on the road when the train ran alongside it. When we got to Gorlitz, on the border between Silesia and Saxony, they opened the doors and unloaded us. They pushed us into a barn for the night and the colonel managed to persuade the guards to allow a party to scavenge for food. The farm was abandoned but the animals were still there. We butchered a cow and two pigs and found a store of potatoes and turnips which gave us all one big meal before we set off the next day, on foot, in the snow, heading west and north – towards Berlin we thought.'

He halted, with his fingers tugging at his top lip in contemplation. He reached out his other hand to hers.

'I don't think any of us thought we'd survive it. I can't describe the cold. I've never felt anything like it: relentless wind and an endless white and grey stretching to the horizon. We overhauled another column of prisoners: Russians. Some had no boots, only rags wrapped around their feet; others without anything to cover their heads. All were starved, with just white, staring eyes out of hollow bearded faces. One stopped to tie up the bandages around his feet. A guard clubbed him unconscious with the butt of his rifle. There was a roar of anger from our side of the road and we started to throw food or cigarettes to them. You cannot imagine what that meant – throwing food to someone else. A packet of cigarettes fell short and one of the poor wretches ran out to grab it. One of our guards – an old *Volkssturm* conscript, not an SS – stamped on his fingers just as he was reaching out to pick them up. There was nearly a riot. What was strange was that we had got to know the guards quite well. They were in as bad shape as we were – worn clothes, no food, freezing – and yet he looked at us completely baffled. Just brutalised, I suppose. How do humans get like that? Easily, I think, all too easily: when food disappears even your friends, men with whom you have been through so much already, will steal food from you. Even Pierre. And me.'

He stopped and stared out of the door at the spring sunshine beyond.

'I'm not sure where the guards thought they were taking us. We just got up in the morning and headed in a westerly sort of direction; anywhere that was away from the Russians and towards the heart of Germany. We grew to dread the towns: hard cobbles underfoot and civilians who were more and more aggressive and angry the farther west we went. Women and children threw stones at us and we really thought that it was only a matter of time before they lynched the pilots among us. There was fear everywhere: fear of the Russians and the Nazis, fear of bombing and, above all, we realised, fear of the millions of prisoners who were now everywhere in Germany. Up until last winter most of them had been spread over the extended Reich, particularly in the East – in Poland and the occupied Soviet Union – out of sight. Now they were in Germany; marching like us, in miserable temporary camps, or just abandoned and sleeping in barns or old factories – anywhere where they could get shelter; desperate; nothing to lose. And what I've learnt is that people most hate those they fear. You'd think there'd be pity. No. Not much. Some gave us food. More threw things at us and, in the bombed cities, screamed at us that we were murderers. Escape? No one thought about it. The opposite. We were terrified of being left behind. Safety in numbers.'

He shook his head as if to clear it of its memories and sighed. 'I'd love a cigarette. And coffee?'

Marie-Louise shook her head. 'No coffee. Even papa can't get it now. But a cigarette – yes. And I can do a sort of tea with honey.'

He smiled at her and reached out to touch her hand. 'Anything.'

She looked at him with the first real happiness that she had felt in years lighting up her face. There was a gentleness there that was new in him. She bustled by the range, conscious of his eyes on her and, with a tea of sorts, they both settled into a domestic huddle, smoking, with the child playing between them in the naturalness of a long-standing family. A cloud of memory settled over him again.

'Do you want to hear the rest?'

She nodded.

'Torgau. That's where we ended up. On the Elbe, about two hundred kilometres south of Berlin. We were at the end of our tether, finished. Two months of freezing marches, little food. Disease. Pierre died in a barn one night. In February. I can't even remember where it was. The ground was too hard to bury him. So we just had to leave him. I think about it . . . him . . . often. Still.'

He halted, blinking and swallowing before he could go on.

'We were in a barracks on the outskirts of the city, on the east side unfortunately: the Russian side. We heard them first in the distance. Artillery. Low-flying bombers and then the sound of those terrible rockets – *Katyushas*; Stalin's organs they called them. I don't know how the Boche ever had the nerve to stand up to a bombardment from them. By that point we were too tired and ill to care. So were our guards. A tank smashed through the gate followed by . . . it's difficult to describe them. They were armed to the teeth but one was wearing a dress and a woman's fur hat with his steel helmet over the top. Another had a German general's uniform – red-striped trousers and grey field-coat along with one of those padded helmets made for tank personnel. We thought they were going to shoot us all at first. We looked pretty strange, I suppose, a mixture of uniforms and hats that weren't that different from our guards. I had a British greatcoat – the one I appeared here in – and a

Wehrmacht forage cap with a balaclava underneath. It became pretty obvious who was who: we just stood there stupidly but the guards had their hands up shouting *"Kamerad!"* The first thing they did was to take everyone's watches. Your wedding present to me went, I'm afraid, to a boy who was hardly old enough to shave. He had a dozen on each wrist. Then they pushed the guards into a corner and forgot about them. It was late afternoon and they'd obviously decided that this was their billet for the night and they made themselves at home. Strapped to the back of the tanks were cases of drink and the most extraordinary loot: I saw a piano, curtains, women's underwear, old-fashioned corsets and a sofa. To make firewood, they just drove a tank track over a cupboard and then lit a bonfire on the floor of the hall we were in – even though there was a perfectly good fireplace in the corner. It didn't take them long to get comfortable – then they started drinking: industrial quantities. They made us join them – one of them made me finish the best part of a bottle of schnapps while he pushed a machine pistol in my face: a sort of joke. He was splitting his sides with laughter as I nearly choked. I wasn't sure whether we were prisoners or allies at first. It was like sharing a cage with a friendly hyena that wants to play with you: the bite might be amiable – but it could still take off your arm. They unstrapped the piano from the tank and got the guards to manhandle it on to the ground. They signalled that one of them should play: the law of averages meant that someone in the fifty or so prisoners they now had would be a musician. A boy – no more than fifteen of sixteen – volunteered. Or rather the others pushed him forward. He started to play: beautifully. And he carried on for two days. Every time he wilted one of them would pour schnapps down him or hit him: sometimes with a slap, other times with a bottle or a pistol butt. Finally, he collapsed. Two of them dragged him outside and shot him.

'Almost everyone was asleep – mostly comatose with drink – when the Americans arrived. The luck of it. We just happened to be at the very point where the Allies linked up. They walked into the hall not believing their eyes. It must have been a sight: bonfire smouldering; Russians lying drunk everywhere wearing a kaleidoscope of clothes; German prisoners huddled in a corner terrified of what was coming next; American, British and French POWs not much better than the Russians. When the Russians realised what had happened, the party started all over again. Their capacity for drink was prodigious. It only stopped when some military police arrived – I think they were the NKVD – and beat them into sobriety. They'd have nothing to do with any of us, or the Americans: no drinking toasts or even shaking hands. They looked on us as something contaminated and pointed their guns at the Americans – who seemed to be baffled by it. I got the feeling that they were naïve, to say the least, about their allies. They'd had a diet of propaganda too – just at the opposite end of the scale from the Germans – and the reality of what their allies thought of them must have been a shock. The Russians were all for taking us with them but our American colonel came to the rescue again and insisted that all of us, including our guards, were going with the Americans. They must have been relieved that they'd treated us well. There were some pretty tense negotiations but the Russians backed down and, for the first time in three months, we really thought we might survive. God bless America.'

He said the last without irony. Marie-Louise looked at him with surprise, as his pre-war attitude to America had been reactively hostile. This brush with the reality of the Communist brotherhood had cleared some illusions. He then asked her about Montreuil, about the changes and the news of friends and relations. When the sun came out, projecting thin shafts through decades of grime into the granite gloom of the kitchen, he suggested that they go outside and lie by the river.

By a pebbled pool, darkened by the sinuous shadows of grazing trout and shaded by rippling willows, they lay in the grass and wild flowers with Philippe paddling in the shallows in the perfection of peacetime. As their bodies absorbed the sun, Jerome continued intermittently through the morning and into the afternoon to tell her the rest of his story.

He told her about the frustration and boredom of the holding camp where they awaited the final collapse. Food was there, but not enough to cure the effects of five years of deprivation. He described his decision to escape and make his own way back to France rather than await the bureaucratic grindings of the post-war Allied machine. He had gone out with a volunteer work party to help mend bombed railway lines and slipped away during a cigarette break to join the chaos that was Europe in the first days of peace. He described the cascade of humanity on the roads – on foot, in carts, on bicycles; trains bristling with the destitute, on roofs and boarding plates, heading back to the corners of a continent from where they had been exiled; military convoys pushing past carts and prams carrying disintegrating suitcases and children with ricket-twisted legs; the taunts of GIs sprawling in health and victory, sneering at humiliated French soldiers wearing rags and exhaustion; menacing bands of Displaced Persons, toothless from malnutrition and still wearing the striped prison clothes that were the Nazi mark of shame; the indifference of soup kitchens; puddles of fear within groups of former slaves from territories now under the Soviet yoke, arguing with bored military bureaucrats against repatriation to the certainty of the Gulag; dull-eyed victims of rape; feral children combing the ruins of cities in hungry packs; the stink of excrement and buried cadavers blooming in the early spring heat.

He described his journey, mainly by train but also on foot and in the back of empty lorries heading westward to the Channel coast for food to feed a starving continent; the awful necropoli that had been the cities of Germany, seemingly destroyed beyond renaissance; endless waits, days sometimes, in dusty sidings – thirsty and hungry and itching with impetigo. He told her about the France she had not seen: the devastation and guilty misery in Alsace-Lorraine, whose mainly Francophone male population had been drafted into the *Werhmacht* and the SS – to cover themselves in notoriety in some cases; the self-serving greed of peasant farmers hoarding their food in expectation of the speculator's profit; suspicious closed doors and turned backs to requests for shelter; indifference to the suffering and humiliations of the army by civilians who felt their own experiences to have been their equal; the scars of the *épuration* all too apparent in taunts across cafés and bowed women wearing headscarves in the sunshine to cover their humiliation. He described to her a defeated country playing the victor: bankrupt, morally and economically – but acting out the part of resurrected heroism.

'A country fit for heroes? No. Not too many heroes; and not much of a country at the moment. Funny, isn't it? We must have known what it would be like but we chose to see it through rose-tinted spectacles. We all remembered the bitterness of the previous decade. How could we not when it was played out in the camps all over again? But somehow we . . . I . . . imagined France in a different light; that life would be going on as normal but with a glow around it: all the best bits, the bits in the sunshine. I wasn't the only one. It was a sort of ideal in which we invested all our hopes, an antidote to the grim reality of our day-to-day lives. We had to believe it, I suppose . . . to keep sane. When it was fractured, it sent men over the top. One of those I was captured with – a *notaire* from the Ardèche – got a letter one day from his wife saying that she was leaving him. No reason. Just the fact. He hanged himself with his belt in the latrine.'

Marie-Louise felt a surge of guilt rising and the familiar pounding in her temples. She sat up to shade her eyes as if in concern for the child who was nonchalantly stirring the mud at the edge of the pool. Jerome remained lying on his stomach with his chin in his palm, his view of the river framed by grass-stalks, oblivious of the turmoil his last remark had caused. She felt an almost over-whelming urge to tell him everything – but fought it down.

He rolled over on to his side and faced her. 'Your letters. Thank you. You managed to keep the illusion for me. Keep me sane perhaps. I know it was lonely. Your father. Food. All sorts of difficulties. I saw men go mad trying to wrestle with domestic things in the camps. A wrong phrase, an insinuation, a casual remark would be worried over for weeks, built up into something it wasn't. By the time it could be cleared up, the damage had been done and a worm had bored its way into the back of the brain and a sort of madness taken hold. You shielded me from that. I know you did. Thank you.'

He reached up to her and pulled her head down towards his and they kissed, tentatively at first and then deeply. She lay down next to him, with the chattering of the water and the humming of her son as the aural backdrop, and allowed the sun and his lips to caress her into a sensual trance, free of thoughts and full of happiness.

20

Montreuil. Three weeks later. Mid June 1945

If a farmer, or someone checking rabbit snares, had passed the old mill in the valley below Montreuil in the early morning of the summer solstice, he might have come across a woman sitting on a low-swept branch of an ancient hornbeam that provided a seat and also shelter from the light drizzle. It was also a vantage point, allowing her to see the mill without being seen herself. She was wearing a coat and hat against the rain and the unseasonal chill. Every few minutes she would stand and walk a circle with a slight limp before resuming her vigil.

At about ten o'clock the door opened and a small child appeared, minded by a woman dressed similarly to the one under the tree, carrying a small suitcase and followed by an older man who shut the door behind them. They walked slowly down the path that led to the road and the town until the shadows of the wood enfolded them. The woman under the tree waited for a few minutes, smoking and pacing, before throwing aside her cigarette. She walked quickly down the riverbank to the massive elm door and knocked, waiting with her fist against her mouth. A man opened the door and they stared at each other without speaking before he stood back and she walked past him into the dark of the interior.

Marie-Louise could feel a blister bubbling under her heel as the mill-house came into sight. Philippe was grizzling gently beside her, holding on to her free hand with both of his, allowing himself to be pulled along. The arm holding the suitcase was aching and, despite the cool weather, she was hot with the exertion and relieved at the prospect of being able to sit down. It was a long walk from the station. The train to Honfleur had broken down. Her grandmother was ill – again – and concern about her heightened the discomfort of her feet. She opened the door and pushed her son ahead of her into the cave-like interior, smelling the familiar cocktail of tobacco and wood smoke melded with damp. As her eyes adjusted to the gloom, she saw her husband standing by the range with a look of surprise, and opposite him a woman, wearing a buttoned coat and a similarly startled expression.

'The train. It was cancelled.'

Jerome blinked before recovering himself. 'Your suitcase. Here. I'll take it.'

The woman looked down as he bustled the case into the corner. She took a step towards Marie-Louise and held out her hand. 'My name's Mimi. I know you're Jerome's wife. I'm sorry to surprise you.'

The woman's voice had the tincture of an accent that she had heard in eastern France. Marie-Louise nodded and took her hand briefly before dropping it to attend to Philippe who was tugging insistently at the hem of her skirt. With a dozen thoughts criss-crossing her mind, she crouched down to undo the child's coat, grateful for the interruption. By the time it was removed and she had straightened, Jerome was back by the range.

He gestured towards the table and chairs. 'Please. Let's sit down. Wine? And water?'

Both women nodded and sat either side of the table, silent as he worked the pump to fill a jug and pushed beakers and a plain bottle of wine into the middle of the table. Marie-Louise stole a glance at the interloper. There was an alertness about her, despite marks of privation and still unhealed wounds, that reminded her of Ghislaine; an elegance in her bearing that trumped uneven features that were less than the sum of the parts. Some sixth sense told her that this woman represented something important – and dangerous, perhaps. There was meaning in the glance that she had seen her dart at her husband as he had stood by the range and an intimacy in how he reciprocated. A familiar apprehension crept over her.

'Who are you? Not your name. Why are you here?'

'I'm German. Jerome worked on my farm; towards the end of the war.'

'The library?'

She nodded.

'So why are you here?'

'I didn't know . . . if Jerome had a wife. I guessed perhaps. But I didn't know – until yesterday. I didn't intend to see you. But I needed to see Jerome. I'm sorry. I really am.'

Marie-Louise believed her. 'What about?'

Jerome spoke. 'She's pregnant. That's what she came to tell me.' A pulsing cloud in her head and the skin of the bubble of self-protection undulating in her vision; the insistent sound of the child scraping the edge of the wood box. 'I was going to tell you. I was waiting for the right moment. But I didn't know about . . . '

She could feel herself nodding and a rippling calm coming over her. 'It's . . . OK.' Echoing around the bubble. 'It's the war.' She gave out something that could have been an ironic laugh – but could also have been a sob. 'I met someone a few years ago who used to say the war was a bad excuse – but he said it anyway. Is it the war?' Neither answered. 'All the things that have happened – they wouldn't have happened without it, would they?'

Mimi looked at her. 'No. They wouldn't. This certainly. And . . . I'm not here to take him from you, I promise. Please believe me. It wasn't about that. Isn't about that. I needed to know if there was . . . if he was married. Then I was going back to . . . I'm not sure. Maybe to my friend. Somewhere.'

'When?'

'September. I'll manage. With my parents, if necessary. It won't be the only baby in Germany without a father.'

'It has a father.' Jerome was looking down at the table as he spoke.

Marie-Louise placed her hand carefully on his. 'I have something to tell you too. I was going to tell you. Later. Once we'd settled. Got used to each other again. It's about Philippe.'

The bubble again. Roaring silence.

'I think . . . I knew. Something. I don't need to know more.'

'You do. He was German. He's dead. No one knows, except papa.'

The three of them looked at each other, now in a balance of uncertainty and revelation, the silence only broken by a nervous laugh from Jerome.

'Quite a morning.'

Marie-Louise glanced at the interloper but couldn't hold her eye.

Mimi spoke. 'I don't even know your name.'

'Did Jerome not tell you?'

'We never talked about you.'

'Do you . . . have a husband?'

'I don't know. He's missing. In Russia. Was missing. Who knows now? He may be a prisoner . . . but probably dead.'

'How will you . . . explain . . . this?'

Mimi shrugged and sighed. 'I don't know. I'll have plenty of time to think about it . . . if I . . . if we . . . want to live together again. I don't think I do. Too much has happened. I think I've become a different person. Does that make sense? It sounds very . . . brutal.'

Marie-Louise looked up at her in surprise at the intimacy of these revelations. The openness of the woman opposite her was allaying some of her fears. She found herself responding.

'No. It sounds like the truth. I too worried every day . . . about what would happen afterwards, after the war. I've changed. Both of us have: difficult to spend five years in prison and not change; maybe too much; too much to be able to fit together again afterwards. But we have managed it. So much better than I thought we would. Now this. It looks as if I was worried about the wrong things, doesn't it?'

'No.' Jerome spoke. He had been listening quietly to the two women. 'You don't have to worry. Mimi's right. I worried too. About us. About myself. I was terrified – wondering whether I'd be able to make it without a breakdown of some sort. And what would happen afterwards. Whether I could cope with the disgrace – about what happened at Sedan.'

Both women looked at him in surprise. Marie-Louise spoke for them both. 'Sedan?'

He looked away. This was a raw wound. 'I haven't talked about this to a soul. I wanted to share it. So wanted to. Maybe now I can.' He stroked the beaker as he talked. 'It happened on the day that Robert and I were captured.' He pushed his two index fingers and thumbs together and gazed through the delta they formed at the contents of the table. 'Our unit was detailed to cover a bridge over a small river. Not much more than a stream: deep enough to stop a tank though – with steep sides. The Boche had broken through and we were covering the retreat. The machine-gun detachment.

Key. Two of us. One to fire and one to feed the belt. Me. The others had rifles – and a few grenades. The Boche got across the river somehow and outflanked us. A bullet hit the side of my helmet. Glanced off. I ran. Panicked. Left the others. All of them were killed except Robert, who managed to crawl into a ditch and ended up next to me. I thought he'd kill me there and then. He put his rifle between my eyes.' His finger was pressed hard against his forehead so that a halo was forming white around the pressure of his finger. 'The only reason he didn't shoot me was that the Boche were all around us. By the time they'd moved on, he'd calmed down. You know Robert; he's not easily angered.' Ghislaine's husband was a placid man of gentle hands and calm judgements. 'We were left behind the front and it was only a matter of time before we were picked up and packed off to a camp near Darmstadt. Together. He never mentioned it again. And I don't think he will now he's back. I love him for that. But it doesn't make it any better for me. I think of it . . . every day. Three of them were friends of mine – and I killed them.' He looked at each woman in turn. 'I think you can say that I didn't have a good war. Did I? Now this.'

There was a lull as they pondered. Philippe left his scraping of the wood box and moved next to his mother, hauling himself on to the chair with her. He sat on her lap and twisted round to face her, with his fingers manipulating her bottom lip.

Mimi broke the silence. 'Does anyone have a good war? Maybe some have a war that's less bad than others. I have my dirty little secret too. I was a Nazi. Not one that killed Jews in concentration camps, but one of the millions that allowed the whole thing to happen in the first place. Just as guilty. I should have known better. Of course I should. I should have done something – anything – to stop it. I didn't. I just sat in Silesia pretending to be a grafin, being bowed and scraped to as if I was something special. Especially bad, in fact, as I did have the opportunity to make a difference – but I did nothing. And now I'm here. Why? Because I still don't have the courage to deal with the consequences of my actions on my own. That's a bad war.'

She reached into the pocket of her coat and pulled out a packet of American cigarettes. She offered them round. Marie-Louise was shocked to see still the livid welt marks of barely healed burns on her hands

'This would be like burning money in Germany. It's the only currency. And only women can earn it. By whoring themselves.'

The implication sank in as Jerome rasped the flint on his lighter and the satin smell of paraffin filled the space between them.

She sat back and blew smoke towards the roof beams. There was a matter-of-factness in the way she then looked at each in turn as she spoke. 'I was raped. By two GIs. They chucked me a carton of cigarettes as they left. These are the last of them. Maybe it made them think that . . . that it was consensual. Who knows?'

They smoked quietly, absorbing the enormity of all that had been said. Marie-Louise could sense the fury and the absorbed hurt in her husband. With it she recognised the depth of his feeling for this women. The intensity of his stare and his evident anguish on her behalf could have raised a billow of jealousy – but she too felt a surprising empathy for this woman. Compassion began to overwhelm fear. Philippe provided a pressure-release of sorts, a distraction, as he tried to grab the lighter that was still too hot to hold, climbing on to the table so that they had to move the bottles and pewter mugs away from his exploratory hands and scrambling legs. He sat on the edge facing Mimi, who offered him the packet of cigarettes to explore and watched him with a tired half-smile as he twisted it in curiosity.

Marie-Louise spoke. 'It's the same here in France. No. Not the same. It can't be. No camps. But not many covered themselves in glory. A few did – like Ghislaine. I think it's why everyone seems to hate the Tommies and the Americans so much – almost as much as the Boche. They hold up the mirrors everyone has to look into every day. Remind us of all the little humiliations and mean-minded things we thought and did just to get by. De Gaulle tells us that we liberated ourselves; but we know it's a lie – but it's a lie we need to give us back our self-respect. Maybe that's why so many joined in the dolling out of the *tontes*. It made them feel better that there was someone else who'd done something worse than they had. Like the hierarchy of a prison: murderers can feel better about themselves by beating up rapists. A bad war? Maybe. But we're alive – which is more than can be said for millions of others. Is the war and all we did – or didn't do – something that we have to carry with us for ever? I hope not.'

'But we do, don't we?' Jerome stood and walked around his chair, smoking as he spoke. Marie-Louise recognised this familiar trait as he marshalled his thoughts with knitted eyebrows. 'We can't just leave this behind.' He waved the two fingers holding the cigarette at the child on the table and, by imputation, the swelling beneath Mimi's coat. 'I'll see the wives of those men I killed every day. Their children – I'll have to watch them grow up knowing the truth. How can I draw a line under that? *Pas possible.*' Marie-Louise put a hand out and held his arm, stopping his pacing. He continued his theme. 'How can I forget or forgive what the Germans have done? Or forgive myself for what I did?'

Marie-Louise kept her hand on his arm. 'All Germans? This German?' She pointed at Mimi.

'Of course not.'

'Then it's some Germans. That's a start. And who says that you have to forgive them? All you, and enough people all over this ruined continent, have to do is stay your hands; not seek revenge. That's enough. Enough to halt the cycle. She put another hand on his arm as if to implore him. 'And you, *chéri*, what about you? You have to work out some way of dealing with this otherwise the guilt will eat you up. It's only about what you've just told us – certainly not about me. I've enough guilt for all of us. You have to park it in a siding or hand it over. My grandmother would pack you off to confession to wipe the slate clean – but unless you've become a Catholic, you're going to have to work out something or . . . ' She hesitated as the spectre of mental illness hovered in the air.

Mimi saw in front of her a gentle face, pinched by hunger and nerves. She felt her turmoil in her own heart. The woman she had imagined during the long journey had been harder and more brittle, not someone so *sympathique*. There was something in her raw vulnerability that touched her and she felt herself reaching out to her, her response articulated in a hand that moved tentatively across the table.

Mimi spoke quietly. 'I had a friend, a dear friend, who was with me for part of my journey here, who had a similar experience in the last war, in the trenches. He said he blamed himself for years, accused himself of killing his men. But of course he didn't. The enemy did. The war did. It's the war. It's just the war. We didn't choose it. Well if anyone did, I did. And that led, inexorably, to what happened. It depends on your perspective doesn't it? Guilt.'

'The Jesuits would make mincemeat of that, wouldn't they?' observed Jerome

Marie-Louise replied, '*Chéri*, you're not a Catholic. If you are, go to confession. The Jesuits would be right if there's an immovable canon of right and wrong – and God's up there, clicking his abacus of good and bad. You did something you were ashamed of, in extreme circumstances. Maybe if you hadn't run, all of you would have been killed. Who knows? Regret it. Resolve to do it differently if something like that happens again. But don't drag it around with you like a ball and chain. Because that is what guilt is, a ball and chain that will destroy you . . . and us.'

He blinked at the last two words and some of the anger visibly dissipated. He sighed and smiled ruefully at her, and at Mimi too.

'Those Jesuits leave their mark though, don't they? You can't completely put it behind you; no matter how hard you try. I've tried – but maybe I've got to work at it a bit harder.'

'If we don't put all this guilt somewhere,' Marie-Louise continued, 'how can we deal with everything peacetime's going to bring? None of us . . . ' her finger made a circular motion on a horizontal plane ' . . . are exactly free of sin, are we? None of us would be in a position to cast the first stone. But we're lucky. All our sins are private. None of us has to face an *épuration*, a court martial or a *tonte*. The guilt may be there, but it's something about which we have choices. It really depends on what we want to do with each other, doesn't it?' She looked carefully at her husband and at Mimi. 'We can tear each other apart – in recriminations now or, worse, slowly and deliberately in a drip of cold, jealous poison. Or we can say, "It was the war," and live out the little lies we have to. We won't be the only ones doing it. It won't be the same as it was before the war. How could it be? But I don't think there's any other way.'

Jerome looked at her with curiosity. 'I would never have expected this. You . . . you used to be . . . conventional . . . very much so. You've changed.'

'I've . . . I've learnt a lot. Over the last five years. From papa. From grandmama. Mainly from Philippe's father. He made me see that jealousy is only about possession. If you feel you don't possess someone, then anything's possible. I thought it wasn't – until you came back. What I've realised over the last month is that I love you . . . very much . . . and I love him still. There's no conflict. There really isn't. Or there needn't be. We can choose to be jealous – or not. It can be how we want it to be. We don't have to follow a script written by others. We can write our own lives if we want to. That's what I've learnt.'

Mimi felt a hot film of tears in her eyes at these words and when she glanced at Marie-Louise she was surprised to see the same. Two unwiped streaks ran past the sides of her mouth that was trembling with emotion. She spoke with a catch in her voice. 'My brother used to say the same thing. He was younger than me, but wiser. I used to think it was wishful thinking, for the fairies. But he was right. I used to say to him that jealousy is hard-wired – that you can't avoid it. I still think you can't avoid it completely, but what you can do is work at it . . . work at cutting it out. It's not a very enjoyable sin after all.'

'It's complicated.' Jerome was pushing the stub of his cigarette around the wooden bowl they were using as an ashtray. 'Is it too complicated?'

Mimi answered. 'Complexity's for grown-ups: that's what my brother also used to say. Nothing's simple – that's for certain. Simple answers to complicated questions end up with . . . Hitler. Maybe that's the lesson of the last decade: welcome complexity and compromise, develop a bad memory and selective vision, get used to shades of grey. Good for politics . . . and for people too.'

'No ideals?'

'Less patriotism and more humanism; no miracles; less genius. More boring people working hard at compromises. I think we've all had enough of "interesting times". I have. Though I think they aren't over yet. In Germany anyway.'

Mimi was moved to see the emotion in Jerome's face as he spoke. 'You cant go back there. I've seen what it's like. Nothing. No food, no houses. Nothing.'

'I'll work it out. I'll have to. We're all – all us Germans – going to have to face the consequences. Many – most – are worse off than me. I'll manage.'

'No.' Marie-Louise was quiet but firm. 'You can't. Jerome's right. I know. I know what it's like; on your own. I had my grandmother. And papa. And this is Jerome's child. How can I have my child here and live with Jerome while his is . . . ? You have to stay. At least until the child is born.'

There was a slow silence. Mimi looked at Marie-Louise, her mouth quivering with emotion. 'I still don't know your name.'

'Marie-Louise.'

'Thank you.' She looked up at the dark timbers of the ceiling. 'I've had a lot of time on my own since January: horrible times; lonely times. Plenty of time to think – and imagine. What would it be like? What was I going to find if I got here? This is very . . . unexpected. Undeserved. More than that. I'd imagined every possible permutation. Apart from this one. There's not much generosity of spirit around at the best of times. And I think we can say that these must be the worst of times, mustn't they?' She halted, deeply moved. 'This kindness . . . I don't deserve it.'

Philippe climbed off the table and picked up a toy horse that was on the floor. They watched him place it on the table and gallop it across its width.

Jerome spoke. 'What do we deserve? Any of us? We didn't deserve to get born during one war and then have to go through another. But it happened. No one deserves anything. They just get dealt a hand that they have to play. I used to think that we were free agents, that we could "write our own lives", as Marie-Louise put it. But I'm not so sure. I think we're more like a rock trapped in a glacier, moving forward but imprisoned in the ice that finally deposits us downstream with all the other pebbles and rocks that thought they controlled their destiny. But they didn't. The glacier just carried them.'

They considered this as they watched the child offer a wine cork to the horse. Mimi answered, 'I heard this sort of thing in a different context: this idea that we are some sort of collective, and that we're shaped by it. Destiny. In the case of us Germans, to rule the world. But a glacier only moves in one direction and rocks can't change. They can't learn either – collectively or individually. That must sound a bit optimistic, mustn't it, at the end of a war that's killed more people than any other in history? But what this war may also have killed is faith in any big idea, any ideology. We now have to take responsibility for what happens to us, individually, and not hand over our critical faculties to the Hitlers of this world – nor to popes for that matter.' She paused. 'I met a man on my travels. We shared a cattle-car for nearly a week. He was a rabbi who'd survived; but his faith hadn't. He was a man without illusions, without a faith that God would provide. He said that the responsibility was now ours, not God's. It was up to us to make sure it never happens again. He'd looked in the camps for God – but there was nothing there. Just a massive collective cruelty and indifference offset by tiny drops of occasional kindness. It's up to us. A glacier allows you to avoid that responsibility. But you're not a boulder. You're a human with the privileges of choice. A river's a better analogy; it was one that was used by the same friend who was in the trenches, in the same context as you're using it. There are rapids, strewn with boulders. God knows we've had those. Then there are the long meandering sections where the current is still running but where, if we exert ourselves – paddle if we've the means, swim if the boat's sunk – we can control things. Take responsibility. Write our own lives even.'

Jerome was silent – but Mimi could see he was affected. His naturally sceptical, even cynical, cast of mind, that had had five years of confirmation of the worst that human nature could contrive, was struggling to accept this idealistic alternative; this lily in the swamp. He shook his head. 'I'd like to believe you but . . . I can't. The meek don't inherit the earth, do they? They end up in gas-chambers.'

He was still standing with his hands on the back of the chair, gripping it with emotion. Marie-Louise put her hand on one of his whitened fists. She held his eye and with a slight movement of the head indicated that he should sit down. She poured him some wine before answering. Mimi saw in her a firmness that her gentle diffidence had disguised.

'It's not meek to believe that tearing each other apart to be the last predator left on a pile of corpses is madness. We've done that enough already. Surely? We could go on doing it for generations. It's not meek to say no to that. What you can say is that we can all do with a little less; forgive a little; try to forget a lot. We can make – we have to make – different choices.'

'Love thy neighbour?'

'No. Just not hate him. That's enough.'

He was about to reply, but checked himself, considered for a moment then continued. 'There is something: someone who's here – but not here. He's important, isn't he?' He looked at Marie-Louise. 'Maybe there's been enough said for one day. Tell us another time.'

In the past, Marie-Louise would have flushed and stammered with embarrassment. Now she sat serenely, with her hands on her lap, watching her son as she spoke. 'I . . . I'd like to tell you . . . both. I don't think it can do any harm to us; no more harm than has been done already. Though it is . . . was . . . complicated . . . I don't think I feel any shame about it now. It wasn't a seduction. It was something that I'll hold precious all my life. He was the father of my son. How could I disown that? If I cause hurt to you, *chéri*, or shame to my father, I regret that. Of course I do. But in itself, it was good. I know it. My grandmother would have none of it. The Jesuits again. We talked about it often when I was staying with her until Philippe was born. We used to talk about our inner gyroscope that tells us what's right and wrong. That's what he was . . . is . . . to me. A compass as well. When I want a guide . . . need some help in working out what I should do or say, I think what he would have done or what he would have said.' She looked up at the other two. 'He's never let me down yet.'

21

Montreuil. Eight years later. Christmas Eve 1953

The floor of the old grain store was strewn with papers – yellowed copies of *Le Figaro* protecting the floor from the industry in progress. Two boys were cutting shapes out of cardboard and using paint-brushes more suited to covering walls with whitewash than painting Christmas decorations. In the corner stood the crest of a larch tree, brown-needled in its deciduous winter colours, embedded in a small oil drum that Mimi was corseting with waxed tissue paper that crackled as she tightened the string that secured it in place. All were focused on the tasks in hand with only the hissing and occasional crack of damp wood in the corner stove to distract them. The room was cold, despite the stove, and all were wearing scarves and coats.

The younger of the two boys laid his carefully painted star on the newspaper and twisted towards her. 'Mama, can we open our presents after church this evening. It's too long till tomorrow.'

'I don't see why not. What do you think, Philippe?'

The older boy shrugged and continued painting. Deferred gratific-ation was his speciality: sooner or later made little difference to him.

The younger leapt to his feet and boxed the air in delight. But a cloud passed over his face. 'Will Uncle Jerome or Aunt Marie-Louise mind?'

Mimi shook her head and smiled. 'Uncle Jerome? Never. He can never wait to open his presents. You remember what he was like on his birthday.'

The sun came out again and she watched him spar with an imaginary opponent in a *dance de joie de vivre*. Christmas, for him, was something to be looked forward to from the previous Boxing Day – and she took vicarious pleasure in his enthusiasm. His coat was open: he never seemed to feel the cold even though the frost still lay on the ground outside, despite the afternoon sunshine that had melted the skin of ice from the casement windows of the former storeroom. The floors were bare elm boards, softened by a heavy magenta rug by the stove, and the furniture was heavy Empire in mahogany tones. Two prosperous epitomes of respectability, one in a high cravat and collar, the other in a crinoline, stared out from either side of the stove, and a *faux*-Gobelin tapestry covered the bare stone of the wall opposite – a hunting scene of Burgundian splendour. The velvet of the monumental sofa was worn to the nap and the cushion on the high-backed chair displayed its stuffing.

Mimi looked on her shared home and her son with contentment. This time of year created a unity around the children that banished some of the tensions in their careful *ménage à trois* that bedevilled the rest of the year. The mill-house had grown during the nineteenth century to house not just the mill-owner, but also his two sons and their families. She and Theo, her son, had lived in one part until Marie-Louise's father had died of lung cancer the previous year. She had then spread into what had been his rooms as well. The old storeroom, where they now were, was a communal drawing room of sorts, used for birthdays and Christmas. Despite the extra space, she missed Michel Annecy. He had taken a shine to her; partly, they couldn't all help feeling, to needle his son-in-law, but also for genuine reasons of affection. He admired her spirit and, despite his visceral hatred of Germans and Germany, he seemed to have persuaded himself that she was what she pretended to be to the outside world – a cousin from Mulhouse in Alsace who had lost her husband to the war. He treated her with a courtesy and gentleness that, even in his mellower latter years, he only partially extended to his daughter and son-in-law. With Jerome's return, some of the intimacy that he and Marie-Louise had achieved after the blows of the *épuration* had evaporated and his exaggerated praise of Mimi was an unexpected source of jealousy to his daughter. Mimi attempted to laugh it off, but the truth was that she had developed a tenderness for him that she had never enjoyed with her own father and they spent many contented evenings arguing or reading quietly in one or the other's sitting room. His illness had been heralded by a cough that failed to respond to treatment and a gaunt cast to his face. One day, over dinner, he announced that he was putting himself in the hands of the mendicant sisters who specialised in nursing the terminally ill – and died quietly in their hospice, fortified by extreme unction and the blessing of his old friend, the Bishop of Amiens. He explained, at the same dinner, that as he had come into this world alone he wanted neither his daughter nor anyone other than the sisters at his bedside when he died. Three friends, his immediate family and the officiating bishop were the only mourners at the funeral in the Abbatiale St Saulve. His *Croix de Guerre* lay on his coffin and the theme of the address was *Sic transit gloria mundi*.

The first year of Mimi's time in Montreuil had been spent in domestic arrangements – looking after a sickly baby and making the mill-house into a home that would suit their particular arrangement. There had been no direct discussion as to what would happen after Mimi's arrival, but her physical state and Marie-Louise's steely kindness silenced the genesis of an objection from Michel Annecy. Economic necessity, as much as anything, shaped their *modus vivendi* thereafter. Michel Annecy's business had collapsed under his post-war disgrace and any capital they had was tied up in the town house. The week before her confinement Mimi placed a pinch of diamonds on to the kitchen table and it was the proceeds of the sale of these that saw them all through the threadbare post-war years. Further offerings at crucial moments when bankruptcy threatened made her an economic lifeline rather than an object of charity and provided a practical bridge of necessity that spanned what could have been a cataract of emotional difficulties. She was also instrumental in financing and managing a magazine of literary criticism that became their livelihood and connection with the outside world. Locally they remained, if not ostracised, then isolated – physically, in their solitary house in the wooded countryside below the town, and socially, in the post-war disgrace that hung like the valley's marsh-mist around Michel Annecy. Provincial conversation had never held great appeal for any of them, other than for Marie-Louise's father – so this was not missed much – though the taunting of their children when they reached school age was wounding. The magazine was an outlet for their respective talents. Jerome provided the creative flair and the editorial edge that made it the organ of choice for writers of the centre-left. He crossed swords with censors, politicians of all stripes and writers incensed by reviews that were often acerbic and never dull. Mimi, the driving force in its foundation, discovered an unexpected aptitude for managing the business, for which neither of the others was temperamentally suited. Marie-Louise, always more domestic by inclination, remained in Montreuil and provided the intellectual backbone, writing reviews and conducting epistolary exchanges under a variety of pseudonyms.

She and Jerome lived as man and wife but the business of the magazine meant that Mimi and Jerome travelled regularly, mainly to Paris, where the Bohemian circles that they frequented asked no questions of their relationship which remained charged with a voluptuous sexuality. This they kept strictly in a Parisian compartment unless Marie-Louise was visiting her grandmother in Honfleur, which she did regularly as the old lady's periods of ill-health became more frequent. The Bishop of Amiens himself would have found nothing to complain of in the outward appearances of the extended Annecy family. The tensions between them were rarely between Mimi and Marie-Louise – and then only stirred up by a mischievous Michel Annecy. Their complex relationship was never discussed – it slowly evolved out of necessity and a mutual pragmatism that chose to see what it wished. They shared the upbringing of their respective children and a developing friendship that replaced for Marie-Louise that of Ghislaine; Jerome's awkward relationship with Robert, tinged with unspoken guilt, and hers with Ghislaine, that laboured under a shared secret knowledge, made anything other than the exchange of social niceties a strain – though the surface remained amicable.

Jerome himself, rather than their unorthodox domestic arrangement, was the usual source of friction. His relationship with Michel Annecy had always contained a *froideur*: both men were opinionated and intolerant but the peace was kept with a formal *politesse*. Both women continued to be drawn to, and captivated by, his energy and originality. He engaged them, intellectually and sexually, with an intensity that they both recognised as being, if not unique, then certainly rare. Allied with this were mood swings that swept from ecstatic highs of loving affection for the children, adventurous expeditions, both physical and mental, and an outpouring of ideas and enthusiasms, to the depths of melancholia where he would sometimes spend days alone with a pall of gloom hanging over the household. But the ups outweighed the downs and, by now, both women and their children recognised and interpreted the warning signs and had learnt to trim the sails or batten down the hatches when they recognised a shift in the barometer. They were just emerging from a depression and were looking forward to sunnier times over Christmas than had prevailed throughout Advent.

Mimi heard the sound of dogs barking outside. A visitor. She knew that Marie-Louise was downstairs and carried on watching the two boys hang their home-made decorations on the tree, which was now lit by a brilliant shaft from a sun that rarely at this time of year raised itself high enough to light, let alone warm, the valley floor. She half returned to her book and drifted contentedly between the gentle pleasures that the room offered. Footfalls on the stairs. She and the two boys looked up as the door opened. Marie-Louise was holding the boys' two-year-old half-sister, Thérèse, on her hip. Her fine beauty had filled out since they had first met in the hungry aftermath of the war. Her open face was troubled as she took in the room and its activities. 'There's someone to see you, Mimi. German. He won't tell me who he is. He . . . he doesn't look very well.'

'Thank you. Will you . . . stay here while I . . . see what he wants.'

Marie-Louise stood aside as Mimi passed her and halted at the top of the stairs. Both knew that a German was likely to be a messenger – and that the news would inevitably be bad. She felt Marie-Louise's hand on her arm. 'I'm here if you need me.'

She acknowledged the offer with a small wave and took each step slowly, trying to compose herself for what was coming. With each step down, the chinks round the door at the stair's head shed less light until, at the kitchen's door, there was barely enough for her to find the latch. She pushed open the door and paused as her eyes adjusted. A man was sitting at the table. He stood as she entered. They faced each other for some seconds as recognition sank in.

He spoke first.

'Hello, Mimi. I'm sorry to surprise you.'

She had the back of her hand against her mouth in shock. It was as if she had seen a ghost – which, in a way, she had. It was her husband. She found she was unable to make the right sounds and continued to stare at him. He moved towards her and she felt his lips against her cheek. He stepped back and she recovered enough to speak.

'I . . . I'm so sorry. But it was such . . . this is . . . a shock. I thought you . . . that you were dead. Oh, Eric . . . '

She wept as she looked at the ruin of a man in front of her. He was eighteen years older than her, nearly fifty now, but looked seventy. His mane of blond hair had gone. Thin tobacco-coloured strands were combed over a scalp that displayed blotched patches and flaking skin. His eyes were luminous in their deep sockets and his lips out of proportion to his sunken face. The suit he was wearing fitted him in the vertical but drooped off the sides of reduced shoulders. He had been nearly a head taller than her, upright, with the powerful frame of an athlete. He now seemed curved in every plane. She noticed he leant against the table for support.

'May I sit down? I broke a leg in the mine a year ago, and it never set properly. I can walk. But not for too long.'

She looked down, using the opportunity to run the sleeve of one arm across her tear-logged eyes, and saw that one foot was not aligned with the other, pigeon-toed on one side. She indicated the chair on which he had been sitting.

'I'll get you some wine.'

'Thank you. But water it for me, please. A little alcohol goes a long way.'

She busied herself with finding a glass and bottle, in a state of shock. Nothing could have prepared her for this; in the immediate aftermath of the war, perhaps – but now? She gripped the sideboard, fighting to align a tumult of thoughts and emotions, and groped for a kitchen towel to deal with the tears that had left dark marks on her shirt. By the time she turned back to face him, some of the initial surprise had abated.

Mimi found, however, that she could not meet his gaze. 'How did you know . . . how to find me?'

'Your father.'

She shook her head. She had written to her parents explaining her circumstances in the autumn of 1945 – not without doubt and angst. She had expected nothing but rejection and cold disapproval from her father – and had not been mistaken. Her mother had replied, clearly behind the back of her husband, in a quiet agony of curiosity about her grandson. But she had contracted pneumonia in the freezing post-war winter – and died: she was buried and was decomposing in the iron soil of the Lutheran cemetery in Baden-Baden before word arrived in Montreuil. Subsequently, her father had refused even to concede his daughter's existence, or that of his grandson. Out of filial duty only, she wrote a letter once a year – but had never received even an acknowledgement.

'How is he?'

Eric shrugged. 'He exists. He lives alone with a housekeeper; a refugee widow from Pomerania. He reads the newspaper all morning, walks in the afternoon and listens to the wireless in the evening: a shrivelled little man, with a shrivelled little life. He didn't even offer me a meal; but I wasn't expecting much.'

Her father and his son-in-law had only ever been coldly polite with each other.

'Did he . . . did he say anything . . . about me?'

'He gave me your address. And he said things about you that I refused to listen to. Disgraceful. That he should say such things. About you. In that way.'

'Maybe they're true?'

She forced herself to look at him, into eyes that were set shadow-deep in hollowed sockets. He shook his head. 'True? He said you had a child. But there are ways of saying that, aren't there?'

They contemplated the floor.

'Would you like some food?'

He nodded

'Nothing that needs too much chewing. I had scurvy and lost too many teeth to deal with meat.'

She realised that when he had smiled, it had been more of a grimace. Now that her eyes had adjusted to the light she could see intermittent discoloured pegs. Three in front were broken – evidence of a blow.

'Soup?'

'That would be . . . very good. Thank you.'

Nothing was said as she stirred the saucepan and arranged the simple meal. She was conscious of his eyes following her, hungry in more ways than one. She busied herself as he ate, sensitive to his enforced clumsiness and difficulties with masticating the bread, even when it was soaked soft by the soup. He had been thirty-eight when they had married, physically youthful but with a prematurely aged cast of mind that was profoundly conscious of his position. This was not snobbery – he mixed evenly, but not easily with all – but rather a sense of familial obligations and expectations that made him pompous at worst. She had been attracted by his intelligence and certainties but, as she had got to know him better, those certainties had lost their appeal. They had held him back, anchored and unevolved, while she had matured over the five years that they were together into a woman of broader views and tastes than the one he had married. Her failure, as he saw it, to produce an heir had become, if not a grievance, then a nagging reproach that began to sour some of the affection between them. He was always kind and gentle with her, avuncular rather than passionate. What she realised now was that the glue of sex had been missing, the uninhibited physical release that might have mortared the interstices between them. As she had extended her horizons with voracious reading and enriching friendships, he had begun to resemble, in her mind, the portraits on the walls of the schloss – conservative to the point of reactionary, and imbued with the values of a caste that had reached its apogee in the summer of 1914. In the raw new world it floundered like a brontosaurus in the age of the sabre-toothed tiger. His mother, who had lived with them for the first years of their marriage, while always courteous, had never quite forgiven her son for marrying out of the circle. As each year went by without children, her silent condemnation drove a wedge of conflicting loyalties between them. Whatever the tensions, there was never enmity. Over the long years after the war she had thought about him often, concluding that enmity might have come later if their differences had had the time to mutate into conflict. But affection remained her dominant memory – and was there now as she stole glances at the ravaged physique painfully spooning soup into a shattered mouth.

While nothing could have prepared her for this, the gossamer-thin possibility of his return had always been there. After the final collapse in May 1945, there were known to be over a million prisoners held by the Russians. No Geneva Convention had been signed between Germany and Russia – Hitler's war of annihilation allowed for no such niceties – and the number was only a guess as almost no word came from behind the Iron Curtain as to their fate. Batches of desiccated men were released over the years that followed, arriving home with tales of starvation and slavery in the reconstruction of countries that they had helped so comprehensively to destroy. Whispers of cannibalism came too. And of a breakdown of military discipline and any human decency: a freezing, bitter hell-on-earth that raised shudders even in a country that was itself barely alive in the shattered aftermath of war. By 1950, the number of returnees had become hundreds rather than thousands, and those hoping against hope that a husband, son or brother might see their home again resigned themselves to mourning their dead. Mimi had heard few of these stories, living as she was in France and cut off from Germany other than through an occasional letter from Eva. French newspapers contained little about the fate of German prisoners: sympathy was limited in countries that had suffered under the German yoke. In her mind, he had been ten years in an un-marked grave, somewhere in the western Ukraine. Now he was here, in her new life, bringing with him resurrected guilt and a slew of complicated emotions. She sat down at the table opposite him.

He was the first to speak. 'You look . . . wonderful. I've thought of you every day.'

She looked away, embarrassed. She had not done the same. The anticipation of endearments that could not be reciprocated filled her with dread.

'I had a photograph of you with me until . . . last year; of you in your wedding dress.' She could feel knives of guilt slicing into her. 'A guard took it from me and pushed the end of a lighted cigarette through your face. I had to rely on my imagination from then on. It was a cruel thing to do.'

She forced herself to look at him and deflect this flow of pitiable sentiment. She could see that he wanted to touch her, embrace her. She was glad of the width of the table between them. She hated this dilemma. Her instincts were to comfort the man in front of her but she knew that could – would – be misinterpreted.

'Where's your child?'

'Upstairs.'

'A boy?'

'Yes.'

Another knife; this time plunged into him. There was a sad silence.

'So it was me.' He made a mirthless laugh. 'After all my mother said – and I thought. It wasn't meant to be, was it, Mimi? After all. How old is he?'

'Eight.'

He registered no emotion as he ran the calculation. She found she could not look at him and stared out of the narrow window where the midwinter shadows were lengthening.

'Where are you . . . staying?'

'In the town. In the hotel where Victo Hugo wrote *Les Misérables*. Rather suitable in the circumstances. It's comfortable. Anything is after the last few years.'

She reached over the table and put her hand on his. They looked at the contrast of the elegance of her fingers over his knurled claw.

'I'm sorry, Eric. I really am.'

'Why should you be? It's been nearly ten years. I was dead. As good as anyway.'

'You know why. It happened. I can't turn the clock back. And I don't want to. That's why I'm sorry. It wasn't anything you did. Ever. I've just become a different person. Changed. I'm not sure you'd love that person. I'm not the person in the photograph any more.'

It was his turn to look away with pain in his squinting eyes. 'Was it wrong of me to come?'

'No. I did a similar thing.'

'With a different outcome?'

She nodded.

'Is he here?'

'He's out. Until later. That was his wife, the woman who met you.'

'How . . . ?'

'How did we meet? He was a prisoner working on the farm. That's why I'm sorry, Eric. I'd hoped that I'd never have to tell you that.'

'It was the war.'

'Yes, it was. But not entirely. That's what you have to understand. It was more. There were other things. I don't think we would have made it, Eric. Happily anyway.'

He slowly withdrew his hand from under hers and stroked the thin hair on his temple as he replied. 'If you say so. I had this illusion that we were happy. Was that just wishful thinking?'

She shook her head, searching desperately for the right words.

'No. We had many times of happiness. That's why this is so . . . difficult for me . . . for me to say in the right way. I so don't want to hurt you, really I don't, but what I have to say is hurtful however I put it. It can't be anything else. What I'd like you to understand is that then I didn't know any different. Now I do. Knowing what I know now, I can't go back to what I knew then. It's not possible. Life, the war, him – they've changed me. I can't unknow what I now know. The point is that I think I would probably have got to know some – not all – of what I know now anyway, without the war, without him. And I don't think you would have been with me on that journey. That's not your fault. It wouldn't have been anyone's fault. It's just what happens when you marry too young.'

'So it was an illusion. But maybe I needed that illusion; to get me through.'

She moved her head as if she was weighing an argument. 'No. Not an illusion. What we had then was real enough. I loved you in the way I understood love then. But my understanding's changed. It would have changed because change is what happens between people, isn't it? It's how you adapt to that change that determines whether a marriage is a vessel for exploring life or a straitjacket that imprisons. This is me now, Eric: the real me. I'm the mistress of a Frenchman with a bastard child – not a child-bride in a wedding dress. Is that what you'd want?'

'You're sounding like your father.'

'I'd be surprised if he put it that nicely.'

'So I'd have been a straitjacket?'

She reached over the table again, wanting to soothe the hurt she was causing. 'Eric, I don't know. That was a clumsy expression. Who can ever know these things? I married you because you were a man of certainties, moral and principled – a good man. That hasn't changed. It's me that's different. I thought that you and all those good things were what I wanted, needed, for my life. I wasn't disappointed – ever. What I know now is that I needed more. It's about my needs, not your failings. Can you understand that?'

He did not reply immediately but traced a figure of eight on the table with his finger. 'I shouldn't have come, should I? After I'd seen your father, what was the point?'

She hesitated. 'It depends. If you thought – think – that we could carry on as if nothing – this, the war – had ever happened, then no, of course not. But if, in your heart, you can understand some – even a little – of what I'm trying to explain, then it may have been worthwhile.'

He made no reply. None was necessary. The clock, the same that had watched over Marie-Louise and Adam Kohl in the parlour of the town house, whirled and rattled out the hour. Mimi stood and fed logs into the range. The flare at the inrush of oxygen threw a yellow flickering light into the room that was now almost entirely dark: little of the twilight outside penetrated. She lit two candles and offered him a cigarette. They smoked, initially in silence.

Mimi spoke. 'It's been nearly ten years. I still don't know what happened to you.'

He stared at the glowing end of his cigarette before answering. 'Do you mind if I don't tell you the details? It was more horrible than I thought was possible, lonelier and more hopeless; colder and crueller than you can imagine.'

'Only what you can.'

He told her about his capture: his tank and he were knocked out by a glancing shell. He told her how he survived the initial cull of the wounded, shot where they lay, and the sodden wretchedness of the early days as he and thousands of others were left to rot in the open as the spring rain soaked them to the skin.

'No worse, I suppose, than we had done to prisoners captured by us.'

They were marched east and south along roads that had turned into the traditional quagmire of the Russian spring before they metamorphosed yet again into a choking dust swirl that added thirst to the ever-present hunger; thirst that became an exquisite torture when salted fish drove some men to insanity. Stalingrad was their destination.

'Not a building standing. Not one. Yet there were people living there: children mainly; orphans that were like packs of wild dogs foraging for what they could among the ruins.'

There he spent four bleak years clearing rubble and rebuilding the tractor factory that had been the epicentre of the eponymous battle and that was intended to become the phoenix-like symbol of the city's renaissance. They were treated with indifferent brutality, draft animals to be worked until illness or exhaustion finished them off, the end hastened, if necessary, by a single shot to the nape of the neck. In winter they shivered around inadequate stoves alongside Soviet prisoners who had had the misfortune to have been captured by the Germans and survive. They had exchanged one hell for another as the very fact of imprisonment by the Nazis condemned them to the Gulag or a bullet on their supposed liberation. To the litany of miseries was added that of civil war among prisoners. In such a world, kindness rarely showed its face, illness was a death-sentence and the search for food the only concern. Beasts of burden have no antecedents or family, so to physical deprivation was added the despair of abandonment.

In the summer of 1949 he was moved, this time by train, to a coal mine in Upper Silesia, barely a hundred kilometres from Breslau and a home that was no longer in Germany but part of a newly-formed Poland. Any remaining Germans who had not fled in the trek west ahead of the bow-wave of the Red Army and who had survived the rape and murder in its wake, had simply been transported west and dumped in destitute family knots to fend for themselves in an occupied Germany. Poles, themselves dispossessed, from eastern provinces that had been annexed into the Soviet Union, replaced them. There he laboured, in suffocating dust and under the Damoclean sword of premature burial, in tunnels that were inadequately shored-up through lack of timber. One collapse had broken his leg. His faculty with both Polish and Russian had saved him: he had convalesced while undertaking the bureaucratic tasks that were part and parcel of the Communist machine. One day, without warning or explanation, he, and the handful of remaining prisoners who had survived, were told they were free to go. On foot, or crutches in his case, they headed west.

'Breslau's gone. Just ruins. Hanke's handiwork. Apparently he didn't surrender the city until three days after the war was over. His idea of heroism. The Poles have taken all the bricks they could find to rebuild Warsaw. I knew that there was nothing left for me at home – but I had to go. Mimi . . . it's gone!' There were tears in both their eyes as they remembered the arcadia that had once been their home. 'There were three families living on the farm: poor Poles who had been peasant farmers on the Belorussian border. But the house is burnt to the ground. Just fire-blackened roof timbers. The stone and bricks, those that weren't split by heat, have been looted. No one knew what had happened. It's a foreign land now, with no collective memory. I found this in the ruins.' He handed her a small gold cross; the chain that had held it as a necklace had gone. 'My grandmother's. I'd like you to have it.' Mimi took it, not trusting herself to speak. 'I dug up a box of gold coins and precious stones that I'd buried on my last leave. I want you to have some of those too. I've more than enough for my own needs.'

She looked up at him and, making no effort to staunch the flow of tears that was staining her shirt once more, she shook her head as she took his hand. 'No. I can't take more from you than I have already. No.' In the candlelight she could see his ransacked face softened by the flame's gentle light. It repaired some of the damage wrought over the last ten years. He did not press her. She asked softly. 'What will you do now?'

He considered. 'I don't know. I'm qualified to be a coal miner, I suppose. Live? My sister has invited me to live with her in Hamburg. Georg was killed in Italy, so she's a lonely widow. I may just go somewhere warm, the Riviera perhaps, and repair some of the damage; if I can. But when I look in the mirror, I wonder if it's possible. I remember my mother saying that she always felt young, even in her seventies. And that she would look in the mirror and think, "Who's that old lady?" I feel even older than I look: everything sucked out; sucked dry; a sterile old husk.'

Mimi looked down at the table. There was no reply that could give any comfort, no contradiction that was credible. The logs spat and crackled, easing the discomfort of the silence that Mimi broke.

'You can stay here, of course you can . . . ' she saw a flash of hope in his eyes . . . 'in the cottage by the bridge. It's part of the demesne. It would take some time to get habitable again but . . . '

Her voice trailed off as he shook his head and placed his hand once again on the back of hers. In the silence they could hear the sound of children's feet and the animated shouts of a boys' game above them. The candles trembled in sympathy.

'I'm glad I came, Mimi.'

'I wish I . . . '

'No. No apologies. Not needed. I know. I knew.'

They sat for some moments in silence. Both were aware that this was the final click of the latch as the door to the past fell shut behind them; that this was an epilogue of sorts to a life that had been over for many years, existing now only in the memory. Neither could bring themselves to throw the bolt and turn the key. They stood up either side of the table with no words for dissolution. Eric limped to the wall against which a walking stick was leant. There was a metre between them as they faced one another. His eyes travelled over her as if to fix her on the photographic plate of his mind. He put out a hand and touched her cheek. He made no attempt to kiss her but, in one movement, turned on his sound leg and swung the door open, disappearing into the ebony cavern of the night. She heard his uneven, dragging steps as they scraped the rust on the metal footbridge, tapping into silence as the moss-strewn footpath absorbed him. She listened for a few moments before closing the door on the hypodermic cold.

The flames in the range were now tugging hard, and a steady orange light bathed the room. She pulled a chair close to the fire and stared into its now white centre, conscious of, but not listening to, the vibration of the game going on above her head. She registered Marie-Louise's progress down the stairs but remained gazing into the bowels of the range as the door was tentatively pushed ajar. Seeing she was alone, Marie-Louise came in and drew a chair alongside her; she too stared into the warmth.

'It was my husband.'

Mimi felt a hand on her arm and the slight pressure of empathy. They sat like this for some minutes until a thump on the floor above called them back to the present.

Marie-Louise stood and placed her hand on Mimi's shoulder. 'If we want to go to mass, then we need to set off soon. Would you rather stay here?'

Mimi shook her head and stood up. 'No. I'd like to go.'

*   *   *

Once inside the church, the bell lost its metallic timbre and boomed around darkened vaults that were barely touched by the candlelight below. Children wriggled on packed family benches and the rumble of a hundred conversations counterpointed the tolling above. The tingling of a treble bell and a roll of incense smoke from the thurible chattering against its chain, heralded the entrance of the priest and his entourage, white, red and gold amid the smoke of candles, frankincense and condensing breath.

'*Christus natus est!*'

The refrain reverberated around the Abbatiale, acclaiming the arrival of the Saviour at the same time as chairs rattled and scraped in response to the introductory notes of the organ rising against the fading bell. Missals were explored and throats cleared in anticipation of the joyful carol, '*Il est né, le divin enfant. Jouez hautbois, resonnez musettes*'. Mimi put one hand on Theo's shoulder as the first phrases filled the church, and with the other surreptitiously dabbed her handkerchief against tears she could no longer hold back as she imagined the arctic loneliness of her husband. The contrast of the surrounding family warmth choked her, allowing her only to mouth the words as best she could. Half blinded by tears, she stared fixedly ahead at the priest and his acolytes as they formed in front of the altar to await the dying bars of the antiphonal carol. She dared not look either side of her as they sat once more. She could feel her son looking at her anxiously amid the shuffling of shoes and anticipatory coughs.

As a prelude to the mass, the priest held up both hands and once more greeted the birth of the Christ-child, calling down a blessing on his flock. He reminded them of the poverty of the birth of Jesus, the homelessness of his family and the simplicity of the first disciples. He spoke also of the needs of travellers and the holiness in hospitality – every word a lance-wound in Mimi's side. The priest finished and motioned the congregation to stand as the organist made out the gentle harmony, in flute tones, of the universal Christmas hymn. From the darkened choir, rising out in treble purity from a single voice, came the first bars.

Silent Night. *Sainte Nuit.*